本书系河南省哲学社会科学规划项目
（2021BWX006）研究成果

A Study of Peter Carey's Neo-historical Fiction
from the Perspective of Cultural Memory Theory

彼得·凯里新历史小说的文化记忆研究

郭云仙 著

河南大学出版社
HENAN UNIVERSITY PRESS
·郑州·

图书在版编目(CIP)数据

彼得·凯里新历史小说的文化记忆研究:英文 / 郭云仙著. -- 郑州:河南大学出版社, 2024.6. -- ISBN 978-7-5649-5971-5

Ⅰ. I611.074

中国国家版本馆 CIP 数据核字第 2024PU7295 号

彼得·凯里新历史小说的文化记忆研究
Bide Kaili Xin-Lishi Xiaoshuo De Wenhua Jiyi Yanjiu

责任编辑	马　博　时二凤
责任校对	王　珂　张　远
封面设计	高枫叶

出版发行	河南大学出版社
	地址:郑州市郑东新区商务外环中华大厦 2401 号　邮编:450046
	电话:0371-22860116(南方出版中心)　网址:hupress.henu.edu.cn
	0371-86059701(营销部)
排　　版	郑州市今日文教印制有限公司
印　　刷	广东虎彩云印刷有限公司
版　　次	2024 年 6 月第 1 版	印　次	2024 年 6 月第 1 次印刷
开　　本	787 mm×1092 mm　1/16	印　张	23.5
字　　数	457 千字	定　价	68.00 元

版权所有·侵权必究

(本书如有印装质量问题,请与河南大学出版社营销部联系调换。)

前　言

　　全球化浪潮在促进不同文明、文化交流互鉴的同时，也引发了知识分子对文化同质化和传统断裂的警觉与思考。具有浓厚历史意识和深切文化关怀的各国作家，充分发挥虚构文学作品调度多种叙事策略再现民族记忆的独特优势，创作出了一批享誉全球的新历史小说，对此进行间接、诗性的回应，使得文学与记忆的互动成为21世纪最热门的文化议题之一。而扬·阿斯曼和阿莱达·阿斯曼夫妇创立的文化记忆理论，以其固有的跨学科优势，或可成为阐释新历史小说的有效工具。

　　彼得·凯里是上述作家中比较有代表性的一位。他是当代澳大利亚文坛"最富独创性，最有才华的作家之一"，被认为是继帕特里克·怀特之后最有实力角逐诺贝尔文学奖的澳大利亚作家。迄今为止，凯里已出版长篇小说十四部，短篇小说集和非虚构作品各两部。他曾凭借《奥斯卡与露辛达》和《凯利帮真史》，在1988年和2000年两次摘得布克奖的桂冠。他的作品在创作手法上常融黑色幽默、寓言式小说和科幻小说元素为一体，擅长运用魔幻现实主义和超现实主义的表现手法，将历史与幻想糅合交织，模糊现实与非现实之间的界限。就作品主题而言，凯里的小说因其对澳大利亚历史和文化的独特诠释而受到广泛赞誉。迄今出版的十四部长篇中，有九部被评论家称为"历史小说""新历史小说"或"编史元小说"。他也因此在批评界享有"澳大利亚文化代言人""澳大利亚神话制造者"的美誉。然而，现有研究更多关注小说中"写回帝国中心"的解构性倾向，从文化记忆视角对其中建构性层面的剖析尚不多见。

本书将前文提到的九部历史题材作品统称为新历史小说,援用文化记忆理论,对其中着重表征澳大利亚文化记忆的七部进行研究,即《魔术师》《奥斯卡与露辛达》《特里斯坦·史密斯不寻常的生活》《杰克·麦格斯》《凯利帮真史》《健忘》《漫漫回家路》。本书将沿着从外部关照到内部辨析的进路,从对小说发生的思想文化语境和政治社会现状的透视,到深入文本辨析各自因应变化所呈现出的独特文化记忆景观,再到对应副文本的外应佐证,力图更全面、深入地呈现凯里作品的独特魅力和丰富内涵。全书共分三个部分:绪论、主体和结论。其中,主体部分分三章呈现,分别研究澳大利亚的殖民记忆、原初记忆和新殖民记忆。其中殖民记忆是澳大利亚最早的集体记忆,从很大程度上也决定了其原初记忆的形态,两者又共同构成了澳大利亚文化记忆的内向度。新殖民记忆是澳大利亚的晚近记忆,亦是其文化记忆的外向度。与此相应,七个文本则依据它们所表征的文化记忆的侧重点,分列入以上各章进行讨论。

本书绪论由六个小节组成。第一小节简要回顾彼得·凯里的生平和创作,扼要介绍了本研究没有涵盖的七部长篇小说。第二小节梳理国内外彼得·凯里的研究现状,指出现有研究存在研究视角单一,对作品的建构性主题和文化关怀探讨较少,对作家的创作缺乏整体性、历时性把握等不足。第三小节从后现代历史书写的记忆和叙事双重转向、澳大利亚历史之争和新历史小说作为一种后现代文学题材的兴起等方面交代了本书的研究背景。第四小节介绍了本书的理论框架,简要分析了文化记忆理论的源起,其最重要的重构性和功能性向度和其对于文学研究的适用性。第五小节说明了本书的理论、现实意义和创新之处。第六小节交代了本书的结构安排。

第一章,寻根、重估和发明传统的澳大利亚殖民记忆。本章共分三节,重点研究凯里如何通过《奥斯卡与露辛达》《杰克·麦格斯》和《凯利帮真史》重构帝国远征、流放犯和丛林传奇等记忆,表明澳大利亚文化与不列颠和爱尔兰文化一脉相承的关系,批评性重估欧洲文明在澳大利亚的传播、英国的流放制度和帝国对澳大利亚的殖民统治,发明澳大利亚的反专制传统。

第二章,确认身份、超越和治疗的澳大利亚原初记忆。本章共分两节,着重探讨《魔术师》和《漫漫回家路》中对澳大利亚的民族谎言、民族主义、多元文化、囚禁感和原住民等文化记忆的重构问题。分析作者如何召回这些记忆以确认澳大利亚的多元文化身份,发明民族主义传统,抚慰那些承受历史之重的灵魂,探讨澳大利亚何以通过寻求白人和原住民的对话与协商,超越历史保守主义和狭隘的民族政策,建立和谐共生的多元文化生态。

第三章,指责和照亮当下的澳大利亚新殖民记忆。本章共分两节,重点分析作者如何在《特里斯坦·史密斯不寻常的生活》和《健忘》中重构澳大利亚的"美国化"记忆和"盟友"记忆,以谴责美国通过文化输入和跨国资本主义的形式对澳大利亚实行"自我殖民",批判国人遗忘历史和文化谄媚,探索如何通过构建文化主体性和积极抵抗等方式摆脱美国霸权。

最后是本书的结论部分。通过对上述内容的研究,本书有以下发现:首先,彼得·凯里的新历史小说不仅是叙述性的,还具有鲜明的述行性特点。作品通过召回澳大利亚的殖民记忆、原初记忆和新殖民记忆,构建了澳大利亚文化的主体性。这种主体性包含内和外两个向度。就其内向度而言,通过寻根确认了澳大利亚文化的欧洲源头,借此发明了民族主义和反专制主义传统;通过白人和原住民的对话、协商,建立和谐共生的多元文化生态;通过对其文化遗产的批判性重估和叙事治疗,澳大利亚人得以从历史重负中解放出来,克服文化自卑情结和自身局限性,重建文化自信,"追求超越"①。从外向度上说,澳大利亚文化的主体性同对美国霸权的批判和抗争密切相连,具有鲜明的反新殖民主义的特点。其次,凯里的新历史小说具有鲜明的后现代主义和存在主义特征。文本中元小说、戏仿、拼贴、魔幻现实主义等叙事策略的运用既体现了文本自身与后现代智识语境的连续性,也蕴含了作者的历史观和哲学观。一方面,他将元小说的自指性和历史小说的似真性并置,制造矛盾张力,突出了历史真实的复

---

① "超越"概念借自阿尔弗雷德·阿德勒,指人们在自卑情绪的驱使下,不断超越自我,变成更好的自己的状态。

杂性、模糊性和不可通达性。另一方面，他又像不知疲倦的西西弗斯一样，坚持不懈地追求这一真理，从追寻本身中获取意义。最后，20世纪90年代初是凯里新历史小说创作的分水岭。此前，他关注的重心是对帝国记忆和官方记忆祛魅；此后，他在重构澳大利亚文化记忆方面发挥了更为积极的作用，以祛魅为起点，对澳大利亚如何摆脱当前困境进行更深入的诗学探索。凯里的新历史小说是他对多元文化和全球资本主义语境下澳大利亚文化记忆生态的象征性文学演示。作品中对澳大利亚文化主体性的诗学建构，也是作者为世界贡献的文化间性主义智慧。

最后，由衷感谢河南大学高继海教授对笔者的倾心指导。从商讨选题、研究设计到定稿，笔者无不深深受益于高教授的博学多识和不懈鼓励。特别感谢中国社会科学院陆建德教授，中国人民大学郭英剑教授，杭州师范大学周敏教授，国防科技大学胡亚敏教授、石平萍教授，广东外语外贸大学邱业祥教授和河南大学焦小婷教授。他们阅读了笔者的部分书稿，并提出了非常有建设性的意见和建议。他们的专业知识、审慎思考和孜孜不倦的精神，都给予笔者深刻的影响。本书的责任编辑马博先生和时二凤女士为本书的编校付出了辛勤劳动，在此一并致以诚挚的谢意。书中有不当之处，恳请读者批评指正。

郭云仙
2023 年 12 月

Foreword

While sweeping globalization promotes exchanges and mutual learning among different civilizations and cultures, it also arouses contemporary intellectuals' vigilance and reflection on the threat of cultural homogenization and the rupture of traditions. With solid historical awareness and deep cultural concern, writers from all over the world have made full use of the unique advantages of deploying various narrative strategies to reproduce national memory in literary works and created several world-renowned neo-historical novels, which indirectly and poetically respond to this issue. This makes the interaction between literature and memory one of the hottest cultural issues in the 21st century. Cultural memory theory initiated by Jan and Aleida Assmann, with its inherent interdisciplinary advantages, may be an effective tool for interpreting neo-historical novels.

Peter Carey is one of the most representative authors of the type. He is "one of the most ingenious and talented writers" in the contemporary Australian literary world, and considered as the most competitive Australian writer to compete for the Nobel Prize in Literature after Patrick White. Carey has published fourteen novels, two short story collections and two non-fictions. With *Oscar and*

Lucinda and *True History of the Kelly Gang*, he won the Booker Prize twice, in 1988 and 2000, respectively. Carey often integrates black humour, allegory and science fiction elements into his works. And he is good at using magical realism and surrealist techniques to interweave fantasy with history, blurring the boundary between reality and non-reality. In terms of their themes, Carey's novels have received widespread praise for their unique interpretation of Australian history and culture. Nine of the fourteen fiction are frequently referred to as "history novels", "neo-historical fiction" or "historiographic metafictions" by critics. He, therefore, enjoys the reputation of the "spokesman of Australian culture" and "Australia's national Myth-maker" in academia. However, existing studies paid more attention to the deconstructive tendency of "writing back to the Empire" in his novels, and scarce research has been directed towards the constructive aspect from the perspective of cultural memory.

The above nine novels are termed uniformly as neo-historical fiction in this research. Adopting cultural memory theory, seven among the nine that are concerned with the reconstruction of Australian cultural memories are brought under examination in this study, namely, *Illywhacker*, *Oscar and Lucinda*, *The Unusual Life of Tristan Smith*, *Jack Maggs*, *True History of the Kelly Gang*, *Amnesia* and *A Long Way Home*. The research methodology integrates extra-textual investigation into textual analysis. Overall, the examination of the ideological and cultural context as well as the political and social status quo of each fiction, the in-depth analysis of the unique cultural memory landscape presented within each text in response to the political, social and cultural dynamics, and the external evidence elicited from corresponding paratexts, is integrated closely in this research, with the endeavour of presenting the unique charm and rich connotation of Carey's works more comprehensively and profoundly. This monograph consists of three parts: the introduction, the main body and the conclusion. The body part comprises into three chapters, devoted to examining Australia's colonial memory, original memory and new colonial memory, respectively. Among them, colonial memory is the earliest collective memory in Australia, which also determines the form of its original memory to a large extent, and both types of memory constitute the introversion of Australia's cultural memory. The neo-colonial memory is Australia's recent memory and its cultural memory's external dimension. Accordingly, the seven texts are allocated to the above chapters for close examination according to the emphasis on the cultural memory they represent.

The introductory part of this book comprises six subsections. The first section is Peter Carey's biography and his writings. The seven novels that are not covered in this study are introduced briefly. The second section combs the research status of Carey's criticism at home and abroad, pointing out that only minimal research perspectives have been employed by critics, that quite few discussions are directed to the constructive themes of his works and even fewer to their cultural concern, and that there are very few holistic and diachronic studies of Carey's writings. The third section explains the research background of the book, which includes the double turn to memory and narrative of the postmodern historiography, Australian history wars, and the rise of neo-historical fiction as a postmodern genre. The fourth section introduces the theoretical framework of this research, analyzing briefly the genealogy of the cultural memory theory, its most significant reconstructive and functional dimensions, and its applicability to literary studies. The fifth section sketches the theoretical and practical significance of this research and its innovations. The sixth section introduces the layout of this book.

Chapter One is "Australia's Colonial Memories to Trace Origin, Re-appraise and Invent Traditions". This chapter consists of three sections. Research attention is focused on how Carey reconstructs Australia's memories of the imperial expedition, the convict stain and the bushranging legend in *Oscar and Lucinda*, *Jack Maggs* and *True History of the Kelly Gang*, respectively to demonstrate the consistency between Australian culture and the British and the Irish culture, re-evaluate critically the advancement of the European civilization in Australia, the Transportation System and the Empire's ruling of Australia, and invent the antiauthoritarian tradition.

Chapter Two is "Australia's Original Memories to Concrete Identity, Surpass and Heal". This chapter comprises two sections. It is oriented to examine the recuperation of Australia's memories of the national lies, the nationalism, the multiculturalism, the sense of imprisonment and the Aborigines in *Illywhacker* and *A Long Way from Home*. The analysis goes to how the above memories are retrieved to concrete Australia's multicultural identity, invent the nationalist tradition, soothe those souls that burden the historical weight, and explore how Australia can transcend its historical conservatism and provincial ethnic policies to build a harmonious and symbiotic multicultural ecology via dialogue and negotiation between White Australians and the Aborigines.

Chapter Three is "Australia's Neo-colonial Memories to Blame and Illumine the Present". This chapter consists of two sections. It studies mainly how Australia's "Americanization" and "ally" memories are reconfigured in *The Unusual Life of Tristan Smith* and *Amnesia* by the author to condemn the United States for its "auto-colonization" of Australia through cultural input and multinational capitalism, blame Australians for forgetting history and cultural cringe, and explore how Australia can get rid of the American hegemony by constructing cultural subjectivity and active resistance.

The last part of this monograph is the Conclusion. Studies of the above issues lead to the following findings. First of all, Peter Carey's neo-historical texts are not only narrative but also distinctively performative. Australia's colonial, original and neo-colonial memories are recuperated to construct Australian cultural subjectivity, which consists of both the internal and the external dimensions. In terms of its internality, it concretes the European origin of Australian culture by root-seeking, upon which Australian nationalist and antiauthoritarian traditions are created; it establishes a harmonious and symbiotic multicultural ecology through dialogue and negotiation between Australian Whites and Aborigines; Australians who are freed from historical burdens through a critical re-evaluation of its cultural heritage and narrative therapy overcome the cultural inferiority complex and their limitations, restore their cultural confidence, and "strive for superiority"[①]. From the external perspective, the subjectivity of Australian culture is closely linked to the criticism of and resistance to American hegemony and has a distinctive anti-neo-colonialism characteristic. In addition, Carey's neo-historical fictions have distinct postmodern and existentialist flavours. The writerly strategies he

---

[①] "Superiority" is a conception borrowed from Alfred Adler. It refers to the state in which people driven by the feelings of inferiority transcend themselves and transform into bettered beings.

deploys in the texts, such as metafiction, parody, pastiche and magical realism, manifest both their consistency with the postmodern intellectual milieu and the author's historical and philosophical outlook. He juxtaposes the self-consciousness of metafiction and the verisimilitude of historical fiction to create a tension highlighting the complexity, ambiguity and inaccessibility of historical truth. At the same time, he is in pursuit of that truth unremittingly, like the indefatigable Sisyphus, prioritizing the meaning of pursuing itself. Lastly, the early 1990s marked a turning point in Carey's creation of neo-historical fiction. Carey has played an overtly more progressive role in reconstructing Australia's cultural memories since then. He has shifted his preoccupations from a pure disenchantment of the imperial and official memory to taking this engineering as a threshold to launch further a poetic exploration of Australia's way out of its current predicament. Carey's neo-historical fiction is a symbolic literary demonstration of Australian cultural memory ecology in the multicultural and global capitalism context. The poetic construction of Australian cultural subjectivity in his works is also the wisdom of interculturalism that the author contributes to the world.

  Finally, I would like to express my sincere gratitude to Prof. Gao Jihai of Henan University for his guidance to the author. Throughout the whole process of choosing the research topic, planning the research, and finalizing the manuscript, I have profoundly benefited from Mr. Gao's remarkable expertise and unremitting encouragement. My great thanks would definitely go to Prof. Lu Jiande from Chinese Academy of Social Sciences, Prof. Guo Yingjian from Renmin University of China, Prof. Zhou Min from Hangzhou Normal University, Prof. Hu Yamin and Prof. Shi Pingping from National University of Defense Technology, Prof. Qiu Yexiang from Guangdong

University of Foreign Studies, and Prof. Jiao Xiaoting from Henan University. They have read some of the manuscript and offered remarkably constructive suggestions to improve it. Their extensive expertise, meticulous contemplation, and unwavering diligence have exerted a profound influence upon the author. Finally, I would like to express my sincere appreciation to Mr. Ma Bo and Ms. Shi Erfeng for their indefatigable work in editing the manuscript. There might be some inadequacies in the book, and readers are kindly requested to offer criticisms and corrections.

Guo YunXian
December, 2023

Contents

Introduction ·· (1)
    The Author and His Works ··· (1)
    Literature Review ·· (11)
    Research Background ·· (17)
    Theoretical Framework ·· (26)
    Significance and Innovations ··· (36)
    Layout of the Monograph ·· (39)

Chapter One   Australia's Colonial Memories to Trace Origin, Re-appraise and Invent Traditions ·· (42)

    1.1   European Civilization Remembered as a Double-edged Sword: *Oscar and Lucinda* ·· (44)
        1.1.1   Preliminaries of the Fiction ······························· (45)
        1.1.2   Christian Civilization as a Sugar-coated Bullet ······ (53)
        1.1.3   Gambling as a Home-grown Religion and Victorian Transmission ··· (67)
        1.1.4   Misogyny as Punishment for Bush Intruders and Victorian Transgressors ··· (75)
    1.2   Convicts Recollected as Scapegoats for the Empire: *Jack Maggs* ··· (85)

1.2.1　Preliminaries of the Fiction ……………………（87）

1.2.2　Scapegoats Expulsed for Good …………………（96）

1.2.3　Convicts' Homesickness ……………………………（110）

1.2.4　Reorientation to Embrace the Adopted Land ………（118）

1.3　Outlaw Recalled as a National Hero: *True History of the Kelly Gang* ……………………………………………………（130）

1.3.1　Preliminaries of the Fiction ……………………（131）

1.3.2　Colonial Australia as a Dystopia ………………（140）

1.3.3　Death of the Outlaw as a State Murder …………（150）

1.3.4　Monument to the Antiauthoritarian Hero …………（155）

Chapter Two　Australia's Original Memories to Concrete Identity, Surpass and Heal ……………………………………………（166）

2.1　Underpaintings of Australian Memory: *Illywhacker* ……（169）

2.1.1　Preliminaries of the Fiction ……………………（170）

2.1.2　Lies as Part of Existence ………………………（176）

2.1.3　Utopian Nationalist Dream ………………………（184）

2.1.4　Multi-cultural Genes ……………………………（199）

2.1.5　Nation in Gaol ……………………………………（209）

2.2　Aborigines Remembered as Victims of European Australians' Racism: *A Long Way from Home* ……………………………（217）

2.2.1　Preliminaries of the Fiction ……………………（218）

2.2.2　Victims of the White's Racism …………………（225）

2.2.3　Deferred Reconciliation between the Whites and the Aborigines ……………………………………………（237）

2.2.4　Aborigines' Salvation by Carving Their Cultural Memory ……………………………………………………（246）

Chapter Three Australia's Neo-colonial Memories to Blame and Illumine the Present (257)

  3.1 Americanization Recollected as a Crippling Force: *The Unusual Life of Tristan Smith* (260)

    3.1.1 Preliminaries of the Fiction (261)

    3.1.2 Mania for the New Empire (270)

    3.1.3 Hybridized Cripple of Imperialism (276)

    3.1.4 Culture as Armour (285)

  3.2 Ally Recalled as the Imperialist: *Amnesia* (294)

    3.2.1 Preliminaries of the Fiction (296)

    3.2.2 Forgetting as a National Ill (303)

    3.2.3 Cost of Oblivion — Carnival of Humiliations (310)

    3.2.4 Birth of the Overman (318)

Conclusion (327)

Reference List (333)

Introduction

The Author and His Works

Carey is "one of the most ingenious and talented writers" in the contemporary Australian literary world. He is considered the most competitive Australian writer to compete for the Nobel Prize in Literature after Patrick White. With European ancestry, he was born in 1943 in Bacchus Marsh, a small working-class rural town in Victoria, Australia. He went to Geelong Grammar School, which boasted as Australia's Eton at the age of ten, and was enrolled to Monash University after graduation in 1961, majoring in chemistry and zoology. Nevertheless, a serious car accident combined with his lack of enthusiasm for science led to his dropping out in the first year. Thereafter, he began his work experience in an advertising agency, which facilitated his socialization with writers like Barry Oakley and Morris Lurie. His acquaintance with Oakley and Lurie further offered him great convenience to read works of European and American writers like Samuel Beckett, Vladimir Nabokov, Jack Kerouac, William Faulkner etc., which turned out to be a big boost in his subsequent writing career. The expanded horizon gained through reading helps to open his eyes to a wide range of literary possibilities and further prompts his departure from the Australian bush-realist tradition started by Henry Lawson and even the modernist tradition consummated by Patrick White.

Another event that has exerted a considerable impact on Peter Carey's writing is his travel across Europe towards the end of the 1960s. The Second World War has propelled Australia to change its insularity and open up to the outside world. The previously isolated country lying on the southern land starts to involve itself in international affairs, which preludes the booming of Australian culture. Among the actions that Australia has taken to get itself out of isolation and included in the global stage, its participation in the Vietnam War as America's ally is a milestone in its political as well as cultural history. That political event has induced Australia's in-depth cultural interactions with America and European countries and consequently triggered a prevailing complaint about the government especially among the intellectual youth. Their discontent eventually ends up with the breakout of the nation-wide anti-cultural protests. Disappointed with the repressive domestic politics and social mores, Carey left for Europe in 1968 and did not return until two years later. During his travels, he witnessed the cultural mania sweeping the European continent in the following two years. That eye-opening experience has exerted a profound influence on his writing career.

In addition, Peter Carey's literary creation has drawn considerable benefits from the unprecedented cultural prosperity and the political milieu of the 1970s. The newly-elected Whitlam government tends to be politically tolerant and culturally liberal, and it pours enormous funding to encourage creative writing. Furthermore, the 1970s has also witnessed the loosening of censorship restrictions. (Hergenhan, 1988: 540) A wide range of subject matters such as sex and drugs, which were regarded as taboos in the 1960s, have been allowed to be dealt with in the avant-garde fiction, the deliberately playful "narrative artefact". The above intellectual conditions have combined to boost the flourishing of fictional publishing. In response to that culture climate, *Tabloid Story*, co-launched by Michael Wilding (1942-) and Frank Moorhouse (1938-), begins accepting stories of a broad range of themes and shows great interest also in non-Australian writers like Jorge Borges and Gabriel Garcia Marquez. The introduction of Latin American writers into the literary circle has further paved the way for the flourishing of the new type of fiction featuring magical realism, and Peter Carey has cut himself a figure with his crafted mastery of this textual strategy.

 Finally, Peter Carey's emigration to the United States in 1990 also had positive influence on his writings. He sold his share of the advertising agency and accepted the job of teaching creative writing at New York University. He has settled in there with his family after that and is now frequently referred as to an expatriate writer. The expatriate life has equipped his writings with bigger visions and broader humanistic concerns ever since.

 Peter Carey has published fourteen novels, two collections of short stories, and two non-fiction monographs so far. He is one of the five writers who have won the Booker Prize twice — including J. G. Farrell, J. M. Coetzee, Hilary Mantel, and Margaret Atwood. He was first awarded the Booker Prize in 1988 for *Oscar and Lucinda*, and the second award came in 2001 for his *True History of the Kelly Gang*. Peter Carey has also garlanded multiple Australian literary awards. He has won the Miles Franklin Award three times with *Bliss* (1981), *Oscar and Lucinda* (1988) and *Jack Maggs* (1998). *Jack Maggs*, together with *True History of the Kelly Gang* is also a Commonwealth Writers Prize winner. His *Parrot and Olivier in America* (2010) has been a finalist for the 2010

National Book Award and on the shortlist of the six books for the ManBooker Prize of the same year. All his other eight novels: *Illywhacker* (1985), *The Tax Inspector* (1991), *The Unusual Life of Tristan Smith* (1994), *My Life as a Fake* (2003), *Theft: A Love Story* (2006), *His Illegal Self* (2008), *The Chemistry of Tears* (2012), *Amnesia* (2014) are either Australian national or provincial literary award winners or included on the shortlist of those awards. His latest novel, *A Long Way from Home* (2017), has acquired very positive reviews, too. Carey was nominated for the Best of the Booker Prize in 2008, and he is frequently named as Australia's next contender for the Nobel Prize in Literature after his precursor, Patrick White.

Peter Carey touches on a wide range of motifs in his literary works, ranging from writing back to the Empire to cyber activism, from the construction of the Australian identity to the marital relationship. Nevertheless, what the author preoccupies himself with most in his literary world are Australia's cultural memories, either those inscribed in its memory book or those concealed in the recess of history. He has made up his mind to resume writing stories and air "the sound of the Australian voice and freedom from the dead hand of history pressing (our) noses into the past" (Woodcock, 1996: 4) ever since his return to his home country in 1970. He does return to the country's past obsessively and interrogates the nation's collective memories with great fervour in his works. As Mary Ellen Snodgrass observes, he "fills his works with the perspective of an underappreciated South Pacific culture and its colonial history" (2010: 3). His works envelope proximately two hundred years of Australian history, ranging from as early as the arrival of Captain Cook 1830s in *A Long Way from Home* to that of the twenty-first century in *Amnesia*. They incorporate an inventory of the nation's cultural memories: the lying and forgetting complex, the convict trauma, the aboriginal dispossession, the multicultural reality and the xenophobic ethnic policy, the infertile nationalist dream, the English and Irish inheritances, the Kelly Gang legend, the Battle of Brisbane and the constitutional crisis, the most recent Julian Assange's cyber-activism and so on. It is not surprising for Andreas Gaile to review that "[T]he vision of Australian experience that emerges from Carey's fiction is so comprehensive his oeuvre makes up nothing less than a fictional biography of the country" (2010: 5).

Since this study is dedicated to mainly seven of his fictional texts, the ensuing paragraphs will be devoted to a brief sketch of his short stories with which he rose to fame and the other seven novels that will not be seriously covered in this monograph. Though Peter Carey took to writing in the 1960s, the publication of his first collection of short stories, *The Fat Man in History*, in 1974 has made him an instant celebrity in Australian literary world. Five years later, the second collection, *War Crimes*, was even more widely lauded, wining him the New South Wales Premier Award in 1980 and confirming his place as an eminent avant-garde writer of Australia. His rebellion against the realist tradition with experiments in forms first seizes the critical attention. He estranges the actual world in his stories by blending reality with fantasy, science fiction, fable, satire and nightmares, demonstrating an innovative and refreshing bizarreness. As Craig Munro observes, Carey's stories "fuse the past, present, and future into super-real scenarios in which the gap between the observed and the imagined disappears" (1981: xii). Some reviewers even label him as a fabulist or surrealist. However, this assignation is contended by other critics who tend to believe that there lurks Carey's realistic concern behind his grotesque artistic form. Kate Ahearn, for instance, argues that his stories are "more like straight parables" (1980: 16-17), infused with allegorical and didactic implications, though Carey once denies the direct connection between his works and the outside world and contends that his "stories are only about what they seem to be about" (Evans, 1984: 8). Despite Carey's own declaration of his detachment from the experiential world, renowned Carey critics like Anthony Hassall and Bruce Woodcock pinpoint, either from the repetitive themes or the hybrid forms, the connection between the author's literary creation and the cultural trend of that period of time (Hassall, 1997: 6) or the "distinctively political edge" (Woodcock, 1996: 17) of his stories. More recent researchers loosely follow their path but relish the artistic feast of Carey's short fiction either from the perspective of the cohesive devices of systemic functional linguistics or from the angle of cognitive science. Carey's short stories are appreciated through his crafty manipulation of the interaction between their unique forms and the resultant "cognitive" (Margarete, 2005: 169) implications and the "social and emotional validation" (Martin, 1988: 3).

Though his remarkable reputation as a writer begins with his novellas, Carey confesses that writing stories does not really interest him because they are not as "serious" as novels in fulfilling a writer's ambition of "going to do anything" (Munro, 1976: 7). This starting point foregrounds his political and ethical concerns in the novels. As a matter of fact, in spite of the "apparent move into a more realistic narrative practice" (Woodcock, 1996: 37) in his long fiction, Carey retains and makes better use of some of his earlier textual strategies. Moreover, there is continuity between his short stories and fiction in their repetitive motifs, such as the Americanization, the late capitalism, power and authority, and gender issues except that they are investigated with more complexity and profundity. He never seems to have altered his obsession with creating poetic authenticity with the apparent dislocation of reality and engaging in the experiential world with his writings as a literary discourse.

Bliss (1981) is Carey's first shot since he turns to prose fiction, and it is a great success, garnering the Miles Franklin, the National Book Council and New South Wales awards. Francis King acclaims that "[N]ot since Patrick White's *The Aunts' Story* has a novel so much convinced me of the emergence of a potential major talent" (1981: 21). This debut consolidates Carey's reputation as an outstanding contemporary novelist. The fiction was adapted for a film in 1985 directed by Ray Lawrence and won the Best Film, Best Director and Best Adapted Screenplay Awards from the Australian Film Institute. *Bliss* is a novel about writing novels or, in other words, about story-telling. It marches into the literary world with both a flauntingly postmodern playfulness and an overt postcolonial undertone. Its metafictional textual strategy, its satire and critique of late capitalism and its moral implications are frequently explored topics among critics. (Hassall, 1994; Natale, 1994; Woodcock, 1996; Fletcher, 2007) *Bliss* relates the story of Harry Joy, an advertising executive in an anonymous Australian city. He is best known for his ability to tell stories. He used to believe that he had been leading a happy life with a successful career, a charming wife and a pair of adorable children. However, a severe heart attack brings him to the recognition that that is only an illusion and that he has been actually living in Hell. He finds with his own eye that his wife Bettina commits adultery with his partner Joel, and his son David, a drug dealer, and his daughter Lucy, a communist, are incestuous. Moreover, he finds his agency involved in advertising business with a company manufacturing carcinogenic products. After his wife, his son, and his business partner kill themselves, he escapes from the city with his lover, Honey Barbara, into her hippy commune to live a blissful life, where he takes delight in telling the tribal stories. *Bliss* can be interpreted as Peter Carey's literary declaration of telling Australian own stories. By disclosing the discursiveness of widely accepted normality and assuming the role that literary discourse might play in inventing an alternative version of truth, this novel sets the tone for his ensuing artistic creation. As suggested in *Bliss*, passing down his father's stories is his obligation as well as his redemption.

Presumably, because Australians are in desperate need of something jolly to boost them up, *The Tax Inspector*, published in 1991, is not greeted with much applause. The novel relates the stories of the three generations of the Catchprices, a dysfunctional family owning a car dealership in Franklin, New South Wales. All stories happen within four days, especially when the family come into contact with Maria, the beautiful and very pregnant tax inspector of the Australian Taxation Office who is sent to audit their business. The whole novel is pieced together more by episodes giving the backgrounds of the characters and the relations between them, depicting an apocalyptic montage of guilt, frustration, sexual perversion and delusional dreams. Portraying a dystopia in the actual world, *The Tax Inspector* is a coal-black humour that directs its satiric target to "yuppie culture", skewering "the concept of romantic epiphany and its implied escape from history" (Marx, 1992: 346-348). This motif is consistent with Carey's historical outlook suggested in his neo-historical novels — facing up to all historical inheritances, favourable or unfavourable.

Published in 2003, *My Life as a Fake* might not be a commercial success without the halo of literary awards. However, it has been a darling of critics for its overt postmodern flavour. The novel is inspired by the most notorious anti-intellectual affair in Australian history, the

Ern Malley hoax.① The frame narrative of the novel is told in the first-person from the focalization of the young woman Sarah Wode-Douglass, who is the editor of *The Modern Review*. Also inspired by Mary Shelley's *Frankenstein*, the novel is about how the hoax poet, the created being, Bob McCorkle, mysteriously materialises and haunts his creator, Christopher Chubb, stalking him menacingly and kidnapping his daughter. It is also about Sarah's discovery of her own history, which she counterfeits to protect her from the remembrance of her mother's horrifying suicide. Most of the story is located in Kuala Lumpur, Malaysia, a city full of bandits, superstitious yet sophisticated villagers and Cambridge-educated rajas. Though *My Life as a Fake* is a neo-historical novel (Gaile, 2010: 286), it is excluded from the current research because Carey preoccupies himself in this fiction not with the cultural memory itself but with the "issue of authenticity in literature" (ibid.: 288), with the relationship between art and the real world, and between author and text, and with the function of narrative in constructing truth, lie, history and identity. (Ashcroft, 2004; 彭青龙, 2011; 张计连, 2015; Osteen, 2017)

Published three years after *My Life as a Fake*, *Theft: A Love Story* (2006) continues with Peter Carey's fascination with the "issue of authenticity" (Gaile, 2010: 289), which he takes as a linguistic construction. The novel narrated alternatively by Butcher and Hugh tells

---

① In 1944, two Australian conservative poets James McAuley and Harold Stewart who detested modernist literature picked out lines from books handy randomly, scrabbled up sixteen poems under the title of *The Darkening Ecliptic* in one day and submitted them to *Angry Penguins*, a cutting-edge literary magazine, under the name of a fictitious poet, Ern Malley. Max Harris, the glamorous young poet, champion of modernist poetry and editor of the magazine was so impressed by their experimentalism that he arranged a special edition to be devoted to Malley's work. The hoax was revealed soon after in newspapers, resulting in the humiliation of Harris, who was put on trial, convicted and fined for publishing the poems on the grounds that they contained obscene content. *Angry Penguins* folded in 1946. The prank arguably undermined the cause of literary modernism and experimentation in Australian literature.

the story of an Australian painter, Butcher Boone, known in his hometown of Bacchus Marsh as Butcher to acknowledge his father's trade. Fresh out of prison for having robbed his ex-wife of his own paintings that were in her possession when their marriage fell apart, Butcher has been working feverishly to get his life and career on track. Simultaneously, he manages to take good care of his mentally handicapped brother Hugh and not be distracted by the attractive art dealer Marlene. *Theft: A Love Story* is concerned both with the authenticity of works of art and with the demonically transformative power of it, which makes it a satire of the venality of the international art market.

His Illegal Self (2008) was published two years later. Set in the 1970s, it is briefly about the story of Che, the abandoned son of a couple who are radical Harvard activists in the 1960s. Left in his grandmother's custody in New York, Che is suddenly abducted by a woman named Dial, who intends to take advantage of him to lure his mother. However, his mother gets killed when attempting to plant a bomb. Dial then takes the boy away from New York and flees to the Australian outback to hide out in a hippy commune.

Parrot and Olivier in America (2010) again witnesses Carey's literary success, winning the author the 2010 National Book Award and being shortlisted for the 2010 ManBooker Prize. The novel is a "comic historical picaresque" (Wood, 2010: 107) which is improvised on Alexis de Tocqueville and Beaumont's 1831 sojourn in America. Throughout the novel, the narrative voice switches unevenly between Olivier (Tocqueville) and Parrot (Garmont), an English engraver who is appointed by Olivier's mother to act as his servant and secretly keep an eye on him and report back to her. Through the peculiar journey of Olivier and Parrot, Carey sketches the genealogy of American democracy. (Wood, 2010; Jones, 2010; Mathews, 2012)

The Chemistry of Tears (2012) tells the story of a spinster in her 40s, Catherine Gehrig, who buries herself in work to eliminate the grief of losing her married lover and colleague, Matthew Tindall. While Catherine preoccupies herself with the task of restoring an automaton from the mid-nineteenth century assigned by her boss Eric Croft, the head curator of horology at the Swinburne Museum of London, the novel unfolds another plot. In the embedded plot, Henry Brandling, the younger son of a wealthy railway family of the nineteenth century and father of the ailing boy Percy, travels to Karlsruhe, the birthplace of the cuckoo clock, with the slim hope that a mechanical entertainment built there might save his son when all the usual Victorian therapies have failed. The story Catherine discovers behind the automatic duck bears peculiar parallels with that of her own.

Literature Review

As a highly esteemed writer, Peter Carey has attracted much academic attention on his writings. Searches in AustLit① and EBSCOhost show 435 entries in the criticism section and 248 entries in academic journals, ranking only second to Patrick White. Up to now, most of Carey's critics have been in the English world, where he has been the subject of eight monographs, one of which evolved from the doctoral dissertation. Carey's works have also been brought under the research interest of eight dissertations, among which only one focuses on how Peter Carey invents Australia's mythistory in five of his fictions dealing with Australian history as well as in 30 *Days in Sydney: A Wildly Distorted*

---

① AustLit is a searchable, scholarly source of authoritative biographical, bibliographic, critical, and production information about Australian writers and writing. The database is collaboratively built by the top eight Australian universities and the National Library of Australia.

Account. Moreover, the rest of them take one of Carey's texts together with novels of other writers to conduct a comparative study from typically the postcolonial perspective. Carey has also been the subject of an essay collection, more than two hundred scholarly journal articles, and several hundreds of reviews in major dailies and weeklies in the English world.

The vast majority of the research interest in the English world is centred on his novels revisiting Australian history, especially the earlier ones like *Illywhacker* (4), *Oscar and Lucinda* (22), *The Unusual Life of Tristan Smith* (4), *Jack Maggs* (13), *True History of the Kelly Gang* (28), and *My Life as a Fake* (13) and the literature of the two ManBooker Prize winners accounts for more than half of the total.① Studies of his newly published fiction of this genre, *Amnesia*, which draws on the 1942 Battle of Brisbane and Kerr's Dismissal of the Whitlam government and *A Long Way from Home* which deals with Australia's xenophobic ethnic policy in the twentieth century, have been brought under way quite recently, yielding, for now, quite a limited amount of research achievement. Carey's other novels, like *The Tax Inspector*, *Theft: A Love Story*, *His Illegal Self*, and *The Chemistry of Tears*, have received considerable reviews and commentaries, favourable or unfavourable. Nevertheless, none of them have attracted much attention from serious critics.

When delineating overseas criticism, Carolyn Bliss and Andrea Gaile

---

① In the brackets are the number of academic journal articles of that particular novel collected from the EBSCOhost databases, accessed on 30 May 2019.

have slightly different yet simplified classifications of Carey critics.① I am in debt to them both for concluding that Carey studies in the English world have evolved from the intrinsic criticism in the early period to the present parallelism of the intrinsic and extrinsic criticisms, and both the depth and breadth of research have been effectively expanded. Critics of the intrinsic persuasion led by Helen Daniel, Christer Larsson and Sue Ryan Fazilleau mainly focus on the formal dimension of his novels, for instance, the author's deployment of the textual strategies of metafiction and parody or his manipulation of readers' expectation to defer the authenticity. Later, critics led by Anthony Hassall, Paul Kane, Bill Ashcroft, and more recently Andreas Gaile, explored in further depth the complexities of Carey's fiction. They identify Carey's adept postmodern narrative strategies to excavate how the cultural and political implications of his writings are achieved accordingly with these manoeuvres. Though Carey's experimentalism in forms exhilarates the critics first, criticism of both denominations has been running parallel with each other in the last thirty years. The difference is that new varieties of research interests continue to be brought under way and stale topics are renewed from new perspectives and with more depth. Apart from the cliché of "writing back" to the Empire, the postmodern playfulness and authenticity, topics like morality (Bliss, 2004), cross-dressing (Smyth, 2009), reading

---

① According to Carolyn Bliss, the first school of Carey critics focuses on the author's postmodern writing techniques; critics of the second school concentrate on the implications of Carey's narrative techniques for character, theme, and ethical vision; the third persuasion meshes the two and studies both the postmodern form and the postcolonial theme of Carey's fictions. See Carolyn Bliss, "'Lies and Silences': Cultural Masterplots and Existential Authenticity in Peter Carey's *True History of the Kelly Gang*," in *Fabulating Beauty: Perspectives on the Fiction of Peter Carey*. Ed. Andreas Gaile (New York: Rodopi, 2004): 275-276. Andrea Gaile brings Bliss's pigeonhole down to two denominations, namely the critical approach oriented towards the aesthetic dimension of Carey's writings and that integrating his narrative strategies with the cultural and political implications of them. See Andrea Gaile's *Rewriting History: Peter Carey's Fictional Biography of Australia* (New York: Rodopi B.V., 2010) : 10.

ethics, canonical rewriting (Pellow, 2013), and even the methodology of teaching Carey's canonical novels (O'Reilly, 2007) have also aroused academic interests.

As a renowned novelist, Peter Carey has also received considerable research attention in Chinese academia ever since he was introduced to readers via *World Literature* in 1988 by Zou Hailun. Up to now, he has been the subject of three monographs, sixteen dissertations, dozens of journal articles and book reviews. Domestic Carey criticism is initiated by Xiao Feng and Xiao Yan, who translate Edmund White's interview with Peter Carey into Chinese, in which the writer professes that as an author, he is duty-bound to discover Australia, create her and shape Australians' national consciousness. (怀特, 晓风, 晓燕, 1990: 70) This article, coupled with Ye Shengnian's recognition of both Carey's remarkable writing style of fusing realism, surrealism and futurism perfectly and his progressive historical consciousness demonstrated in his works, sets the tone for the ensuing Carey criticism in China. (叶胜年, 1992: 89-92)

Echoing Xiao Feng, Xiao Yan and Ye Shengnian's initiative introduction of Peter Carey and his writing characteristics, the overwhelming majority of Chinese Carey critics led by Peng Qinglong and Zhang Jilian approach his fiction from the postcolonial or new historical perspective or focus their research attention on the identity issue. Renowned domestic Carey critic Peng Qinglong (2005; 2008) has deployed the methodologies of neo-colonialism and new historicism and later Michel Foucault's "madness" to examine the theme of "writing back" to the Empire, the narrative strategies and Australia's postcolonial cultural identity in Carey's novels in his doctoral dissertation and later post-doctorial research report. Gong Jing (2015) has examined the relationship between masculinity and Australia's national identity in his colonial trilogy. Zhang Jilian (2015) has conducted a close study of

Carey's representation of Australia's national, ethnic, cultural and individual identity in her monograph. Though a couple of minor themes such as morality, motherhood, and Australia's Americanization have been brought under investigation occasionally, the motifs that are examined untiringly and most deeply by Chinese critics are the author's deconstruction of the imperial narrative and his obsession with the issue of identity. That leaves the discussion of cultural memories or narrative techniques far less explored.

Like that in the English world, academic interest in Carey's fictions in China is not performed evenly. Since the author was introduced to China at the very end of the 1980s, studies of his works proximately began with his first Booker Prize winner, *Oscar and Lucinda*, with only one journal article on *Bliss* and *Illywhacker*, respectively, by Peng Qinglong. Similar to that of the English academia, most research attention of Chinese critics is also paid to Carey's fiction dealing with Australian history before 2010, especially the two Booker Prize winners and *Jack Maggs*, which have been the subject of more than half of Chinese academic journals and approximately all the dissertations. In contrast, very few research achievements have been found in other novels of the same genre, for instance, *The Unusual Life of Tristan Smith*, *My Life as a Fake*, *Parrot and Olivier* or *Amnesia*. This is probably because most of these works have not been translated into Chinese, and they enjoy a limited number of readerships. And Carey's most recent fiction in the same genre, *A Long Way from Home*, is still waiting to be introduced to Chinese readers. Like the case in the English world, Carey's other novels, *The Tax Inspector*, *Theft: A Love Story*, and *The Chemistry of Tears*, have not been received warmly in Chinese academia. They are known to Chinese readers via only one or two reviews in prestigious journals. It is worth noting that, presumably owing to Chinese critics' preoccupation with the issue of "identity" in Carey's writing, *His Illegal Self* has drawn considerably more critical interest in China than in the English world. ①

Taking together the current literature on Carey's neo-historical fiction in both the English world and China, it is not difficult to conclude that both the critical aesthetic features and the political edge of his writings have received considerable academic attention. The latter finding is further justified by the authorial claim in an interview where Carey professes to be a "political writer" (Allington, 2015: 157). However, it's not hard to find that approximately all such thematic studies have been conducted from the perspectives of neo-colonialism and new historicism centring on Australia's poetic break through the imperial hegemony, which is embodied in the author's "writing back to the Empire" (Ashcroft, 1996: 194). They are apparently inadequate to exhaust the richness and complexity of Carey's literary works of art.

A novelist with historical consciousness and nationalist sentiments like Carey, he is more of a world-famous writer who has gradually gone beyond purely provincial yarning and infuses his works with a broader international vision and humanistic concern. In addition, since such thematic studies have usually been conducted on a particular text or several texts individually and statically, they are unavoidably fragmentary and unable to sketch the dynamics of the author's writing career. A fuller interpretation and appreciation of Carey's neo-historical fiction is impossible without tackling the above two problems. These are the gaps where the present study jumps in and it is in line with the tradition of fusing intrinsic and extrinsic research. Using and abusing its past, Carey is first reconstructing Australia's cultural memory to discover and invent

---

① According to the data from CNKI (accessed on 30 May 2019), there are twenty-four journal articles and dissertations for *Oscar and Lucinda*, nineteen for *True History of the Kelly Gang*, thirteen for *Jack Maggs*, seven for *His Illegal Self*.

Australia. Moreover, his spectacular narrative performs the therapeutic function that liberates Australians, the White and the Aborigines alike, from the shackles of their traumatic memory. Though wrestling with imperial discourse is inevitable in these processes, he must also declare war against Australian official memory to offer his version of memories. More importantly, judging from the evolvement of his neo-historical fictions, his ultimate ambition lies not so much in deconstructing the old order of discourse as in constructing a new one from which Australia is created and Australians are emancipated from the burden of memory.

Research Background

Literary criticism, either "extrinsic" or "intrinsic" (Wellek & Warren, 1985: 65/139) approach, is unthinkable to detach itself from the social dynamics when the literary works of art are created or interpreted. Domestic scholar Geng Zhanchun (2019) also argues it is impossible to appreciate Chinese literature in the 1980s without correlating it with the social milieu of that epoch since literary practice is a constituent part of a society's historical potential. Likewise, the prime time of Peter Carey's writing career coincides with the postmodern era when the objectivity of knowledge gets dubious owning to its liaison with power, the grand narrative is increasingly replaced by tiny narratives owing to its overarching totality, and modernity remains an "unfinished project" (Habermas, 2009: 96) owing to its mesmerizing yet unattained commitment to progress and emancipation. Accordingly, this research of Peter Carey's neo-historical fiction from the perspective of cultural memory theory is contextualized in the postmodern intellectual milieus where historiography turns to both narrative and memory and increasingly raging history wars triggered by the intellectual condition mentioned above have been sweeping Australian academic and political circles since the mid-1990s. Since the power mechanism is unveiled to come into play in traditional historiography, the self-claiming objective historical metanarrative is dismantled. As Brenda K. Marshall argues, "[W]e no longer are able to speak about absolute and unquestionable 'facts' or 'truths' of history, speaking now of 'histories' instead of 'History'" (1992: 147). Consequently, there arises a recurrence of historical fiction featuring revived personal memories of past experiences usually marginalized and silenced in official documents, and aiming both at a re-evaluation of history and earning their place in the nation's collective memory as a whole. This is even true in Australia's contemporary historical writing and literary practice. This research background will be delineated in detail and more in-depth in the paragraphs that follow.

The rationalist trend of thought consummated in the eighteenth century and combined with the positivism methodology originating from the early nineteenth century brought forth the golden age of history in the nineteenth century, which is characterized by its scientific objectivity as other social sciences. As Georg G. Iggers observes, "[W]hat was new in the nineteenth century was the professionalization of historical studies and their concentration at universities and research centers" (1997: 1). In Germany, "the term Geschichtswissenschaft (historical science) replaced the term Geschichtsschreibung (the writing of history) to describe what professional historians were doing" (Iggers, 1997: 99). The historiographic principle of showing *wie es eigentlich gewesen* (meaning "how things actually were") (1957: 57) initiated by Ranke, founder of modern source-based history, was soon taken by many historians as the golden rule to abide by. He is viewed as "the most important historian to shape [the] historical profession as it emerged in Europe and the United States in the late nineteenth century" (Hoefferle, 2011: 68), and his doctrine has exerted a dominant influence in the Western historiography until the 1960s.

However, with dramatic and destructive social upheavals, especially the two overshadowing World Wars, optimism towards the progressiveness of history and objectivity of historical writing prevalent in the previous century is held sway. Traditional historiography is at the same time under increasing attack. Based on a comparative analysis of historical discourse and literary discourse in the dimensions of speech-act, statement, and signification, Roland Barthes challenges the uniqueness of historical writing as a narration of past events compared with epic, novel or drama. Instead, he argues that the self-claiming objective history is nothing but an ideological and imaginary construction. "In 'objective history,' the 'real' is never anything but an unformulated signified, sheltered behind the apparent omnipotent of the referent" (Barthes, 1989: 139). Furthermore, Jacques Derrida, a precursor of deconstructivism, hammers the traditional historiography from linguistics perspective by deconstructing the relationship between the signifier and the signified. He takes language as a self-contained system of signs and claims that "[T]here is nothing outside of the text" (Derrida, 1976: 158). Derrida insists that it is the language that constructs reality instead of the vice versa. This renders historical writing no reference to the objective world outside of its text.

The illuminating insights of the above scholars have shaken the foundations of the objectivity of traditional historiography. The observations made by Hayden White, a historian and prominent scholastic figure in American New Historicism and French philosopher Jean-François Lyotard, have further induced the "turn to narrative" of historical studies in the 1980s. Defining history as "a verbal structure in the form of a narrative prose discourse" (1975: ix), White's argument that historical writing is influenced by literary writing in many ways and shares the firm reliance on narrative for meaning, therefore eliminates the possibility of objective or genuinely scientific history. He also argues that history is most successful when it uses this "narrativity" (1980) since it is what allows history to be meaningful. Categorizing the historical writings of the four leading historiographers of the nineteenth century, namely Michelet, Ranke, Tocqueville and Burckhardt, into the corresponding narrative archetypes of romance, comedy, tragedy and satire, respectively, White claims that the manifest historical texts are marked by strategies of explanation, which includes explanation by argument, explanation by emplotment, and explanation by ideological implication. (1975: 7) Working under the motto of "the historicity of texts and the textuality of history", new historicists contend that history is, in its essence, a discourse, and it interplays with other discourses like anthropology, politics, art, literature and so forth. The borderline between historical narrative and literary narrative is henceforth obscured. They differ from each other "only in emphasis not in content" (White, 1975: xi). The historical narrative for White does not distinguish itself from the fictional narrative with reference to the actual past. Instead, "metahistorical" elements can be found in all discourses. As White contends, historical narratives are "verbal fictions, the contents of which are as much invented as found and the forms of which have more in common with their counterparts in literature than they have with those in the sciences" (1978: 82).

While Hayden White points to the discursiveness of historical writing, Jean-François Lyotard goes a giant step further to declare war on all the totalizing theories of cultural thought. In *The Postmodern Condition: A Report on Knowledge*, he proposes the highly simplified version of "postmodern" as "incredulity toward metanarratives"

(Lyotard, 1984: xxiv). According to him, our technical and technological advancement since World War II has compromised our needs for and confidence in meta-narratives. "The narratives we tell to justify a single set of laws and stakes are inherently unjust." (Williams, 2002: 210) For Lyotard, "[T]he grand narrative has lost its credibility, regardless of what mode of unification it uses, regardless of whether it is a speculative narrative or a narrative of emancipation" (1984: 37). Grand narratives cease to be adequate to represent us all since everyone has their own aspirations, beliefs, desires, and their own perspective and story. To delegitimize the universality of grand narratives, Lyotard proposes competing plural mini-narratives to make an entrance. Illuminated by the sharp insights of Lyotard and other postmodern pioneers, there erupts the explosion of micro-narratives that characterize post-modernity.

With traditional trust in the objectivity and continuity of history toppling down, historical narrative is being dismantled, and historiography is getting fragmentized. Various histories with personal experience walk into the horizon to replace History. Right against this backdrop, historical memory steps into the spotlight of postmodern historiography and historical studies and draws considerable attention from historians and theorists alike. With the scholarly boom of memory since the 1980s, a diversity of individualized and private memories carrying their own histories have flooded into the public to claim their rights. As Klein observes, "[W]here we once spoke of folk history or popular history or oral history or public history or even myth we now employ memory as a metahistorical category that subsumes all these various terms ... And yet by the end of the eighties, memory has become the leading term in our new cultural history" (2000: 128). This memory "mania" is termed as "memory turn" (彭刚, 2014: 1) in academia. At the same time, New Historicists pinpoint the textuality of history after examining the part that the narrative forms of modern historiography play in domesticating historical experience and denying historical representation the monopolization of historians, which opens literature up to history revisiting. The scholastic advancement in New Historicism induces the "narrative turn" of postmodern historiography and historical studies. (ibid.: 2) The double turns to memory and narrative in postmodern historical practice and theory contribute to the rise of certain literary genres featuring revisiting history and reconstructing collective memory, neo-historical fiction being one of them.

Echoing the postmodern intellectual milieu, the past few decades have seen a remarkable recrudescence of historical novels. A growing number of renowned writers such as Peter Carey, Hilary Mantel, and John Coetzee, to name a few, have won the Booker Prize and been winners of other key literary awards with their re-appropriation of the past. Moreover, the Walter Scott Prize for Historical Fiction was founded in 2009 by Sir Walter Scott's distant relatives, the Duke and Duchess of Buccleuch, to reward yearly "writing of exceptional quality which is set in the past" (http://www.walterscottprize.co.uk). Boasting one of the most prestigious literary prizes in the world, the Walter Scott Prize is an indicator of how historical fiction has become critically recognized and commercially successful. Amidst this recent booming of historical fiction, one coherent and recognizable sub-genre — "neo-historical fiction" (Pierce, 1992) has come into prominence. This trend includes the neo-Victorian novel, which has recently received significant critical attention, and other incarnations like the neo-Tudor, the neo-Georgian and the neo-Forties novel. It resembles the historical novel in that it is "written from a modern perspective" and "implies a modern interpretation of the past" but with a varied degree. (Gilmour, 2000: 190). Neo-historical fiction is "characterized by its critical re-appraisal of specific historical periods and their social, cultural, and political contexts" (Rousselot, 2014: 1). The proliferation of such texts and their authors' prominence achieved in the literary marketplace and at award ceremonies confirms the importance of this new literary trend.

To cite Ann Heilmann and Mark Llewellyn's definition of the neo-Victorian novel, neo-historical fiction is a type of fiction that "must in some respect be self-consciously engaged with the act of (re) interpretation, (re)discovery and (re)vision" (2010: 4) concerning the past. Robin Gilmour argues that it is "self-consciousness" that distinguishes neo-historical fiction from historical fiction. (Gilmour, 2000: 190) There are two salient features interrelated with each other in this genre. To begin with, different from traditional historical novels employing verisimilitude to create the illusion of reality, neo-historical novel, however, is characterized by the "self-analytic drive" (Heilmann & Llewellyn, 2010: 5). This doesn't mean that the neo-historical does not appear genuine, but means that the verisimilitude it operates solely "aims at conveying a surface image of the real" and is usually "endowed with subversive capabilities". (Rousselot, 2014: 4) To conclude, neo-historical fiction is inherited with the paradox of demonstrating "a vivid awareness of the problematics involved in seeking and achieving historical knowledge" and remaining "nonetheless committed to the possibility and the value of striving for that knowledge". (Mitchell, 2010: 3)

Since neo-historical fiction is "[T]he research novel" (Gilmour, 2000: 190), the other indispensable element, also the most important one, lies in its active interrogation and re-appraisal of the past. Different from traditional historical novels, it does not intentionally rebuild history faithfully. As Junot Diaz points out, "For those of us doing this kind of work, what we are thinking about is what it means to recover lost narratives, lost people, lost memories. When we enter historical cracks, we have to accept that what we bring out is not necessarily going to resemble anything we wish it to resemble" (McCormack, 2013: 37). Rather, neo-historical fiction revisits the past and reinterprets history from the standpoint of contemporary time in order to answer the needs and preoccupations of the present and serve the immediate future. This is not the least something new since Edward Said has assumed that "[a]ppeals to the past are among the commonest strategies in interpretations of the present" (1993: 1-2). Alternatively, in Linda Hutcheon's words, it "uses and abuses the material it draws from to enable a powerful cultural re-contextualization" (1988: 118), ultimately leading to a compelling "critique of ideology" (LaCapra, 1987: 128).

Another backdrop that this research is situated in is Australian history wars. According to the nation's documented memory, Australia came into being as a penal colony; thus, part of the glory of the British Empire and Australian history begins with Captain Cook's discovery. Australia is the land of the White and thus mono-cultural, with the main task of its historiography to celebrate the grand narrative of achievements made by its white ancestry and their decedents. As Stuart Macintyre points out, the version of Australian origin "taught to generations of school children and set down in literature and art, memorials and anniversaries — would have it that Australian history commenced at the end of the eighteenth century" (1996: 1), to be more accurate, on 26 January 1788 when the First Fleet anchored the Sydney Harbour. Even Manning Clark, Australia's most famous historian and leading progressive who is criticized by the conservatives to be the godfather of the "Black armband view of history,"[①] claims that "[C]ivilization did not begin in Australia until the last quarter of the eighteenth century" (1968: 3). However, he is more

---

[①] Edward Kynaston attacked Clark in *The Australian* (24 Oct. 1981). The phrase "black armband" is coined by Australia's leading orthodox historian, Geoffrey Blainey.

liberal than his orthodox counterparts in acknowledging that peoples like Negrito, Murrayians and Carpentarians inhabits this continent before the coming of the European. For him, "[T]he early inhabitants of the continent created cultures but not civilization" (Clark, 1968: 3).

Though orthodox historiography tends to take the successful European settlers' stand and document their experience of this southern land, it could not cover up the fact that there have been other ethnic groups who have inhabited here and have their own differentiated experience and sensibility of the continent. The fracture between the multiformity of ethnic experience and sensibility and the monolith of their representation creates a potential for contradiction and resistance, leading to divergent views as to how to interpret Australia's past and what should be inscribed into the nation's memory book among the country's historians and politicians, which eventually triggered Australia's "history wars"[①] in the mid of the 1990s. Different parties involved in this historiographic battle have been divided into "a progressive and a conservative camp" (Gaile, 2010: 4). The conservatives tend to abide by the "positive ... balance sheet" (Howard, 29 Oct. 1996) of Australia's history, whitewashing Australia's flaws and ignobility, and write its history from a clean and optimistic point of view. They "emphasised the successful European settlement, the Anglo-Saxon legacy, the monarchy, and the sense of national unity and the pride in (their) achievements" (Macintyre; Clark, 2003: vii). On the contrary, the progressive camp points out the ruptures between the hegemonic "great narrative of achievement" (Gaile, 2010: 4) and Australia's multicultural present and proposes that Australia's historiography should include the marginalized

---

① The history wars started with the public controversy stirred by Paul Keating and John Howard in the mid-nineties and culminated with the dismissal of the aboriginal director of the National Museum, Dawn Casey, in 2003.

groups and communities, as well as its defects and traumas, which have been cast in national oblivion.

For one thing, this historiographic battle exerts a prevailing impact on Australians' experience and sensitivity. In the age when "[A]nxiety is essential to the human condition" (May, 1996: 15), it also aggravates Australians' anxiety about who they are and who they ought to be. For another, Australia's raging history wars lay an ideological foundation for ensuing historical rewriting as well as the literary practice of revisiting history, leading to the prosperity of neo-historical fiction, which spawns remarkable literary works of art by great novelists like Peter Carey, David Malouf, Rodney Hall, Thomas Keneally etc. Basically, these writers take the progressive ideological side of the history wars and plough in their literary world laboriously to represent both the formerly marginalized or excluded human experience and strive for their place in Australia's collective memory and the predicaments facing contemporary Australians. Among them, Peter Carey is no doubt the most outstanding one. His whole career is "made out of making [his] anxieties get up and walk around" (Carey, 1994: 342), and he cuts himself a figure in the literary world.

Theoretical Framework

Memory is as old as the emergence of human beings, yet scholarly fascination with it is relatively new. Furthermore, it roughly began in the early twentieth century. Memory studies have gone through various stages, evolving from being the research object of psychology, to sociology and then cultural studies. The research orientations in this field have been switched from initially individual memory to collective and social memory and finally to cultural memory. French sociologist Maurice

Halbwachs' concept of "collective memory", ventured in the 1920s, lays the foundation for social memory theory. Quite different from Henri Bergson's mind and body dualism and Sigmund Freud's interrogation of memory through clinical psychoanalysis, Halbwachs includes it in sociological investigation and contests that both the preservation and retrieval of collective memory is conditioned by the social framework of a particular society and "[N]o memory is possible outside frameworks used by people living in society to determine and retrieve their recollections" (1992: 43). Maurice Halbwachs further argues that collective memory is not a given notion but a constructed one. It is "essentially a reconstruction of the past in the light of the present" (ibid.: 34). Families, religious groups and social classes are institutions of collective memory. He also points out that the collective memory is not some mythical group mind. Although it "endures and draws strength from its base in a coherent body of people, it is individuals as group members who remember" (Halbwachs, 1980: 48) and pass on the memory. In other words, individual memory is a part or an aspect of collective memory. It is not hard to understand this because even the seemingly most exclusive memory of a particular person is left or relived to a certain extent that it is in line with the social milieu.

It was not until the late 1970s, when autobiography, oral history and museums began to thrive with the popularization of "new history" contended by the third generation of the Annales School, that academic interests were drawn to memory. What genuinely led to the explosion of memory and memory studies were the two literary events in the 1980s: the publication of Yosef Hayim Yerushalmi's of *Zakhor: Jewish History and Jewish Memory* in 1982 and Pierre Nora's *Les Lieux de Mémoire* (published in part in English translation as P. Nora, *Realms of Memory: Rethinking the French past*.) As Aleida Assmann puts it, Nora has shown in her studies that "what steers the memory of a group is neither a 'collective soul' nor an 'objective mind', but a society with its signs and symbols. Through these shared symbols, the individual participates in a common memory and a common identity" (Assmann, 2013: 122). What is significant of Nora's contribution to memory is that by introducing "the realms of memory", he bridges the gap between memory and culture. Starting right from this point, Jan Assmann and his team dive into culture from the perspective of memory, aiming to investigate how memory plays its part in forming and stabilizing a nation's "diachronic cultural identity" (阿斯曼, 2016: 26) throughout the history. Those studies lay the rudiments of cultural memory.

Jan Assmann and his wife, Aleida Assmann, proposed the cultural memory theory at the end of the 1980s after their delineation of previous memory and cultural theories. Cultural memory theory emerges naturally when memory studies have reached a higher level of profundity. It is also deeply rooted in contemporary social needs. Since the end of the cold war and the reunification of East and West Germany, collective memory has aroused unprecedented interest in academia. How to face up to the crimes that the Nazis committed in the Second World War, reflect on the tribulations that plague us one after another in the twentieth century, and construct a future-oriented memory have become the most pressing issue ever for Germans and the entire human race. Coincidentally, with more and more witnesses of the world war and survivors of the holocaust passing away worldwide, communicative memory is outrunning its life span of forty years and under the severe threat of dying out. That further means history and tradition are facing the danger of breaking off. How to establish a long-term remembrance mechanism to preserve and stabilize the past memory and maintain the flow of tradition has been a matter more urgent than ever. Just as Pierre Nora argues, "[M]emory is constantly on our lips because it no longer exists" (1996: 3). It's safe to conclude that cultural memory comes into existence with the booming of memory discourse in response to the "acceleration of history" (Nora, 1996: 1). The last but surely not the least, intense attention to cultural memory has been made of acute necessity owing to the explosion of electronic mass media. The new media characterized by its stunning storage capacity and unprecedented speed of information distribution has shattered the borderlines of cultural memory and transformed its modes and contents. In a world organized by an excess of confusing, even opposing information provided by mass media, "memory is dissolved in accelerated cycles of production and consumption" (A. Assmann, 2011: 203). As a matter of fact, mass media culture has posed such an unimaginable threat to memory that organized amnesia is being produced in the endless cycles of remembering and forgetting.

Based on the above analysis, it can be inferred that the cultural memory theory has come forth with the evolvement of memory studies and as a timely tentative remedy to various contemporary social appeals. It is concerned with the diachronic transmission of culture from the perspective of memory, contesting that it is the memory carrying culture heritage that moulds people, unites them, and guarantees their continuous existence throughout history. Jan, Aleida Assmann and their partners have devoted themselves to cultural memory studies and yield prolific illuminating works. Among them, Jan Assmann's *Cultural Memory and Early Civilization: Writing, Remembrance, and Political Imagination* (1992) serves as the cornerstone of this theory. A little bit deviating from her husband's concentration on the theory constructing and Ancient Egypt civilization as a case study, Aleida Assmann draws on literature texts and works of art under the timeframe dating from the Renaissance to the contemporary era to examine the function, media and storage of cultural memory in her *Cultural Memory and Western Civilization*: *Arts of Memory* (1999). With its interdisciplinary background, cultural memory theory has received considerable critical attention from the western academia ever since it was brought under the spotlight and exerted far-reaching influence on memory and cultural studies. Moreover, scholarly interest in the theory is also growing among Chinese memory and culture specialists, historians and literary critics.

Jan and Aleida Assmann define the concept of cultural memory by distinguishing it from communicative memory and science. According to them, cultural memory comes into being when "the extension of the communicative situation requires possibilities of intermediate, external storage of information 'of cultural importance' which can be 'processed through forms of coding, storage, and retrieval'"(Assmann, 2011: 8). In *Collective Memory and Cultural Identity* (1995), Jan Assmann further argues that.

[T]he concept of cultural memory comprises that body of reusable texts, images, and rituals specific to each society in each epoch, whose "cultivation" serves to stabilize and convey that society's self-image. Upon such collective knowledge, for the most part (but not exclusively) of the past, each group bases its awareness of unity and particularity. (Assmann; Czaplicka, 1995: 132).

It can be inferred here that cultural memory refers to the crystallized past of a group, may it be a family, a religious group, a social class, or a nation, which is shared by all the members, binds them and defines who they are. According to Jan and Aleida Assmann, collective memory can be approached from the following dimensions.

To begin with, cultural memory is concrete, and it manifests itself in "figures of memory" that emerge out of the "interplay between concepts and experiences" (Assmann, 2011: 24). Figures of memory are indivisible unities of image and symbolic meaning. They are "models, examples, and elements of teaching. They express the general attitude of the group; they not only reproduce its history but also define its nature and its qualities and weaknesses" (Halbwachs, 1992: 59). Cultural memory does not live in the thin air. It is abheres to those "points of crystallization", substantiated in concrete space, realized in concrete time and related to a real and living community. As Halbwachs puts it, "if a truth is to be settled in the memory of a group it needs to be presented in the concrete form of an event, of a personality, or of a locality" (1992: 200). Thus, cultural memory lends support from concrete realms, or media to be encoded, stored and retrieved. That includes rituals, festivals, texts, images, bodies, places etc.

The second dimension of cultural memory lies in its "reconstructivism". Neither can memory come out of blank, nor can it preserve the past intact. It works through reconstruction. Just like "[A]ll history is contemporary history", all memory is a contemporary improvisation on the vestiges of the past. It is continually subject to reorganization according to the changes taking place in the frame of reference of each society, and "only those recollections subsist that in every period society, working within its present-day frameworks can reconstruct" (Halbwachs, 1992: 189). Personages and events from a remote time and space are remembered only when they relate to present needs and the situations in which they find their echoes. "Cultural memory works by reconstructing." (Assmann, 1995: 130) What shall live on in the minds of group members is selected and moulded by present social frameworks. "Remembering is basically a reconstructive process." (A. Assmann, 2011: 19). Whenever a particular memory is retrieved, it is always related to the knowledge of an actual and contemporary situation thus, it inevitably involves "shifting, distortion, revaluation, reshaping" (ibid.). As is argued by Aleida Assmann, "[I]n the period between present action and future recall, memory does not wait patiently in its safe house; it has its own energy and is exposed to a process of transformation" (2011: 19). What we call cultural memory is nothing more than constant reconstructions of the traces of cultural significance that past experiences have left on people's brain. This vision echoes Friedrich Nietzsche's comment on the principle of using history that "the understanding of the past is desired at all times to serve the future and the present, not to weaken the present, not to uproot a forceful living future" (1998: 15).

The past is never remembered purely for its own sake, which brings us to the third dimension of cultural memory: its functions. To quote Henri Bergson, the past "might act and will act by inserting itself into a present sensation from which it borrows the vitality" (Boym, 2001: 151-152). "Either it becomes the driving force of development or it becomes the basis of continuity" (Assmann, 2011: 58). The potential functions that cultural memory might perform can be understood in the light of power. A widely shared insight of Nietzsche is that man's basic, natural disposition would seem to favour forgetting rather than remembering, which makes the motivation of the latter worth investigating. According to Jan Assmann, "[O]ne strong incentive for memory is power" (2011: 53). Just as Peter Burkes' statement that history is written by the victors, either memory or forgetting is in alliance with power. This assumption is not new. It echoes some core concerns of poststructuralists like Michel Foucault and Jacque Derrida. Michel Foucault argues that memory is one of the key elements people contest restlessly for. "He who controls people's memory will have command of their behaviour. So, possessing, controlling and managing memory is concerning life and death." (Foucault, 2000: 207) Even the apparently neutral archives, as typical realms of cultural memory, can never be made devoid of power operation. As Jacque Derrida points out, "[T]here is no political power without control of the archive, if not of memory" (1998: 4). The remembrance mechanism is permeated with power. What should be retrieved to the foreground to relish people's commemoration and what should be cast off their minds, gathering dust, depending on who is in charge of memory. Memory's alliance with power sets the political tone for its functions, though the political edge is not the whole picture.

Since cultural memory gives human life a second dimension or a second time, Jan Assmann argues that one of its universal functions is the "heterogenization of time, the production of nonsimultaneity, the possibility of living in two times" (2011: 68). Moreover, since culture is the basic foundation of our human existence, the cultural references of a group's past helps to "create a self-image" on which the individuals build their personal identity and provide "support for hopes and for intentions" (Assmann, 2011: 62). Besides, since the connective structures like "contra-present memory" and "anachronous structures" are the "enhanced, artificial forms" (ibid.: 10) of cultural memory that cultural memory studies are preoccupied with, another function of cultural memory is to "contrapresent", to gain "freedom through memory". (ibid.: 68)

To further illustrate the functions of cultural memory, Aleida Assmann first distinguishes between two complementary modes of memory, namely, functional memory and storage memory, corresponding to memory and history, respectively. Functional memory is "inhabited memory", thus "connected with individual persons who re-embody it as its bearers and addressees", possessing the features of "being grouped, selective, normative and future-oriented". (A. Assmann, 2011: 123-127) Functional memory constitutes the meaningful elements of memory. In contrast, storage memory is rendered secondary. It is uninhabited and has temporally lost living relevance to reality. It is more like an amorphous repository of functional memory rather than the opposition to it. It is not actualized partially because it contains the "extremely heterogeneous elements" (ibid.: 127) that do not fit in a society's frameworks or need to be buried owing to the possible pain and shame that they may incur. The relationship between functional memory and storage memory is like that of foreground and background. Storage memory provides a prerequisite for cultural renewal, change and renaissance. It can also "verify, support or correct functional memory" (ibid.: 129). Moreover, "functional memory can orient and motivate storage memory" (ibid.: 132). They are interconvertible. However, it is the functional memory that performs certain functions, such as "legitimization, delegitimization, and distinction" (ibid.: 128). To quote Aleida Assmann, "'legitimization' is the immediate concern of official and political memory", and "delegitimization" concerns itself with "unofficial remembrance" that might be invested with a substantial potential of subversion. (2011: 128) Aleida Assmann is in line with Jan Assmann in that she relates either official or unofficial memory to the claim of power. The third function of "distinction" echoes Jan Assmann's idea of creating self-image or identity political imagination.

Apart from the three dimensions above, it is also necessary to relate cultural memory to the other form of collective memory, for instance, the communicative memory, because it is an essential way of using the past in literary works involving biographical memory. Communicative memory consists of memories of the recent past, of which the most typical instance is "generational memory" whose maximum time span of existence is proximately eighty years before a "floating gap"[①] comes

---

① According to the ethnologist Jan Vansina, floating gap refers to the gap between the time of origin and recent times where little information is given with hesitation.

next. (Assmann, 2011: 33-36) Communicative memory is shared by all the members of a group though their participation in it varies considerably owing to their differences such as age. It depends on social interaction to circulate, even in a literate society. Furthermore, it has been the subject of "oral history" owing to "the directedness of experience" (ibid.: 37). In contrast, cultural memory tends to stretch for two or three millenniums and even more. More importantly, different from communicative memory which concerns the synchronic relationship between a group and its memory, cultural memory examines diachronically from the perspective of culture how memory has been constructed, transmitted and oriented for the future.

The interaction between literature and memory has become one of the most popular cultural issues at present in the twentieth-first century. Narrative is where cultural memory interacts with literature, and literary works exemplify how the past is retrieved through various narrative strategies. Jan Assmann argues that the "internalized", or in plain words, the remembered past, "finds its form in narrative". (2011: 58) In other words, narrative is one of the critical forms in which memory manifests itself. According to Astrid Erll and Ann Rigney, literature has three roles to play in the production of cultural memory, which comprise "1) literature as a medium of remembrance; 2) literature as an object of remembrance; and 3) literature as a medium for observing the production of cultural memory" (2006: 112). Renowned Chinese scholar Feng Yalin (2013; 2017) further points out that fictional literary works have their unique advantages in representing memory through various narrative strategies which can give the reconstructiveness of memory an entire play. According to Feng, in literary works, different times and spaces can be connected, the feelings of the recallers can be related to that of the recalled, and the boundary between memory and reality can be crossed.

Since memory is allowed to deviate from facts, it can relive past events, evaluate or correct them. The burgeoning cultural memory theory co-initiated by Jan and Aleida Assmann may prove to be an effective tool for interpreting neo-historical fictions with its inborn interdisciplinary advantages.

Significance and Innovations

Up to now, Peter Carey has produced nine neo-historical fiction.[①] This study aims to take seven of them in which Peter Carey revisits Australian history with the overt cultural and political concerns, namely, *Illywhacker*, *Oscar and Lucinda*, *The Unusual Life of Tristan Smith*, *Jack Maggs*, *True History of the Kelly Gang*, *Amnesia* and *A Long Way from*

[①] Present Carey studies argue that six of his novels, namely *Illywhacker* (1985), *Oscar and Lucinda* (1988), *Jack Maggs* (1998), *True History of the Kelly Gang* (2000), *My Life as a Fake* (2003) and *Parrot and Olivier in America* (2010) clearly qualify as historical fiction or historiographic metafiction (coinage by Linda Hutcheon used frequently as a synonym of neo-historical fiction). See, for instance, Andeas Gaile. *Rewriting History: Peter Carey's Fictional Biography of Australia*. Amsterdam, New York: Rodopi B. V., 2010; Peng Qinglong. *Writing back the Empire: Textuality and Historicity in Peter Carey's Fiction*. Shang hai: East China Normal University, 2005. This study includes *The Unusual Life of Tristan Smith* (1994) in the genre of neo-historical fiction for the reason that multiple textual clues can be found to indicate that the author is in fact dealing with Australia's political and social upheavals during the 1970s in his fictional world and its relationship with the United States, although it uses pseudo toponyms like Efica and Voorstand etc. For detailed analysis, see James Dahlstrom's "The Unusual Life of Gough Whitlam: Peter Carey's Tristan Smith" in *Journal of Language, Literature and Culture*, 2015, Vol. 62, No. 1: 32-47.

Home, to examine the author's reconstruction of Australia's cultural memories.① To elaborate, I conduct my analysis along the following three lines: what cultural legacies Peter Carey attempts to inscribe into the Australian memory book, how he reconstructs them in texts to interact with present social dynamics and what functions this unique reworking is supposed to fulfil with regard to Australians' contemporary preoccupations and the nation's need in the immediate future.

To achieve this, this study adopts the methodology of close reading and analyzes each text from the perspective of cultural memory theory. In addition to that, paratexts of the seven novels like authorial interviews, epigraphs annotations, acknowledgements etc., historical intertexts and his non-fictional monographs, for instance,30 *Days in Sydney: A Wildly Distorted Account* (2001) are all employed to evidence relevant analysis, making it better founded.

A study of the seven texts suggests that Peter Carey's neo-historical texts are not only narrative but also distinctively performative. Australia's colonial memories, original memories and neo-colonial memories are recuperated to construct Australian cultural subjectivity. Moreover, Australian cultural subjectivity consists of both the internal and the external dimension. In terms of its internality, it concretes the European origin of Australian culture by root-seeking, upon which Australian antiauthoritarian and nationalist traditions are created; it establishes a

---

① *My Life as a Fake* (2003) is excluded from the current study because it preoccupies majorly with issues such as the of authenticity in literature and the power of literary texts in inventing identity. See, for instance, Robert Macfarlane. "Dangerous Inventions" in *Times Literary Supplement*, 12 September 2003, 23; Bill Ashcroft, "Reading Carey Reading Malley" in *Australian Literary Studies*, 2004, Vol. 21, No. 4: 28-39; Mark Osteen. "Hideous Progeny: Forgery, *Frankenstein*, and Peter Carey's *My Life as a Fake*" in *Papers on Language & Literature*. Fall 2017, Vol. 53, No. 4: 347-382. *Parrot and Olivier in America* (2010) is excluded since it is concerned with Peter Carey's interpretation and exploration of America's democracy.

harmonious and symbiotic multicultural ecology through dialogue and negotiation between Australian Whites and Aborigines; Australians who are freed from historical burdens through a critical re-evaluation of its cultural heritage and narrative therapy overcome the cultural inferiority complex and their limitations, restore their cultural confidence, and strive for superiority. From the external perspective, the subjectivity of Australian culture is closely linked to the criticism of and resistance to American hegemony and has a distinctive anti-neo-colonial characteristic.

This research is expected to be of both theoretical and practical significance in the following aspects. To begin with, a holistic and diachronic delineation of Carey's neo-historical fiction to explore their constructive element and cultural concern is expected to deepen Carey studies in that it facilitates a fuller comprehension of his thematic preoccupations and a more dynamic grasp of his writing career. Secondly, interpreting Carey's writings from the perspective of cultural memory theory might help broaden the research horizons of Carey critics at home and abroad. Thirdly, the current research is supposed to contribute to the discussion of how the burgeoning theory interacts more effectively with literature and how societies recollect their past through literature. Last but not least, the excavation of Carey's efficient textual techniques in the light of expressing thematic visions might offer feasible references for novelists to tell their national stories in their writings.

This study is, to some extent, innovative in the employment of the cultural memory theory, the encompassment of relevant paratexts and historical, the preoccupation on the constructive and cultural themes of Carey's neo-historical fictions and the holistic and diachronic delineation of them.

Layout of the Monograph

This monograph is aimed to study Peter Carey's reconstruction of Australia's cultural memories in his seven neo-historical fictions. The memories represented in the texts are classified into Australia's colonial memory, original memory, and neo-colonial memory, corresponding to the First, Second and Third Chapter of the main body of this monograph. The seven texts are allocated to the three chapters for close examination according to what kind of memories are retrieved in them. Colonial memory is the earliest of Australia's collective memory, and it also determines the morphology of its original memory to a large extent. They combine to constitute the introversion of Australia's cultural memory. Neo-colonial memory is Australia's late memory and the extroversion of its cultural memory.

This monograph consists of five parts: Introduction, Chapter One, Chapter Two, Chapter Three and Conclusion. The introductory part comprises six subsections. The first section is Peter Carey's biography and his writings. The second section combs the research status of Carey criticism at home and abroad. The third section explains the research background of the monograph. The fourth section introduces the theoretical framework of this research, and analyzes briefly the genealogy and main dimensions of the cultural memory theory and its applicability to literary studies. The fifth section sketches the theoretical and practical significance of this research as well as its innovations. The sixth section introduces the layout of this monograph.

Chapter One studies how Carey reconstructs Australia's colonial memories to trace its cultural roots, re-evaluate them critically and invent the antiauthoritarian tradition. This chapter is divided into three sections.

The first section is devoted to the analysis of how the Empire's expedition is recalled in *Oscar and Lucinda* to demonstrate the consistency between Australian culture and the Victorian tradition and denounce the Europeans for their genocide of the Aborigines and destruction of the indigenous culture to transplant European civilization. The second section analyzes how Carey mythologizes Australia's convict memory in *Jack Maggs* to consolidate Australia's European origin and the unbreakable blood between Australia and Britain, criticize the harsh and unfair Transportation System and emancipate Australians from the traumatic past by exonerating Maggs therefore their convict ancestors. The third section is an examination of how Australia's bushranging legend is remembered in *True History of the Kelly Gang* to establish a monument to the alienated Irish and Irish culture in Australian collective memory, invent Australia's antiauthoritarian tradition and criticize the colonial government whose corruption and abuse of justice have rendered Australia a living hell.

Chapter Two is the study of how Australia's original cultural memories are reconstructed to concrete identity, heal, and surpass. This chapter comprises two sections. The first section focuses on how Carey recalls Australia's national lies, nationalism, multiculturalism, and the sense of imprisonment in *Illywhacker* to evoke Australians' resonance to confirm their collective identity, heal those whose nationalist dreams have been repeatedly shattered and those who have suffered from the sense of imprisonment, and reappraise Australia's historical conservativism and provincial ethnic policy in order to encourage a surpassing of the existing limitations to construct a new subjectivity for the future. The second section concentrates on how Carey reconfigures the Aboriginal memory in *A Long Way from Home* to monument the Aborigines whose land has been appropriated and who have been slaughtered or "stolen", cure them, condemn Australian racist policies and alert the world to racial violence.

Chapter Three examines how Carey reconfigures Australia's neo-colonial memories to blame and illumine the present. This chapter consists of two sections. The first section investigates how Australia's "Americanization" memory is restored in *The Unusual Life of Tristan Smith* to condemn American imperialism, alert Australians to the colonizing risks of "Americanization" and remind Australians of the significance of adhering to their cultural traditions and maintaining cultural subjectivity in the context of global capitalism. The second section is devoted to the analysis of how Australia's "ally" memory is recuperated to connect the Battle of Brisbane and the constitutional crisis with the forgetting tradition to condemn the political hegemony of the United States and criticize Australian for forgetting history and cringing.

The fifth part of the monograph is the Conclusion which relates the major findings. First of all, in his neo-historical fiction, Peter Carey constructs Australian cultural subjectivity through the retrieval of Australia's colonial memories, original memories and neo-colonial memories. It consists of both the internal and the external dimensions. Secondly, Carey's neo-historical fictions have distinct postmodern and existentialist flavours. Thirdly, Carey has played an overtly more progressive role in reconstructing Australia's cultural memories ever since the early 1990s. He has shifted his preoccupations from a pure disenchantment of the imperial and official memory to taking this engineering as a threshold to further launch a poetic exploration of Australia's way out of its current predicament. Carey's neo-historical fiction are symbolic literary demonstration of Australian cultural memory ecology in the multicultural and global capitalism context. The poetic construction of Australian cultural subjectivity in his works is also the wisdom of interculturalism that the author contributes to the world.

Chapter One　Australia's Colonial Memories[①] to Trace Origin, Re-appraise and Invent Traditions

Australian official memory begins with Captain Cook's discovery of the *terra nullius* which preludes its status as another convict dump of Great Britain after the independence of the penal colonies in North America. However, that is only part of the story. Australia is "a place not just for the punishment and reformation of British criminals but also for the profit of merchants interested in the riches of the East" (Clark, 1973: 3). For a long time in the colonial period, it has considered itself and has been considered as a "new province of Britain's gentry" and "an echo of Old England" in the Antipodes. (ibid.: 17, 116) Colonial Australians preferred to regard themselves first as "Britons" and then as "Victorians" (张计连, 2015: 27). Australia's strong attachment to Britain did not fluctuate much until the Second World War when Australians realized that they had to count on the more powerful United States for their national security. The Commonwealth of Australia participated in the First World

---

① By "colonial memories" I refer to Australia's cultural memories of the colonial period. They are mainly represented by Peter Carey in his colonial trilogy, namely, *Oscar and Lucinda*, *Jack Maggs* and *True History of the Kelly Gang*.

War out of "ethnic loyalty" (Macintyre, 1999: 166). To testify that Australians are "the most loyal and devoted to the King and the Empire", they sacrificed themselves savagely as sons and daughters for "[g]lory, honour and a place in humanity's hall of renown" (Clark, 1981: 377).

The peculiar relationship between Australia and Britain throughout history makes it impossible to understand Australian culture without reference to its British inheritance. To a great extent, Australia and Australians are defined by their connection with Britain. David Carter points out the unbreakable bond, "[T]hough ever since early 1960s, the British connection has ceased to the source of anxiety, envy or even interest to writers, artists and intellectuals, to many till today, Britain was still their spiritual home that they often haunted" (2000: 68-69). This is especially true for Peter Carey, who has drawn endless inspiration from his nation's colonial memories and represented them with remarkable richness and complexity. In the colonial trilogy, he restores Australia's collective memories of the Christian civilization, the gambling and the misogyny tradition in *Oscar and Lucinda* to suggest the continuity between Australian culture and its British ancestry and critically reevaluate the Empire's civilization advancement on the southern land. He reconfigures Australia's convict memory in *Jack Maggs* first to denounce Britain's Transportation System for scapegoating and alienating the minor offenders to serve its own interests. This recuperation also serves to indicate Australia's unbreakable spiritual connection with its cultural ancestry and prelude the author's poetic remedy of embracing the prospering Australian culture to build a blissful life. Australia's European origin is not confined to the British heritage as is recorded in official memory. Carey bridges the gap by reworking Australia's bushranging memory in *True History of the Kelly Gang* to monument Australia's cultural debt to Ireland, especially for its antiauthoritarian tradition which is considered of practical significance in the contemporary epoch when hegemonic threat still exists.

In addition to the functions discussed above, Peter Carey's recuperation of Australia's colonial memory also serves as a therapeutic power. Through the recollection of Australia's collective memory, the expatriate author is able to bridge his break with his native culture in the poetic space. Nestling himself again in the spiritual home cures his homesickness and soothes his anxiety of influence from the overwhelming imperial culture. The following three sections will be devoted to a detailed examination of how the author reworks those memories to perform the relevant functions discussed above in the three texts.

1.1 European Civilization Remembered as a Double-edged Sword: *Oscar and Lucinda*

For Australians, the time when Great Britain tried to plant European civilization in Australia, to quote Charles Dickens, "was the best of times, and it was the worst of times", depending on whether they were appropriators or genuine owners of the land. Using convicts in New South Wales and Van Diemen's Land created both enormous wealth and moral evils of slavery. Moreover, making land grants to Britons of capital in Western Australia boosted the colony's economy while causing settlement dispersion and reducing the supposedly respectable immigrants to a way of life "indistinguishable from that of the barbarian" (Clark, 1973: 43). To perform an act of mercy for the downtrodden indigenous peoples and saving British workers from their brutality, the colonization commissioners decided on bringing their holy faith, Christianity, to southern Australia to establish a virtuous and enlightened society. However, as is reviewed by Manning Clark, "between the conception and the creation fell the shadow of human behaviour" (1973: 48). And that gap is where Peter Carey dives in.

Carey travels back to the Victorian age in *Oscar and Lucinda* to excavate Australia's Christian inheritance. Through the extradiegetic and intradiegetic narrator's recollection of his great grandfather's life story, he pastiches the Empire's expedition to the Antipodes, which has implanted Christianity into the southern continent, and Australia's gambling as well as misogyny traditions. With the deployment of surrealism, parody, and metafiction, the restored collective memories function primarily to suggest the continuity between Australian culture and its English ancestry. Moreover, Britain's civilization advancement on the southern land is also recuperated for an incisively critical re-evaluation in that Christian civilization is established at the cost of numerous aboriginal lives and their ancient culture. Based on a close reading of the text, I will analyze how these functions are achieved through the author's reconstruction of Australia's Victorian memories in the three parts following a brief introduction of the basics of the fiction which includes a plot summary, how the paradox of self-referentiality and verisimilitude is created to fit it into neo-historical fiction, and a brief literary review. ①

1.1.1 Preliminaries of the Fiction ②

Carey's monumental masterpiece *Oscar and Lucinda*, published in 1988, later turned out to be a huge success, winning the author his first Booker Prize and three other Australian awards, including the Miles

---

① The analysis of each of the seven fictions begins with this three-phase pattern in the "Preliminaries of the Fiction". I prefer not to restate them to avoid unnecessary repetition.

② In this research, the analysis of every text begins with "Preliminaries of the Fiction". "Preliminaries" is an expedient conception of the fundamental information of the fiction which includes a plot summary, how the paradox of self-referentiality and verisimilitude is created to fit it into the genre of neo-historical fiction, and a literary review.

Franklin Award. Don Anderson proclaims that this novel "outshone even his own prior creations" and Carey's virtuosity and stylish writing even eclipsed John Barth. (1988: 71) It was adapted into a film under the same name directed by Gillian Armstrong and starred Ralph Fiennes, Cate Blanchett, and Tom Wilkinson, which received considerably good reviews. *Oscar and Lucinda* is Peter Carey's most lauded work and is widely viewed as a monument to the Australian bicentenary of the white establishment, though it is far from being a eulogy of that chapter of history.

The novel relates Australia to its English ancestry both in motif and form. Apart from structuring the fiction in accordance with Christianity (张计连, 2015: 140), the author acknowledges that he draws inspiration partly from *Father and Son*, the autobiography of the English poet Edmund Gosse. Set both in nineteenth century Australia and England, it tells a beautiful love story yet a romantic tragedy between the Victorian Anglican priest Oscar Hopkins, an obsessive gambler, and another compulsive gambler, the young Australian heiress named Lucinda Leplastrier. Their story is retold from the memory of the narrator Bob, the great-grandson of Oscar Hopkins. As reviewed by Angela Carter, with "extraordinary richness, complexity and strength... it brings the past, in all its difference, bewilderingly into our present" (Carey, 1988: cover).[①] The fiction deploys post-modern and neo-colonial strategies to address Australia's nineteenth-century colonial past and presents readers Australia's cultural mosaic at that period of time. It stirs Australia's cultural memories of the imperial expedition, the Christian advancement, and other social mores such as the pervasion of gambling in Victorian Australia and the infamous misogyny, only that the author offers another

---

① The following quotations from *Oscar and Lucinda* in this section are annotated with only the page number.

version of narrative that deviates from the official memory.

Oscar Hopkins is the only son of Theophilus Hopkins, minister of an Evangelical church in Hennacombe, Devon, England. Dubious about his father's faith, he runs away from home and lives with Mr. Hugh Stratton, an Anglican Church minister, and his wife. Mr. Stratton fathers him and later sends him to Oxford to study theology with the intention of making him a reverend. However, influenced by his roommate Wardley Fish, Oscar takes to horse races and later gets compulsively addicted to gambling. Gambling is considered the unforgivably vilest evil by Christianity, not to mention the evangelicals. However, Oscar soon manages to achieve equilibrium by giving out most of the money he earns to help the poverty-stricken Mr. and Mrs. Stratton and other poor people, leaving himself only enough quids to support the necessities for life. Immersed in the pleasure of helping others out, Oscar firmly believes that gambling is "imbued with God's grace" (179). He thus exonerates himself from the sin or guilt completely. He believes he is answering God's call to win money at races to feed and clothe himself and save others who are suffering from poverty. "He knew that God would give him money at the races and thereby ease the burden that the Strattons had placed upon themselves... God would do this just as He has told Moses to divide the land between the tribes of Israel... The Almighty would be Oscar's source of information." (114) He is assured that he is the chosen one, the shepherd appointed by God. It is this belief that prompts him to sail across the sea to the Antipodes when he is 22 years old. He is convinced that "God was sending him to A New South Wales" (189).

Lucinda, who is orphaned and bequeathed a considerable inheritance by her English parents, usually kills her loneliness and boredom by playing cards with her neighbours. Gambling, especially losing money in games, seems to be the only thing that makes her happy. She goes to London to visit her relatives and her parents' friends with the hope of meeting her Mr. Right there but returns with great disappointment and hurt. Owing to their common interest in gambling, the two gamblers, Oscar the compulsive and Lucinda the obsessive meet and share a pleasant journey on the ship named Leviathan which carries tons of English passengers and fauna to Australia. Back in South Wales, Lucinda busies herself with her investment in the glassworks in Darling Harbour. She consults Reverend Dennis Hasset about the "physical properties and manufacture of glass" (132) and gradually develops an affection for him. But her "less well-developed moral sense" fills Hasset with the resolution that "they were too queer a pair to contemplate" (154), and finally, he leaves for Boat Wollahra vicarage to avoid her and possible scandal. Her thwarted love entices her into going to a Chinese trot to forget all about the rejection and humiliation and the overwhelming solitude. There, he meets Oscar who is appointed by the bishop Dancer to fill the vacancy Hasset has left. To flee from her fear and loneliness and his futility in this alien land, they engage themselves in gambling again, and that leads to Oscar's dismissal by the bishop who himself is a card player. Out of guilt that she has caused Oscar to lose his job, Lucinda employs him as her clerk responsible for mixing ink. They gradually become friends and later develop a romantic affection towards each other though neither of them is brave or intelligent enough to take the initiative to confess.

Possessed by the misunderstanding that Lucinda is still in love with Hasset, Oscar proposes Lucinda for manufacturing a glass church for the former reverend. In order to demonstrate his selfless love for her, he volunteers to escort it to Bellingen. Knowing that this mission may expose Oscar to unpredictable dangers lurking in the journey, which is the last thing she'd like to see, Lucinda prays to God to guard his safety and wagers all her inheritance on that. For her, the church "was not a celebration of sacred love, but of their own" (455), and all her possessions and her worldly goods are Oscar's dowry. However, Oscar fails to read her mind. Having survived Jeffris' drug and torment and New South Wales' brutal bush, he is easily compromised by the cunning widow, Mariam, and ends up marrying her soon after he arrives at Bellingen. The glass church cracks and water seeps in. Guilt-smitten Oscar eventually sinks into Bellinger River with the church. His wife and son inherit all of Lucinda's inheritance according to her promise.

In critical academia, scholars like Trevor Byrne (2001) and Andrea Gaile (2010) have examined the problem of history involved in *Oscar and Lucinda* by categorizing this novel into a "historiographic metafiction"[①], a "sub-genre" (Rousselot, 2014: 1) of the more umbrella neo-historical fiction. Like other neo-historical novels, *Oscar and Lucinda* have the inherent paradox of self-referentiality and verisimilitude. Peter Carey exposes the novel's artificiality in and out of the text. Within the text, the extradiegetic narrator Bob warns readers at the threshold that he inherits the "story" from her mother, who has "an excess of emotion in her style" when telling her family stories and that "there was something false" (2) in them. He also reminds readers to take caution against his narrative since even "local history" (ibid.) tends to record things selectively. In fact, the narrator is "sufficiently self-conscious to remind the reader of its mediating presence throughout" (Hassall, 1994: 122). What the implied author tries to convey through the narrator is the constructiveness of memory as well as the fictionality of this novel.

Since paratexts of a novel are taken as "the threshold of

---

① Historiographic metafiction is the coinage of Canadian scholar Linda Hutcheon. This postmodern genre is used to refer to "those well-known and popular novels which are both intensely self-reflexive and yet paradoxically also lay claim to historical events and personages" (Hutcheon, Poetics: 5).

interpretation" (Genette, 1997), the metafictionality of *Oscar and Lucinda* can also be approached in the light of the authorial "interview" which is "one of the most familiar forms of public epitext" (ibid.: 3). "Characterized by an authorial intention and assumption of responsibility" (ibid.) and usually containing the author's "motivational analysis" (ibid.: 363) as well as the anatomy of his creative practice, interviews shed considerable light on the interpretation of literary works. In the interview with Eleanor Wachtel, Carey states quite frankly that, as an author, he is more "inventing" history and "re-shaping it" and that, like all other writers, he is making things up on the "blank page" (1993: 103-104). His statements in the interview make clear the fictional status of this novel, however serious he has been about certain historical facts involved in the text.

Nevertheless, while disclosing the work as an artifice on the one hand, the author spares no effort in directing readers' attention to its authenticity on the other. And the verisimilitude is not just created by his reference to authentic geographical names such as Bellingen and the Crystal Palace, but also historical figures such as Marian Evans (George Eliot). That the novel is designed to be Bob's critical remembrance of his family history and also invites readers to acknowledge his sincerity. In addition, the paratextual "Acknowledgements" in which the author proclaims his "intellectual backing" (Genette, 1997: 136) from Keith Hall the Australian historian, Edmund Gosse, the English poet and author, as well as Henry Philip Gosse, the English naturalist, are not unimportant in suggesting the truthfulness of the novel. If to say that the author exposes the artificiality of his literary work to unveil ruthlessly a more prevailing postmodern belief of the discursiveness of history, he is practically possessed by the same amount of enthusiasm for excavating truthfulness from the ashes of history.

Chapter One Australia's Colonial Memories to Trace Origin, Re-appraise and Invent Traditions

Owing to the social backdrop concerning the creation of *Oscar and Lucinda* combined with the overt motif it is engaged with, most previous critics approach this fiction with the critical tools provided by neo-colonialism or post-modernism. Most overseas critics are fascinated with Carey's dealing with history but this results in competing arguments. Scholars like Bruce Woodcock (1996), Trevor Byrne (2001; 2013), Andrea Gaile (2010), Jessica Cox (2017) etc. contend that Peter Carey makes use of postmodern techniques to re-evaluate Australia's nineteenth-century past and offers an alternative version of hidden imperial history to challenge metanarrative. As Linda Hutcheon argues, this espouses "a postmodern ideology of plurality and recognition of difference" (1988: 114). While other researchers like David Callahan (1990) tend to argue that Carey's intention of subversion is even subverted by his parody of the English canon, and the overt self-consciousness also undermines his neo-colonial drive owing to its inadequacy to represent historical knowledge. Differentiated from the mainstream trend of study relating textual analysis to the outside world it represents, there are researches in recent years that are mainly aimed at aesthetic appreciation of the novel. Scholars like Erica Lombard and Mike Marais (2013) and Sue Fazilleau (2005) either probe into the work from the perspective of reading ethics to study how the author deploys narrative deception and irony to achieve a systemic frustration of readers' expectations or investigate how the author plays on readers expectations aesthetically and thematically using parody and the transgression of Victorian literary tradition.

Domestic researchers proximately follow the same route and examine the novel mainly from the postcolonial perspective, investigating how the imperial order or grand narrative is contested or subverted within the text. Research conducted by Peng Qinglong (2005; 2009), Li Mingxing (2014), Du Guochao (2007), Hua Juan (2018) etc. falls under this denomination of criticism. Either the political metaphors of the Victorian expedition, the representation of neo-colonialism through the "mixed identity", the "splice plots", and the "hybridity of narrative language" (李明星,2014), the imperial lies, or Australia's neo-colonial identity is brought under discussion. Undoubtly, the postcolonial angle does not exhaust the various points of view that domestic scholars approach in this monumental novel. Interpretations from the perspectives of "the reception theory" (张计连,2010), the cultural identity (张计连,2015), the "barriers of communication" metaphorized in the glass church (刘阳, 2014), the feminist criticism (祖华萍,2014), and the "spatial narrative" theory (范丹丹,2016) to analyze the love tragedy between Oscar and Lucinda etc. are all inspiring and valuable practices to replenish the repertoire of Carey study. However, the complexity and richness of this monumental masterpiece is far from being fully excavated.

Oscar and Lucinda was published in 1988, the year of the bicentenary of the white occupation. It is also the era when Australian academia and the political field are possessed by the frenzy of skepticism about and re-evaluation of history. The history wars turn out to be a common theme of many neo-historical fictions. Trevor Byrne argues that this new genre "ironizes history, interrogates it, and highlights that the very possibility of communicating anything concrete about it is problematic" (2013: 209). The historical and intellectual backdrop provides Peter Carey with the necessary frame of reference to relate to the past. As Ruth Brown argues, "*Oscar and Lucinda* is not about finding new cultural allegiances: it invites a fresh look at the old ones" (1995: 140). This authorial intention can be better illustrated in Carey's confession of why he is so fascinated with the church that inspires his creation.

[A]lthough I was no longer a Christian, the image of the church evoked a great deal of my own cultural and spiritual history.

If white Australia had a "culture" it was predominantly a Christian one — it had destroyed 40,000 years of Aboriginal culture to establish itself. Now, it seemed the Christian culture was dying. This seemed an interesting site for an exploration, which is what *Oscar and Lucinda* is — not so much saving history as inventing it, re-shaping it, creating ways of looking at it ... in young countries it seems more important to find ways to look at your past ... It's not always clear what it means ... But it's a great thing for the writers. You have a sense ... that you can do anything. The page is still blank. We really can make ourselves up. (Wachtel, 1993: 103-104)

Both the close reading of the text and the stated authorial intent in the excerpted interview suggest that what Peter Carey revisits is Australia's cultural memory in the Victorian epoch. Christianity being one of the central aspects of Victorian tradition, it is not exaggerating for Sue Ryan Fazilleau to argue that the novel "is itself a bicentennial monument to the memory of the white Christian cultural heritage" (2005: 27). Other issues which are not unimportant like gambling and misogyny are also remembered to be part of Victorian tradition which the author retrieves through Bob the narrator's rewriting of his family memory. For one thing, Australia, as a colony of the British Empire, passively receives and interiorizes the Victorian cultural inheritance which arrives simultaneously with the imperial expedition to this southern hemisphere. For another, the Australian local culture that has nurtured this land over thousands of years comes into contact and wrestles with the imported one. The following sections will be devoted to the examination of those issues from the perspective of cultural memory.

1.1.2 Christian Civilization as a Sugar-coated Bullet

The 1840s witnessed Great Britain's accomplishment of the industrial revolution and the unprecedented economical and cultural prosperity that follows. Ambitious bourgeoisie are bursting with confidence in the industrial advancement they have achieved and the Christian belief that provides them with high moral standards. For one thing, they are in desperate need of setting up colonies throughout the world to dump goods and plunder raw materials to sustain the industrial development. For another, they are more than eager to spread their economic and religious civilization to help those "backward" regions develop and redeem the souls of the "barbarians" out there. According to Manning Clark, "barbarism was gaining the ascendancy in huge portions" of the southern land and "a strange assemblage of human beings was glorying in lawlessness, and inflicting the most hideous cruelty on defenceless savages" (1973: 245) by the 1840s. This backdrop brings the advent of Oscar Hopkins as well as Lucinda's glassworks, which makes the central image and structure metaphor of the novel, the glass church, possible.

For any form of community, "Memory needs places and tends toward spatialization" (Assmann, 2011: 25). This particular setting provides the base for the group members to interact with each other and the spatial reference points for their memories. "Group and place take on a symbolic sense of community" (ibid.) so that when that place is absent from the group's material life, it is remembered symbolically as "home" to host its members' nostalgic sentiment and as a holy site for them to pilgrimage. The place where Bob's family memory inhabits is "the little church of St. John's", which makes his mother proud, his father jealous, and him skeptical. The glass church is actually devised by the author as a double-meaning symbol which emblemizes both the expansion of the Empire's industrial accomplishment and the extension of its Christian civilization to the southern continent, though Trevor Byrne considers it as a metaphor highlighting the author's "doubts about history" (2001: 133).

Chapter One Australia's Colonial Memories to Trace Origin, Re-appraise and Invent Traditions

The author shows his extraordinary ingenuity in representing Australia's most significant collective memory of its Christian heritage in the nineteenth century in the narrator's family memory of the glass church that his great-grandfather Oscar escorts across the inland of Australia. Scattered memories like the implantation of Christian civilization, aboriginal dispossession, as well as imperial exploration, are collaged into his journey to produce a bizarre spectacle of the imperial expedition in the Victorian era.

Only that Bob is "rewriting" his family memory in which his mother wishfully describes Oscar "to be a "missionary" and a pioneer Anglican", and the whole family is fed on the myth that he is "crowed in amongst poor immigrants" "with his map and celluloid, his Bible, his Book of Common Prayer" (190). Family memory is subject to renewal and change as its members turn to a different reference framework. Consequently, in Bob's memory, the glass church thrusts in Bellingen as an unacclimatized alien, Oscar stumbles in the antipode as an impotent clown, Jeffris ventures into the southern continent as the Empire's ruthless military proxy, and the muted black souls are able to tell their own sad stories. It is safe to conclude from Bob's recollection that the Christian civilization is like a sugar-coated bullet shot in the heart of the indigenous peoples and in aboriginal culture. This idea is embodied in the glass metaphor:

> The glass was by way of being a symbol of weakness and strength; it was a cipher of someone else's heart. It was a confession, an accusation, a cry of pain... glass is a thing in disguise, an actor, is not solid at all, but a liquid, that an old sheet of glass will not only take on royal and purplish tinge but will reveal it true liquid nature by having grown fatter at the bottom and thinner at the top, and that even while it is as frail as the ice on a

Prarramatta puddle, it is stronger under compression than Sydney stone, that it is invisible, solid, in short, a joyous and paradoxical thing, as good as a material as any to build a life on. (132-133)

Lucinda's above reflection on the nature of glass foreshadows both the sufferings that the implantation of Christian culture is doomed to cause to the indigenous peoples and the far-reaching influence it exerts on Australian culture. The author unfolds this picture roll through Oscar's escort of the glass church to Bellingen.

Oscar sets his foot on New South Wales, in his own words, to answer the call of God. However, the real picture is symbolically foreshadowed by the ship he takes, the Leviathan, which is a vicious sea monster in the Hebrew Bible. Oscar's journey to the southern hemisphere is bound to be imbued with evils. When it comes to the interaction between Christianity and Australia, according to Bob's narrative, this imported religion turns out to be incompatible with the antipodes. The incompatibility between Christianity and Australia is firstly embodied by the surrealist use of the glass church. Then, it is embodied by Oscar who is the incarnation of Christianity and is ironically and fatally flawed. He is addicted to gambling, and he is adept at absolving himself from sin. He casts doubt on God's existence and questions the meaning of religious belief. On Leviathan, after hearing Lucinda's confession of her obsession with gambling, he questions her "with angry sort of passion" that "Where is the sin" (261). He claims passionately that "our whole faith is a wager... we bet there is a God. We bet our life on it. We calculate the odds, the return that we shall sit with the saints in paradise... I can't see such a God, whose fundamental requirement of us is that we gamble our mortal souls ... we must stake *everything* on the unprovable fact of His existence" (261-262).

His compulsive infatuation with gambling, combined with his

skepticism of his religious belief, exposes the problems of Christianity itself in the nineteenth century. It also indicates that Darwin's evolution theory has exerted a considerable impact on people's cognition. It surely preludes his subsequent being dismissed as an imperial reverend.

Christianity is incapable of saving the local Australians since it is problematic in itself. It is too weak to acclimate itself to the harsh environment of the continent. Its impotence is embodied by Oscar, the reverend. When further put under the surveillance of those Australian workers in Lucinda's glassworks, he appears too "young, inadequate, inexperience" (307) for the industry. In the eyes of the Australian girl Lucinda, he is "immature and frivolous", and "the furnishings of his vicarage were vulgar in the extreme" (309). People find his "form of service as unappetizing as unbuttered bread" (307). He may be meant to spread the glory of God to benefit more people and bring those poor and unblessed souls of those blacks under the shepherd of God. However, in order to "guarantee his place in history" (481), his protectors turn the church into a plausible justification for their massacre of the people he claims to redeem. Moreover, he is completely impotent to stop that except to benumb himself with opium. Preaching sermons of Christianity while the British invaders are expelling the blacks, appropriating their land and causing them detrimental disasters only adds to the hypocrisy of Oscar and his religion. That explains Lucinda's observation that "Sydney was a blinding place … The stories of gospels lay across the harsh landscape like sheets of newspaper on a polished floor. They slid, slipped, did not connect to anything beneath them" (307).

On the contrary, Christianity is, to some degree, the root of white men's cruelty to the defenceless aborigines. Moreover, Oscar, the supposed missionary, stands witness to white men's lowering them to the levels of beasts. As Jeffris lectures on Oscar, "churches are not carried by choirboys; neither has the Empire been built by angels" (482). Jeffris' ruthless exploit of this land and ferocious slaughter of those blacks shock him and cause him overwhelming agony. Many a time, Oscar sees "the knave was disposed of before a soul came out to see the sunlight" (492). He "saw, in every blackened stump, every fallen log, in every shadow beneath a she-oak or turpentine, the same crumpled dark bodies, the frail and tender envelops of human souls... He imagined he could smell the blood" (482). Oscar protests on behalf of the aboriginal that "[I]f it was my country, sir, I would be feared to see you coming... And I would pray to God to forgive you, and all of us who are of your party" (481). Seeing too many innocent creatures being shot or speared to death, Oscar condemns Jeffris as a "murderer" (487) and tries to stop him from more slaughters of the native. Christianity is only a cover for white men's greed for land and wealth. However, he is too weak to do that. Jeffris orders his men to tie him up and feeds Oscar with laudanum to stop him from interfering in his business. Nevertheless, his impotence and powerlessness render him permanent yet futile pain, outrage and hatred. Later, helpless Oscar, who is "pressed by a crushing weight of evil" (484), "had administered his own laudanum... he sipped on it from time to time" (479) to mask the smell of blood and to hypnotize his conscience as a clergyman. When he preaches to the young fellows about Jesus and other Christian stories of martyrs, he actually plays the part of an accomplice of the murder in that his sermons mesmerize the natives so that they regard the sufferings inflicted by the white people as God's tests on them, take them for granted and interiorize them into part of their natural existence. Through Oscar's pacification of those smitten souls, Christianity plays the part of cultural domestication to dissolve their possible revolt. It paves the way for the Victorian Empire's conquer of Australia and its peoples having inhabited there for thousands of years. In

Bob's memory, his great-grandfather's transportation of the glass church across the Australian bush is never an innocent journey, not to say a scared one. Neither his reverend great-grandfather nor Christianity is able to save the downtrodden souls. On the contrary, the establishment of the Christian culture in the new land frequently involves violent confrontations and even massacres. If Oscar symbolizes the Victorian cultural infiltration into Australia, Jeffris would represent the concomitant political and economic colonization descending upon the land with that cultural tour. The advent of Christianity couples with the Empire's appropriation of the land and conquering of the indigenous peoples, as the glass church arrives simultaneously with the imperial explorer, Jeffris.

More than a bodyguard that Lucinda hires to safeguard her beloved Oscar and transport the church, Jeffris is an ambitious explorer and an aggressive colonizer of the Empire, so he recruits a team including blacksmiths, carpenters, and collectors of plants, birds etc. Escorting the glass church is only the cover that Jeffris has to take to conduct a deep exploration of the new continent and realize his ambition. He does not like the church at all. He considers it the "silliest thing he had ever heard of" (449). He is a canonical type of imperial conqueror: ambitious, arrogant, aggressive and brutal. He cares only "to make a name of himself with his trigonometry and explorations" (442). "His great obsession in life was that he should be an explorer of unmapped territories. He was not tall like Burke or educated like Mitchell. But you could not hear him talk and doubt that he would finally triumph." (168) Even his great passion for the widow of Captain Burrows is kindled and maintained by his interest in the late Captain's diaries containing sketches of the bivouacs and creeks, the description of his journey and the records of raids against the blacks. Jeffris dreams of being a hero like his idol, Sir Thomas

Mitchell, surveyor and explorer of south-eastern Australia during the 1830s-1840s. He schemes to be an author of this land and do something useful to explore and settle his posterity. That is why "all his adult life had been spent in preparation for the day when he should survey unmapped country, have a journey, publish a map" (410).

Having Lucinda's capital as backing, Jeffris is with his might doubled. He engages himself in a thorough exploration of the outback of Australia which he has planned for his whole life. He surveys the altitudes of every peak and saddle precisely, and he keeps records of the birds and plants unique to this continent. "He had put names to several largish creeks. He had set the heights of many mountains which had previously been wildly misdescribed... His sketches of the countryside, the long ridges of mountains etc. were as good as anything in Mitchell's journals" (480). While Jeffris is surveying the landscape, recording its creatures and naming them, he is assuming the position of God, declaring himself as the author and claiming his right to this land. In other words, he is colonizing this territory since, according to Elleke Boehmer, colonialism could be a "cartographic undertaking": to map or spatially conceive a territory using figures which harked back to home ground. (2005: 17) Instead of contenting himself with solely objective statistical recording, his depictions are biased and involve distortion, symbolizing the Empire's discursive power over the natives. "His journals recorded that he had 'given better than we took' from the 'Spitting tribe'. Also: '6 treacherous knaves' from the Yarra-Happini had been 'dispatched' by their guns. He had also successfully defended the party from the 'murderous Kumbaingiri'" (480). Jeffris' knowledge of this land lends to an impromptu manipulation, and it lays a foundation for the Empire's historical narrative which is premised on the binary oppositions of civilization versus savagery, centre versus periphery, and superiority versus inferiority. Australia's locality is eroticized and described "as delicate as violet petals" (420). Aborigines are demonized and stigmatized as "spitting", "treacherous", and "murderous" creatures and considered unworthy of the land and history. The author deploys irony to satirize the despicable explorer and imperial hegemony and disenchants the pretentious European civilization. Jeffris' explorative behaviours throughout Australian bush signify the process of the Empire's colonization of this continent both by way of mapping and through the manipulative narrative, which is as hard and sharp as the "spine of steel" (420). However, the above presentation portraits only the seemingly tranquil proportion of the whole panorama of the imperial expedition in the name of spreading religious civilization. More brutality and massacres are recollected from the memory of its victims, the indigenous people. After all, they are the ones who feel this pain most authentically.

In the homodiegetic narrator, Kumbaingiri Billy's memory, the Europeans are brought under the gaze of the aborigines and show their "otherness". They are totally "strangers" (476) in the Antipodes, like "spirits" and "dead men" (475). They climb hills, chop down trees, and make maps, just like clowns. They are ferocious. Wherever they go, there are left only "dead trees" (ibid.) and "removed bees" (476). They treat the aboriginal as castles. A young guide from the Narcoo tribe who is ignorant of their intention is hired to show them the way to Kumbaingiri, but "this fellow had to lie on his back first" (ibid.), Whenever they cross a river. When the Kumbaingiri people come with torches at night to talk to them, they do not even have the patience to understand the little blacks, and they say these disgusting knaves give them a fright. "Then there was a lot of shooting ... Then they went back and fired more rifles at the Kumbaingiri" (478). It is evident that the aborigines have witnessed the plague inflicted upon them by the civilization-coated imperial expedition. They understand that it is this glorious mission of spreading Christian civilization that has caused ecological detriment to their country and led to the dispossession and death of their people. "They saw the glass was sharp. This was the first thing they noticed — that it cuts. Cuts trees. Cuts the skin of the tribes"(477). Bob's remembrance of the aborigines serves, first of all, to claim their original ownership of this land. Secondly, this counter-memory serves to refute the official lies of Christianity spreading the imperial civilization to the Antipodes.

The Empire's grand religious mission eventually fails with the sinking of the glass church and the drowning of the reverend, which metaphorically alludes to the incompatibility of Christianity with the southern land and further implies the genuine ownership of this *terra nullius*. As Lucinda pictures in her memory, this is

> not a Christian land at all... in this place, the water had been dark and still, brown from tannin, cut by church-like motes of sunlight... this was the year when blacks of Parramatta were defeated. Their trunks were brown with mud, cracked like iron bark... you could still feel it in the still shadows along watercourses. She felt ghost here, but not Christian ghosts, not John the Baptist or Jesus of Galilee. There were other spirits, other stories, slippery as shadow. (161)

However, the author does not scramble to equate the abortion of the Empire's Christian mission with its heterogeneity or wrap up by revealing who the actual owner of this land is. He delves deeper into Australian cultural memory and investigates the profound impact the exported religion has rendered on this continent. Apparently, the church appears and disappears, but the religious ghost has already infiltrated into the soil, nurturing the souls inhabiting this land. "When she saw the glass church built she became a Christian" (496). Mary Magdalene, Kumbaingiri Billy's aunty, is only one of those who experience the transformation of Australian culture brought about by the Christian church.

It not only transforms the inhabitants of this continent. It changes the course of its history. Even for an explorer like Jeffris, who does not fancy church, he

> was certainly not without a sense of history. Each pane of glass, he thought, would travel through country where glass had never existed before, not once, in all time. These sheets would cut a new path in history. They would slice the white dust-covers of geography and reveal a map beneath, with rivers, mountains, and names, the streets of his birthplace, Bromley, married to the rivers of savage Australia. (450)

The imperial expedition is founded on the Victorian confidence in its civilization and its ambition to extend that civilization to shelter more territories and a larger population, making them affiliated with the glorious history of the Empire. As Elleke Boehmer argues,

> the fragility and preposterous incongruity of this object reflect the ambition, artifice, and invasive profligacy of the colonial mission of which Oscar composes a small part. But even though it shatters on arrival at its destination, the church also signifies a symbolic investment, however wayward, in the new territory. What emerges from the botched encounter between glass, a dreamer, and the vast continental mass of Australia is a new history of the land, a tale which Oscar's descendants will use to explain their belonging to it. (2005: 17)

Australian history is so short, bloody and trivial that it is usually treated as part of the grand history of the Empire, which records it to witness the outstanding achievements made by Great Britain. According to the documented memory:

> Australian history began with Cook's discovery. But since the aborigines were and since most of conquest in Australia consisted of massacre, or in relentless if scattered guerilla warfare, and even this potential history remained unacknowledged and unwritten. With no traditions, no ruins, and no civilization, Australia is a brief chapter in England's glorious narrative, and most of that chapter was devoted to explorers. The aboriginal past and the genocidal and eco-catastrophes of white invasion were not considered. The dates of the reigns of English kings and queens, however, matters. (Brydon, 1993: 49)

However, Bob's family memory is part of Australia's collective memory of the Victorian religious transmission. Instead of recounting the great merits of those pioneers and eulogizing the grace of imperial civilization, which occupies approximately the whole space of the official memory, the once marginalized or silenced memories are retrieved to counter the documented one. In the restored remembrance, the precursors of the Empire are depicted as ruthless savages who change and destroy the primitive landscape deliberately and shed the blood of the natives at their own will; the missionary of imperial civilization is ignorantly impotent in redemption but complicit in the explorers' ferocities; the Empire is doing nothing more than establishing its Christian culture at the cost of the original one that has nurtured the land for thousands of years. This reconstruction of Australia's Victorian memory is pretty significant in that "[R]edescribing a world is the necessary first step towards changing it" (Brady, 1996: 79). What the author intends to "change" is the prevailing status quo that Australia's collective memory records only the white's achievements on the land, leaving the aboriginal tradition as well the detriments caused by the white invasion in oblivion. The reconstructed cultural memories function primarily to delegitimize the biased documented one infused with the white hegemonic ideology. In addition, since "the making of the alternate realities of art becomes politicized [and, I would add theological]. 'The struggle of man against power [and against false gods] ... is the struggle of memory against forgetting'" (ibid.). These memories are restored to claim their deserved stroke in the nation's memory book.

In the postmodern intellectual conditions where the metanarrative has collapsed any recuperation of the past may involve the hazard of being problematic itself. Peter Carey knows well enough not to set up a "new metanarrative" in his recuperation. He revisits the Christian memory not "in the attempt to re-establish a single, monolithic, and legitimizing discourse" (Ashcroft, 2002: 164), but to provide an alternative version through which he invites a critical re-evaluation of that imperial cause that used to be enshrouded in halos. The systemically forgotten memory may appear filthy, shameful and disturbing. Yet it constitutes the other integrated side of the coin without which a complete picture of the Victorian Christian civilization is impossible. Only when Australia's collective memory encompasses that marginalized and discarded past and those downtrodden souls can history do justice to those wronged and forgotten.

Moreover, only when Australia gathers the courage to face up to its natural rather than the selected past, can it mature and find its right place in the world. That brings us to another task that the recuperated memory is supposed to fulfil: to trace and redefine the "Australianess". When imperial pioneers carry cages of rabbits, pigeons, and pheasants on Leviathan to "a body known as the Acclimatization Society of New South Wales" (203), it symbolizes the continuity between Australian culture and British traditions. To be more specific, as a significant aspect of Victorian culture, the Christian spirit is made overtly an integral part of Australian culture. Though Christianity turns out to be out of phase with this land, it does cast its seed in it which is bound to sprout. It may not flaunt itself, but it flows in Australians' blood vessels. This can be metaphorically illustrated in Lucinda's explanation of the aftermath when Price Rupert's drops explode, "you have grains of glass in every corner of the workshop — in your eyes if you are not careful — and what is left in your hand you can crumble — it feels like sugar — without danger" (129). Since "Group and place take on a symbolic sense of community" (Assmann, 2011: 25), Australians do not need to take a tangible church to associate themselves with Christianity. It has been imbedded in their cultural tradition. Any recollection is able to reproduce the church symbolically as the base upon which they rely to confirm and consolidate their "identity" (ibid.). This explains Percy Smith's response when Oscar questions where the church is on which account so much blood has been spilt. "It is all around you. Do you not recognize a pane of glass?" (492)

While neo-colonial texts are widely claimed to be genetically subversive, it's still early to jump to the conclusion that *Oscar and Lucinda* is aimed at an overall subversion of the imperial narrative. After all, Carey's parody of the Bible and Edmund Gosse's *Father and Son*, suggests the intimate relationship between Australian traditions and that of the British. As is argued by David Callahan, Peter Carey uses the imperial cannon with "comfortable assumption that English writing is also Australia's just as the earlier history of colonized Australia is also English history" (1990: 21). Remembering could be revolutionary. By reviving those counter memories of the Christian transmission, the author does interpolate the overarching metanarrative, which focuses on the eulogy of the pioneering exploration of the southern hemisphere. However, he is highly conscious of the cultural debt that Australia owes to Great Britain, and he is ambivalent about the debt.

While scolding the ferocity the Empire inflicted on the aborigines during the advancement of Christian civilization, Carey also recognizes its significance, identifies with it and credits its place in creating Australian culture. He also suggests reconciliation between the blacks and the white people. This can be briefly glimpsed when Mary Magdalene is eventually "very taken with Oscar", sees him as "a good man", names him "Bushfire", and believes that "glass could be good" (495-496). By retrieving the nation's Christian memory, Carey is more motivated to acknowledge that English heritage as part of Australian cultural tradition, reappraise it, modify it and supplement it with the aboriginal voice rather than subverting it and replacing it with his own version, since there is no future in denying history. Since Australians can not still disregard the hard fact that "the country was thick with sacred stories more ancient than the ones he (Oscar) carries in his sweat-slippery leather Bible" (500), the author's reconfiguration is aimed at replacing the monolithic white Australian cultural memory with the heterogeneous Australian cultural memories which celebrate its multiple roots of tradition. After all, that is what Australia really is and what it should be like. Christianity is only one of the many aspects of Australia's English inheritance. Peter Carey works on the gambling and misogyny traditions, too.

1.1.3 Gambling as a Home-grown Religion and Victorian Transmission

Another Australian tradition Peter Carey reworks on is gambling. It runs through the whole fiction as a lifeline, threads the seemingly irrelevant characters and stories and prophesies the destiny of the male and female protagonists. Oscar and Lucinda make their initial acquaintance on Leviathan through gambling; they are reunited with each other in a Chinese den in Sydney; despite being unaccustomed to Oscar's untidiness and moderate taste, Lucinda resonates with his passion demonstrated in gambling; the misfits eventually gamble on their love for each other which takes a toll on their fates. Sue RyanFazilleau argues that gambling is one of the "thematic preoccupations" (2005: 12) of the Victorian novel, and she attributes Oscar's death to his "dependence on games of chance and literal interpretation" (ibid.: 21). Gambling is recuperated to Australia's cultural memory as a local carnival as well as an imported tradition from the Victorian Britannia. It is reconstructed both literally to represent Australia's status quo in the nineteenth century and emblematically to signify the uncertainty of and pervasive anxiety over Australia's national and individual identity.

Australia's endless stretches of the wild bush, the rare human presence, coupled with the monotonous life, make various forms of gambling a common occurrence, even a fashion of life. According to Paul Delfabbro and Daniel King, "[G]ambling has been a feature of Australian life since settlement, and very probably before this. Historical evidence suggests that gambling was common in Aboriginal communities before British settlement" (2012: 1556). Apart from being a perfect leisure activity to kill time, gambling has special significance for those gold diggers flooding into Melbourne from different countries around the mid-nineteenth century. The temporary community formed through gambling serves as a momentary consolation to their displacement and homesickness. Moreover, the prevalence of gambling in Australia is associated with opportunities and risks concomitant with the gold rush, and it is a manifestation of the Australian mentality of doubt and uncertainty towards the significant changes imported from Victorian

Britain. That makes it plausible that "[A]mong Europeans, gambling is known to have been common in the gold rushes of the 1850s (playing-cards) and the Melbourne Cup has been a national event ever since the 1860s" (Delfabbro; King, 2012: 1557).

According to Bob's recollection of his great-grandfather's life story, gambling is in vogue in both Australia and England. To begin with, Lucinda's obsession with gambling can be the best illustration of that fever. Having lost her parents and been isolated by people around her, who either hold conservative grudges against her since she is a heretic sympathizer towards the blacks, like Mr. Tomasetti, or are frightened by her strident conduct to keep at a distance, like her consultant, reverend Hasset, she is possessed by an overwhelming loneliness and melancholy. Playing cards saves her from boredom and indignation. Since she is able to control cards and win her hand solely with her willpower instead of kissing up to the people she dislikes, it makes her feel happy and even look prettier. Gambling brings her aesthetic pleasure. When gambling, "[S]he could feel her transformation ... She was moved by playing cards in a way she could not explain even to herself" (159). In addition to killing time and gaining a sense of self-control, Lucinda obtains from gambling a therapeutic power. Knowing that her immense fortune is not earned from the innocent labouring on the natural resources but made by her parents' appropriating the land violently from the aborigines, subdividing it and selling the small chunks off to other free settlers, Lucinda is haunted by guilt. She is anxious to "slough off the guilty weight of her inheritance, drop it like a rusty armour that she does not need" (455). Gambling is, for her, a physical expression of this oppressed feeling, which winning any hand will aggravate, making her feel like a robber. But losing money in games provides her the momentum of redemption. When losing money, "she felt so light, an airy, dragon-fly wing of feeling" (266). When she finally stakes all her ill-gotten fortune on Oscar, she has the sensation of being "light as a feather, as uncorrupted as an empty purse, unencumbered" (455). Losing all her inheritance is, for her, an ultimate redemption, through which she washes away all the sins she inherits from her parents and has the chance to embark on a happy life with her own bare hands.

Within the text, Lucinda is undoubtly not the only Australian who abandons herself to gambling. Bob recollects that it had already been a prevailing obsession among people from all walks of life across Australia when Oscar set foot in New South Wales in the 1860s. When Oscar assumes his responsibility as a priest to preach sermons against the unforgivable evil to set up his authority as a clergyman and restrain his own inflaming compulsiveness, his house keeper warns him that it is too pervasive to stop. He is also informed that "generous gents" often donate their earned money to the church. This echoes John O'Hara's observation that "[E]ven though the evangelists tried to attack gaming and betting in Australia too, the Anglican church supported the gentry and accepted the tenets of conservatism because it needed the protection of the 'old order' in the colonies" (1988: 47). Apparently gambling is not restricted to the upper-class gents at all. It is a carnival for all people from all classes. When Oscar is taken to the racecourse, he finds that "there was fan-tan town on Gorge Street. There was swy and poker and every card game to be imagined among the taverns down the Paddington. Oscar had never seen such a passion for gambling. It was not confined to certain types or classes. It seems to be the chief industry of the colony" (308). Even bishop Dancer, who dismisses Oscar for gambling out of public pressure, is a crazy "card player himself" (324). That probably explains why John O'Hara (1988) states in the preface of *History of Gaming and Betting in Australia* that "Australians have long thought of themselves as a nation of gamblers — perhaps even the world's greatest gamblers."

Back in England, Bob recalls that horseracing was very popular around the 1860s among gentlemen like Wardley Fish, who "had been corrupted from birth" and "got his pomade and slicked down his hair" (101). Though Oscar, a young from a humble origin, does not even know what a flutter is when Fish makes the first introduction, he soon picks up the "gambler's disease" under the influence of his friend. He learns, through thick travelling, how prevalent wager is among both the upper and the lower classes in England. Oscar is so addicted to gambling during his years in Oriel that he travels across the south England by train, by coach, and by foot to bet. Furthermore, his journeys could be made into a map as thick as a spider web. He is seized by the game and has

> produced sixteen smudge-paged clothbound notebooks in which were recorded not the thoughts of Divine Masters, not musings on the philosophy of the ancients, but page after page of blue spidery figures which recorded... the names of horses, their sires and dams, their position at last start, the number of days since the last start, the weight carried at the last time, whether they were rising in class, or falling in class, who was the owner, who the jockey and so on. (178)

Though gambling was considered to be the worst evils of Victorian society and relevant laws were passed consecutively in the mid of the nineteenth century to forbid betting or bookmaking, it is undisputed that Victorian culture is imbued with betting and sporting. Ironically, the effect of parliament legislation is that "gambling could no longer be conducted as a glamorous public spectacle, but was driven underground, to flourish only in seedy 'hells' or at furtive private parties" (Dingley, 1996: 18). As a matter of fact, that "hidden" part is what Fish enjoys most about the track. "The whispered conversations, the passing of 'tip for tips', the grubby low-life corner" (114) gives him momentary manic elation. During the nineteenth century, despite all the aversion and legal restrictions,

> [G]ambling, then, gradually developed into a capitalistic enterprise where a whole betting industry developed. The sporting discourse of this new enterprise would eventually come to dominate not only the market, but common language as well. Sporting papers evolved to publish tips on races and encouraged gambling and betting throughout the country. (Jodi L. Wagner, 2008: 25).

Traces can be found in the novel's depiction, "Notting Hill derives its distinctive street plan from the racehorse ... a ghostly imprint of a racehorse lay over its streets" (178). Unlike the eighteenth-century, when horseracing was mainly a leisure activity confined to the gentry, a multiplicity of gambling like horseracing, bookmaking, wagering, betting, and flutter swept all classes in England in the nineteenth century. Gambling mania even causes detrimental consequences to families. This is represented in *Oscar and Lucinda* by the death of the reverend Mr. Stratton, who kills himself for losing all his money in horseracing.

Multiple social and philosophical backdrops contribute to the prevailing gambling in Victorian England. However, the most prominent reason lies in the contradicted antithetical ideologies between utilitarianism and Evangelicalism. "The ideology behind Utilitarianism is the cold, analytical, reasoned pursuit of happiness for the greater good... Evangelicalism, on the other hand, stressed the value of morality, work, frugality, and self-denial." (Wagner, 2008: 23) Obviously, that doesn't exhaust the logic under the Victorian inconsistency. The arising of Darwin's evolutionism also exerts a great impact on the intellectual world of the century and induces people's skepticism about the suffocating religious rigidity and insecurity about the possible uncertainty and change. These factors contribute to Oscar's indulgence in gambling. He has both belief in and doubt about God. Knowing that gambling is viewed as malicious and immoral by his religion, he also believes it is the only way God provides him to get funds to support himself and redeem others. It is the "something-for-nothing" (ibid.: 24) attitude that Victorian orthodox goes strongly against that he relies on "to accumulate money in order to dare the formless terror of the ocean, to bring the word of Christ to New South Wales" (181).

Canonical Victorian literature refers to gambling as a symbol of "doubt and uncertainty of the changes occurring within the Victorian period"(2008: 32). Nevertheless, the gambling memory is reconstructed tactically by the author to perform different layers of functions. To begin with, the gambling metaphor, with its embodiment of the philosophical and psychological uncertainty of the human condition, is used here to problematize and suspense the legitimacy of the self-assuring documented memory regarding Australia's origin mythology and the spreading of the Victorian Christian civilization. Despite the revelation that the aborigines are authentic masters of the continent, that the imperial expedition involves civilization-coated barbarianism, and that Christianity is a sugar-coated bullet at the micro-text level, the gambling reference running through the fiction also serves to encapsulate the overall skepticism about the metanarrative and encourage a re-evaluation of it. It embodies "the plurality of cultural narratives and a decentring of authorial style" (Boym, 2001: 336) in the postmodern epoch.

Gambling memory is also reworked to show Australians' anxiety over their identity. Moreover, the combination of gambling with the orphanage of the three main characters, Oscar, Lucinda and Miriam Chadwick, further enhances this implication. Orphanhood is a classical obsession of Victorian novels, and according to Sue Ryan Fazilleau, it "symbolizes rootlessness and a search for identity at a time when society was undergoing profound changes. The father figure represents the law and reality. If he is absent or lacking then the orphan has difficulty fitting in and has to found his own values" (2005: 12). As the narrator claims at the beginning of Chapter 83, "Our history is a history of orphans" (395). Lucinda loses both her parents consecutively and when she chooses to lose all her fortune more than willingly to Oscar, she is thinking about giving him "all her armour she had hitherto to keep herself safe... She would be looked after" (ibid.), still her wishful dream vanishes; Oscar chooses to be self-orphaned by getting away from his oppressive father after he loses his mother; Miriam loses her father in England, and again, her mother is drowned in Bellingen Heads. The juxtaposition of gambling and orphanages indicates Australians' insecurity and uncertainty when it comes to their identity. They crave a solid home to nest their fragile souls, yet end up losing them one after another. As the condition Oscar meditates upon, "we are the creatures of our own situation, one minute all snug and warm, worthy of affection and the esteem of total strangers, granted respect without question, credit without a pause, and the text, the most despicable creature on whom it is quite permissible to spit" (325). No matter for Lucinda, who was born in Australia, or for the British immigrants, Oscar and Miriam, there is no such thing that something is built on certainty or that he is one of the chosen. They are all regarded as the "Other" either in their home country or the adopted one, publicly cast out and condemned to be permanently rootless.

To recuperate the gambling memory at the bicentennial of Australia's white establishment, the author is further dedicated to a sketch of his assumption about Australia's cultural identity apart from showing its inherited inconsistency. Australia features prominently in its multicultural genes. For one thing, Australian culture shares the British origin.

It serves as the extension of the imperial culture to the southern continent, passively undertaking the radiation and influence of Victorian industrial expansion and the spread of Christian civilization. For another, it's undeniable that the aboriginal culture that suffers from the devastating disaster along with the imperial expedition survives in the cracks of the seemingly monolithic imperial culture. It keeps popping up to claim its own right to the continent as well as its place in Australia's collective memory. Carey does his poetic justice in his recuperation which renders it strongly reasonable to encompass the multiplicity of memories in the nation's cultural memory reservoir.

1.1.4 Misogyny as Punishment for Bush Intruders and Victorian Transgressors

Unremitting feminist movements worldwide keep reminding us that women have long been rendered to disadvantageous circumstances. Australian women are no exception. As a matter of fact, Australia has a long-standing tradition of misogyny, which is inseparable from its colonial backdrop. Britain did not intend to compose the penal colony of male and female convicts at the very beginning since the government never thought the outcasts of the old society would serve as the foundation of a new one. As a result, the proportion of men and women convicts transported to the Antipodes between 1788 and 1852 was seven to one. (Hughes, 2003: 504) The absence of women caused a series of social problems, such as drinking, whoring and fornicating. Later, women were sent to the Antipodes for "social control", "preventing men from turning homosexual" (ibid.: 505). Under this circumstance, both convict women and aboriginal women fell prey to men's brutality. They received "rape rather than help from men", and the only right had they had was "to be fed" (ibid.: 504/528). "It was as though women convicts had passed the ordinary bounds of class and become a fiction, not far from pornography: crude raucous Eve, sucking rum and mothering bastards in the exterior darkness." (ibid.: 504) Although women convicts and female free settlers from the British middle class laboured as hard as men and played their part in the construction of the colony, they have long been misrepresented by the male-dominated discourse system as "degenerative, incorrigible and worthless" (ibid.). According to Benjamin McHutchion, "[F]rom early in Australian history, female migrants, especially convict women, had been associated with prostitution, leading to what has been termed the 'damned whore' stereotype" (2005: 24).

Moreover, during the Irish Great Famine between 1845 and 1852, England government was under tremendous pressure from the fact that Irish workhouses had been over-crowed with people tormented by impoverishment and starvation. Many of them were children. At the same time, Australia had an acute shortage of domestic servants and the demographic imbalance between the sexes had been ever since going on convict transportation became increasingly severe. Earl Grey, Secretary of State for the Colonies, proposed the famous Earl Grey Scheme which "oversaw the arrival of a total of 4175 Irish orphan workhouse girls in the Australian colonies between 1848 and 1850" (Farrell, 2000: 74). However, these orphan girls suffered unprecedented discursive violence from the politicized Anglo-centric colonial newspapers. These public media directed tremendous enmity towards them, and they were constructed to be "[A] set of ignorant creatures... coarse, useless creatures, whose very personnel, with their squat, stunted figures, thick waists, and clumsy ankles, promises but badly for the physique of the future colonists of Victoria" (McHutchion, 2005: 21) and were subjected to public derision and resentment in Australian colonies. Owing to their negative image, they were considered by the white immigrants unqualified for marriage, and many of them, who could not even find a decent job to support themselves, ended up making a living by prostitution. The influence of the Whore stereotype of Australian women is so far-reaching that "[M]any Australians still think their Founding Mothers were whores" (Hughes, 2003: 503).

Hostility towards women is still being expressed in the contemporary public life. Sawer Marian argues that women are frequently misrepresented in politics and fall victim to various forms of sexual vilification on talkback radio and the internet. (2013: 105) Her data show that "Australia slipped from 15th to 45th place in the Inter-Parliamentary Union ranking for representation of women in national parliaments between 1999 and February 2013" (ibid.). This inherited misogyny is like shackles put on women, denying them the deserved place in Australian history. That is what Peter Carey is preoccupied with in most of his writings. Female characters either feature in his neo-historical texts, like Lucinda in *Oscar and Lucinda*, Gaby in *Amnesia*, or Irene in *Long Way from Home*, or plays a critical role in deciding the fate of the male protagonists, like Leah in *Illywhacker*, Felicity in *The Unusual Life of Tristan Smith*, Mercy in *Jack Maggs*, or Ellen in *True History of the Kelly Gang*. In the fiction, Australian misogyny grows out of the colonial soil. It is also connected to the Victorian femininity. The author reconstructs this tradition through Bob's recollection of his family memory to perform a couple of functions.

Australian women's status represented in the fiction can be primarily glimpsed through Lucinda's mother, Elizabeth's description that "Irishmen had their women walk after them with their heads bowed like prisoners of war" (86). It is also suggested in her letter to Marian Evans, explaining why she and her daughter must go "Home" (London).

> My daughter lives in a fairy world I have made for her, and they would not tolerate her in open society in New South Wales where they hate women like us with a passion you would not believe without seeing their angry resentful little eyes. It would chill you, Marian, to walk down a street in Parramatta. (88)

It is widely believed that the Australian feminist movement began in the late nineteenth century, though some scholars argue that Australian women had participated in business and articulated demands for political rights since the gold rush in the 1850s. (Bishop; Woollacott, 2016: 84) Both the time of correspondence (1850s) and reference to George Eliot suggest that the awakening of Elizabeth's female consciousness is under the influence of the British women's movement since the mid-nineteenth century.

Australian misogyny is epitomized in the fiction by people's enmity towards Lucinda. To begin with, the law made by men prevents her from getting her mother's inheritance until she reaches the age of eighteen, which means she has to be under the tutelage and control of her mother's strict solicitor, Charles Ahearn, after her death. Then when Lucinda steps into society, she receives all the hatred that her misogynist folks, either in Parramatta, Sydney or London, throw at her. Even before she does anything inappropriate, she is condemned to be a symbol of degradation because any single young female who is "travelling without protection of a family, either of a father, a male relative or a spouse, was to be seen as potentially immoral" (McHutchion, 2005: 24). They give no care to the fact that she is an orphan without any possible family for company. More importantly, she is judged, demeaned, and isolated because she transgresses the Victorian borderline prescribed for a "perfect woman". In his narrative poem *The Angel in the Home*, the English poet Coventry Patmore (1823-1896) depicted the Victorian feminine ideal — a wife and mother who is obedient, charming, unselfish, sympathetic and pure. Women's roles are positioned as "angels at home". They are supposed to be submissive to their husbands and devoted to their children, and their existence is only a foil for men. However, Lucinda is a spinster, and there is no evidence to suggest that she is charming or obedient. She wears rational bloomers instead of respectable bustle; she walks in her stride; her hair is inadequately coiffured, like "a sea of little snakes, each one struggling to insist on its freedom" (125). She is indeed sympathetic, but most of the time, her compassion is directed towards the downtrodden indigenous peoples. Influenced by her feminist mother, she never defines her role as "the angel at home". "She knew better Greek. She seemed well schooled in theology. She played cards with cool elegance and skill" (315). Most of all, she is passionate for industry and considers it a ladder through which women gain their independence. Those are sufficient reasons to condemn her to being alienated and "pinned and crippled by her loneliness" (124).

When Lucinda meets Hasset to consult about glassworks, she is brought under the gaze of the reverend and constructed to be the Other. Both her "unusual garment" (139) and her less than perfectly tidy hair produce "an unsettling impression", which leaves the vicar in the conjecture that its owner is "at once wealthy and not quite respectable" (140). For him, her plump lips release the information of "disturbing sensuality" (ibid.). Though Hasset confesses that it is the passion he sees in her that kindles his desire to assists her with her glass factory, it is also the same sentiment which is taken as a Victorian taboo, frightens the vicar off and eradicates in his head any thought of marrying her for fear of the threat that any possible scandals might ruin his reputation. The reverend warns her that passion is "not an admirable thing, a dangerous thing" (146). Her awakening feminist consciousness to strive for independence through industry is viewed as the evil fire that Victorian Australian society is bound to put out.

Lucinda is more hated because she is a woman who exercises her autonomy in life, which often, if not always, involves her breaking into the territories traditionally dominated by men. She often stays up late to handle those glass bottles and falls asleep by the fire in his consultant's study out of fatigue. These conducts are all regarded by the bourgeois as improper and morally flawed. Her friendship and frequent associations with Hasset are considered unacceptable and induce rumours that partly contribute to his exile by Bishop Dancer. When she gambles in Chinese dens, she is disgusted by other gamblers who "felt her otherness, her womanness" (300). On seeing her, she feels their "bodies move aside. Where there been a hot press, she now experienced a distinct and definite cooling" (ibid.).

Lucinda is alienated even by her employees. When she goes to her own factory to inspect how the workers labour, she finds herself not welcomed, even resented by her employees. His accountant, Mr. d'Abbs, "was flustered because he did not like the routine of his arrival interfered with... He did not like what he did not expect" (359). She is informed that her surprise visit to the clerks is disturbing.

> [She] earned Jeffris' hate just by opening his door. She felt the eyes of all the clerks. She smelt the alleyway, the sour smell of urine. She felt their scorn for her small body, her womanliness, for the sound of her tread on their boards. She nodded to Mr. Jeffris, and to Mr. d'Abbs who returned to the open door like a dog forbidden the parlour. (361-362)

Her glass blower Arthur Phelps "orders" her "not to attend her own works without prior notice" (369) but he would like her and Oscar to visit together. Moreover, when they are in the presence of her employees, they offer Oscar "a fellowship they had denied to her" (379). As a businesswoman, she is regarded as a gender transgressor and reaps all the contempt and repulsion that men are capable of.

George Eliot writes in the prelude of *Middlemarch*, "[M]any Theresas have been born who found for themselves no epic life wherein there was a constant unfolding of far resonant action" (2008: i). Lucinda is a woman of integrity, disdaining those white parasites who make a fortune by subdividing and selling off the land stolen from the blacks. Though orphaned, she is tough and independent, getting herself learned in glass and earning her innocent money by establishing a glasswork all on her own. Though having suffered countless adversity, she remains sympathetic and pure. While she feels pain, grief and loneliness, she imagines herself "a heroine at the beginning of an adventure" (128) and re-accumulates energy to carry on. She is like a woman warrior. However, the desk, various bureaux, cabinets and samples of manufacture in her office, which are supposed to be the physical monument to her success and solidity, turn out to be "theatrics" and stand witness to her despicableness, her exile. Her versatility, potency and optimism are turned against her solely because she is a woman. In the eyes of the men around her, she is forever a girlie still wet behind her ears. Lucinda is determined by their gaze, and it is from the gaze that she is "photo-graphed" and receives its "effects". (Lacan, 1998: 106) She feels "the power of men" (144), and their gaze reduces her to anxiety and shame. "By the way they looked at me, by their perception of me, they would make me into the creature they perceived. I would feel myself becoming a lesser being." (ibid.) Suffocated by men around her, "[S]he felt humiliated and powerless, like a child dragged down the street by a large dog on a leash" (378).

Misogynists are not confined to men. Lucinda is also discriminated against and repelled by people of her sex. Her maid, Mrs. Smith, despises her for lodging homeless and infamous Oscar, and finally quits her job out of indignation, because she cannot bear to share a roof with the "immoral" girl. Even Gorge Eliot, the English Victorian novelist who lives a life against social customs and encourages women in her writings to surmount society constraints, is mean to her, criticizing her for her social inadequacy and disobedience. Lucinda's "bits-and-pieces accent, her interest in trade, her lack of conversational skills, her sometimes blunt opinions or her unladylike way of blowing her nose — like a walrus" (202) makes her feel uncomfortable. That the Australian girl has a "quite peculiar tendency to stare" instead of lowering her eyes in deference to hers like other young ladies makes her completely an "alien" to George Eliot (ibid.). When Lucinda does lower her eyes, for Eliot, "her lids were heavy and sensuous", producing an effect which she "ungenerously described as 'sly'". (ibid.) The Victorian writer attributes all her bad luck in courtship to these personality flaws and deems her unworthy of people's natural sympathy.

Lucinda is not the only female character who falls victim to Australia's misogyny. Mariam, the narrator's genuine great-grandmother, is another. She would have been one of the ordinary girls who immigrated to the new continent with their family to earn a living if Death had not claimed the lives of her grandmother, father and mother consecutively. Unfortunately, she is not loved by God. She is orphaned the minute she is saved from the sunken ship and left alone in a "hard and hostile environment amongst people" (396). Consecutive adversities render "almost all her adult life in black" (ibid.). With the help of the agent, she finds a position as a governess in the Trevis family in Boat Harbour, but her employer acts like a bully and Victorian moralist. Mrs Trevis is convinced that twenty-year-old Mariam should spend her life in mourning after her mother's death. She "filled her copper with black dye and put her lovely new clothes into the copper, one by one" (ibid.) on her first morning. She tries her best to extinguish Mariam's hope to start a new life. With the black "got into her skin" and making her feel "sick at heart", (ibid.) she feels her life like a fallen bloom, withering before even blossoming. When her first husband dies of a snakebite later, Mrs Trevis considers it Mariam's duty to show her continuous loyalty and devotion to her late husband. She "cautioned her against ripping up her old mourning clothes for dusters" (399) and urges her to retreat to "her cage of deep mourning" (400). When poor Mariam finally throws her mourning weeds, her employer regards it as bad luck and requests her to stay in black to mourn forever to show her "humidity" (396). In addition, the Trevis family show no respect for Mariam. They are inclined to view her as a "labourer" and "would request her to do something more practical around the place" (400). Feeling "depressed and unstimulated" and "continually weary" of her laborious and meaningless governess life, Mariam gathers the "zest ... in her optimism" (399) and determines to count on the only "option" left to transform her fate, that is, to marry vicar Hasset. However, Mrs Trevis perceives her plan to pursue happiness as "nabbing" the reverend Hasset for remarriage and judges her as "harsh and scheming" (400). She ridicules Mariam and tries unsuccessfully to bring her governess to a "proper understanding of her place in this society" (497), which is the predestined role for Victorian women.

Like the Christian civilization and the gambling tradition, misogyny is remembered first of all to suggest the inseparable connection between Australian cultural tradition and Victorian heritage. Colonial Australian culture and Victorian culture come down in one continuous line. The misogyny tradition has its roots in Australia's gender environment. It is also the result of the rigid Victorian moral rules transported to the continent with cultural and religious transmission. Colonial Australian women are disciplined both by the bushmen and by Victorian limitations for femininity.

Moreover, the misogynic memory is restored to insinuate the presently alienated relationship between Australia and Britain. Either Lucinda's being rejected by George Eliot or Mariam's being abandoned by her English mother symbolizes the orphanhood of Australia itself. It is like the declaration that God is dead and there is no exterior assistance to count on for salvation. That they take sovereignty over their own lives despite the harsh environment is a fable suggesting Australia get independent and move forward with its own tradition and the English heritage instead of immersing itself in excessive nostalgia for the once grand Empire. After all, it is important for orphaned Australia to look at its "options" (400). As Lucinda reassures herself whenever she gets skeptical about her crazy decision of striving for freedom, "it was frightful city to contemplate madness, all hard with eucalyptus, snapping sticks, sandstone rocks with fractured faces and cutting edges. You could not, not in Sydney, dear God, allow yourself to fall into such a weakened state" (296). Lucinda's condition in Sydney is the metaphor of the environment that Australia is rendered in the contemporary era.

The misogyny memory is also retrieved for a critical re-evaluation. Either Lucinda or Mariam is most hated because they disdain the hypocritical moral rules and trespass the borderline set for Victorian women. However, Peter Carey reconfigures their transgression as their active and autonomous choice to transform, and change their predestination when they are confronted with hostile environment. This manoeuvre not only exonerates them and delegitimizes the misogynic tradition stigmatizing and shackling women but also acknowledges appreciatively their place in history. Though they might be considered as indecent and immoral by their mediocre folks, the author suspends his moral judgement of their transgression. This is best illustrated in Lucinda's reconciliation with Miriam, who compromises Oscar and usurps her inheritance. "There is no disputing that you are a thief, but a thief, I think, made so by fear and weakness and as I too understand the terror you have felt in your soul to contemplate a woman's life alone in New South Wales, then I forgive you" (515). The author points to the transformative power underlying transgression by criticizing misogyny. To quote Michael Foucault, "... at the root of this discourse on God which Western culture has maintained for so long ... a singular experience is shaped: that of transgression. Perhaps one day it will seem decisive for our culture, as much a part of its soil, as the experience of contradiction was at an earlier time for dialectical thought" (1980: 33).

The transplanting of European civilization to the southern land makes Australian culture somewhat an extension of the Victorian traditions. However, that comprises only part of Australia's cultural connection with its English ancestry. Another issue that has exerted considerable influence on Australia and Australians is Britain's Transportation System which is widely deemed to have set the keynote for Australia's origin myth.

1.2 Convicts Recollected as Scapegoats for the Empire: *Jack Maggs*

Australian history begins with its convict origin. The Australian Day is set to commemorate the landfall of the first fleet of eight ships containing hundreds of convicts in Botany Bay on 26 January 1788, commanded by Captain Arthur Phillip. Between 1788 and 1868, 160,000 British convicts were transported to the southern land. (Hugues, 1988:

13) This makes it impossible to bypass the convict chapter to have a full grasp of Australian history and culture. However, convict history had been a taboo for historians until 1962 when Manning Clark unveiled the dark episode in his *A History of Australia*. Before that, convict experience remained the territory of journalists and novelists. It had been the "folklore" of the Transportation System that had kept the convict memory alive before historians drew it into the light of inquiry from the 1960s onward. (Hugues, 1988: 13) Concerned with social and political respectability, not a single Australian would like to admit their forebears are convicts. For most Australians, their convict ancestry is a "stain" (ibid.: 256), "a moral blot soaked into [their] fabric" (ibid.: 14). It has dominated the argument about Australian selfhood so that they have been possessed with the feeling of inferiority. This by-product continues affecting contemporary Australians who believe that the only cure for their "colonial double bind" is "amnesia — a national pact of silence". (ibid.: 256)

Nevertheless, the past cannot be past because those who have experienced it choose to forget. The historical brand has been so deeply ingrained in Australians' table of memory that it has been an archetype of their collective unconscious and literary creation. It is one of the most important threads to unlock Australia's contemporary predicaments, such as its problematic national and individual identity and cultural cringe. The convict experience is also one of the most recursive motifs of Peter Carey's novels. As Peter Carey's "vision of his native land calls back to its roots overseas" (Porter, 1997: 5), a large bulk of his attention to the convict past is directed to nineteenth-century England, which gives the southern hemisphere a convict European beginning. Unlike his fellowmen who would rather bury the ignominious part of history in oblivion or his peers who focus on the "horror" (Hugues, 1988: 17) of the Transportation

System, he continues with his rebellious style and chooses to "mythologize" the convict memory in *Jack Maggs*.① He changes Charles Dickenson's *Great Expectations* to be an original Australian narrative in which he revives the convict experience through Maggs' individual memory. This section will focus my analysis on the following three questions.

To begin with, how does Carey's paradisiac rewriting of the Victorian cannon reappraise the Transportation System by reconfiguring the convict protagonist to be a scapegoat of the Great Empire? Next, how is that reconfiguration intended to suggest the unbreakable bond between Australian tradition and English culture and heal Australians by narrating the traumatic story of their ancestors and exonerating them? Last but not least, how is Carey's reconstruction intended to reorient Australians to face up to the imperfection in their culture and their resultant feeling of inferiority, and embrace the heritage they have received from their convict ancestors to embark on new life in Australia.

1.2.1 Preliminaries of the Fiction

Peter Carey never ceases to provide his readers with a pleasant surprise. His canonical rewriting of Charles Dickens's *Great Expectations*, renamed as *Jack Maggs*, hails another success, winning him multiple literary awards, including the Miles Franklin Award and the Commonwealth Writers Prize. The novel receives strong positive commentaries and captures top places on best-seller lists in Europe and America as well. A. S. Byatt reviews in *Sunday Times* that this story is "sensationally bold and brilliant" (Carey, 1998: cover).② Peter Kemp

---

① According to Robert Hugues, when it comes to Australian stereotype of convict identity, there are two paralleling trends to historicize it, "to forget and to mythologize" (1988: 257).

② The following quotations from *Jack Maggs* in this section are annotated with only the page number.

commends it highly for the author's "empathy with the characters, combined with his psychological sharp-sightedness ... and his style" and claims it "a triumph of ebullient incident, humane insight and creative generosity". (ibid.) *New York Review of Books* compares it to a "Christmas pudding stuffed not with nuts and raisins and candied peel but with dark, succulent, dense, pungent, knobbly, inscrutable characters every one of whom has come from a Dickens novel" (ibid.). Caryn James proclaims that the novel "has become the hallmark of Carey's best work" and comes to the point that within the novel "a bright 19th-century surface masks a world-weary 20th-century heart" (1998: 10).

Jack Maggs is a rewriting of Charles Dickens' *Great Expectations*. Unlike Dickens' overt preference for Pip and the demeaning of the Australian convict transported from England, Abel Magwitch, Peter Carey does totally the opposite. In Carey's reworking, Jack Maggs, a character who is loosely based on Dickens' marginal character Magwitch, is restored to be the protagonist with multiple merits such as intelligence, loyalty and bravery. In contrast, Henry Phipps, whose archetypal character is Pip in *Great Expectations* is rendered to be hardly visible and depicted to be an arrogant and heartless gay. Set in the nineteenth-century London, *Jack Maggs* employs the narrative, and the novel mainly takes the titular hero's point of view to relate his story, centring on the hero's exile experience and what he goes through when he returns to England with the attempt to meet his adopted son Henry Phipps and recover his childhood fantasy. He is not welcomed by his foster mother, Ma Britten, and considered a disgrace and threat. To wait for Phipps, who has closed up the mansion he offers him and mysteriously disappeared, Maggs allows himself employed as a footman to Percy Buckle, who lives next door. It is where he meets Buckle's friend, the novelist and mesmerist Tobias Oates, who is a thinly disguised Charles Dickens, desperate for material for his new fiction. He eventually secures a deal with Tobias Oates in which he promises to accept the novelist's mesmeric experiment in exchange for his assistance in finding Phipps. Nevertheless it never occurs to Oates to cure Maggs' facial tic. On the contrary, the novelist preys selfishly on his traumatized criminal mind as the inspiration for his new novel and plans to earn good fortune from his anguished memory. To maximize his profits from this story, he keeps a distorted account of Maggs' memory, alters it in the process of mesmerism and even plants a phantom in his mind to aggravate his pain.

It is widely agreed that British canonical literature in the nineteenth-century played an indispensable part in rationalizing and consolidating its imperial domination. Postcolonial critics point out that Victorian cannon writers like Charles Dickens, consciously or subconsciously, have "participated in the representation of British global power mainly by taking it for granted. The integrity, superiority and the strength of the West, the expanded new geography of the Empire — these were Victorian Givens" (Bohmer, 1995: 24). To quote Edward Said, "Mainstream realist novels, therefore, could be of imperial domination though they are not about it" (ibid.: 24). As a convict dump of Great Britain, Australia has frequently been mentioned in the nineteenth-century British literary cannon and treated as the stereotypical Other, like exotic Asia or Africa. It is belittled and regarded as a "down under" (Brydon; Tiffin, 1992: 62). In Henry Kingsley's imaginative construction, it is "the most wonderfully scentless cesspool for a vast quantity of nameless rubbish, convicted or unconvicted" whose discovery "ranks in importance, after the invention of soda water" as "a sort of escaping cheaply from the consequences of debauchery for a time". (1973: 238-239) In order to fight against the colonial power that British literary cannons have exerted on Australia, Australian intellectuals have embarked on a literary revolution since the 1950s and devoted themselves to deconstructing and rewriting conical Anglo-European narratives complicit in British domination and colonization. "Historians and anthropologists have turned to oral sources to refute 'authoritative' accounts of European invasion and settlement. Documentary evidence has been reinterpreted, and a picture of both atrocity and Aboriginal resistance on scales vaster that had been previously acknowledged is emerging"(彭青龙, 2005: 78). Fictional writers like Peter Carey rewrites the imperial cannons more to rectify the distorted history in the imperial narrative and to pay homage to the cannon. *Jack Maggs* is one of these operations.

Except from the glimpse of the atrocious criminal image of Magwitch, we hardly get any clue of his past in Dickens' fiction. However, Carey breaches the gap by presenting the convict's history to his readers through his reconstruction. For one thing, through Tobias Oates' account of Maggs' recalling of his earlier life when he is mesmerized, especially in colonial Australia, those painful flashbacks, Carey metaphorically implies how the Empire manipulates convicts' memory or Australian memory in a larger picture. For another, Oates' biased and distorted story is challenged and rectified through the letters Maggs writes in person to his adopted son in which he mainly pours his remembrance of his childhood life in London. The fiction reaches its climax when Phipps finally presents himself at the mansion. He considers it an ignobility to accept any penny from the criminal and points his pistol at his benefactor, Maggs. Mercy, Buckle's maid, saves him from Phipps' gun and brings him to the awareness that his real responsibility, decency and destination lies in Australia, where they later return together. Jack Maggs ends up with a very successful businessperson and a prestigious president of the shire. They start a new life, civilize their children and evently have a happy life there in Australia.

Jack Maggs falls under the category of neo-historical fiction with its re-appraisal of the past as well as its self-analytic drive. Its motivation for interrogating Australia's misconceived convict history can be first glimpsed by Carey's statement of the authorial intention in an interview:

> Then one day, contemplating the figure of Magwitch, the convict in Charles Dickens' *Great Expectations*, I suddenly thought THIS MAN IS MY ANCESTOR. And then: this is UNFAIR! Dickens' Magwitch is foul and dark, frightening, murderous. Dickens encourages us to think of him as the 'other', but this was my ancestor, he was not 'other'. I wanted to reinvent him, to possess him, to act as his advocate. I did not want to diminish his 'darkness' or his danger, but I wanted to give him all the love and tender sympathy that Dickens' first person narrative provides his English hero Pip. That's where I started. The journey itself is, of course, far more complicated. (Author Q & A, n. d.)

Though opinions may vary regarding to what extent Carey's rewriting pays homage to the British cannon, there is a consensus among previous critics that Carey's interpretation of that history has a postcolonial flavour. The imperial narrative has always condemned transported convicts to be devious criminals who are excrescent and poisonous tumours of the glorious Empire and unworthy of God's savour. However, by re-evaluating that history, Peter Carey offers an alternative explanation of their offences to ascribe their crimes at least partially to the Empire's purposeful manoeuvre, de-stigmatize them and re-enchant them with favourable merits. Kathleen J. Renk observes by exercising the right of the colonial rendered in the postmodern epoch to map their own world, Peter Carey employs the "post-imperial Gothic fiction as a way of critiquing the imperial mindset of the writer/conjuror who plundered the lives of the marginalized" (2004: 69).

With his neo-historical fiction, Carey bridges Australians' connection with their past. As noted by Andreas Gaile, "[S]tories are the exclusive carrier medium of history in Carey's writings — his narrators' tales and those embedded in them constitute the author's version of Australian history" (2010: 103). As for *Jack Maggs*, apart from the author's implicated endeavour to represent an alternative version of truth concerning the convict's past, he also deploys postmodern metafictional techniques craftily in the novel to add to its aesthetic value and complicate the fiction's motifs. Though self-reflexivity has been overtly or covertly a consistent thread shared by most of Carey's other fictions as well, he exploits this strategy to a much fuller degree in *Jack Maggs*. By exposing how and why the fictional author Tobias Oates, who is modelled on Dickens, composes his story of Jack Maggs based on his memory recalled in the mesmerisation as well as how Maggs writes his own past to his adopted son, it is safe to argue that *Jack Maggs* is a typical metafiction, which is roughly a novel about writing novels. As Anthony Hassall concludes, "[I]n *Jack Maggs* ... the business of writing is insistently foregrounded. The book is full of the actual mechanics of Maggs and Oates' writings ... no other work is as deeply concerned as *Jack Maggs* is with the actual processes by which novelists gather, transform, and inscribe their material" (1997: 131).

The novel reveals its fictive status first by making a parallel between Peter Carey's composition of *Jack Maggs* and how the nineteenth-century fictional novelist, Tobias Oates, writes his ongoing novel concerning Jack Maggs. Instead of hiding his status from readers, he exposes it fully by making explicit his purpose of writing to perpetuate the memory and boasting that he is the best "carver" (280) in the whole Empire. Readers are told that "He wrote full-steam, brazenly"(231). Quite intriguingly, the novel's metafictive status is further exposed through the competing storytelling between Oates and Maggs himself. As Rene Girard argues when pointing out the rivalry and conflict resulting from mimetic desire, "[T]wo desires converging on the same object are bound to clash. Thus, mimesis coupled with desire leads automatically to conflict" (Fidyk, 2009: 146). When Maggs learns that Oates has "burgled" him by having "plundered" (32) his past life, he realizes that he must be his own cartographer to make the true picture of his life known to his son Phipps. Though Maggs, the narrator, casts doubt about the truthfulness of realist writing itself by informing his readers that "writing is a distrustful art", he insists on dipping "the great albatross quill into the apothecary's bottle" and pouring out his real story to his son as well as to readers and he "wrote fluidly" (74). The first draft of Oates' novel regarding Maggs begins in quite a Dickensian way:

> It was a dismal day in the year of 1818, and the yellow fog which had lain low all morning lifted a moment in the afternoon and then, as if the desolate pile of rock and stone thereby revealed was far too melancholy a sight to be endured, it descended again like a shroud around the walls of Newgate Prison. (223)

However, afraid of Maggs exposing his scandal, Oates submits his manuscripts for the former convict's scrutiny. Dissatisfied with Oates' treating him like a compulsive criminal and his god-like patronizing tone in the previous drafts, he snatches his book and threatens him into burning it. As a result, the published version of *The Death of Maggs* starts like this: "As certain birds do declare themselves unto their intended, so the Murderer returned to court his beloved England, bold as cock robin in his bright red waistcoat." (231) This beginning is brought to Maggs' content and bears much resemblance with the opening of Peter Carey's *Jack Maggs*:

It was a Saturday night when the man with the red waistcoat arrived in London. It was, to be precise, six of the clock on the fifteenth of April in the year of 1837 that those hooded eyes looked out the window of the Dover coach and beheld, in the birth aura of gas light, a golden bull and an overgrown mouth opening to devour him — the sign of his inn, the Golden Ox. (1)

In the contest between a British novelist and an Australian convict to relate the genuine story of that convict, the latter wins the game despite a series of torture, and wrestling and the muted Other gets the chance to voice his version of his past to rectify the Empire's distorted narrative.

As a matter of fact, the novel ventures to expose its self-reflexivity even to such a playful degree that it threatens to run into the cliché of postmodern "language game". When Maggs accuses Oates of thieving his painful past and including him and Sophina in his ongoing convict novel, he also tells Oates defiantly that he is "just a character" (280) to him, too. However, "language game" is not what Carey intends the novel to end up with. The author's real intention lies both in deconstructing the overarching imperial narrative as well as in constructing the Australian narrative. This can be seen from some details of Maggs' cartography of his own story. He writes it on the handle of a mirror in a backward script, and the handwriting is designed carefully to avoid possible attempts to tamper so that "fresh lines fade, first to lilac, then to white; until, that is, they became invisible" (74). His adopted son Henry Phipps is instructed to squeeze lemon juice on it to "read a different type of story in the glass" (ibid.). Here, Carey metaphorically points out the challenges that (Australian) writers are confronted with when representing the historical truth and the zigzag process for readers to get access to that truth. It becomes something that is shrouded in a certain sort of secrecy.

According to the imperial narrative, Australia has been a "shadow image of English society's criminality — not just a physical locus for penal servitude, but also a psychic escape valve that allowed middle-class England to persuade itself that society could be purified by the banishment of 'evil' to the hellish, nethermost regions of the earth" (Thieme, 2001: 106). However, to fulfil certain political functions in *Jack Maggs*, Peter Carey revisits Australia's convict memory, reconstructs it in a postmodern text in a refreshing way that deviates from the overarching imperial narrative by giving voice to the disenfranchised, launches a re-examination of the convict history, and points out a feasible way for Australians to get out of the entrapment. The subsequent parts in this section are devoted to a detailed investigation into the above facets.

Influenced by postcolonial theories, especially Bill Ashcroft's theory of "writing back" to the Empire, the most critical attention of *Jack Maggs* is devoted to investigating Peter Carey's reusing of the past and rewriting of *Great Expectations*. Regarding the novel as a postcolonial response to the Victorian cannon, critics (Thieme, 2001; Peng Qinglong, 2005; Ho, 2013) argue that Peter Carey reverses the roles of Pip and Magwitch in his narrative to write back to the Empire and deconstruct Charles Dickens as well as his imperial narrative. There are exceptions, though. For example, Wang Liya argues that Carey's rewriting of *Great Expectations* is not so much a subversion as a supplement of the pretext. (王丽亚, 2017: 12) Other critics (李晓娟, 2008; Fidyk, 2009; 郭梅; 2012; 刘芳, 2015; Pellow, 2013; 赵晶, 2018) focus on how Peter Carey uses the past in a postcolonial way to decolonize Australia and Australian culture. Other motifs such as Carey's deconstruction of "the imperial hegemonic masculinity" (龚静; 向晓红, 2012), his deployment of "domesticity" (Myers, 2011; 陈栩, 2019) as a political metaphor to explore the negotiation between Australia's national identity and its English heritage, have also attracted some research attention.

When critics investigate Carey's use and abuse of Australia's past with a postcolonial concern, they are carried away by the deconstructive aspect of his work. However, deconstruction or subversion is only one side of the coin. Textual clues suggest that the author concerns him equally, if not more, with the constructive side of his rewriting. Moreover, owing to Australia's undeniable ties with the English inheritance, it is unreasonable to jump to the conclusion that the author disavows everything that is English, though he denounces the imperial mindset. Approaching this work from the perspective of cultural memory can breach the gap between the author's deconstructive and constructive motivations. Though what the author revives is Maggs' personal memory, his recollection is impossible unless he has recourse to the thought of his group since individuals need to be "located in a specific group context, draw on that context to remember or recreate the past" (Halbwachs, 1992: 169). Since individual memory is a "conglomeration that emerges from participation in different group memories" (Assmann, 2011: 23). Maggs' personal memory of his convict experience is also Australia's collective memory of its penal past. How the author reconfigures that tradition to fulfil his authorial intention will be discussed in the three sections coming up.

1.2.2 Scapegoats Expulsed for Good

Transported convicts, males and females alike, are condemned to be social transgressors in imperial texts, and this overarching imperial ideology has long dominated the documented memory of penal colony Australia and continues inflicting further psychological colonization over the continent. However, when Peter Carey embarks on his project of writing Australian stories, he reconfigures Australia's convict memory from the perspective of the convicts. Compared to the imperial narrative or Australian documented history, the reversed point of view foregrounds the convicts' individual memories and allows them to juxtapose with the metanarrative. These plural tiny narratives give voice to the formerly marginalized and silenced lesser beings and transform their identity from "social transgressors to heroes, from victimizers to victims" (Fidyk, 2009: v), considering the social and historical context they are forced into. When Percy Buckle denounces the Empire's Transportation System, which has dumped his sister on that barren land owing to an unwarranted minor offence, he claims it unbelievable that "Mother England would do such a thing to one of her own" (89). Through his focalization, Carey alludes to the excessive severity of the government's punishment system and the injustice possibly involved. Then, he strides forward to reconstruct Australian convicts to be the scapegoats of the Empire who possess favourable merits like any other mortal being.

Unlike Abel Magwitch, whom Charles Dickens depicts to be an Australian convict stained with the odour of a ferocious criminal without leaking to us any of his history, Maggs is allowed by Carey to give a full account of the backdrop of his transportation, which suffices to convict the Empire of subornation of and complicity in his crime. Maggs writes his story on the handle of a mirror in a backwards script, and Henry Phipps needs to squeeze some lemon juice on it to make the words visible. The handle of mirror is the metaphor of Thomas De Quincey's "palimpsest" of the human mind, and Phipps' lemon juice is the restorer's chemical that makes the images of Maggs' life, which has stored themselves layer by layer readable again. When Maggs is orphaned at three years old, the wretched little boy is rescued by Silas from his mud flats beneath London Bridge and then adopted by Ma Britten out of his benefactor's bribe. However, either his benefactor, Silas, or his foster mother Mary, Britten, does not adopt him out of humanistic kindness or any Christian creed. Instead, they raised him solely for self-serving purposes. As Maggs recalls, "Silas' comfortable way of life was paid for by my labours" (214). Ma Britten goes much farther. Hardened by the poverty-stricken life she scrambles for with his slow-witted son Tom, she sees Maggs as an instrument to earn her material gains and an "arm" for his own son. She implemented her scheme first by having Silas train him to be a masterful thief when he was just six years old and had already gotten accustomed to a life of crime (Both Silas and Tom make a living by thieving.). This can be evidenced by Ma Britten's contradictory statements in a situation when Tom shows extreme jealousy of Maggs because he is the one taught how to recognize valuables silverware and gets his mother's adoration and affectionate hug and extra meat in his meal when he proves himself to be "useful" (104) by bringing home those items and threatens to kill him. Ma Britten tells Tom, "You are the man that gets the meat... You may kill him, but you may as well cut off your arm, for it is this sooty fellow who is going to take you out of this pit. It was what he was raised to be. It was what you carried home his meat for" (105-106). Her hurtful speech makes "the little nipper" know crystal clear that he has been made a thief and "raised for a base purpose like a hog or hen" (106). If he wants Ma Britten to love him, he has to exchange it with more valuable silverware in his hessian sack. Moreover, Maggs would instead take the adventure to win his mother's affection. As he confesses, "I am an old dog[...] who has been treated bad, and has learned all sorts of tricks he wishes he never had to know" (72-73).

Both Silas and Britten are well aware that burglary is a crime that may result in the perpetrators' transportation. So, they just coach them, Maggs and later Sophina (Silas's biological daughter and later adopted by Ma Britten after he is locked in prison out of Tom's betrayal), plot behind the scenes, and then profit from their labour. As Maggs says, Silas and Britten's very original ambition is "to do a series of clever burglaries without laying fingers on the goods. And once they got Sophina and me properly trained-up to the art, it was, so Silas said like having ferrets, except that he was excused the bother of carrying the cages" (153). When their life is bettered, she stops her son Tom from thieving and sends him as apprentice of a carpenter. Even when Tom returns to his previous occupation because he is unable to put up with a "useful, honest sort of life" and always intends to "set on bigger things" (209) like his mother, Ma Britten arranges for him to solely unlock the door with his carpenter's craft and leave the most hazardous bulk of job done by Maggs and Sophina. When Sophina is pregnant with Maggs' child, and Britten immediately feels her vested profit endangered, she kills that baby boy with her poisonous sausage while having Tom assault Maggs and make him listen to Sophina's deafening bawling painfully yet helplessly. Maggs is forced later by Tom to see for himself that the boy's "sweet little cheek is cut open" (204). "The flash of terror makes a photographically precise impression" (A. Assmann. 2011: 236) that inscribes on his cheek "the same wound" (205). She perpetrates that hideous crime solely because "She did not wish to lose her little girl-thief to motherhood, or me to Sophina. She needed both as servants to her cause" (239). Later on, it is Tom again who betrays Sophina out of jealousy and hatred and causes her arrest and being hanged. Maggs attempts to save his love by assuming all the perpetrations himself but ends up with his own transportation.

In Peter Carey's reconstruction, it is effortless to tell that Maggs has been converted by his foster mother, Mary Britten, from an innocent nipper into a habitual thief rather than born with a criminal mind. He is raised in a family where crime is an integral part of his life and trained to be one of the perpetrators on purpose to support that family with continuous material gains. For him, burglary is an offence he has to commit for his livelihood, either in the material or spiritual sense. He has to trespass the law to earn himself extra meat and win over Ma Britten's affection. Thieving also provides him chances to flee from the suffocation of his highly taxing and confined life, designed elaborately by Britten. Since he and Sophina are always worked hard by Ma Britten, charged with the care and cleaning of the household and detained on the upstairs floor without any amusement at all when their jobs are done, "the tedium of close confinement" (213) makes burglary something they look forward to rather than fearing much of its consequences. As Maggs contends, it is not their "bloodline" or their "criminal craniums", but their natural human desire for something other than the boringly confined life Ma Britten has rendered them that makes burglary a rather attractive adventure for them. "They were the sweetest thing in all my life, to go burgling with Sophina and to flirt with the great dangerous web of sleep which came down to claim us afterwards" (216). The author deploys irony to accuse Ma Britten, thus, the Empire of abetting the innocent of committing crimes for her own benefit and invite readers' sympathy towards the convicts.

Carey does not stop with exonerating Maggs by representing him as a scapegoat for Silas and Ma Britten's crime. He further re-enchants the former convict with creditable merits. Maggs is made not only a devoted son but also Sophina's loyal and gallant partner. Even after he is transported and flogged and brutally abused, one "will find him of a very decent disposition" (163). His relationship with heartless Ma Britten, who is often called "the Queen of England" by her young customers, and ruthless Tom, is made an emblem of the association between the convicts and the penal colony and the Empire. As Tobias Oates describes, Ma

Britten remains a "shadow, passion, hurt, an inky malignancy" (230) in Jack Maggs's dreams. She is the trauma carved into his body. Maggs' experience metaphorizes Great Britain's total patriarchal domination of the downtrodden and, symbolically, the penal colonies as well. Convicts are first exploited to the full to satisfy the Empire's thirst for the primitive accumulation of capital. Then, they take the blame for the Empire's corruption, crime, and incompetence in solving its own problems. Eventually, those lesser beings, perpetrators either with severe or minor offences, paupers, and young famine girls eligible for domestic life, are picked out as unwanted populations and banished to the vast and barren space of penal colonies permanently to resume their service for the more significant benefits of the Empire.

Maggs' recollection of his early life makes it convincible that, like other lesser beings that are at the Empire's disposal, convicts are actually the scapegoats rather than the devious monsters. When they finally find their way back to the homeland that they have been pining for all these years, what awaits them there is a second-time alienation. Once transported, like Jack Maggs, they are perpetually crossed off from their motherhand that they have once ploughed laboriously for. Maggs' image as the inferior Other is co-constructed by three important figures he is confronted with, his foster mother Ma Britten whose name emblemizes Britain, his foster son Henry Phipps and the imperial writer Tobias Oates.

Even though Ma Britten has named him after the foul smell of the herbs she works on, maltreated him and his Sophina, and eventually killed their son, she remains one of the two critical figures he has long been craving to meet. After all these years, Maggs never falters his affection for her, as he admits to Oates, "I'd rather be a bad smell here than a frigging rose in New South Wales" (230). An analogy is made here between Maggs' uncritical love for Ma Britten and Australians' blind worship of their British ancestry. However, when Maggs finally finds his way to her house and presents himself at the door, he is the brusque Other, harshly questioned on his purpose of returning back to London instead of being invited home for a proper chat. Though Maggs states repeatedly that he returns only for a reunion since England is where he belongs and he intends to catch up with the culture, she turns a deaf ear to his solicitude and insists on judging him with the victimizer stereotype she holds against him. Ma Britten calls him "varmint" and persists in her mistaken assumption that he comes back to "put the bite" or "play the old dart" or "have a bone to pick with" her (4-5). She threatens that she might still use her "Bilboa" against him or report to the police to get him hanged if he dares to bring her trouble. After that bitter speech, she closes the door in his face, leaving merely "the heavy clanking of some chains which seemed to amuse the visitor" (5). No matter how hard he tries to win her favour, he remains the vicious Other who is predestined to rest in eternal banishment.

The other figure that fuels his pining for his native land and propels him to risk his neck back there to meet is his adopted son, Henry Phipps. Saved by little Phipps' food and touched by the undamaged goodness he has seen in him, he promises that he will come back from exile, "take him from orphanage", "spin him a cocoon of gold and jewels", "weave him nest so strong that no one would ever hurt his goodness", and "clad him in a scholar's robe and learn him his numbers and letters, not only English, but Greek and Latin too" (264). For Maggs, Henry epitomizes the good vision he has for his home country, and he is the bridge by which Maggs reunites with it. Phipps is also made by the author as another symbol of ungrateful Great Britain. Maggs does keep his promise by taking him out of the orphanage, providing him with a bountiful life and getting him educated in Oxford. However, the English gentleman he has taken enormous pains to cultivate never tries to accept him. All he was capable of is taking advantage of him, like Ma Britten. When he was young and under the tutelage of his Oxford tutor Victor Littlehales, they laboured together to invent "lies" (325) in his letters to gratify Maggs' needs to obtain generous funding. When he grows old enough, he becomes very skilful in doing it by himself. The picture he sends to Maggs, which is supposed to represent himself, turns out to be a portrait of King Gorge IV. While Maggs celebrates the enormous comfort and joy that Phipps has brought him and grows grateful because fancying himself to be accepted and loved by his English son has kept him alive in the last twenty-four years, he is, in fact, self-deluded in "a flight of fancy" (ibid.) conceived by Phipps. This is only part of the enmity that Henry Phipps directs against his benefactor.

He has always known that Maggs is a convict transported to Australia and forbidden to return to England for the rest of his life. When he learns that Maggs has been back in London, he hides himself from him. When Edward Constable, out of sympathy for poor Maggs, finds Phipps secretly, delivers him the letters Maggs has meant for him and pleads him earnestly to meet the wretched man who has been pining to meet him, the gentleman demonstrates his "churlishness" (162). He first pretends that he never knows such a criminal yet assumes him to be a "ruffian" (163). Later, when Constable indicates that he has a document from Maggs, Phipps gets excited because he thinks it is the legal document to grant him the freehold of the mansion his benefactor provides him on Great Queen Street. He turns atrocious again when he is told that they are just letters intended for him and howls that he cannot correspond with such a "dangerous man" (164). He asks Constable to tell him that he is "not fond of him", and he finds the "very notion of him vile" (ibid.). Only when he is disclosed to have lived a leisure life with Jack Maggs' financial support, does he consider it a gesture of lowering himself to maintain a comfortable life with money from a banished convict. To save himself from the disgrace of being "a dancing boy for a criminal" (295), he immediately decides to repudiate the connection with him by joining the army and becoming a soldier of His Majesty. However, he does not report to his regiment as expected. When Percy Buckle, who feels humiliated for losing his favourite maid, Mercy's fancy to the former convict, persuades him to kill Maggs to usurp the mansion. He rekindles his "passionate desire to ensure his own comfort" (320) without any labour again. This time, like Ma Britten, he would rather commit a murder to sustain his leisurely life. As instructed by Buckle, he attempts to shoot Maggs dead on sight to take "his" house back by accusing him falsely of burglary. Dressed in his uniform of the 57th Foot Regiment, Phipps steps into that mansion, pointing his gun at Maggs' heart. The wretched man is paralyzed since he resembles the Phantom, who keeps hunting him in his memory. "There, in the firelight, he beheld his nightmare: long straight nose, fair hair, a brutal dreadfuluniform of the 57th Foot Regiment. The Phantom had broken the locks and entered his life" (323). Fortunately, Mercy is aware of Buckle's whole scheme and appears timely to save Maggs from Phipps' pistol. Under the gaze of Henry Phipps, Jack Maggs remains a demonic criminal regardless of all the tender feelings he has shown him and the fine dispositions others credit him with. He always treats him as an inferior creature that he can exploit and juggle with to his heart's content and get rid of anytime his interest might be jeopardized. He is isomorphic with Ma Britten. However, neither Ma Britten nor Henry Phipps exhausts the list of characters in the novel that alienate the home-coming convict. Among them, the imperial writer Tobias Oates is another crucial figure who treats Jack Maggs as the Other and exploits him relentlessly.

Tobias Oates is a writer and a fetishist of Animal Magnetism, which he believes to be a modern science effective to dig out all truth deep buried in any criminal's mind. The first impression he gives Maggs is being unsettling and condescending. "He was edgy, almost pugnacious, with eyes and hands everywhere about him as if he were constantly confirming his position in the world, a navigator measuring his distance from the chair, the wall, the table." (26) Oates is a typical imperial writer, like Charles Dickens. He regards Maggs as the object on which he can conduct experiments. When he detects Maggs' contorted face on his mentioning of a criminal mind susceptible to magnetism, he diagnoses it as "tic douloureux". He assures Maggs he can take away the pain from him. Nevertheless, the fact is, he decides to deviate from his initial orientation of curing his pain the moment he finds the man to be a transported convict in mesmerism. Instead, he intends him and his previous life experiences to be the raw material for his future novel. He foresees a reservoir of exotic stories, characters and landscapes in Maggs. As he assures Percy Buckle, "[T]his Australian of ours holds his life in his cerebrum. He carries pelicans and parrots, fish and phantoms, things the Royal Botanist would give a sov or two to hold" (88). However, Oates is not content with the sole inventory of exoticism Maggs gives up to him when he is mesmerized. He sees in Maggs' traumatic memory his chance for fame and wealth. Like Ma Britten and Henry Phipps, he is determined to take advantage of him. He is thrilled to tell his friend Buckle, "[W]hat you have brought me here is a world as rich as London. What a puzzle of life exists in the dark little lane-ways of this wretch's soul, what stolen gold lies hidden in the vaults beneath his filthy streets... It is the Criminal Mind... awaiting its first cartographer" (90). Blithely likening himself to Thackeray, Oates is determined to push into the musty corridors of that mind and labour like an "archaeologist inside an ancient tomb" (91), treating Maggs "like a blessed butterfly he has to pin down on his board" (39). Both the "tomb" and "archaeologist" are the spacial metaphor of memory, which leads readers to the discovery of how the imperial version of the convict memory is constructed.

Complacent about mesmerism being the scientific method leading him to Maggs' compressed unconscious, Oates is fascinated with the prospect of being the first one to map the criminal mind. Oates, the fictional writer's digging of Maggs' unconsciousness, is the analogy of the Empire's intrusion into the Antipodes in the name of civilization. He does not hesitate a bit to achieve the goal by foul means. He first cheats Maggs into believing that he means to remove the tic on his face through mesmerism. When Maggs denounces Oates for having pried into his private life and stolen his secrets when he is mesmerized, he continues bewitching him with an attractive deal, promising the poor man to help him find Phipps in exchange for his secrets. Maggs continues his labour as the object of the writer's scientific experiment. Since memory is malleable and "it is reconstructed not only under the pressure of the present but also within particular institutional frameworks that guide selection and fix contours" (A. Assmann, 2011: 253), Oates tries to manipulate Maggs' memory to write a sensational story. He plants a Phantom, which takes the shape of a soldier from the 57th Foot Regiment, in Maggs' mind to evoke his extreme horror and excavate his most painful memories of the punishment he has received in the penal colony. The instant that the Phantom is planted in his brain, Maggs revives the most painful memory of the tremendous torture inflicted on him by his flogger Ruder in Morton Bay and ends up weeping and begging him to show mercy. That is also the excellent timing for Oates to sketch rapidly in his notebook, totally disregarding the poor man's aggravated convulsion on his face he initially promised to cure. When Maggs gets suspicious that he is the victimizer that has introduced this creature into his mind through some "Magical Arts", Oates deceives him by saying that the beast has long lived in him and caused his convulsion and he is the only one he can count on to depict it and drag it out. To make things worse, the Phantom Oates turns into a personification of pain and begins invading Maggs' everyday life. The wraith keeps appearing in his dreams and sleep, staring at him, devouring him. Oates dominates and reconstructs Maggs with his discourse.

Oates is also confronted with Maggs' resistance. Discovering that the writer has used his painful memory for the material of his fiction, altering it randomly to make it more attractive, Maggs reprimands him for having perpetrated such a low scheming, thieving thing. However, Oates flaunts his discursive power, contending that he is making a memorial to immortalize him and his Sophina. "I write that name, Jack, like a stone mason make the name upon a headstone, so her memory may live forever. In all the Empire, Jack, you would not have employed a better carver"(280). What Oates shows off is the moulding power of the imperial narrative. Then it is this best "carver" who ascribes Lizzie, his wife's sister and his lover's death to Jack Maggs owing to the fact he brings the girl abortion pills out of sympathy. Oates exerts his power as a writer on Maggs in his fiction, groundlessly condemning him to be a "murderer" and ending his life burnt in flames.

At the very beginning of their acquaintance, Tobias Oates sees in Maggs nothing but a treasury vault filled with exotic stories, which he blackmails him into pouring out from his memory with the help of Animal Magnetism. To obtain the most thrilling ones, he plants a phantom in Maggs' mind which intimates the poor man's desire to squeeze more of his painful experiences. In the end, he asks Maggs to take the blame for his moral stain in his fictional landscape, demonizing him to be a hopping "devil", a gimp with a transmogrified head that still carries the heavy convict chains. Though he has once been a citizen of the Empire and transformed into a gentleman, Maggs remains an outsider for Oates, serving solely as "an exotic collectible that can be controlled by the writer/conjuror who plunders marginalized lives to make art" (Renk, 2004: 63). The imperial writer Tobias Oates grows complicit with the Empire in stopping him returning to the imperial centre by alienating and demonizing him in texts.

To obtain a better insight into the functions that Peter Carey intends his reworking of Australia's convict memory to fulfil, it is necessary to review the principle Friedrich Nietzsche sets for revisiting history:

> The utterance of the past is always an oracular pronouncement. You will understand it only as builders of the future and as people who know about the present... It is appropriate now to understand that only the man who builds the future has a right to judge the past. In order to look ahead, set yourselves an important goal, and at the same time control that voluptuous analytical drive with which you now lay waste the present and render almost impossible all tranquillity, all peaceful growth and maturing. (1998: 27)

Carey's recalling the convict memory in the twentieth century echoes Nietzsche's golden rule of starting from the present to serve the future. In Peter Carey's recuperation of Australia's convict memory, the binary opposition of the victimizer and the victim is dismantled. The boundary between the two gets very fuzzy. Different from the metanarrative which pronounces convicts as malicious law breakers or social transgressors, Carey takes into account the social dynamics that they are situated in his reconstruction. Convicts are, alternatively, depicted to be the disadvantageous people who are instigated or forced to be of complicity with the Empire to commit minor offences and then demonized by the imperial narrative. They are not as many victimizers as victims. On the contrary, embodied in Ma Britten, his son Tom, Henry Phipps amal Tobias Oates, the Empire itself is portrayed as the most greedy and vicious victimizer who perpetrates the crimes of thieving and plundering resources from colonies worldwide. To serve the larger picture of its hegemonic ambition or its immediate dirty little schemes, it chooses those vulnerable ones as scapegoats, frames cases against them, banishes them justifiably to the end of the world and forbids them from returning for ever.

Carey's primary function in recuperating the convict memory is to consolidate Australia's cultural and national connection with Britain. Australia and Australian culture are part of the continuum of the Empire and British culture, which extend in a peculiar way in the Antipodes. Convicts are contributors to the creation of Australia and the Empire's capital accumulation. Moreover, this engineering suggests that the "convict" tag is enforced in Australia historically and culturally. The author intends to legitimize the alternative version of the scapegoat memory while he delegitimizes the imperial narrative, claiming transported convicts to be victimizers. Through legitimizing Maggs' individual memory and rectifying the overarching metanarrative, Carey's reworking aims at exonerating Australians' convict forebears and uprooting the negative element of Australia's collective memory concerning its convict origin, which has long clouded its fostering of cultural confidence and building of a positive self-image. By rewriting their convict ancestors to be victims of certain historical periods with heroic and righteous merits, he invents Australia's cultural memory with the attempt to exert positive influence on the nation's pessimistic mentality and equip Australians with enough confidence to embrace their new life in the future. Carey's reconstruction aims to break Australians free from the bondage of history, appease their guilt and anxiety, unite them and produce a power to live a life with sovereignty.

Apart from recuperating the scapegoat version of Australia's convict memory, Peter Carey portrays those former banished convicts as alienated Other under the gaze of the Empire. They are prohibited by law from coming back to their native land and further nailed up on the column of history disgracefully, which symbolizes crime and immorality by imperial writers. This engineering first serves to disclose the Empire's political and discursive hegemony. Just as Ma Britten would not invite Maggs in for fear of the trouble he might bring to her, the British Empire is preoccupied by the anxiety that the prolonged re-connection with the supposedly lesser beings may induce domestic moral corruption, which threatens its superiority. Then, Carey's reconstruction of former convicts received as others in the Empire serves as an allegory of Australia's contemporary status quo. It depicts or foresees the predicament that faces Australians who crave to seek comfort from their mother land and count on her assurance of them as her offspring to ease their unsettling souls, or the Australian government, which continues implementing a cultural cringe towards Britain. The author sobers Australians to sit up for his moral lessons by disillusioning their nostalgia or cringe. Since relying on Britain for salvation is impossible, they might as well give up that illusion as soon as possible for a fresh self-supporting new start. This can be better illustrated in Maggs' recognition with the help of Mercy and settling down eventually in Australia, which will be delved into in the following section.

1.2.3 Convicts' Homesickness

Another dimension of the convict memory that Peter Carey explores through his reconfiguration is the ambivalent cultural identity of those displaced creatures, since most of them, like Jack Maggs, who have English blood flowing in their vessels, start a new life and set up a family on this continent as the sentence ends. On the one hand, England still attracts them with the scared halo of "motherland" though it has once deemed them as victimizers, cast them out of the Empire as unwanted criminals and transported them to the corner of the world. On the other hand, the alien land on which they have an in-process new life also stands witness to their being brutally flogged and traumatizes them for a second time. In Carey's reconstruction, convicts are possessed by an irrepressible impulsion to return to their England home owing to complicated psychological reasons. Tormented by a sense of loss and displacement, they often suffer from the "incurable modern condition"(Boym, 2001: 8) of nostalgia. Living in Australia, they have a "metaphysical yarning for the Old World" (Clark, 1973: 136). Australia cannot be like "home" since there are no palaces, cathedrals, old country houses, or Oxford. For Maggs, everything related to his homeland, "the culture", "the opera", and "the theatre" is all that he longs. He is more than willing to make reckless sacrifices, even risk his neck to ease his homesickness. What underlies this reconstruction is Carey's interpretation of Australia's unbreakable ties with its English ancestry. Carey depicts Maggs' "disease" of nostalgia with considerable profundity and exhibits it in multiple layers.

As a former convict transported from Great Britain, Maggs has transformed into a considerably successful man in the secular sense. He possesses a good fortune and owns a grand house in Sydney where a street is named after him. He ascends to the Australian upper-class, keeping a coach and two footmen and being addressed as "Jack Maggs Esquire" (281). He fathers two children. However, as a transported convict, he is also the sufferer of the penal colony's brutal punishment, which writes into his body overwhelming traumatic memories. In one of the cases when he is mesmerized by Oates, Maggs recalls one of those ferocious floggings that he receives as a daily routine in penal Australia. Seeing "[T]he small red button at the apex of the flogger's forage cap, the worn supple thongs which bound his wrists and ankles to the triangle" (321) could have horrified him. Just as "the unheroic memory blocks integration of the traumatic experience and prevents the possibility of constructing an identity" (A. Assmann, 2011: 249), Maggs, the former convict, loses track of who he is. Throughout his lifetime in Australia, he is filled with nothing but tremendous "pain" and "horror" and hunted by an extreme anxiety of rootlessness. As the omniscient narrator reveals, "It was not a horror of anything or about anything, but a horror so profound that a certain time elapsed during which he hardly knew where on earth he stood" (29). Just as Svetlana Byom suggests, "creative rethinking" coming from nostalgia can be "a strategy of survival" (2001: 8). Maggs' homesickness and his dream of returning "home" is a therapeutic prescription to sustain him, soothing his wretched soul and helping him survive the horrific experience in those years in the penal colony. The wretched man begins to "build London in his mind. He would build it brick by brick... Underneath the scalding sun, which burned his flesh as soon as it was mangled, Jack Maggs would imagine the long mellow light of English summer" (322). Nostalgia for the domestic idyll in his native country ascribes him the sensibility he imagines he could share with his folks back in England and that serves to pacify him and counteract the violence he is being inflicted.

> The flies might feast on his spattered back; the double-cat might carry away the third and fourth fingers of his hand; but his mind crawled forward, always, constructing piece by piece the place

wherein his eyes had first opened, the home to which he would one day return, not the mudflats of the Thames, nor Mary Britten's meat-rich room at Pepper Alley Stairs, but rather a house in Kensington whose kind and beautiful interior he had entered by tumbling down a chimney, like a babe falling from outer darkness into light. (322)

His longing for a return to that house hovers around him like a halo and pumps him with tremendous willpower to save his breath in any condition for that exciting prospect. Despite all the thick and thin he has gone through in Australia, it seems that a rediscovery of his English identity through imagining "I am a fucking Englishman" (128), and that he is returning home anyway will remedy all the suffering he has long endured. He dreams of, to quote Svetlana Byom, "repairing his longing with final belonging" (2001: 8).

For a criminal who is banished from his motherland, Maggs' unheroic memory produces a "diminished self" who "calls for an entire complex of redefinitions and new perceptions, a modernized or modernistic view of ethical discursive possibilities and limits" (A. Assmann, 2011: 247). Consequently, the house that suffuses his fantasy and feeds him with endless artistic imagination is not at all any decent home that ever hosts him. Instead, it is the mansion that he had been instructed by his foster mother, Britten to burgle when he was a kid. He degrades the traumatic memories into false ones to cut his connection with the traumatic past because only in this way can he unload the burden of memory and go through purgatory with the pure and unburdened present.

Apart from taking nostalgia as a therapeutic mechanism for the brutal torture he has suffered in penal Australia, Maggs underpins this sentiment and tries to cure himself of the convict trauma in Australia by reconstructing his bond with his home country. Though deprived of any chance to be a decent English man himself, he compensates for his loss by funding his foster son, Henry Phipps, in secrecy to be a gentleman. All his fantasy and nostalgia for England and Englishness are incarnated in Phipps, with whom he intends to resume his unaccomplished dream. To appease his homesickness and meet his foster son, he runs the risk of being hanged and sneaks back to England, disavowing his prosperous natural home in Australia and leaving behind his two sons born on that land. He is obsessed with an imaginarily bright future that he will build with his adopted son. The idyllic life that he has been denied spending with his dear Sophina, he now fetishizes to living with his beloved English gentleman, Henry Phipps. He is so intoxicated with that illusion that his safety, his home and his family all eclipse in front of his fascination with that prospect:

> When I was imagining my lovely English summers — and I did meditate on this subject an awful lot, my word-I would be suffering the mosquitoes and the skin-rot, to mention two of the least of my discomforts, but I would oft-times make a picture of me and Henry puffing our pipes comfortably in the long evenings. (291-292)

As nostalgia tends to "produce 'erroneous representations' that caused the afflicted to lose touch with the present" (Boym, 2001: 11), Maggs' homesickness is unveiled ruthlessly by Peter Carey to be nothing but an illusion related to his traumatic experience. As a matter of fact, the brutal life he has led in England with Ma Britten before transportation, especially seeing with his own eyes the death of his still-born son with Sophina, severely traumatizes him. That trauma is written into his body, which remembers his past as extreme pain. As a PTSD (Post-traumatic Stress Disorder), he selectively represses that painful memory deep down and disguises other traumatic ones in his consciousness. When the repressed memory is aroused by Oates' mesmerism, tics emerge on his face consequently. Possessed and blinded by the traumatic convict experiences, he consequently confuses his actual home with the imaginary one. It is quite necessary to disguise his awful memory of England and paint it rosy to justify his nostalgia and place his rootless and unprotected soul. As Michael Kammen argues, the heritage of nostalgia is "something suffuses us with pride rather than with shame" (1991: 688). Clouded by homesickness, Maggs conceives every object related to his homeland in an idealized manner despite their true colour.

Maggs' idealization does not take root in reality or can be traced back to any of his childhood experiences. Instead, that rosy picture-book image of England and Englishness he has been long pined for fervently is his imaginary invention because he needs new perceptions to justify his compelling nostalgia. This can be illustrated in one of the highly symbolic scenes in which Maggs and Tobias and their fellow passengers abandon their comfy coach and walk in ankle-deep mud down the road to Gloucester to visit a thief-taker whom Maggs pins his hope to find Phipps. When "the *True Briton* descended with all its locked brakes screaming against wheels" (242) and "[T]he slippery surface of Burlip Hill muddied the backside of more than one passenger" (ibid.), they are supposed to be upset by the harshness and inconvenience. For Maggs, the grass is always greener on the other side of the fence. All the harsh sound of the wheels and the inconvenience brought about by the sticky mud is filtered out automatically. He is pretty "excited" and intoxicated. What emerges in his horizon instead is "as pretty a scene as you would see in all of England — the land divided by hedges into fields and orchards, and the whole picture, with the Cathedral in the middle and the Morvan Hills of Wales in the distance, 'was worth the price of twice the mud'" (ibid.). It is safe to conclude with Janet Myers' observation "Maggs possesses an emigrant's nostalgia for home that clouds his judgment and encourages him to believe in the myths promulgated by fiction" (2011: 463).

When talking about historical writing and its connection with the time it happens, Italo Svevo comments, "[T]he present conducts the past in the way that a conductor conducts an orchestra... The only part of it that is highlighted is the part that has been summoned up to illumine and distract us from, the present" (1967: 302). His anticipation finds an echo in subsequent memory theory, which stresses the constructiveness of memory based on the immediate time it is recalled. To quote Aleida Assmann, remembrance "always starts in the present"(2011: 19). As one of the critical facets of Australia's convict memory under Peter Carey's recuperation, the sentiment of nostalgia that former convicts harbour for their native country is revisited to answer Australians' contemporary preoccupations. Parallel is drawn between former convicts' desperate nostalgia for the Empire and contemporary Australians' prevalent idolatry for Britain and British culture. Seeing that his titular protagonist, Jack Maggs' experiences leave him with perpetual trauma and evoke his enormous sentiment of loss and displacement, Carey tries to show considerable understanding and sympathy towards the wretched man bearing an uncontrollable sense of nostalgia toward his native land. Similarly the author makes allowance for his fellow citizens who are haunted by the sense of rootlessness to harbouring worship of their British ancestry when unresolved historical issues and the raging "Australian history wars" (Gaile, 2010: 1) amongst the academics and politicians problematize their identity. Maggs' nostalgia for his native land serves to heal him by offering him temporally an imaginary shelter to warm his soul and an illusion to confirm his identity. It is used by Carey as an emblem suggesting that Australians' worship of Britain may help them expediently appease their sense of rootlessness and simultaneously obtain a sense of belonging before they could define who they are. Though the

Chapter One Australia's Colonial Memories to Trace Origin, Re-appraise and Invent Traditions

author deploys narrative as a therapy either for his protagonist within the text or his fellow folks out of the text, it is far less to be his central preoccupation. By a feat of aesthetic revelation and plot reversal, Carey has a far-reaching intention to conceive.

According to the third-person omniscient narrator, Maggs' nostalgic sentiment is exposed to be his PTSD. Suppose it does have some connection with the material world. In that case, it roots in nothing more than the fictionalized stories he has read by British authors to advocate the idealized Englishness of the Victorian epoch, consciously or unconsciously. Here, the author points to the transformative potential of literature of the experiential world. Maggs' nostalgia is further revealed to be an utter illusion upon his home-returning. When feverishly nostalgic Maggs finally makes it to his native land at the risk of his life, what awaits him there is nothing more than a disillusion of all his longing. Because he used to be a transported criminal, he is given a cold-shoulder by his foster mother Britten and denied entrance into her house to avoid being implicated.

Moreover, she accuses, though wrongly, Maggs of instigating some villain to kill her son Tom solely because he used to be a victimizer. Tobias Oates, who fetishizes mesmerism like science, takes advantage of Maggs' eagerness to meet his adopted son to trick him into accepting his magnetic experiment. However, his real intention is to evoke Maggs' painful memory and use it as raw material for his new novel delving into the criminal mind, regardless of the tremendous torture it inflicts on this wretched soul. When Henry Phipps, the English gentleman he has splashed his cash to cultivate and has been yarning to meet day and night, presents himself in front of him, he points his pistol at Maggs, his benefactor, and threatens to claim his life. Carey's reconfiguration of Maggs' nostalgia for the Empire, which has originally cast him off, serves as an allegory of the idolatry of the British prevailing amongst Australians. Though they are depicted to be sympathetic owing to the dilemmatic context they are situated in, the author exposes ruthlessly that their reliance on their English ancestry for a secure sense of belonging is bound to end up with disillusion. Through this reconstruction, Carey echoes Vico's argument of memory as a "genuinely productive faculty" rather than "a reproductive", and he evokes Australians' nostalgic memory as, in Vico's words, "the civilizing force" (Assmann, 2011: 22) to preach his own moral lessons on his fellow folks. Just as the god-like narrator in the novel is quite aware of the illusive nature of Maggs' nostalgia as well as what he has left behind to satisfy that sentiment, the reasonable distance Peter Carey maintains with his mother land allows him a more rational perspective to re-examine that national sentiment critically. Nostalgia being one of the critical dimensions of Australia's convict memory, the subsequent section is devoted to Peter Carey's interpretation of the root of the convict system as well as its impact on the convict Australians.

1.2.4 Reorientation to Embrace the Adopted Land

Unlike Abel Magwitch, who dies a wretched death lonely, though spared from hanging, Peter Carey's canonical rewriting of *Jack Maggs* has a happy ending despite a series of twists and turns in the plot. The former transported convict is offered a chance by the author to be brought to the recognition of his memory as well as the actuality ahead of him and to experience the catharsis of reorientation to embrace a decent and meaningful life in his adopted country. Furthermore, this dramatic reversal begins with the author's deconstruction of Maggs' "home", which holds his incurable nostalgic sentiment and obsessive longing for return.

The home Maggs has long dreamed of returning is dismantled by Carey as a mere illusion, and he does this through two accentuating layers. First of all, the "home" that suffuses his memory with gorgeous imagination and provides sources for his compelling nostalgia is not at all the mud-flats he is found lying under London Bridge or that "damp and low-ceilinged little place" where he shares "one bed and two chairs" (99) with Ma Britten and Tom in Pepper Alley Stairs in reality. Instead, it is the affluent Kensington mansion that he has been sent into from the chimney to sack priceless silverware when he is too young to make sense of burglary. That experience is an eye-opener, and what he smells and sees first when he falls from the sooty chimney onto the floor was brought from the utter darkness into light is crystallized in his memory as the archetype of his English "home". Even after all these years, the frozen memory remains vivid and clear to him. The distinguishable smells of "apples and oranges, and what may be called cinnamon", give him "a feeling of almighty comfort" (ibid.). He still remembers

> the long double room with great glass doors... there was enough upholstered seating to accommodate half the population of our little court. All around the room there were armchairs, sofas, chaises, love-seats — none of which I could have named for you, never having seen such things before. In my enchantment, I sat on each of them, each one. (99)

He can even picture the "sooty mess" he might have left behind in his imagination. All these years, it is that luxurious mansion with an extreme sweet aroma he burgles instead of the filthy and smelly room he actually lives in that fills his imagination and dominates his illusory thirst for a home-coming and being an Englishman.

The "home" crystallized in Maggs' memory is his invention grounded on his burgling experience to resist the body writing of trauma when he witnesses the death of his in-born son. That illusory image is further echoed and consolidated in English fiction he reads, which promulgates high-profile Englishness, highlighting its unparalleled superiority and genteel domestic life. He uses those works of art to bridge his gap with his native land when he is banished to the end of the world, though the truth is they estrange him even afar from it. Both his invention and the myths he fetishizes in the textual world disavow the realities of his home country. In addition to that, his former identity as a thief and transported convict further shatters his fantasy of returning home and being held dear by his mother or motherland as her long-lost beloved boy. However, he is received by his "home" with remarkable alienation and hostility, totally in opposition to the landscape stamped in his memory.

When he walks into the street of London, he does not see any scene corresponding to the picturesque home country filling his imagination. Instead, London impresses him with a picture of decay. "All around him was uproar, din, the deafening rush, the smell of horse shit, soot, that old yellow smell of London Town." (2) He has to blow his great hawk's nose from suffusing soot and dust his face occasionally with his Kingsman handkerchief. He keeps tugging himself free from child paupers or short-legged streetwalkers to make his way forward. Britain is still infested with crimes. At the shining black door of Ma Britten's house on Cecil Street, he hears a young woman weeping over the death of her unborn baby or the pains caused by the abortionist's poisonous pills. His actual childhood home is aligned with exploitation and brutality rather than humanistic tender feelings. When he takes so much pains to present himself at the door, his "mother" rejects his pleading to come home even for a proper chat. However sincere and fervent he appears to be, he remains a bullshitting varmint for her. While he acclaims, "[T]hat's a nice home-coming" (2), she bolts her door to avoid any possible implication and threatens to disclose him if he dares to conceive of any perpetration. No matter how anxious he has been about comting back, he is banished from home by her for ever.

Maggs' dream of home-coming is not only denied by his mother Britten, and it comes close to claiming his life. His house in London is the mansion he purchased on Great Queen Street which shares similar ostentation of the Kingston one that is framed in his memory. It is under the freehold of his adopted son, Henry Phipps, and it is meant to be a home in which he returns to enjoy the rest of his life with him. However, Phipps is no longer the little boy with "undamaged goodness". He takes advantage of Maggs' kindness and obtains his funding fraudulently to support his extravagant life with an easy conscience. He regards Maggs as a villain and sees his connection with him as a degradation, not to say sharing a room or an idyll life with him as he envisages. When instigated by Buckle, he attempts to deprive Maggs of his ownership of this mansion by killing him. For him, the former convict deserves to be homeless. Consequently, the only contact Maggs has with his grand home is that he occasionally sneaks in it to write letters justifying himself to Phipps. Instead of bringing him any domestic happiness or any genuine sense of belonging, his home stands as a witness to his perpetual banishment. What he has been longing for all these years, a place called home, is in fact a mirage that he is never able to reach. It may be difficult for him to recognize that his heart-felt nostalgia and the painstaking elaboration that has kept him alive all these years is merely an illusion. Maggs' journey back to London is greeted with Ma Britten's indifference, Phipps' hostility and Oates' exploitation rather than any warmth and comfort he craves from his native home.

Not only does Peter Carey sober Maggs by exposing the illusiveness of his nostalgia for Britain, but more importantly, he also introduces the female character, Mercy Larkin, into his life to guide him. Mercy is Percy Buckle's maid. Like most other feminine figures in Peter Carey's fiction, she is intelligent and sensible. She switches her affection for her master to Maggs after she obtains a good knowledge of the wretched man's character and sympathetic experiences. It is remembering, not forgetting, that cures the trauma, and bringing traumatic memories from the unconscious and admitting them into the conscious is the only way through which the traumatized reinstate themselves in the society. (阿斯曼, 2016: 325-327) However, Maggs, as a severely traumatized subject, is no longer "the man of action"① who has the ability to keep his memories under control. It calls for the heroine, Mercy, to bring him to his senses. Reminding him of the lashed scars on his back "glistening like torture" (318), Mercy brings him to face up to the harsh reality that all his suffering in Morton Bay is actually inflicted by the English King whom he adores and is more than ready to serve and that what his native country is capable of is bullying him, causing him intense pain instead of loving him.

Moreover, Mercy uses Maggs' consciousness of kinship to weave a therapeutic web that grows bit by bit until it covers the wound of his soul. She reminds him that his two sons of "That Race" (327), Dick and John, are adorable and in desperate need of their father. She reminds him that the bullet blowing away her wedding figure has been intended for him by his "better class" (318) son. She reminds him how he has pranced around England for people unworthy while leaving behind those who love him dearly. Mercy brings him to the recognition that there are naturally

---

① Men of action is initiated by Henri Bergson to refer to people who are characterized by the "ability to invoke pertinent memories while maintaining an insurmountable barrier in his consciousness that separates him from his chaotic and incoherent memories" (A. Assmann, 2011: 268).

imperfections in human history and there is nothing shameful to have feelings of inferiority since they are all what human culture is based on. (Adler, 2014: 35/115) Maggs realises eventually it is high time that he should break up with his illusion and go back to his real sons of the "Australian race" (313) to "kiss them good night" (327). With the help of Mercy Larkin, Maggs recognizes that it is his adopted home where he is supposed to attach himself to rather than the estranged native land. He gives up his burdensome past by admitting it into his memory, from which he gains infinite therapeutic force.

Once Maggs is freed from his illusion about his native England, he flees from London with Mercy Larkin and weds her in Wingham, where he comes from in Australia. Since he breaks off his connection with Oates and Phipps, who emblemizes the colonizing power of the Empire, and returns to his honest work in Australia, he is spared from the torture and exploitation that have plagued him in England. Anthony Hassall depicts the transformation succinctly, "[H]is return to the social order which made him a criminal, which he has romanticized from afar, enables him to recognize the freedom offered by the social order of his former prison, which has itself begun to metamorphose from a penal colony into a site of liberation" (1997: 134).

Back in Australia, Maggs turns his idyllic fantasy of England into his real life. He and Mercy settle down in the new town and build a new, prosperous and decent life together. "Jack Maggs sold the brickworks in Sydney. In Wingham, he set up a saw mill and, when that prospered a hardware store, and when that prospered a pub. He was twice president of the shire and was still the president of the Cricket Club"(327). Mercy also finds herself a proper place in the new town. She assumes the responsibility of taking care of Maggs' other two sons, John and Dick and applies "herself to being their mother with a passion... It was she who moved the family away from the bad influence of Sydney. Moreover, in the new town of Wingham, where they shortly settled, she not only civilized these first two children but very quickly gave birth to five further members of 'That Race'."

With the prospering industry, pubs, and Cricket Clubs, Wingham is a thriving town like any one in London during the Golden Age. They construct a grand mansion on Supper Creek Road with servants meticulously selected and a particular library. It satisfies all what Maggs has expected from a "home" in England, and his awakening repays him with an extra bonus. His real sons are civilized and outstanding. His succeeding generations prosper on the fertile river flats, with their stories relished by their folks. As Anthony Hassall comments on the close of the novel, "[D]oubly unexpected, the ending is determinedly Australian and optimistic" (1997: 129).

As pointed out by Peng Gang, all kinds of power in the modern nation state and modern society have a positive and clear consciousness of the competition for the dominant power of shaping people's memory and how to shape historical memory. (2014: 10) Literature, with its "privileged position" (Erll, 2008: 318) in representing cultural memory, has engaged itself in the rivalry for the domination of a nation's memory. This is true for Peter Carey's rewriting of *Great Expectations*. Unlike Dickens' omission of Magwitch's history, Carey's *Jack Maggs* is not only devoted to the invention of that history. It is also involved in a contention as to who is the one that should be endowed with the privilege to write that history. Within the text, this is embodied by the rivalry between the imperial writer Tobias Oates' mapping of Maggs' memory and his own documentation of his past life intended for his adopted son. As Kathleen J. Renk observes, "Carey invokes the trope of invisible writing to dramatize the question of who Jack Maggs' story belongs to — Oates or

Maggs, Dickens or Carey, England or Australia" (2004: 69). The answer is obvious: Carey, as an Australian writer, is prioritized to reclaim Maggs' convict memory for Australia. He reconfigures it in a version that is different from and even opposite to the imperial metanarrative. As stated in previous sections, Australian convicts are reconfigured by Carey to be the scapegoats of the British Empire; though framed by their native country, they still see it as their spiritual home, harbouring nostalgic sentiment toward it and waging whatever they can to reunite with it. However, they are denied entry and treated as inferior Other. Only when they are awakened from that home-coming illusion and realize who they really are can they embrace a prosperous and meaningful life in the adopted home.

Commenting on the memory turn in historiography in the 1980s, Henry Rousso argues that when the entanglement with the past is expressed in memory, it is probably propelled by the subject's desire to redefine public space; those minority groups believe they have been excluded from that space by Histoire, and they demand to gain a foothold in it by looking to the past for resources; they reinterpret a particular kind of history resorting to primarily their own oral memory which is distinct from the traditional and written History. (黄艳红, 2017: 143-144) Australian convicts are depicted to be social transgressors and victimizers in the imperial narrative. They are convicted to be criminals who are liable to corrupt social morals and pose a threat to the Empire's integrity and supremacy. They well deserve the banishment to the end of the world to assume penal servitude and receive severe punishment in that most hostile environment. However, Carey's recuperation of Maggs' convict experience first provides readers with the social backdrop where he is instigated and forced to commit thieving to survive and then framed to be the fallen guy. A couple of binary oppositions are made here by the author to strengthen the conflicts of the context story behind his transportation, for example, the opposition of Maggs' innocence and Silas and Ma Britten's shrewdness, and the opposition of Maggs' faithfulness and bravery, and Tom's disloyalty and cowardice. Nevertheless, the most remarkable conflict comes from the opposition made between burglary as a crime and as a salvation. When Maggs is forced into servitude for the comforts of Ma Britten, and Tom yet denied any amusement or affection in confinement, he sees burglary as a temporal emancipation from the estrangement and isolation he feels at home rather than a crime. Seemingly absurd enough, he would rather intoxicate himself with burgling. "It is our great fancy that the houses where we exercised our craft belonged to us, and thus, even in the selection of the silver plate we were to steal, we acted the parts of a lady and a gentleman choosing which items to send to their country estate." (216) Then, Carey contrasts the brutal scars lashed on his back and neck sharply with his creditable merits, such as being grateful, being faithful and being gallant. All the conflicts, contradictions, and absurdities demonstrated in oppositional scenes enhance the tension between Maggs' innocence and creditable merits and the punishment he is inflicted on.

As is argued by a group of American doctors, psychologists and cultural historians when they make reference to the increasingly significant role that memory plays in our public life and culture, "[M]emory is invoked to heal, to blame, to legitimate. It has become a major idiom in the construction of identity, both individual and collective, and a site of struggle as well as identification" (Antze; Lambek, 1997: Ⅶ). Carey's crafty engineering serves ostensibly to denounce the British brutal penal Transportation System for transporting those petty larceny offenders for life to take the blame for their own crime and incompetence and leaving sometimes kind people tormented in inhumane conditions of the colony. However, he goes far beyond the cliché of simple denouncement of the unjust system itself. By delegitimizing the metanarrative, he simultaneously aims at legitimizing his alternative version of the convict memory as the scapegoat, which is oriented further to liberate Australians from the traumatizing bondage of regarding themselves as descendants of felons. Consequently, Carey's reconfiguration of the convict memory delegitimizes Australians' self-depreciation resulting from their historical bondage, which has long made their cultural confidence groundless and encourages them to get rid of the historical burden that is wrongly imposed upon them. Peng Qinglong points to the author's primary concern, "*Jack Maggs* is more concerned with writing back against the negative representations of Australia as antipodean penal colony" (2005: 83). It draws on support from Carey's own contestation concerning what motivates his rewriting of the English cannon. *Great Expectations*

> is not only a great work of English literature; it is (to an Australian) also a way in which the English have colonized our ways of seeing ourselves. It is a great novel, but it is also, in another way, a prison. *Jack Maggs* is an attempt to break open the prison and to imaginatively reconcile with the gaoler. (Author Q&A, n. d.)

Nevertheless, Carey's purpose of resorting to the past is multi-layered, as is analyzed above, and it rests more on the construction than on the deconstruction. Apart from "rectifying the misconceived and distorted image of Australia by the Empire" (彭青龙, 2005: 78), Carey is also concerned with the therapeutic effect that his recuperation is supposed to exert on contemporary Australians and the positive role it may come to play in their struggle for a better future. His future-oriented inclination to revisit Australia's convict memory is externalized fully through Maggs' nostalgia and eventual embracing of his adopted land.

As Astrid Erll argues, "[N]umerous studies of various epochs and authors have shown that literature, both thematically and formally, is closely interwoven with the thematic complex of memory and identity" (2008: 333). Renowned critics such as Anthony Hassall and Peng Qinglong have unanimously made reference to the identity issue in *Jack Maggs*. The former concludes that "Jack himself is finally transformed from an Englishman into an Australian, opting for the more open, generous and egalitarian Australian culture he has come to recognize" (Hassall, 1997: 134). The latter also argues that "Peter Carey's rewriting of *Great Expectations* is for a re-inscription of an emergent identity as an Australian" (彭青龙, 2005: 78). However, there needs an elaboration on Carey's manifold exploration into Australia's identity by resorting to Maggs' experience.

Maggs' nostalgia is not reworked solely as his own private sentimental obsession. Instead, it is an emblem of his identification that is called into question. In a broader sense, it emblematizes the problematic identification that contemporary Australians are afflicted with. As embodied in Maggs' case, they would rather not accept themselves as descendants of the continent with the ignoble convict origin or rub shoulders with the blacks in the adopted land, although they have procreated there and neighboured with them for generations. Instead, they tend to identify themselves with their supposed superior British ancestors who gaze at them as the colonized Other. As Maggs' tic trope shows the conflict between what Maggs longs for and what he gets in return causes him tremendous pains embodied in his incurable facial convulsion, Australians' confusion in their identity is supposed to cause them undesirable anxiety that jeopardizes their personal wellbeing and Australia's national identity. Compared with the earlier phase of Carey's writing, when his novels are more preoccupied with problematizing the documented memory, Carey ventures a remedy for their predicament.

Since "[T]he stability of his identity is often called into question when the remembering *I* is not able to adjust his memories to his current needs in a meaning-creating manner" (Erll, 2008: 337), Carey's reconstruction eliminates Maggs' identity anxiety right by reconciling his current need with his revived memory. He is brought to the recognition that he is the desperately needed father of the two teenage boys left behind in Australia rather than an undesirable convict who has been banished by his motherland perpetually. This observation partially echoes Janet Myers' observation that "[I]t is through an understanding of what 'home' means that Jack Maggs — and by extension Carey — learn to disavow parts of their English inheritance while reconciling other parts as integral to a uniquely Australian identity" (2011: 457). As is also pointed out by Myers, Maggs does not disavow all his English inheritance to embrace Australia, which is unrealistic since he carries it in his blood vessels. His embrace of Australia is, as a matter of fact, an acceptance of the cultural hybridity that serves as the base for his reconciliation. As is demonstrated in the novel, "[T]he Maggs family were known to be both clannish and hospitable, at once civic-minded and capable of acts of picturesque irresponsibility" (323). Maggs' happy ending is the trope for the prescription Carey writes out for contemporary Australians tormented by their floating identity. Instead of drowning themselves in the delusion of looking up to their English ancestry for salvation, they are supposed to identify themselves with Australia's hybrid culture, which fuses its English inheritance with Australian traditions to embrace a new and prosperous life in this young and promising land. Peter Carey has brought Australia's multicultural background under examination in *Illywhacker*. *Jack Maggs* can be presumably seen as its sequel with regard to its further exploration into the nation's hybrid cultural identity which Carey seems more readily to applaud at this time. He draws on Australia's convict past to disseminate this new mode of identity.

When it comes to Australia's European origin in official memory, it usually refers to the country's bond with Great Britain. It is mainly because the formation of Australia in the nineteenth and twentieth centuries has coincided with Britain's roaring economic and political influence worldwide. This partially because the Irish were rendered as the Other by the Empire as well as the colonial government for political and religious reasons. For an author who has Irish ancestry like Peter Carey, that part of history naturally needs to be revisited and re-examined to serve Australia's present needs, and he does that in *True History of the Kelly Gang*.

1.3 Outlaw Recalled as a National Hero: *True History of the Kelly Gang*

When Australians flaunt their European ancestry, they refer to their bond with England. Whereas Irish Australians have been Australia's "first white minority"(Hugues, 1988: 290) and "the Other of White Australia" (张计连, 2015: 66). Since most Irishmen transported to Australia at the turn of the nineteenth century were political dissidents, their presence in the penal colony continues getting on the nerves of the local government. The Irish's well-known rebelliousness and solidarity make them "treated as a special class", as "bearers of Jacobin contagion", and as "ideologically and physically dangerous traitors" (Hugues, 1988: 290) on arriving in Australia. They are sent out in "dribs and drabs", "oppressed with special vigilance", and served with "unusually hard punishments" (ibid.) from the outset. They are doubly colonized.

The Kelly Gang, which comprises four young Irish, represents the consummation of Australian bush legend. The gang leader, Ned Kelly, has been declared a bandit and hanged by the colonial government. However, he gains immortality by being frequently turned into a conception entailing either an adorable antiauthoritarian hero or a devious bloodthirsty monster. The Kelly Gang has been a barometer of the Australian cultural milieu and has frequently been used by Australians to review their past and redefine their identity since Ned Kelly's death. It unavoidably fascinates Peter Carey, a treasure hunter of his nation's cultural heritage who has Irish ancestry. When he broods over a figure that is able to epitomise Australian national ethos, Ned Kelly comes to his mind. To quote from the authorial interview, "[W]hat is it about us Australians, eh? ... Do we not have a Jefferson?... But I then saw the real point. So many Australians were pleased to see him there as part of the story" (Wroe, 2001: 6). *True History of the Kelly Gang*, to cite Mary Ellen Snodgrass, is Peter Carey's "salute to the enduring folk tradition honouring an underclass martyr" (2010: 24).

Peter Carey uses ventriloquism in the fiction to give voice to Ned Kelly to revive Australia's memory of the Kelly Gang and mythologize the controversial bushranger. This section will be devoted firstly to examining how the author reconstructs Ned Kelly as a gallant and rebellious hero who has martyred for freedom, equality and democracy in the dystopian colony to monument Australia's cultural debt to Irish, especially its antiauthoritarian tradition. Secondly, it is also dedicated to analyzing how Carey's engineering suggests metonymically the significance of antiauthoritarianism in contemporary era when Australia and the whole world are still under the threat of the new hegemonic power.

1.3.1 Preliminaries of the Fiction

Peter Carey's writing career is pushed to its peak by the publication of *True History of the Kelly Gang* (2000). The fiction won him the Booker Prize laureate for a second time and garners more than ten other literary awards, including the Commonwealth Writers Prize. English writer Robert McCrum (2015) includes it into the list of the 100 greatest novels written in English. *The list* acclaims Carey to be "an absolute rhinestone germ" and observes that he "deserves to be listed next to Dickens and Lawrence Stern" (Carey, 2000: cover).① *Scotland on Sunday* also observes that "*True history of the Kelly Gang* should confirm Carey as significant novelist firing on cylinders. It tackles important issues with linguistic verve and emotional complexity" (ibid.). David Coad reviews that "Carey's Kelly is convincing, captivating and one cannot but be impressed by the author's attention to detail in his attempt to retrace the youth and aspirations of Australia's most celebrated criminal" (2001: 314). Anna Mundow (2001) sees this convincing novel "not only as an outback adventure but also as a psychological and historical drama... a spectacular feat of imagination grounded in an Australian landscape that is an astonishing, apparently limitless place with mysteries of its own to reveal".

Ned Kelly is an Australian bushranger, presumably the most famous one by far, an outlaw, a convicted murderer of policemen and the leader of the Kelly Gang. He was sentenced to death by the Government of Victoria and hanged in 1880 when he was twenty-six years old. It is purported that the last words he utters on the gallows are "[S]uch is life" (Wilde etc., 1985: 382-383). Kelly's death signifies the end of Australia's bushranging legend but spawns the composition of his stories in the literary world. As is concluded by Graham Seal:

Every one of the hundred years since his death in 1880 has

---

① The following quotations from *True History of the Kelly Gang* in this section are annotated with only the page number.

contributed something to the Kelly legend. Up till about the time of World War II, most of the material belonged to folk or popular culture. It proliferated often in spite of the efforts of officials and school-teachers to suppress it, and it flourished in city and country areas alike. (1980: 5)

As a matter of fact, Kelly, the figure who has been condemned to be a heresy and dislodged from Victorian orthodoxy, has evolved to be a cultural icon of Australia and gained his immortality through literature and art. This can be better glimpsed form the fact that over twelve hundred books have been composed on Kelly or his place in Australia's bushranging history, in spite of countless popular ballads, poems, and paintings of Sydney Nolan as well as tons of dramatic recreation in plays, films, and TV series. (Gaile, 2001: 37) For Peter Carey who labours with enormous assiduity on his nation's cultural inheritance, as he tells Robert McCrum (2001) in an interview, "it's a book I've waited my whole life to write, say 35 years".

True Story of the Kelly Gang is engineered to be a parody of *The Jerilderie Letter*, Ned Kelly's most famous surviving piece of writing, in which Kelly writes to her unborn daughter to recount his short twenty-six years of life in the first person. He lays bare his purpose of composing these letters, "so when our daughter comes into the world she will always know the proper story of her dad and who he is and what he suffered" (318). The novel consists of thirteen sections, and each is ostensibly in Ned Kelly's hand and preludes with annotations by an anonymous archivist describing the physical condition of the original manuscripts as well as an account of the main events in that part. Before Kelly recounts his history while he is on the run from the police, the novel also begins with a preface by an extradiegetic narrator identified as S. C., presumably a relative of Thomas Curnow who escapes the town of Glenrowan with

Kelly's manuscripts. It ends with S. C. 's frame narrative, relating the events of the Glenrowan shoot-out and Kelly's eventual death sentence.

According to Kelly's own account, born in 1855, he is the eldest son of an Irish family who eventually settled down in the British colony of Victoria. His father, Red Kelly, is a transported convict to Van Diemen's Land to serve his term of sentence. He is eventually destroyed in Avenal lockup and dies soon after he is released, forcing Kelly, aged twelve, into his maturity overnight. The poor selector family must battle against the hostile environment, acute draught, and bushfire to scramble a living. Kelly's mother, Ellen, runs a shebeen and takes on a couple of lovers to provide for her eight children. However, the family still see themselves fall prey to frequent colonial police persecutions and are ruthlessly downtrodden by the colony's Squattocracy. To equip her eldest son with more survival skills, Ellen sends Kelly to be apprenticed to Harry Power, a famous bushranger as well as one of her lovers. He learns from Power a plentiful knowledge of the land, the hideouts, and practical bushranging strategies before he leaves him and returns to his family's settlement. Wrongly charged with stealing a horse, Kelly is arrested and sentenced to three years in prison. After being released from jail, he finds a job in a vicinal sawmill and works doggedly to make an honest living. However, his tranquil life is interrupted soon by a rival squatter who appropriates his herd of horses and later by a local police officer, Constable Alex Fitzpatrick. Fitzpatrick woos Kelly's younger sister, Kate, but is found to toy with her since he takes multiple mistresses in other towns. When Ellen threatens him with violence, he points his gun at the family. Kelly shoots him in the hand in defence, which results in the warrant arresting him and his brother Dan. To elude the police's chase, Kelly and Dan flee to the bush. They are later joined by two other larrikins, Joe Byrne and Steve Hart, and begin their violent confrontations with the corrupt police. The quartet is known as the Kelly Gang.

To entice Kelly into giving himself up, police officers arrest Ellen with her baby daughter and imprison her in Melbourne. Four policemen are sent to kill them, but three of them get killed in the gunfight at Stringybark Creek. After this incident, they are declared by the government outlaws and ordered to be shot on sight. However, the gang earn themselves a lot of sympathizers who would like to offer them shelter from the police owing to their pathetic experience, and more importantly, their exploits to raid banks and give out part of the money to the poor folks. During their robberies, Kelly meets Mary Hearn, the Irish girl who used to be the lover of his stepfather George, with whom she already has a son. After Mary gets pregnant with Kelly's child, she motivates him to write his life stories down for her future child in case he or she will not know what his or her father is like. Mary immigrates to America with her son and their unborn daughter, but Kelly insists on staying in Australia to see to that his mother is released from prison. Eventually, betrayed by Thomas Curnow, the gang fails in the attempt to derail the train-carrying squads of policemen sent to annihilate them. They are besieged in the town of Glenrowan. Thomas Curnow, who is initially kept as a hostage, tricks Kelly into trusting him with his "500 adjectival pages" and freeing him. After Kelly's narrative ends abruptly before the gunfight, the extradiegetic narrator S.C. closes the novel with his recounts of the tale of the furious shoot-out, which kills the other three members of the gang and wounds its monitor Kelly in the leg as well as Kelly's hanging.

Like Peter Carey does in his other neo-historical fiction, he makes crafty use of the metafictional strategy to relentlessly reveal the fictive status of his "true history". Lisa Fletcher and Elizabeth Mead recognize this self-analytic drive and argue that *True History of the Kelly Gang* makes it quite overt in its status as what Linda Hutcheon calls "historiographic metafiction" (2010: 198). To begin with, the novel informs us that it is Ned Kelly who is prompted by his wife Mary to pick up a pen that is "writing" his history while his gang are cornered by the police. In other words, Carey makes Kelly the writer of the history we are reading. We are also informed that the writer is seized by indignation and trying to clear his name to his daughter while he composes his text, which renders readers to conjecture the reliability of his narrative. The novel provides us with further information that what is presented on the pages in front of our eyes may have been adapted to an unknowable degree by Thomas Curnow, who is the caretaker of Kelly's manuscripts and obsesses himself with being a "hero" (415). In the conversation with Kelly before the gunfight breaks out, Curnow promises Kelly to make some "improvements" to make his history less "rough" and assists him with the "parsing" (404). In another instance, S. C., the extradiegetic narrator, tells readers that "[T]he evidence provided by the manuscript suggests that in the years after the Siege of Glenrowan, he continued to labour obsessively over the construction of the dead man's sentences, and it was he who made those small grey pencil marks with which the original manuscript is decorated" (419). In addition to Curnow's trimming of Kelly's letter, the prefatory note of parcel eight also tells readers that "Pages describing the shooting of Constable Fitzpatrick are much revised by a second hand reliably presumed to be that of Joe Byrne" (221). All these pieces of textual evidence point to Professor Paul Eggert's review of the novel as a "self-conscious retrieval" (2007: 125) of the past. The repeated self-referential tendency is so potent that it makes the authenticity of Kelly's history a perpetual deferral. It makes it plausible for Graham Huggan to jump to the conclusion that "the voice through which (the narrative) claims to speak is never Kelly's own" (2002: 149).

However, while problematizing the authenticity and objectivity of Kelly and his historical writing through the textual strategy of metafiction, Carey also demonstrates his perseverance in seeking historical truth through his protagonist, Ned Kelly. As Andrew Dowling notes, Peter Carey creates in the novel "a contradiction between using history to create fiction and using fiction to reveal the 'truth' about history" (2001: 249). Carey expresses his yarning for truthfulness by creating manifold verisimilitudes. At the threshold of the novel, the frame narrator mesmerizes readers by affirming that all the letters contained in the thirteen parcels are "in Ned Kelly's distinctive hand" (4). Then at the beginning and the end of the fiction, a statement is presumably provided by the archive collector to note the sources of these parcels, "Melbourne Public Library V. L. 10453" (4/419), creating an illusion of genuine historical reference. In addition, Carey creates an illusion of truthfulness by structuring the novel not in chapters but according to the archived order of the parcels, each with a prefatory introduction at the beginning describing the physical state of the manuscripts, individually guillotined, crudely bound, soiled, creased, torn, water damaged or stained with ink or tear, giving the impression that the author is solely a ventriloquist who records the voice of Kelly the ghost. Moreover, the illusion of tunefulness is also created through Carey's use of vernacular language. Idiomatic expressions, simple vocabulary, and scarce punctuation combined with deliberate spelling omission to avoid offence in the letters are so mesmeric enough for readers to take them as products of the semi-illiterate Kelly. Apart from creating structural and linguistic verisimilitude, Carey vindicates vociferously the authenticity of his version of history within the novel through the protagonist's self-profession. Kelly swears an oath at the beginning of his account that the history he writes to her daughter "will contain no single lie may I burn in hell if I speak false" despite that he admits that he is raised on "lies and silences" (7). Althrough Carey is contradicted by Xavier Pons who reviews that "[A]nyone who says 'true history' is obviously writing a novel... No historian would ever say that" (2001: 64), it does not seem to eclipse his endeavour to strive for historical truth. Moreover, he seems to have achieved what he aspires. Nathanael O'Reilly, a professor of literature at Texas Christian University, is convinced that *True History of the Kelly Gang* is a canon of Australian literature that lends itself to a couple of pedagogical approaches to teaching Australian literature in America since it "provides students with insight into the colonial period in Australia, including the formation of dominant Australian cultural ideals, such as the importance of antiauthoritarianism and egalitarianism, and the championing of the underdog" (2015: 71).

As one of Peter Carey's most garlanded novels, *True History of the Kelly Gang* earns the author the reputation of "one of the most engaging historical novelists alive" (Knopf, 2001: 90). Novelist John Updike praises the expatriate writer for taking the advantage of his distance from Australia "to contemplate and reshape some notable legends of his homeland" (Harford, 2006: 118). Nathanael O'Reilly notes the counter effect that the novel exerts on Ned Kelly's enhanced iconic image in Australian culture and argues that the critical as well as commercial success of *True History of the Kelly Gang* repositions "the Kelly narrative firmly at the centre of Australian popular culture" (2007: 488) and adds another canonical instance to Australian literature repository for future rewriting. As a matter of fact, the Book Prizer has lent itself to critics approaching it from a variety of perspectives. Since Ned Kelly's death in 1880 proximately coincides with the rise of Australia's nationalism and Peter Carey demonstrates in his works a potent concern for Australia's national identity, a bulk of criticism is conducted from that point of view, though with slightly differentiated orientations or sometimes opposing conclusions. Premising on her analysis of Kelly's unswerving loyalty to his mother, Chinese scholar Zhang Jilian draws a conclusion that Kelly has a clear and resolute identification with Australia. (2015: 114) Heather Smyth delves deeper into this issue and pinpoints the values that Carey intends to derive from Kelly's legend, "antiauthoritarianism, loyal to family and 'mates' and a fighting spirit" (2009: 186), only that he does not elaborate on this motif. Based on his interpretation of crossdressing, Heather Smyth notes how Peter Carey deviates from traditional European nationalism with "manliness" as its constitutive component and argues that "by evoking Irish ritual cross-dressing, he gains an image of revolutionary nationalism routed through powerful images of women" (2009: 214). Another school of critics (Clancy, 2004; Eggert, 2007; Fletcher & Mead, 2010; Antor, 2015; 彭青龙, 2003; 黄洁, 2017; 沈忠良, 2018) approaches the novel from the postcolonial and/or postmodern point of view and they pinpoint how Carey deploys intertextuality and parody to give voice to the historically silenced figure Ned Kelly and transforms him from a villain in official narrative into a folk hero through his own "secret and true history". As observed by Peng Qinglong, "This epic novel, which is to deconstruct the Australia mythology in history, makes itself a new mythology in English speaking world" (2005: 25).

It is worth noting that some scholars have drawn critical attention to several aspects of cultural memory in *True History of the Kelly Gang*. For example, Laurie Clancy emphasizes Carey's "subjective and selective" and "highly partisan" (2004: 58) use of historical facts to transfigure Kelly into a hero. Huang Jie approaches the novel from the postcolonial perspective yet considers the novel as a cannon to reshape Australia's collective memory of bushranging and heterogeneous masculinity. (2017:

36) Peng Qinglong examines how Peter Carey represents Australia's cultural memory of "the cruel histories" that Australian people "have experienced in fighting against their enemies" and argues that his reconstruction "deconstructs the official memory of the past, and constructs a new one through personal narration" (2017: 191). However, he covers in his discussion only a limited number of aspects of the retrieved memory and his examination of the functions of Carey's reworking is confined to the author's deconstruction of the old myth and construction of a new one. That leaves Carey's ultimate purpose of constructing the new myth inadequately explored. The ensuing parts are dedicated to a close examination of how Peter Carey reconfigures Australia's memory of Ned Kelly and the various functions he intends his reworking to perform. The ensuing parts are dedicated to a close examination of how Peter Carey reconfigures Ned Kelly, the outlaw, as a national hero to monument Australia's cultural debt to the Irish, invent the antiauthoritarian tradition and reappraise Britain's colonial ruling of Australia.

1.3.2 Colonial Australia as a Dystopia

John Pilger indicates in *A Secret Country* that in classic Australian myth, Australia is "a veritable land of promise" for battlers, a potential "Utopian under the Southern Cross", and the "workers' paradise". (1990: 313/317/345) Carolyn Bliss also points out that among the legion of Australian masterplots, the popular ones are Australia as "the Lucky Country" or "the Workingman's Paradise" (2004: 278). However, the truth is rather complex and sometimes deviates a lot from idolatry since "conflicting masterplots" (Abbot, 2002: 44) often, if not always, coexist in Australian national culture. For those tormented bitterly in this milieu, Australia could also be a place "'down under' everybody else on the globe and so far away that its very remoteness exercises what Geoffrey Blainey ... called a 'tyranny of distance' over its inhabitants" (Gaile, 2004: 278). In *True History of the Kelly Gang*, Kelly's recollection of Australia's colonial past in the late nineteenth century fits that description impeccably. Australia is remembered to be not the least of the workingmen's paradise, but a dystopia where poverty enslaves the poor selectors and injustice is prevalent. This apocalyptic scene is presented to readers from Kelly's remembrance in multiple facets.

The first key word to summarize Kelly's dystopian memory is "poverty", which is attributed to a couple of reasons. To begin with, poor farmers don't have their own land. Since Red Kelly, the father, is possessed by the fright of being thrown into prison, he transports his family to the outskirts of Avenel and rents a piece of land rather than buying any acre from the government when they are eventually granted the right by the Duffy Land Act of 1862 to select a virgin block for one pound per acre with part of the fee paid on selection and the rest paid off in eight years. He makes that untimely decision because he is aware that "[T]he Quinns attract the traps as surely as rabbit guts will bring the flies" (23), and he believes the least contact with the law will minimize his risk of being bullied by the police. However, by doing so, he renders his family taxed yet vulnerable to starvation. When Avenel is struck by drought, nothing flourishes on their farm. Kelly takes it the eldest son's duty to save his family from hunger, which leads to his first perpetration. He ends up killing Mr. Murray's heifer to feed his family. As he vindicates himself, "I have spilled human blood when there were no other choice at that time I were no more guilty than a soldier in a war" (25). However, this incident ends up with his father's imprisonment, which eventually leads to his death, leaving behind a widow with her seven children.

The second reason leading to their poverty-stricken life in colonial Australia comes from the oppression of the Squattocracy. Through their connections with the government, squatters like Whitty and McBean "made a game of the law getting the best land for themselves" (227). They are permitted to rent soft, rich lands on the common ground, which are not liable to the punishment of drought. However, what is left for poor selectors are those infertile acres vulnerable to lousy climate. When Ellen raises enough money presumably, with the help of her multiple wooers, she finally selects a land of eighty-eight acres in Greta. However, "grass were eaten to the roots" (231) on every acre of her land. In bad years, when the land is stricken by drought, she, like other poor farmers, has to cut down even saplings to feed her stock. If the poor farmers graze their horses even beside the government road, the squatters will take those stocks and lock them away in the pound. As Kelly recalls, "I have known 60 head of horses impounded in on day all of them belonging to poor farmers who was then required to leave their ploughing or harvest and travel to Oxley to release them & so they would have to give a bill of sale or borrow money which is no easy matter" (227). Things also turn out very badly for the Kellys since Whitty impounds all their thirty thoroughbred mares in foal strayed on the common land. That means they have all their hard-earned property stolen by the squatter overnight.

The third reason contributing to the Kellys' poverty is the shortage of financial support. Since she sends her eldest son Kelly to be the apprentice of Harry Power, with the hope of equipping him with survival skills and earning her extra fund, and since she is pregnant while the only specialty of her second husband Bill Frost, the English man, is dancing, Ellen's selection is left very poorly attended and little to profit on. As Kelly sees in his own eyes, "the adjectival pasture is filled with dandelions and docks no one cleared nothing... it were a sad and ruined sight no new fencing not a single acre claimed" (110). To add insult to injury, the Kelly boys are frequently made victims of the police's prosecutions, which costs her extra quids to employ solicitors to get them out of the lockup. What is more, Kelly's unemployment owing to his spoiled reputation of thieving and betraying Power, coupled with Power's imprisonment, which completely cuts off Ellen's extra funds, aggravates the family's poverty. All in all, in Kelly's remembrance, "[O]ur land poor were poor, our purse were empty and many is the night we sat before the fire with no food other than what I shot" (187). During Kelly's third imprisonment, consecutive misfortunes come close to toppling his forty-two-years old wretched mother down. Rats plague descends upon their hut and consumes all their flour, and his brother Jim is convicted of a cattle theft. Even his little brother Dan is forced to steal to help his mother. It is a time when all that refills them with hope for the future is Ellen's stories about those courageous and unyielding Irish fighters.

Suffering from material insecurity and food shortage, the wretched Kellys also find themselves frequently falling victims to the colonial law, which boils down to another key word to sketch their plight, namely, "injustice". As a man with Irish blood in his vessels, he does not need to perpetrate any crime to arouse the attention of the law. His Irish family are judged and discriminated against by their "ignoble" ancestry. They are stigmatized as "This Certain Man" (9) and can not avoid being molested and prosecuted by the police with or without proper excuses. As Kelly complains in indignation and helplessness, "[S]he were a Quinn and the police would never leave the Quinn's alone" (7). His complaint is well based. When his father is released from the Avenal lockup, he is totally destroyed and found dead before long, "bulging with all the poisons of the Empire his skin grey and shining in the gloom" (41). When the police are unable to capture Harry Power, the victimizer who robs the squatter Mcbean of his heirloom watch and horse, they arrest Kelly's uncle Jack as a scapegoat and warrant to hunt his cousin Tom down. Even though Kelly admits his guilt of helping Power in the robbery and gets himself jailed in Benalla, they still threat to lock Tom up and take his mother's selection back from her under the Land Act of 1865 because she "harbours" Tom, the wanted "criminal". As far as the Kellys are concerned, it seems the police show no respect for the law at all. Sergeant Whelan threats that "he would gaol my mother if he so chose and all my brothers & uncles & cousins and he did not care if we should breed like rabbits for he would lockup the mothers & babies too" (165). He abuses his power to such a brutal degree solely because Mcbean is an acquaintance who offers a considerable bribe. In another case, when Kelly is charged with stealing a horse while the truth is he receives it from a friend without being informed that it is a stolen one, he comes close to being murdered by the police. He is eventually sentenced to three years' Hard Labour in Pentridge Gaol. False charges descending on them one after another force them into maturity and harden their heart. However, this incident, in Kelly's own words, strips away his "last hope of youth... I had never kissed a girl but were old enough to be a married man" (194), he is filled with a "rage no rain can staunch" (195).

Not only does the law bias against them and inflict more severe punishment on them for their minor offences, it also takes sides with the squatters and gets complicit in their oppression and depravation of poor selectors. When Kelly protests the police for charging his brother Dan with stealing a saddle while leaving the thief who steals all his horses beyond the law, surprisingly he finds his own name on the list of The Police Gazette without committing any offence. It turns out that Whitty, the squatter who impounds his cattle, frames him for stealing a horse first from Kelly's former employer and then from him so that Kelly is put in jail and he gets all his property without being bothered by the victim. Constable Farrell, the squatter's son-in-law, is well aware of the whole scheme but still warns Kelly, "we are picking on you" (227). Being accomplices of the oppressive squatters does not exhaust the list of malice the law directs against the Kellys. The police treat them as cattle and victimize them brutally. Apart from lodging false accusations of the boys, they harass the females relentlessly. Sergeant O'Neil tries to molest Ellen when she goes to the station to send her brother some food; Constable Flood rapes Kelly's elder sister Annie and causes her death from giving birth to his child; Constable Fitzpatrick takes multiple lovers in other towns but still keeps harassing Kate. To protect her daughter, Ellen clouts his helmet off with a shovel as a warning. However, he draws out his revolver, threatening to kill the whole family. When Kelly could have killed him, he shoots him in the wrist in self-defence and dresses his wound later, sparing him from death. Fitzpatrick feigns his gratitude, but issues warrant to arrest Kelly and Dan for their "Attempted Murder" and Ellen and other males in the family for "Aiding and Abetting Attempted Murder" (276). To force Kelly's girlfriend, Mary to betray him, he confiscates her passbook and threatens to put her baby into an orphanage if she does not obey.

Although, as Kelly confesses, all he wants throughout his life is no more than a "home" (206), "a hearth to sit by in the night" (293), his dream is smashed by the police and squatters. They are the worst people in the world, and the roots of injustice, which lead to their tragic life. As Kelly accuses them:

> And here is the thing about them men they was Australians they knew full well the terror of the unyielding law the historic memory of UNFAIRNESS were in the blood. A man might be a bank clerk

or an overseer he might never has been lagged for nothing but still he knew in his heart what it were to be forced to wear the white hood in prison he knew what it were to be lashed for looking a warder in the eye and even a posh fellow like the Moth had breathed that air so the knowledge of unfairness were deep in his bone and marrow. (359-360)

Consecutive misfortunes imposed upon the Kellys by the police who disrespect the law and the squatters who take its advantage kindle his fury and fire, which he compares to the flame "the government of England lights in a poor man's guts every time they make him wear the convict iron" (187). Kelly complains "[T]hat injustice put me in a rage nothing would ease but danger I now craved it like another man might lust for the raw burn of poteen" (206). The injustice resulting from the arbitrary exercising of power fails to discipline him and produce, in Foucault's words, "subjected and practiced bodies, 'docile' bodies" (Robinow, 1984: 175) but renders him more untameable and opens him up to violent revolts. As Foucault contends, "[T]he prison makes possible, even encourages, the organization of a milieu of delinquents, loyal to one another, hierarchized, ready to aid and abet any future criminal act" (1984: 228).

However, ungrounded prosecutions, imprisonments and tortures are part of the techniques through which the colonial law functions to discipline Kelly's body, or in Robinow Kantorowitz's words, "the King's body" (1984: 176). Since memory usually joins hands with power, the colonial government tries every means to control the Kelly Gang by controlling people's memory of them. It exercises the imperial power on Kelly by forging his soul with "knowledge". To justify its job of hunting him down, the law resorts to newspapers to defame him. All newspapers, without exception, *The Melbourne Herald*, and *The Melbourne Argus*, condemn him to be one of those "Irish Madmen" (313) and declare them "outlaws who could be shot on sight and was entitled to no more mercy than a rabid dog" (315). Newspapers counterfeit ferocious details to depict them as murderous and demonic creatures. According to their documents, Kelly is a ruffian who cuts Constable Kennedy's ear before murdering him and would cause "the people of Jerilderie swim in their own blood" (380); "Dan Kelly was eager for blood, as he expressed a strong wish 'to put a bullet through the — retch'" (351). The official reports result from a series of distortions as memory could be distorted and false, especially when it is usurped to serve the government's reign. As Kelly refutes the media and the government, "the author of this so called LIKENES were not content to show my natural imperfections he must join my brows across my nose and twist my lips to render me the Devil of Horror of Ages" (312). As Foucault contends,

> power produces knowledge (and not simply by encouraging it because it serves power or by applying it because it is useful); that power and knowledge directly imply one another; that there is no power relation without the correlative constitution of a field of knowledge, nor any knowledge that does not presuppose and constitute at the same time power relations. (Robinow, 1984: 175)

The news media function as the colonial power to produce "knowledge" and memory of the Kelly Gang, through which the colonial law exercises its domination over both their souls and bodies. A good example is how Mary feels when she reads the documents, "these sentences like a steel nibbed kookaburra on the fences in the morning sun" (349). For Kelly, "[M]y 58 pages was pinching & cutting me I could feel them words being tattooed onto my living skin" (372). Both his corporal body and "noncorporal soul" bear the effects of the colonial power with reference to the knowledge and memory produced in news reports. To quote

Foucault, what fades in the picture here, is "the machinery by which the power relations give rise to a possible corpus of knowledge, and knowledge extends and reinforces the effects of this power" (Robinow, 1984: 177).

Though not well-educated, both Kelly and Mary are conscious of the power of knowledge, and they fight against it through contending for the authors of their own history. Encouraged by his wife Mary, Kelly writes down his own story and turns to Mr. Donald Cameron, one of their sympathizers who has questioned the Premier about the motivation of the Springbark Murdering, hoping that he could help do him justice and clear his name. However, the British colonial government replies with a confirmation that he is "'a CLEVER ILLITERATE' who is filled with 'MORBID VANITY'" (368). He intends to show the world that they are "driven to the deed that the law was scandalous in our pursuit" (315), yet he is doomed to fail since "'Truth' is linked in a circular relation with systems of power which produce and sustain it, and to effects of power which it induces and which extends it" (Robinow, 1984: 74). But he is the Other who is excluded from the system of power and the object through which the colonial power articulates its sovereignty and consolidates the status quo of the imperial colonialism. This makes it natural that "all the editors had been shown my letter by Cameron but NOT ONE WOULD PRINT MY ACTUAL WORDS instead they was like snooty narrow shouldered school teachers each one giving their opinion on my prose and character" (368). Kelly accuses the media which spread the slanderous "knowledge" of him and his members of being complicit in the injustice of the law of the colonial system. Later, when they capture the town of Jerilderie and take control of the news agency, *The Jerilderie Gazette*, Kelly gives his letter to the editor and forces him to print it out. Nevertheless, he conspires with the police and gives Kelly's manuscripts to them. Disillusioned, Kelly complains helplessly that "I wished only to be a citizen I had tried to speak but the mongrels stole my tongue when I asked for justice they give me none" (394). Kelly's failure to air his own voice in colonial Australia echoes Foucault's argument that "it is not the activity of the subject of knowledge that produces a corpus of knowledge, useful or resistant to power, but power-knowledge, the processes and struggles that traverse it and of which it is made up, that determines the forms and possible domains of knowledge" (Robinow, 1984: 175). Under the domination of the imperial power, he is the object to be spoken, never the subject of speaking.

In *True History of the Kelly Gang*, Carey revives Australia's cultural memory of Ned Kelly. By giving voice to the protagonist, Kelly is made a speaking being and a political being in Aristotle's conception. With the author's "redistribution of the sensible" (Rancière, 2013), the demonized and silenced object Kelly in the official memory is made a subject to speak what used to be muted and bring what used to be invisible visible. Deviating from the official document that stereotypes him to be a bandit, Carey's reconstruction foregrounds Australia's social dynamics around the 1870s and provides the milieu his protagonist is in. Through the author's ventriloquism, Kelly is allowed to reveal what he senses to be the total absence of justice out of the economical oppression of colonial Australia's Squattocracy and the political oppression of its law. He is allowed to make heard their humble dream to make a home on this adopted land, which ends up with abject poverty, frequently imprisoned bodies and repeatedly tortured souls. He is allowed to expose what options are left for them when even the chance to protect them against injustice has denied them. What Kelly presents through his sense experience creates a "dissensus" (Rancière, 2010) with the official sensory regime and its way of making sense of it.

As Jacques Rancière argues in *The Politics of Aesthetics*, any writing aiming at a redistribution of the sensible "destroys every legitimate foundation for the circulation of words, for the relationship between the effects of language and the positions of bodies in shared space" (2013: 34), the most significant function that Carey intends his recuperation to perform is to delegitimize the official memory condemning Ned Kelly as a bandit. By offering Kelly's own vindication that colonial Australia is a dystopia, the darkest society under the sky that preys on the honest poor to nurture the vicious rich, rather than the Promised Land or even a fair land, Carey makes the imperial accusation of Kelly groundless. Simultaneously, Carey's reconfiguration attempts to legitimize Kelly's personal memory to include it in the nation's collective memory to justify his transgressive action. In other words, Carey's reconstruction serves as a poetic exoneration of Ned Kelly, rendering him a sympathetic figure and creating a democracy within the text. To quote Peng Qinglong, "Carey's literary representation of memories implies that Ned Kelly was forced into banditry by his hostile circumstances and oppressive social environment" (2017: 183). By exonerating his protagonist, Kelly, Carey also paves the way for his further and more in-depth exploration of this cultural icon within the text. Carey says in an interview, "[I]f you look at our history, we began as a penal colony, and so our relationship with the law is very complicated" (Wigston, 2002: 14).

1.3.3 Death of the Outlaw as a State Murder

Back in the 1880s, Kelly was declared by the colonial government to be an outlaw and painted by the newspaper as a "demonic kind of man" (312). The stereotype is passed down in Australia's collective memory. In the latter half of the twentieth century, British historian Eric Hobsbawm still classifies Kelly as a "social bandit, an avenger of the lowest and poorest"（彭青龙，2005：109）and equates him with other famous bandits like the British Robin Hood or the American Jesse James. Even in contemporary Britain, Carey mentions when talking about the English reception of *True History of the Kelly Gang* in an interview, that the novel is taken by the English as a "revisionist history... because [they see] Kelly [as] a dirty, smelly Australian criminal" (Wigston, 2002: 14) from their perspective. Though most Australians love Kelly, he remains a controversial figure in Australian official memory, and teachers do not teach him in school. However, Peter Carey recuperates him to be a true-to-life mortal being who possesses a legion of commendatory merits. Moreover, through providing the hostile economical and legal milieus he lives in, he is reconstructed to be a fearless soldier who stands up to oppression and tyranny. Eventually and naturally, Carey's reconfiguration leads it to the assumption that Kelly's execution is the result of the injustice inflicted on him by the colonial government of Australia. He dies from a state murder, and this can be analyzed in the following paragraphs.

In Carey's reconstruction, Kelly is recovered to be a dutiful man. When his family suffer from starvation owing to the severe drought, he assumes his responsibility as the eldest son to be the bread-earner even at a very young age. He kills Mr. Murray's heifer to feed his family, regardless of "his hair and shirt soaked with blood and gore" (25). When her mother sent him apprenticed to Harry Power, he obeys his mother to learn the racks and trails of the hostile landscape and earns her gold to help support the family, though he does not fancy the bushranging life at all. He assumed the responsibility to protect his family since his father died when he was twelve. He does not approve of his mother's husbands, either the good-for-nothing Englishman Bill Frost or the American thief George King, who is of his age, since they both bully his mother, who used to be proud and demanding in front of his father, into an obedient creature to some extent. However, he is willing to leave the decisions to her mother, withdraws from her marital life and stands by to offer her protection. When Ellen distresses herself for Bill Frost's unnoticed disappearance, he turns to Harry Power to inquire about his whereabouts. As he explains to Power, "[H]e is a dreadful mongrel but she is very bad without him. I need to bring him back" (134). He refuses to flee to America with his wife, Mary, when he is able to because he intends to get his mother out of jail. In fact, he is so attached to his mother that a few critics (Pons, 2003; Clancy, 2004; Peng Qinglong, 2017) regard his relationship with Ellen as Peter Carey's parody of the Oedipus complex. Even his brother Dan jokes with him saying, "your ma is your donah" (225). However, this monograph tends to suggest that it is Carey's genius engineering to make reference both to the intimate relationship between sons and mothers in colonial families where fathers are frequently absent for imprisonment and to illuminate his protagonist with a typical humane sentiment. After all, his mother is not the only family Kelly would like to trade his life for. There is his father, Red Kelly, who takes the blame for his offence. Little Dan who is charged with stealing a saddle to exchange several quids for his wretched mother. There is Mary and her boy, who are constantly threatened and tortured by the police to get out of her mouth Kelly's hideouts. He would rather rob the bank to get them out of the police's clutch. "[W]hen I looked in her frightened eyes I knew we could not live like this no more I could not have her follow me as the wives followed their husbands into war in olden days"(338). He is always there ready for all their protection.

Kelly is also recuperated to be a caring and kind man before his goodness is damaged and his heart is hardened by the hostile circumstances he is soaked in. He is responsive to the folks' needs. When eight-year-old

Dick Shelton is washed into the flooded river, he risks his life to save him from drowning. Mrs. Shelton grants him a sash in front of his class as a commendation for his courage. In defence, Kelly shots lascivious Constable Fitzpatrick in his hand for his harassing Kate and threatening his family with a gun, but he dresses his wound. Touched by his tender heart, Fitzpatrick apologises for his character and says he would like to be friends with him. Though he hates the police who have bullied his family repeatedly, he never intends to kill any of them. When the gang are confronted by the police officers who are sent to ambush them at Stringybark Creek, he kills Sergeant Kennedy in the gunfight. According to his account, he does that in defence but his conscience still tortures him. "All night I had bad dreams very confused I saw Kennedy raising his hand to surrender and me shooting him again & again"(294).

Kelly is especially celebrated in Carey's reworking for his endurance, loyalty and bravery. When his father is wrongly accused of stealing a heifer, he brings himself forward bravely to the constable, confessing that he is the real perpetrator and demands that the policeman arrest him. When he is wronged for a Highway Robbery, put into prison, and enticed and beaten up to leak the whereabouts of his mentor, Harry Power, to the police in exchange for his freedom, he refuses to succumb, saying he is "raised on stories of Irishmen being tortured and would not go home a traitor" (121). Even when he is thrown into prison again out of Harry Power's framing and offered handsome incentives for betrayal, he refuses to shop the hateful "liar and thief" (166) to the policemen. His principle is that he does not "trade in human flesh"(167). To highlight his bravery and faithfulness, Carey also juxtaposes his role as a gang leader with that of Harry Power. While his mentor plants robberies on him, exposes his face to their victims on purpose to paint him a criminal and keep him "bound as Harry power's apprentice" (143) without his knowing that he is "a rabbit in his snare" (144), Kelly is very protective towards his gang members. He regards himself as the "Monitor" and "Captain" and them as "children" whom he is supposed to shelter. He is convinced he has "obligations they was no less to my mother than to him" (345). In Glenrowan's besiegement, when he is told Dan and Steve have got out of the hotel to fight the policemen, with his leg bleeding,

> he stumbled out the back door and into the early dawn. Intending to draw the police fire onto himself, he mounted his horse... He walked painfully towards his brother, no longer deigning to take cover or hide himself. He hammered the butt of his revolver against his chest to let Dan hear him coming to his rescue. I am the b-y Monitor, my boys. (417)

When he learns the other three members are shot dead, he could have run away, but he chooses to stay and avenge their deaths. As the frame narrator comments, "[H]e was a Kelly, he would never run" (418). He risks his own life to protect those boys as well as those poor widows and children who are their sympathizers. However, "[H]e could not protect these people against the police, nor could he protect himself. It seemed there was no machine ever invented that could protect these people from the forces of God had placed upon the earth" (416).

As Carey's reworking shows, Ned Kelly is a dutiful, kind, endurable, faithful and gallant Irishman. Like any other poor selectors, he labours assiduously to eke out a living on this adopted land yet falls victim to the oppressive colonial system. Different from other oppressed folks of his class, he is infused with a consciousness of democracy and egalitarianism. When his democratic and egalitarian dream is trampled on, he has the valiance to rebel against the ruling class. What is more commentary, his rebellion does not make him a sociopath for disrespecting law. Instead, he revolts to make the law respected and to make justice done to everyone despite that blood is shed in this process. As he confesses to his wife, "Mary I would never kill no one unless I had to" (312). In Carey's own words, "he operated within the society" (Wigston, 2002: 14). Kelly dies a heroic death. He does not die from the culpable punishment of an outlaw. He is murdered by the corrupted colonial government who hunts down anyone, who challenges their authority or transgresses the colonial status quo. As Carey says, "[I]t is easy to look at this boy as a product of his class and circumstances, one more example of what happens when you can change your penal colony into a decent nation" (McCrum, 2001). Kelly's transgression marks the "limit" of what is lawful and what is prohibited in the imperial colonial system, providing the originally limitless world with a "structure or coherence" (Jenks, 2003: 90). Kelly's persecution fully realizes "the force of a prohibition" (ibid.: 89) and marks the "sovereignty" of the imperial colonial order and serves to maintain its status quo. "At the heart of the procedures of discipline, it manifests the subjection of those who are perceived as objects and the objectification of those who are subjected" (1984: 197). For Kelly, death is a doom inflicted by the Empire that he is unable to escape. As memory could be like "a kind of malignant parasite, insinuating itself into the bloodstream and building its destructive strength from within" (Huggan, 2002: 147), Carey's reconfiguration of Kelly juxtaposes his creditable character with the state's miscarriage of justice to create a tension which first arouses reader's sympathy towards his protagonist and then serves as the denouncement of the imperial colonial system for nipping the bud of democracy.

1.3.4 Monument to the Antiauthoritarian Hero

Carey's reworking of Ned Kelly not just transfigures him to be an ordinary mortal being with bountiful merits or an "antihero of dark and turbulent period" (Peng Qionglong, 2017: 178) who represents the cruel history that Australians have experienced. It goes beyond that by mythologizing him, incarnating him into a national hero who stands up to authoritarian and fights for egalitarianism. This motivation can be briefly glimpsed from the parallel Carey makes in an interview between Ned Kelly and one of the three founding fathers of the United States, Thomas Jefferson. "When he was hanged, there were great protests. And since that time, his popularity has only grown. This is, as I continue to tell my American friends, is not like anything, it is like Thomas Jefferson. That is the sort of space Kelly occupies in the national imagination" (Macrum, 2001). That Jefferson-like image may or may not represent the whole picture of Australia's national imagination of Ned Kelly. However, it does signify the place that Carey restores Kelly to in Australia's collective memory, a national hero, a monument to Australia's national ethos, and a memory figure of Australia's antiauthoritarian tradition.

The first and foremost hallmark Carey endows his national hero with is the gallantry to rebel against authoritarian, and he traces this ethos back to Kelly's Irish ancestry. Born to be the son of an Irish convict, Kelly is doomed to have more exposure to the hostility by the colonial government. Choosing to be a selector, he is doomed to suffer from extra oppression by the colony's Squattocracy. However, the Irish blood flowing in his vessels makes the pain coming from the injustice felt even more tangibly and bitterly. Nevertheless, it also makes the injustice he is afflicted with less bearable. Jan Assmann argues,

> [I]n cases of extreme deficiency, a contrapresent mythomotor may become subversive, for instance under foreign rule or oppression. Then traditional memories no longer support the existing situation but on the contrary throw it into question and call for total change. The past to which they refer appears not as an irrevocably lost

> heroic age but as a social and political Utopia toward which one can direct one's life and work. (2011: 63)

The deficiency that his family experience conjures up Kelly's memory of the Irish mythic "stories of Conchobor and Deriu and Mebd and the tale of Cuchulainn"(29), which his mother raises the children on. Those tales "shed a very different light on the present by emphasizing what has gone wrong, what has disappeared, or become lost or marginalized, and thus there is a deliberate break between then and now" (Assmann, 2011: 62). His remembrance of them provides him nutrients of a rebellious spirit and gallantry and prompts him to rebel against the present order. When his horses are impounded by Whitty the squatter and the police fail to do him the justice to return them and further abuse their power by charging his little brother Dan for a minor offence, he decides to let them reap what they have sown. He learns from his step father George King, a first-class stock-thief, the secret of impounding cattle without a trace and "borrows" fifty best-fed horses from the squatter. His successful revenge fills him with the pleasure of robbing the rich to feed the poor. However, that pleasure comes more from his vision of a new and desirable space in the future. "We was building a world where we would be left alone" (234). Though Kelly does initiate his rebellion by avenging his personal loss, Carey equips his protagonist from the very beginning with a broader vision, a flickering political consciousness. He has a sharp insight into the social evils and envisages his part in the rectification.

> Joe and me occupied the waking world we knew our hard circumstances was made by Whitty and McBean who picked the eyes out of the country with the connivance of the politicians and police. Against their force all this queer boy's daydreaming were no defence at all his Irish martyrs couldn't get us decent land not even remove our cows from the Oxley Pound. (236)

He defies the legitimacy of the squattocracy and contends that "[H]e did not own that country he never could" (234).

When Kelly is propelled to revolt against the Squattocracy and the unjust law, his rebellion is not made a sociopath's vicious revenge on the society that steals his life. It is made a captain's leadership of people from the underclass to fight against the authoritarian to claim their own rights to this land and for their freedom. As a fighter, he never fights alone.

> The British Empire had supplied me with no shortage of candidates these was men who had had their leases denied for no other crime than being our friends men forced to plant wheat then ruined by the rust men mangled upon the triangle of Van Diemen's Land men with sons in gaol men who witnessed their hard won land taken up by squatters men perjured against and falsely gaoled men weary of constant impounding on & on each day without relent. Once they had swore their oath upon my Bible we showed them why they need no longer tremble before the law. We wasn't men with pikes no more and would not repeat the tragedies of Vinegar Hill or the Eureka Stockade. (393)

As a hero is nothing but a product of his time, Kelly's rebellion is merely the externalization of the irreconcilable conflicts between the colonial government and the squatters and the underclass, which Carey embodies with a very poetic depiction. "Throughout the spring & summer certain farmers did secretly construct their ironclads in the quiet gullies of the North East you might hear the lyre bird imitating the ching ching ching of the hammer striking blows. Them suits was made and buried in the soil awaiting resurrection." (393)

Kelly's rebellion is made more constructive towards an egalitarian society while destructing the current law and order. Since the distribution of the sensible is a "delimitation of spaces and times, of the visible and the invisible, of speech and noise, that simultaneously determines the place and the stakes of politics as a form of experience" (Rancière, 2013: 45), Kelly spearheads his rebellion for a redistribution of the sensible to re-delimitate the lawful and unlawful, rights and obligations. As is warned in the "coffin letter".

> Any person... who aids or harbours or assists the police in any way whatever or employs any person whom they know to be a detective or cad also those who would be so depraved as to take blood money will be outlawed and declared unfit to be allowed for a human burial... I wish them men who joined the Stock Protection Society to withdraw their money and give as much more to the widows and orphans and poor of the Greta district. (394)

Carey makes further ostentation of this point in a description of Kelly's self-intoxication with the respect and admiration they win from their people, "[A]nd lo they did applaud us with their eyes bright their faces red bank managers & overseers & ex policemen they stood in the scorching sun and cheered us" (361). Kelly's ambition built in his rebellion is epitomized in his declaration, "we had showed the world what convict blood could. We proved there were no taint we was of true bone blood and beauty born" (387).

The second hallmark Carey endorses in his national hero is his historical consciousness, which Jörn Rüsen defines as "the sum of spiritual (including emotional and cognitive, aesthetic, moral, unconscious and conscious) activities that transform time experience into life practice through memory" (吕森, 2005: 63). Carey suggests how Kelly values his Irish tradition by juxtaposing two opposite episodes. In Kelly's recollection, many a time, he and his family draw on Irish traditions for metaphysical therapy and revivification whenever extreme impoverishment and helplessness on this adopted land drives them to the wall. The Irish stories and poems that Ellen has committed to her memory turn out to be the "treasure" (29) they discover. Kelly recalls an abysmal time on their selection.

> Once again my mother began telling stories as she done when our father were in gaol. I had grown the brave beginning of a beard but were not too old to hear the tale... My mother told these tales the firelight shinning in her eyes and every space inside the hut were taken by a ready ear and beating heart. We was far happier than we knew. (187)

In contrast, Kelly is resentful of his parents for selectively hiding the ugly part of their history from them, leaving the skeleton in the closet rotten in oblivion. Kelly shares Carey's progressive historical vision that amnesia ruptures the young generation from their tradition, thus hiders them from a proper understanding of themselves. "That is the agony of the Great Transportation that our parents would rather forget what come before so we currency lads is left alone ignorant as tadpoles spawned in puddles on the moon"(334). Moreover, Kelly tries to tell his readers that the past that his parents choose to forget cannot be really crossed off. Rather, what is buried is not dead but keeps haunting. Carey first resorts to magic realism, introducing a female spirit in Irish mythology, "Banshee", whose role is to herald the death of a family member, to illustrate Kelly's point and, more importantly, to make his narrative all the more mysterious and enchanting. "When our brave parents was ripped from Ireland like teeth from the mouth of their own history and every clear familiar thing had been abandoned on the docks of Cork or Galway or Dublin then the Banshee come on board the cursed convict ships." (108)

In Carey's reworking, Kelly's historical consciousness also lies in his transcendence of the stained past. When Sergeant O'Neil punishes young Kelly by telling him that his father wears a dress like a woman and gallops off "to be serviced by his husband" (16) and he later uncovers a tin trunk to reveal the exact dress with roses on its hem that O'Neil says, he feels humiliated, gets furious with his father and begins estranged from him. The idea of his father as a transvestist remains a mystery and a knot in his mind, and any trigger of the idea assaults him with horrible visions concerning what his father does in that dress and gets him "restless", his "beard hot & itching" and his "limbs as agitated as a threshing machine" (334). Later, the vision of Dan and his mate Steve dressed like women further disgusts and mystifies him. Steves explains that transvestism is an Irish ritual of agrarian rebels who dressed themselves like women to "scare the bejesus out of" (328) the knights of the Queen of England. They wear those dresses in Australia because they still see themselves, in their own words, as "the sons of sieve" (320) who are haunted by the fear of the murdering police who make the adopted land a Hell like that of Ireland. However, Steve is contradicted by Mary, who contends with the recollection of her own experience with transvestism that the "truth" is that those dressed in women's clothes are "weak and ignorant" Irishmen who do not have the guts to fight against the authoritarian but take it out on the powerless, like other poor farmers, landlords, and cattle. In short, the rebels involve themselves in terrorism. Mary's narrative is evidenced by D. J. Hickey and J. E. Doherty's document that those peasant rebels turned to measures like sending threatening letters, intimidation, assault on landlords and their families, torturing or killing animals and murder between 1761 and the 1840s to protest the unjust land use. (2003: 437) She recommends that they stop seeing themselves as sons of thieves, discard the costume, ease the people's lives and "not bring them terror" (334). As she refutes Steve, "If wearing sheets & masks & dresses were such a powerful remedy ... well then Ireland would be a paradise on earth and all the Kings of England have burnt in Hell" (329).

Moreover, the model Mary sets them is Ned Kelly, who breaks himself free from the bondage of his thieving and convict ancestry, goes beyond those rebellious Irish mollies and transforms himself into a "captain" who has the valiancy to revolt against the authoritarian to build an egalitarian world. That includes his perseverant fight against the overarching and distorted imperial narrative to contend for the power and freedom to write his own history, "a people's history" (Burgmann, 1988).

Throughout *True History of the Kelly Gang*, documented archival discoveries converge naturally with Carey's ingenious fabrication of the Kelly Gang's bushranging tale, and history slides imperceptibly into the distant recesses of folk memory. While the metafictional strategy makes historical truth thickly clouded, Carey reinforces it by framing Kelly's voice. He deploys an ingeniously frame narrative in which Thomas Curnow, the school master who betrays the Gang and leads to their extermination, and suggest that differentiated opinions exist as to how to evaluate Ned Kelly in history. The official memory embodied by Curnow tends to keep concordance with what is passed down from the imperial memory and excludes him from the cultural memory as a heresy. As Curnow contests, "What is it about we Australians, eh? ... What is wrong with us? Do we not have a Jefferson? A Disraeli? Might not we find someone better to admire than a horse-thief and a murder? Must we always make such embarrassing spectacle of ourselves?" (419) However, the official memory is soon deconstructed by the tension created between its conservativeness and "the continuing, ever-growing adoration if the Kelly Gang" (ibid.) of the people. It is further dismantled and completely rendered illegitimate by Carey's ventriloquism to give voice to Kelly himself. Peter Carey's revisiting of Ned Kelly's memory foregrounds the hostile and unjust milieu he is confronted with to exonerate him as an outlaw. It then uncovers him to be a dutiful, kind, brave and loyal citizen to denounce the government for its miscarriage of justice. Finally, it transfigures him into a gallant soldier who fights a just and anti-colonial war on behalf of its people, a national hero. Through Carey's compelling mythic narrative, Kelly is made immortal. As the soldier roars, "he is a warrior he can't die" (391).

It has been agreed that memory is never a single unified force. Instead, one-sided memory is often, if not always, open to the potential for conflict and engages itself with "political motivation and the formation of national identity" (A. Assmann, 2011: 73). As Carolyn points out that, Kelly's legend is often used for Australians "in seeking postcolonial notions of national identity" (Gaile, 2004: 297), Carey's retrieving of Kelly's memory, echoes Nietzsche's antiquarian use of history which functions to fashion a tradition. Carey treats the memory of the Kelly Gang with piety and love, as depicted by Nietzsche:

> he looks back in the direction from which he has come, where he has been... The history of his city becomes for him the history of his own self. He understands the walls, the turreted gate, the dictate of the city council, and the folk festival, like an illustrated diary of his youth, and he rediscovers for himself in all this his force, his purpose, his passion, his opinion, his foolishness, and his bad habits. He says to himself, here one could live, for here one may live, and here one can go on living. (1998: 10-11)

Peter Carey's invention of Australia's tradition consists of two dimensions. The first and primary aspect that Carey's reconfiguration aims to unearth involves Australia's national ethos of being liberal and antiauthoritarian. Carey identifies Australia with that exact antiauthoritarianism by uncovering Kelly's valiant rebellion against the colonial power, while problematizing the popular notion of Australia's inborn cultural cringe. Since invented traditions normally involve "the contrast between the constant change and innovation of the modern world and the attempt to structure at least some parts of social life within it as unchanging and invariant" and "are responses to novel situations which take the form of reference to old situations" (Hobsbawm, 1983: 2), the antiauthoritarian tradition is invented in accordance with the author's anxiety that the new hegemonic power still poses threat to Australian liberty and democracy in the globalizing context. Imaginarily repeating Australian antiauthoritarianism is intended to inculcate the values of liberty, democracy, egalitarianism, and norms of revolting against tyranny. It is also aimed to endow contemporary Australians with, to quote Nietzsche, "power, diligence, desire, judgement" (A. Assmann, 2013: 71) to stay vigilant and stand up to the colonizing power when the time comes.

Since traditions usually are invented with the "attempt to establish continuity with a suitable historic past" (Hobsbawm, 1983: 1), the second dimension of Carey's recuperation of the antiauthoritarian tradition functions to highlight Australia's cultural debt to its Irish inheritance. Carey does this by tracing Kelly's gallantry, his rebellious spirit, and his political and historical consciousness back to his Irish ancestry. By pointing out the Irish contribution to Australia's liberal and antiauthoritarian ethos, Carey legitimizes their status in the historical formation of the Australian nation and tradition while delegitimizing the official memory that alienates Irish Australians and treats them as the Other inside White Australia owing to the fact that most Irishmen transported to Australia are political convicts. As he claims that his fictional project has always been "the invention or discovery" of his own country, *True History of the Kelly Gang* witnesses not only Carey's contribution to the world's literary repertoire, but also his invention of Australian antiauthoritarian tradition.

Australia's original status as Britain's penal colony enables frequent exchanges and profound fusions between the local culture and the British and Irish traditions, which, largely, foregrounds its multiculturality and features its distinct European flavour. Australia's colonial memories discussed in this chapter have, to a great degree, determine the morphology of its original memories which are examined in the ensuing chapter.

Chapter Two　Australia's Original Memories[①] to Concrete Identity, Surpass and Heal

For Australians, their European heritage bequeaths them bitter-sweet collective memories. One the one hand, it gives Australian culture a European universality they pride themselves on. On the other hand, placed in the cultural enclave of Europe, Australians clearly feel the scar of their rupture with their ancestry. That rupture partly comes from Australia's geographical distance from the European continent and is partly attributed to its original relationship with the Old World as well as the southern land. The colonial memories give Australians a historical burden, making them feel like inferior European orphans imprisoned in the Antipodes who need to strive for their freedom. Paradoxically, the colonial past also equips them with the condescension to treat the aborigines inhabiting the land for thousands of years as lesser beings and deny the indigenous traditions that keep dismantling the European universality of Australian culture. The inherent contradictions within

---

① By "original memory" I mean Australia's original remembrance of the southern continent, including the ownership of the land, the sense of entrapment, the striving for national independence, the indigenous peoples, the multiracial reality etc. Owing to the peculiarity of Australian history and culture, there are inevitable overlaps between the original memory and the colonial even neo-colonial memory.

Australian culture define the Australianess yet problematize what Australia is and who Australians are, leaving "identity" a national issue frequently explored by politicians, historians and litterateurs.

"'Identity' remains one of the most urgent — as well as hotly disputed — topics in literary and cultural studies. For nearly two decades, it has been a central focus of debate for psychoanalytic, poststructuralist, and cultural materialist criticism." (Moya; Garcia, 2000: I) It has been the hottest issue in domestic cultural studies in the first decade of the twentieth century. (张计连, 2015:21) Seeing that Chinese academia has been preoccupied with turning to the nation's fine traditions to boost cultural confidence in the new era, scholarly enthusiasm for identity is expected to upsurge in the following decades. The word "identity" comes from the Late Latin *identitas* and Old French *identitas*, and is influenced by the Late Latin *essentitas* (essenee, existence, essence). It is represented by the root *idem* (same), the same as the Sanskrit *idem*. Thus, the basic meaning of identity is "the quality or condition of being a specified person or thing" and "the state of being the same in substance, nature, qualities, etc.; absolute sameness" (Thompson, 2004: 1006). Identity entails both the "difference" between individuals and the "sameness" between them and their community. Identity is always at the intersection of synchronic and diachronic dimensions, including both the present "I" and the "I" in the past. (刘海婷, 2017:56)

In late modern times, identity can no longer be defined with "the characteristics of fixed assets" since it is more like a "transient but highly variegated state" (Aleida Assmann, 2011: 55). Identity is about "becoming rather than being: not "'who we are' or 'where we came from', so much as what we might become" (Hall, 1996: 4). It is a construction, which is "multiply constructed across different, often intersecting and antagonistic, discourses, practices and positions. They are subject to a radical historicization, and are constantly in the process of change and transformation" (ibid.). Since identity is normally constituted within discursive representation, language and literature play a critical part in its symbolic construction. Moreover, either for individuals or for societies, "remembering primarily means the identity-creating constructions of a 'usable past'" (Neumann, 2008: 339). Numerous studies of various epochs and authors have shown that literature is closely interwoven with the thematic complex of memory and identity. Access to and transmission of cultural memory via various media is controlled primarily by the "need for identity" (Assmann & Czaplicka, 1995: 130).

Cultural memory comprises "that body of reusable texts, images, and rituals specific to each society in each epoch" (Assmann & Czaplicka, 1995: 132). It also encompasses the remote, marginalized, exiled, non-instrumental, heterodox and denied memories. (阿斯曼, 2016: 26) What Peter Carey reconstructs in *Illywhacker* and *A Long Way from Home* is the latter case. Positive images in a nation's literary canons play an "active" part in the construction of cultural identity, and negative ones assume the same role yet in more complicated manners. (周宪, 2006: 12) The author retrieves Australia's collective memories of the lying complex, the nationalism, the haunting sense of entrapment, the multi-cultural reality and the racist ethnic policy to return to Australia's roots and come to terms with and surpass its "routes".

For one thing, Australians are able to form an integrative image of their collective past and underscore the commonality of their experience to create a collective identity through intersubjective validation in the textual space. For another, the "reflexivity" of cultural memory makes it possible for Carey to draw on its negative part to "explain, reinterpret, criticize, censure, control, and surpass" (Assmann & Czaplicka, 1995: 132). The construction of identity is "never completed — always 'in process'" and "it can always be 'won' or 'lost', sustained or abandoned" (Hall, 1996: 2). Similarly, Australia and Australians' identity that used to be defined largely by their colonial experience are also subject to evolvement. Australians are expected to be enlightened by the author's representation of their past and construct a renewed identity through their self-examination, striving for superiority and interaction with current social dynamics. In this sense, Australians make use of, to quote Michel Foucault, "technologies of the self" which permit them to "effect by their own means" and with the help of the author's narration "a certain number of operations on their own bodies and souls, thoughts, conduct, and way of being, so as to transform themselves in order to attain a certain state of happiness, purity, wisdom, perfection, or immortality" (Martin, Gutman & Hutton, 1988: 18).

Last but not least, Carey's narration functions as a healing force. To some extent, Australians burdened with the unfavourable historical inheritance are, cured in the textual space by the author's externalization of their otherwise deep-buried melancholy and by imaginarily associating themselves with other fellows sharing the same secret. The indigenous people who have been deprived and silenced by their white fellowmen are also able to draw on the healing power in the sense that the author's narrative, to a certain degree, does justice to them by establishing a monument commemorating their part in Australian history and culture. I will investigate in the following two sections how the author reworks on Australia's original memories in *Illywhacker and A Long Way from Home* to fulfil the functions briefed above.

2.1 Underpaintings of Australian Memory: *Illywhacker*

Consistent with the imperial narrative, Australian official memory has been a monument to the White's settlement and the achievements they have made on the southern land. It has repulsed the more ancient traditions of the indigenous peoples together with those of other ethnic minorities, which are indispensable parts of Australian culture. The inconsistency between the Australian experience and its representation in the official memory has called Australia and Australians' identity into question, which is Peter Carey's starting point. When the author turns to prose fiction, he begins his rediscovery and invention of the Australian traditions on which Australians depend for their political imagination. As he tells the interviewer, "[T]his novel represents me at last coming to grips with what it means to be an Australian and what Australia is" (Sexton, 1985: 41).

Herbert Badgery's family memory retrieved in *Illywhaker* is the epitome of Australian social and cultural milieus in the early twentieth century. Then, I will focus attention in the following parts on how Peter Carey reconstructs Australia's cultural memories of the national lies, the striving for national independence, the multiculturalism and the inherited sense of imprisonment for the concretion of Australian identity, the reappraisal and surmounting of specific cultural heritages for a better future.

2.1.1 Preliminaries of the Fiction

Published in 1985, *Illywhaker* won Peter Carey international acclaim, garlanding three Australian major literary awards and being shortlisted for the ManBooker Prize. The novel has turned out to be a considerable commercial success and received positive critical reviews, too. Howard Jacobson (1985) calls it "a big, garrulous, funny novel, touching, farcical and passionately bad-tempered… Not unlike spending a week in the company of the best kind of Australian". Laurie Clancy, an

Australian mythographer, thus proclaims Carey. The title name "illywhacker" is the Australian colloquial synonym for trickster or bullshit artist, terms which embody in themselves several of the critical aspects of the country's cultural identity. In fact, Carey deliberately uses a large body of Australian vocabulary in this novel to manifest its provincial feature. The epic novel features the adventures of Carey's grandfather, Robert Graham Carey, the first Australian air mail carrier, as the central character, named Herbert Bagery. He is a confidence trickster who professes to be 139 years old and a liar. Through the protagonist's first-person reminiscence of the life and love stories of himself and his family, the author weaves into the novel Australian history of the early twentieth century, for instance, Australian aviation and auto dreams.

Illywhaker is written in the form of a fictional autobiography in which Herbert Badgery, the main protagonist, relates his legendary life story and his breathtaking and fantastic family saga, mixed with satirical fable and fantasy. It chronicles Herbert's life history, beginning with his landing at Balliang East in 1919 and meeting the wealthy former bullock-herder, Jack McGrath, who owns a Hispano Suiza. He is thirty-three years old then, though he counts his adult life from that day. Before that, the former aviator is a Ford agent. Though adept at securing deal after deal of the T-model of Ford to make a living, he has been fud up with selling the Yanks' vehicle because he hates the fact that all the money goes back to America instead of staying in Australia. As a Ford salesman, he is always possessed by complicated and ambivalent feelings toward this American brand.

> The Ford had been a tumour in my life. I had fought battles with it in the way another man would fight battles with alcohol or tobacco. I had walked away from it and returned to it. I had rejected it only

to embrace it passionately. I admired its construction, its appearance, the skill that had produced it so economically. And these were also the things I loathed. (Carey, 1985: 75)①

So much so that he might sometimes persuade his potential customers to buy a domestic Summit instead of the T-model he is promoting. His acquaintance with Jack further rekindles his desire to do something more "decent". He befriends Jack and persuades him to invest in the construction of an aeroplane factory. Their ambition falls through when Jack kills himself in a fight with other investors. Herbert ends up marrying Jack's teenage lesbian daughter Phoebe, and they bear two children, Charles and Sonia. After Phoebe abandons them for her partner Annette, Herbert takes Jack's widow, Molly, as his lover. Taking his two children with him, Herbert goes out on the road to scrape a living as a confidence trickster. That leads to his meeting and then hopeless falling in love with Leah Goldstein, a dancer and trickster playing with snakes like him and a writer who is married to the Communist agitator, Izzie Kaletsky.

His daughter Sonia dies in an accident. Soon after that, Herbert is put into jail for assaulting a Chinese man named Goon Tse Ying. Goon is his childhood mentor who has taught him various skills, the most important of which is to get invisible. In the fight, he tears off Goon's finger and preserves it in a jar that he carries with him in prison. Having remained illiterate for most of his life, Herbert begins to study while he is gaoled and eventually obtains a degree in Australian history. His son Charles opened a pet shop and built a successful business selling animals. Charles later gets married to Emma Underhill despite her father's warning of her fragile mental state. At the outbreak of the Second World War,

---

① The following quotations from *Illywhacker* in this section are annotated with only the page number.

Charles disappears for enlisting without informing his wife. Though he is rejected owing to his defective hearing, his behaviour has traumatized Emma and led to her decision to retreat into the goanna's cage and continue living there for the rest of her life. Leah returns to help Charles but also ends up living in a cage, which is part of Charles' extended household.

After his release from prison in 1949, Herbert goes to live with Charles at the pet emporium. He gets on well with Charles' youngest son, Hissao, who dreams of becoming an Australian architect. Herbert's jar containing Gong's finger falls into Emma's possession, and she contends that she has seen a reptile in the bottle, which is Hissao's half-goanna-half-human brother. This ruptures the nerves of Charles who has been overwhelmingly disturbed by the illegal demands brought forth by his American shareholders. He shoots Emma's goanna and then turns the gun to himself. In order to preserve the family business and maintain the welfare of the family, Hissao becomes an animal smuggler. He sells much of his share to Japanese investors and rebuilds the pet shop into the best emporium in the world according to his own design. It eventually becomes a bizarre museum of Australia, in which "shears, lifesavers, inventors, manufacturers, bushmen, aboriginals" (599) are all on display.

This epic work examines Australia's cultural memory of the early twentieth century and the elements that help this novel fit into the genre of neo-historical fiction are listed below. The first element lies in its employment of the metafictional strategy. Not only does the main protagonist, Herbert Badgery expose his status of fiction at the end of his narrative by complaining that "there was nothing left for me but to teach myself to be an author" (548). He further disillusions readers by communicating with them in the middle of the book. Herbert demands that readers should maintain their patience since it is "not use at all in you skipping the pages, racing ahead, hoping for a bit of hanky-panky" (227). Apart from revealing the artefact state of his story, Herbert Badgery, the protagonist and first-person narrator, opens his narrative with the confession that "I am a terrible liar and I have always been a liar" (11). In addition to that, he mentions this identity repeatedly in the text and sometimes even anatomizes to readers how he has achieved his little schemes. The self-reflexiveness seems to problematize all his narrations as an unreliable narrator. As a matter of fact, the artifice of the text is best illustrated in the self-reflexive image of Hissao's reconstruction of the emporium:

> He built like a jazz musician. He restated and reworked the melody of the old emporium. The creaking galleries were gone now, but you saw them still, in your imagination. He built like a liar, like a spider — steel ladders and walkways, catwalks, cages in mid-air, in racks on walls, tumbling like waterfalls, in a gallery spanning empty spaces like a stainless Bridge of Sighs. (597)

However, it is too naive to jump to the conclusion that Peter Carey is playing purely a game of words in this novel since a salient paradox can be easily detected in it. The author tries almost equally hard to create a verisimilitude to contradict his laying bare the fictive status. He first constructs a sense of authenticity by referring to genuine toponyms and historical events like Australia's budding aviation dream or the Lambing Flat riots. Moreover, Carey tries to peddle the credibility of his story by making Herbert a man with a Bachelor's degree of Arts in History from the University of Sydney and an acquaintance of the progressive historian M. V. Anderson. In addition, Herbert, the salesman, tries to mesmerize readers by declaring that he is indeed a "kind man" (600) and that there is, in his words a "fact you can rely on" (11). Within the novel, the author has been negotiating between historical and cultural truth and his imagination through the tense created by the contradiction of self-referentiality and verisimilitude. Carey's paradox of exposing his works as an artefact and creating in it a verisimilitude has also drawn Helen Daniel's attention in her discussion of *Illywhacker* as a metafiction. She writes in *Liars: Australian New Novelists* that "*Illywhacker* is a play on truth, fiction, lies... it is about the calibrations of the Lie and so about the calibrations of truth" (1998: 167-168).

Previous studies on *Illywhacker* have paid continuous academic attention both to the aesthetic and the political edge of the novel. Critics (Hassall, 1993; Woodcock, 1996; Huggan, 1996; Edwards, 2004; Highfield, 2006; 彭青龙, 2006; Gaile, 2010; 张计连, 2015), though with different research orientations, have devoted their commentary to Carey's play with language games and/or his rebellion against the imperial tradition. It is unanimously believed among them that Peter Carey preoccupies himself with Australia's identity issue. He is trying to define what Australia and an Australian is. Suppose we keep in mind that his novel was composed in 1985, when the author's countrymen and women were prepared to celebrate Australia's 1988 Bicentenary. In that case, that observation makes more sense, only that it fails to encompass the richness and complexity of this splendid family saga. It is argued that *Illywhacker* is actually the site of Australia's cultural memories of the early twentieth-century. The lies, the futile nationalist ambition, Australia's multicultural origin, and the sense of imprisonment that continues entrapping contemporary Australians, are all enwrapped in the text and displayed in the theme-prison-like commodities for tourists to visit. This argument echoes Woodcock's comment that *Illywhacker* "depicts a particular phase of Australian culture and nationalism, a search for identity which went wrong" (1996: 57) and Brian Edwards's insight that the novel is a "postmodernist pastiche of early twentieth-century Australian history" (2004: 150). Moreover, I am incredibly inspired by and indebted to Cliff Lobe (2002: 17), who notes the correlation between the emporium and Australia's memory of its penal-colonial past and the postcolonial period, and Mary Ellen Snodgrass, who argues this neo-historical fiction "merges Australian lore with cultural themes to produce a passionate narrative filled with the ethnic diversity of Europeans, Chinese, and Jews" (2010: 15-16).

The ensuing three parts will be devoted to the investigation of how Peter Carey reconfigures through Herbert's family memory Australia's overt lying complex, its nationalist tradition, its ethnic diversity and haunting sense of entrapment to consolidate Australia and Australians' identity, critically reappraise the cultural inheritances and surpass them to build a better future.

2.1.2 Lies as Part of Existence

Peter Carey states, at the very beginning of *True History of the Kelly Gang*, that it has been an open secret that Australian history is suffused with "lies" or "silences". For one thing, when the grand historical narrative claims that Australian history commences with Captain Cook's great "discovery" of this south-pacific land in 1788, it denies the existence of the indigenous peoples who have inhabited this continent for thousands of years. For another, the ignoble history of racial dispossession and genocide of the indigenous tribes combined with the "convict stain" suffice for them to retreat into cultural self-deception. As Robert Hughes notes in *The Fatal Shore*, "the idea of a 'convict stain', a moral blot soaked into Australia's fabric dominated all argument about Australian selfhood by the 1840s" (2003: xi). As a matter of fact, the lying issue is so prominent in Australian culture that Cliff Lobe even argues, "it is not hard to see that Australian national identity is founded upon substantial fault lines" (2000: 149). This motif has also been Carey's constant preoccupation, recurring in *Oscar and Lucinda*, *30 Days in Sydney*, and lately in *A Long Way from Home*. In fact, the study of the paratextual elements of the novel, which carry "illocutionary force" (Genette, 1997: 10), suggests that "lies" is the most important theme of *Illywhacker*. Peter Carey quotes from Mark Twain's commentary in *More Tramps Abroad* as the epigraph of *Illywhacker*:

> Australian history is almost always picturesque; indeed, it is so curious and strange, that it is itself thé chiefest novelty the country has to offer and so it pushes the other novelties into second and third place. It does not read like history, but like the most beautiful lies; and all of a fresh new sort, no mouldy old stale ones. It is full of surprises and adventures, the incongruities, and contradictions, and incredibilities; but they are all true, they all happened.

Since the functions of the epigraph are "commenting — sometimes authoritatively — and thus of elucidating and thereby justifying" the title, *Illywhacker*, and "commenting on the text, whose meaning it indirectly specifies or emphasizes" (Genette, 1997: 156-157), a brief glimpse at it gives us the hint that this novel is most related to the motif "lies" woven into Australia's cultural memory and ingrained into its national psyche. As a matter of fact, the diffusing of lies in the text is one of the most significant aspects of this fiction.

Families are cells of society whose impact depends on the power of the traditions belonging to each family. Each family may seem to run on its own logic and traditions. However, families have more in common in the sense that the logic and traditions they rely on for their unity and continuity derive from a general society and function to regulate the family's relations with that society. (Halbwachs, 1992: 83) Family memory consists of notions of persons and facts that apparently appear singular to a particular family but actually have the characteristics of thoughts that are common to other groups, since our family recollections must be placed "in the frameworks where our society retrieves its past... We accept remembering in the way society remembers" (ibid: 81-82). The Badgery's memory recollected by Herbert is, in fact, the epitome of Australia's collective memory. Herbert's father was born on York Street, Warrnambool, but he never misses a chance to lie to his sons and others that he is an Englishman. He is ashamed of being Australian and chastises Herbert for his "acquired" local accent. Family memories "express the general attitude of the group; they not only reproduce its history but also define its nature and its qualities and weaknesses" (Halbwachs, 1992: 59). The father's characteristic of being "a liar and a bullshitter" (51) has become a "mysterious symbol for the common ground from which the family members acquire their distinctive traits" (Halbwachs, 1992: 59). Herbert declares at the outset of his narrative that he is one hundred and thirty-nine years old and his age is one fact that the audience can rely on, then he warns his "Caveat emptor" that "I am a terrible liar and I have always been a liar... lying is my main subject, my specialty, my skill" (11). In addition, he contends that his children are "spawned by lies, sucked on dreams, infested with dragons" (359). When he is in prison, he writes about his experience and admits it is "a pack of lies" (409). He is accused by Leah of lying and distorting their lives in his notebook, and most of his activities are wrapped in lies too. Since family memory is a form of collective memory, Badgery's family trait of lies, which defines who they are is also an essential cultural masterplot① that helps shape Australian history and Australians' self-images.

Lying is not confined to Herbert's self-profession or his occupations as a salesman or trickster. They are knitted neatly into the fabric of the text and become a common occurrence involving proximately every character. According to Herbert, he is the "King of Liars" (304). His father lies that he is an Englishman; his son lies when he is caught stealing at school; Phoebe lies to steal Herbert's aeroplane and abandons him and their children; Leah is also a trickster and lies about her age and the situations of Charles and his family when she writes to imprisoned Herbert; even the Sydney city is "full of trickery and deception. If you push against it too hard you will find yourself leaning against empty air" (547); above all, "the whole nation is built on a lie which was that it was not already occupied when the British came here" (307). As Jonathan Highfield reviews, "[I]n Peter Carey's 1985 novel, *Illywhacker*, nation formation is left to a liar" (2006: 130). Herbert cites the work of his mentor, the fictional historian M. V. Anderson, to illustrate this point:

> Our forefathers were all great liars. They lied about the lands they selected and the cattle they owned. They lied about their backgrounds and the parentage of their wives. However, it is the first lie that is the most impressive for being so monumental, i. e. , that the continent, at the time of first settlement, was said to be occupied but not cultivated and by that simple device they were able to give the legal owners short shrift and, when they objected, to

---

① H. Porter Abbott defines masterplots as "recurrent skeletal stories, belonging to cultures and individuals, that play a powerful role in questions of identity, values, and the understanding of life", and further argues that "masterplots can also exert an influence on the way we take in new information, causing us to overread or underread narratives in an often unconscious effort to bring them into conformity with a masterplot". (2002: 192)

use the musket or poison flour, and to do so with a clear conscience. It is in die context of this great foundation stone that we must begin our study of Australian history. (456)

For Australians, lying has a philosophical implication. Lies have been the air that they inhale and prescribe their existence. As Hebert says,

> it would never permit me to be what I was. Everyone loved me when I appeared in a cloak, and swirled and laughed and told them lies. They applauded. They wanted my friendship. But when I took off my cloak they did not like me. They clucked their tongues and turned away. My friend Jack was my friend in all things but was repulsed by what I really was. I admired and loved him … but he could only like the bullshit version of me. (78)

If we take Carey's works dealing with Australian history together, it is safe to infer that the author is critical of and even indignant at Australia's documented memory which tends to lie about the genuine ownership of this continent and excludes indigenous traditions. Nevertheless, he is ambivalent towards the lying tradition ingrained in Australia's collective memory and passed down from generation to generation.

The Australian origin myth of Cook's discovery is deconstructed in *Illwhyacker* as a national lie. However, lying is imbued with much more complicated and profound meanings rather than an unethical human defect. As Phoebe contends, "there are several meanings to the word 'lie'" (519), lying may be a detestable blemish for others. However, for Australians, since lying helps to cover a shared shameful past, it is considered a patriotic duty to observe this national tradition: "[A] liar might be a patriot." (456) Lies also possess some sort of transformative power. Just as Herbert claims complacently, "you call it a lie, I call it a gift" (34). This "gift" is an enchanting virtual with enormous potential of trespassing and transformation. When Phoebe and Herbert are head over heels in love with each other, she writes in her diary, "I like him because probably he is a liar", he has "invented" (91) himself, and he can be anything he wants. What Phoebe says points to the constructiveness of memory as well as its effect on the construction of one's self-image.

Lies, for Australians, can also be a therapeutic power that shelters them from the cruelty of the hard truth. That is why when Herbert is told that Phoebe might have lied to and cheated on him, he "took the lies and held them gratefully. I wrapped them round me and felt the soft comfort a child feels inside a woollen rug. And this, of course, is what anyone means when they say a lie is creditable; they do not mean that it is a perfect piece of engineering, but that it is comfortable" (186). It is not hard to infer that Peter Carey, though critical of Australia's denial of the aboriginal culture and its appropriation of the land, suspends the moral judgement of lying because this tradition has been wired into Australia's national psyche. It is the lies that help define what Australia is and who Australians are and sustain their spiritual wellbeing, at least temporarily. Carey's feelings towards lying are complicated. It involves criticism, self-mockery and helplessness.

Lying is used in this fiction as a pun, which can be first glimpsed from an authorial interview in which Carey mentions what motivates him to write the lies in *Illywhacker*:

> I was sitting in the doctor's office one day waiting, and I suddenly thought, "Damn it, I'll make him a liar." ... That meant I could have the first person, I could have the third person, I could have whatever voice I wanted, because he was a liar. But also by then I had established him as a confidence man, and I was starting to deal with what I regarded as lies we have been told in history about Australia, the lies we've told ourselves. These different aspects of

lying all really arrived in a big tangle, if you like, all at once. (Tautsky, 1990: 32)

This confession points to both the aesthetic and political dimensions of Australian lies. Aesthetically speaking, lying is designed ingeniously in line with the pervading post-structural and postmodern notions constructiveness and deceptiveness of narrative, which defers its authenticity. When Carey integrates all the roles of storyteller, narrator and novelist into his protagonist Herbert and when Herbert repeatedly exposes the fictional status of the text, ridicules his readers occasionally and professes that he, as an author, and novelists in general are all liars, it can be inferred that the author is using the postmodern technique of metafiction to exhibit the fictionality of all texts and indicate that there might not be an entity in the material world corresponding to the floating signifier. By suggesting the arbitrary status of narrative truth or even falsehood, it warns readers of the unreliability of relying on traditional expectations to obtain knowledge from texts, or to be specific, here from neo-historical novels.

However, Carey does not contend himself with the aesthetic play of words. Instead, he digs deeper. While revealing the uncertainty and instability of literary texts, Carey problematizes historiography as a whole, alluding to historical narrative as an artifice. To be more specific, he relentlessly spearheads his attack on Australia's overarching grand-documented history. That makes Carey's retrieval of Australia's lying memory embedded with, consciously or unconsciously, his cultural and political concern. First of all, the "lies" memory performs the function of "differentiation" (A. Assmann, 2013: 129), suggesting the peculiarity of Australia and Australians, though in a negative way. This characteristic relates all Australians to a shared foundational history, differentiating them from other peoples and consolidating their connection with their nation. Since telling the truth involves remembering its penal history and the ignominious genocide, which will hazard the building of a positive self-image, original memories are distorted, even falsified and then suppressed in the collective unconscious, to serve political and moral ends. In other words, lies are invented in response to a dishonourable history and thus are imbedded into the national psyche to replace truths. As Cliff Lobe argues, "white Australia is built into a suitably empty space, to sustain a stable sense of national identity and a clear national conscience" (2000: 151). However, the lying tradition is a double-edged sword. It starts with the intention of building Australia's a positive image. Nevertheless, it ends up problematizing its identity because Australia is deprived of authenticity and compromising its cultural confidence. As Herbert cries helplessly: "we Australians are timid people who has no faith in ourselves." (518) Peter Carey returns to this issue in *Amnesia*.

In addition, though Carey deploys the metafictional strategy frequently and makes Herbert Badgery an unreliable narrator by declaring at the threshold of the text that he is going to tell lies and stories, he deals with Australian history very seriously. That brings us to the second function of his reconstruction of the lying tradition, namely, "delegitimization" (A. Assmann, 2013: 128). By telling the lies that Australia used to be an empty land and its history initiates with the White's discovery and later laborious exploration, the official memory servest to legitimate the White's domination and ruling of this *terra nullius* and immortalize the ruling class on this territory. However, Herbert's remembrance offers another version of memory in which the grand narrative is deconstructed to be nothing but a pack of lies. They are exposed by people with historical consciousness and humane conscience, such as the fictional historian M. V. Anderson, Leah, the former medical student, and Herbert, who obtains a degree in history, for the sake of the conquered and deprived indigenous tribes. Exposing that the Whites have invaded the continent, appropriated the land from the aborigines, taken procession of their cattle and women, and finally dispatched and slaughtered them ruthlessly, Herbert's family memory presents itself as a counter-memory to challenge, criticize and finally subvert the official memory infused with lies. While denouncing the discursive power lurching behind the official memory that is "experienced as tyrannical" (ibid: 129), it simultaneously legitimizes itself as an alternative version of the collective memory striving for its right to be written into Australian memory book. In this sense, the author, by reworking Australia's lying memory, fulfils his poetic justice. It is a pity that Carey is more preoccupied with exposing the problems in Australian collective memory in this fiction. He plays a more progressive role in venturing poetic remedies to solve them in his later writings dealing with the same theme. Not only does Peter Carey concern himself with Australia's struggling to build a positive national image in *Illywhacker*, he is also trying to capture the predicaments facing the nation when it strives for its independence.

2.1.3 Utopian Nationalist Dream

Though lying is a keynote that runs through *Ilywhacker* and that pieces together all the main characters and their stories, the three-generation family saga is threaded by the Badgery's ardent yet compromised dreams told from Herbert's recollection. The main protagonist Herbert Badgery professes that he is a "nationalist" (223) and his children are all "sucked on dreams" (359). Herbert, the grandfather, his son Charles, and then his grandson Hissao have spent all their lives seeking metamorphosis. They do so not to upgrade their own economic or social conditions but with the big vision of bringing positive changes to their nation, Australia, which is stuck in a disadvantageously dependent state. In Anthony Hassall's words, they are "passionate about 'Australian nationalism'" (Hassall, 1994: 87). The Badgery's dreams begin with the grandfather's ambition to build an Australian aeroplane, proceed to the son's management of a pet shop to enhance Australia's publicity, and ends up with the grandson's reconstruction of the pet shop into an emporium to save his family as well as Australia from degrading into obscurity. However, to a certain degree, none of their dreams come through neatly. Herbert's ambition vanishes with the death of his supporter and funder, Jack. Charles' dream is severely compromised because he has to rely on financial support from American firms to save him from the brink of bankrupt and because his business involves him in immoral smuggling, which plays a big part in his suicidal. Hissao's dream ends in futility because he has to sell most of his family (national) business shares to the Japanese company, Mitsubishi, to keep it alive. The Badgery's dreams are in fact the epitome of Australia's collective memory of its budding yet struggling nationalist imagination in the early twentieth century. Moreover, they will be anatomized respectively in the following paragraphs.

Herbert used to make a living as a sales agent for Henry Ford and he is doing pretty well in it, especially before the Great Depression. Selling T Model makes him a lot of dough, but it never makes him happy. As a matter of fact, Herbert often gets broody and even humiliated because it is not an Australian car, and most of the money from the sales goes back to America instead of staying in his country. He has such a solid inclination for selling Australian-made cars that his promotion of the T Model often ludicrously ends up with his persuasion of his fellow man to buy an Australian Summit. In his own words, he is "smitten with desire to do something decent" (72). The complicated feelings of the admiration for Fords' skill and the resentment of its technological colonization of Australian vehicles keep tormenting him and eventually leading to his walking away from it. That brings him "an enormous relief, a lightness" (75) and makes him feel like "a man entering into the first decent chapter of his life" (75).

Among the various factors that induce his resignation, he is most fueled by the rekindling of his dream to "establish a factory that was going to build an Australian-designed aircraft" (34) owing to his acquaintance with Jack McGrath, a rich yet unhappy man "with an obsession, about transportation" (29) who is wilful to back him up financially. His ambition to make Australia strong and independent shines because of Jack, the man who is "enthusiastic, willing, and impressed with the idea of an aeroplane" (30). Their plan commences with how to make a wheel. They go to Belmont Common to take flying lessons. They "tramp around the bush to look at timbers" and decide on "mountain ash or white ash for spars; blue fig for struts; cudgerie for the fuselage" (117). They pay the Forest Commission to conduct tests on the timbers to eusure they meet the "British Aero-nautical Standards". They chase timber suppliers in Queensland and wake up squatters in the middle of the night to lobby them to invest in the new enterprise. They have the solicitors draw up plans for the would-be "Barwon Aeros". With Jack's enthusiasm and Herbert's resolution of "risking his life and his capital by taking to the air" (60), it does not take long for that aircraft factory to take shape. When Herbert's aero dream is contradicted by Cocky Abbot and his English son, who regards the scheme as impractical and suggests that he should set up an agency to import the best planes from Britain, Herbert demonstrates solid political consciousness, refuting that the relationship between the agent and the manufacture is like that of a "child and parent" (136). He argues that Australia will have to serve Britain for its life time like a slave and never grow up if it does not have its own aero industry. Moreover, he "had no intention to die like a silly goat for the British" (ibid.). Herbert and Jack are busy with the big plan of building an Australian aircraft. Herbert's aviation dream is the emblem of Australian flickering craving for independence from Great Britain, which turns out to be premature.

Herbert's inflamed dream is nothing but a flash in the pan and is doomed to end up in abortion owing to a couple of elements. To begin with, Herbert is fundamentally flawed in his personality, which foregrounds the frangibility of his ambition. He is not so much rational as sentimental, getting fuelled easily by the nationalist impulse yet unable to maintain that passion for long. He is the one who brainwashes Jack with flamboyant nationalism, filling him with the burning desire to build Australian-made aircraft. Nevertheless, he is soon frightened by Jack's craze and has to "imitate my former self, counterfeit an enthusiasm to match that of my host" (117). In other cases, his nationalist sentiment turns out to be a physiological urge to impress women with his masculinity. For example, his passion for airplanes fluctuates with his courtship of Phoebe, and he gets manipulated by his eroticism for her. When his infatuation is discouraged by Phoebe, he "couldn't summon up sufficient interest in the aircraft he had so carelessly set in motion" (117). When Phoebe is attracted to the shape of dreams in his eyes, he realizes "a cruelty, a fear of his own weakness" (37).

In addition to Herbert's personal defects, the severe passiveness of Australians contributes to the utopianism of his national dream. Though he and Jack did persuade some people to dive in their adventure, and the trial flight turns out to be successful, they fail to hold the zeal of the people in town for long. Most Australians tend to be content with the status quo of life, and they are not keen on any change that the national industry would bring them. What is worse, since investors are most concerned with the payback, the bleak prospect of making a quid from the so-called Australian aircraft in the short future soon stirs disagreements among them. Even Jack sways under the overwhelming pressure from his partners, who firmly insist on setting up an agency. They are convinced that "we are a young country and we've got to crawl before we can walk" (141). Though Herbert eventually talks Jack into the sense that "if you start out crawling, you end up crawling" (ibid.), his strident nationalism remains the last thing to hold them together.

Moreover, Herbert's nationalist dream was smashed because it is not well-founded. Herbert builds his aircraft ambition practically on the thin air. Despite his fluid enthusiasm, he has to rely totally on others to realize his dream. He steals the registered aileron design originally made by an Englishman, Mr. Bradfield, makes minor adaption and threatens the draughtsman into placing his name as the craft's designer. By doing this, Herbert demonstrates Australia's inextricable dependence on the British Empire, which makes the foundation of its aircraft industry "very shaky" (119). He counts on Jack to fund his aero dream, so he is entirely disillusioned when Jack commits suicide out of disappointment and a sense of betrayal. Ironically, the man who is an ardent supporter of Australian national industry is poisoned by the "true Australian snake" (140), which Herbert calls the once gaoled untameable mean bastard and compares to an ideal Australian. Eventually, the snake bite serves as the embodiment of the unawaken national consciousness among the average Australian which makes Australia's independence from the British affiliation an empty talk. Phoebe is an excellent example to illustrate this. Although she "had no aptitude for things mechanical… only a poetic understanding of machinery, a belief in magic" (164), she demands that Herbert coach her to be a pilot and give her the aeroplane as a gift. Finally, it ends up being abandoned in the grass and eaten by cattle. And Herbert's aero dream vanishes into the air completely.

Herbert's strident nationalism is then relayed to his son Charles. Like his father, he desperately craves attention in his life even from a young age. When he is on the road with his father to a circus performance, he always meditates on how to attract spectators with innovation and seek opportunities to "escape, revenge, triumph and — most of all—making money" (291). Reaching his adulthood, Charles often feels distressed and haunted by the fact that Australia is paid no attention in the world. He beholds a dream to change that situation and make his motherland stand out in the world. He decides to set up a pet shop to exhibit Australian birds and animals, in other words, to present Australian uniqueness and charisma to the whole world so that other countries will sit up and take notice of this forlorn continent. Though he initiates the pet shop with his love for his wife Emma, he grows to pour into this place his much more profound affection for his home country. Charles does not have the aptitude for business at all. "He did not even calculate the money to fix the arcade which had been disused since the depression. He signed the lease without getting a quote for building cages or aquariums. He did not even think about the extra cost of feed" (480-481). However, like his father, he is a dreamer, "an enthusiast, a fan" (480), and the pet shop is built right "in accordance with his dream" (481). It is "an expression of the purest patriotism — pure Australiana" (ibid.).

What occupies Charles' mind is doing anything to change Australia for the better and the pet shop is just one of the tools. He is always ready and resolute to do anything for his dream. When the Second World War starts, he rushes to enlist in without noticing his family because he is not content with being just "a proprietor of a non-essential industry" (480).

Charles' move is the embodiment of Australia's endeavour for a place on the international arena to get away from its obscurity. However, he is rejected owing to his problematic hearing, which makes him feel "embarrassed to be a young man in plain clothes", imagining "himself a coward" (ibid.). He is entirely devoted to the management of the pet shop and takes it more as a battlefield where Australia is going to win its own war. Like what Herbert says about his son, "he was having his own quiet revenge and he was conducting the whole affair with a nicety that would surprise those who thought him clumsy" (446). It is not difficult to infer that Charles' pet shop business is emblematically Australia's business of standing among the nations of the world and that his perseverance or "stubbornness" is the continuation of Herbert's unfulfilled nationalist dream.

However, Charles' national dream is severely compromised, and eventually turns out to be another illusion. As his father sighs in grief, "[A]ny real businessman would have told him that the best pet shop in the world would be a failure" (481). Although Charles does make it that one "can travel all over the world and find Badgerys' birds in all the big collections, Hamburg, Frankfurt, Tokyo" (574), his "success" is impossible without funds coming from America. Only those Americans would like to pay big money for "rosellas and lorikeets, blue bonnets and golden whistles, all varieties of cockatoos, king parrots and western parrots, finches, warblers, even a pair of dancing brolgas" (481). In Herbert's words, it is the Americans who "saved his arse" (ibid). In contrast, his scared mission of making Australia famous fails to win support from his fellow citizens, who get used to taking things as they are and are too passive to envision any positive change. As Herbert observes, "Sydney was not big enough to support such poetry" (481). Most of the time, they flock to the shop, take a quick glance at the local fauna and disappear. Charles' original plan is to introduce Australian exclusive beauty to the rest of the world and show them that his home country matters. However, it turns out that it could not even support itself without the essential assistance of America. Charles used to be resolute in rejecting Nathan Schick's proposal to smuggle Australian endangered birds and animals to America to make a good fortune. However, he is later forced to change them into commodities and sell them to the United States and other parts of the world. His nationalist dream, like his father's, turns out to be nothing but a mirage built into the thin air.

Charles is a man of integrity. The contradiction between getting Australia known to other nations with its unique fauna and flora and smuggling to keep the business alive keeps getting on his nerves and eventually sticks him in a moral dilemma. Moreover, his wife Emma, who is traumatized by his attempt to take part in the Second World War, retreats to the cage with the goanna, causing him continuous spiritual and sexual torment. Emma's repeatedly lunatic behaviour of identifying the preserved finger of Gong to be her half-goanna-and-half-human foetus keeps infuriating him. The accumulated anxiety grows so overwhelming that it drives Charles to the brink of collapse. He shoots the goanna and then turns the gun to himself. Charles' death terminates the utopian nationalist dream of the second generation of the Badgery family, as Herbert wails, "that shiny box (Charles' coffin) contained a man, my boy, a skin-wrapped parcel of fucked-up dreams" (578).

The pupil learns from and outdoes his master. Surpassing both his father and grandfather, Hissao is a young man "all afire with enthusiasm and ambition" (584) and "fuelled by fierce nationalism" (560). Moreover, he is equipped with more explicit historical and national consciousness. Distressed to see that buildings in Sydney are all colonial ones with verandas tacked on, which "seemed merciless and uncaring, like machines of war" (585) and that there is not a single Australian architecture, he is determined to be an Australian architect, designing buildings with pure local style. Unlike his father or grandfather, who is desperate to seek changes yet lack foresight, he has the "ability to draw very fine moral distinctions, and to see very objectively"; he does disapproves of the idea of the pet shop, foreseeing "the damage his father's business was doing to the fauna of the country he loved" and considering "it was one of those great Australian enterprises that generate wealth while making nothing new" (561).

Nevertheless, Hissao understands more than well what his family have preoccupied themselves with. He understands especially his father's helplessness and grief. When Charles dies, he refuses Charles' American partners either to smuggle or to legally export endangered birds or animals to the United States. When *Time* calls his family business into question and accuses Charles of being unethical, he stands up to deal with the interview and tactically defends his father. He plans to go back to university to continue his architect dream after the funeral. However, he could not bear to see that the pet shop "had fibrous matted roots that pushed down into the tank stream. It sweated and groaned and sighed in the wind" (581). In his father and grandfather's shattered dreams, he sees the fading of the Australian dream, which is the last thing he would rather lose. Finally, he decides to sacrifice his personal pursuit and take upon his family mission since "[H]e had loved his country more than he had pretended and had tried to make something fine out of something rotten" (593). The first thing he does is to rectify the damages the pet shop has inflicted on Australian fauna, only that things do not turn out as smoothly as he wishes.

Learning that the pet shop hosts the last-recorded golden-shouldered parrot in Australia and no buyer would like to return a breeding pair,

Hissao decides to take it personally to Rome for breeding to avoid the extinction of this shining species. He puts the parrot in his baggy trousers to spare it from the interception of the customs officers. However, he, who interprets continual love affairs as the proof of his manhood, encounters a fellow passenger, Rosa Carlobene, who "was seeking the warm juices of life, defying the tape worms of habit and order, luxuriating in the complexity of her sexual feelings" (592). Sitting side by side in the first class cabin on the flight to a new and strange city, they are both enchanted with the "limitless possibilities of the erotic future" (590). Rosa thrusts her pelvis sinuously and strongly onto his thighs, which squashes the head of the golden-shouldered parrot which he risks to save and causes its death. Hissao is overwhelmed by guilt and self-accusation. At the same time, he is possessed by hatred, blaming the killing of the creature on anyone related, directly or indirectly, to this incident: himself, Rosa, his family, Miss Grim, who considers his plans for the parrot impractical, and his fellowmen lacking imagination.

Hissao used to love his country ardently. However, now, the unstoppable grief and hatred are as intense as his love. They transform him and induce his revenge scheme, which departs completely from his original intention. Like his fellowmen, he is again "dullness personified", taking pleasure from his "politeness, the excessive courtesies, the slow progress, circular, but sometimes spiral, towards consensus" (596). What is worse, he sells most of the share of his family business to the Mitsubishi Company and ends up with "a great salesman, the best the family had yet produced" (ibid.). That is not the end of the story. After all, "he was his grandfather's grandson and unkindness was his strongest card" (ibid.). Using the Japanese capital, Hissao reconstructs the pet shop into a first-class emporium in which he cages all his fellows: shears, life savers, inventors, manufacturers, bushmen, aboriginals, Leah the Jew, and even his grandfather Herbert, for display. With Hissao's ambition to be an architect winding up as a salesman and his endeavour to protect his family business and save Australia's endangered species ending up in yielding to Japanese capital colonizing of Australia, the nationalist dream of the third generation of the Badgery family also vanishes in utopia. All the three dreamers strive to make their obscure home county matter, but they strive in vain. Australia is "all but invisible", and it is its "destiny" (596).

What Peter Carey weaves into the Badgerys' family memory is Australia's collective memory from the years after the First World War to the 1980s. Through Herbert's remembrance of family's utopian dreams, the author represents and interrogates the nation's cultural memories, ranging from Australia's "entrepreneurial optimistic optimism" (Hassall, 1994: 93) after the First World War to its cravenly "selling out its resources to successive colonial overlords" (ibid.: 96) since the Depression, and to its self-inflicted economic colonizing by post-imperial power continuing to the end of the twentieth century. Owing to the constructiveness of memory and the unavoidable transformation, displacement or even distortion it goes through to represent itself, it is hard to know to what extent Herbert's recollection is identical with how things happened then. The author uses his remembrance of Charles Ulm (the first Australian pilot) to illustrate this point in the text:

> I had known Charles Ulm (the first Australian pilot). Possibly I had known Charles Ulm. To tell you the truth I can't remember whether I really did know him or if I claimed it so often I came to believe it myself. Photographs of Ulm never looked like the man I described but people often blamed the photographers for that, not me. In any case, when the news was over I told them all about Ulm, what he was like as a man, what he looked like and so on.

(36)

Nevertheless, the past is always remembered for some reason. Herbert declares to his audience: "I delivered value." (ibid.) Then, what are the "values" that the author is going to convey to his readers through his reworking of Badgery's utopian dreams?

In the first place, by repeating Australia's fight against obscurity and striving for independence, the author invents its nationalist tradition, which "automatically implies continuity with the past" (Hobsbawm, 1983: 1). Nationalism remains significant in the ear of late capitalism in that Australia is represented as a nation which still needs to get rid of its reliance on the Old and the New Empire to establish a distinct national identity. As is argued by Bruce Woodcock, "*Illwhacker* depicts a particular phase of Australian culture and nationalism, a search for identity that went wrong" (1996: 57). Australia, which has long been tormented by its mediocrity and belittled self owing to its weakness and invisibility, is anxious to step on the international stage and impress the world. This is embodied by Australians who spend every effort to seek transmogrification by doing something "decent" (75), showing the "nicety" (446) of Australia, or "making something fine out of rotten" (593) with the hope of inventing themselves.

Herbert quits his job as a well-paid Ford sales agent to dive into the aviation industry to make autonomous aeroplanes with the intention that Australia can get rid of its dependence on imperial colonizing. He wants to make history. Nevertheless, his scheme is aborted with the suicide of Jack, his financial and spiritual supporter. Charles has been obsessed with impressing others from a young age, and he is assured that he has attracted the world's attention to his obscure home country by exhibiting and selling its unique and beautiful animals and birds throughout the world. However, his business is called into moral question, which eventually leads to his suicide. Hissao dreams of distinguishing himself to be a real Australian by being an architect but has to first devote himself to saving his family business by rectifying the disadvantageous situation where it has rendered Australia's extinct species. But the enormous hate generated out of his failure leads to his selling out his business to Mitsubishi to allow the Japanese to be Australia's new master and caging his fellowmen for exhibition. It seems that they are confronted with immediate disillusion whenever they create something to mark themselves or their nation out. The identity they crave desperately for is always entangled with lies and deceptions and continual colonial dependency that it seems to be out of their reach forever. Leah Goldstein's footnote that "It's not a country where you can rest. It's a black man's country… we can only move around it like tourists" (323) explains why white Australians are so infatuated with their identity and why they could not get the hang of it. Through Goldstein's argument, the author connects Australia's failure in seeking their identity to the national lies that the country keeps telling itself, implying that Australia will find where it stands only when it is brave enough to confront the hard truths.

Nevertheless, Carey's invention of the nationalist tradition parallels his critical reappraisal of the passivity pervading the Australian national psyche for compromising that national ethos. Passive Australians are blamed for being one-dimensional men.[①] They are "culturally and economically a collection of pets who are going around thinking that they are all really wonderful, not thinking they are in cages or on leashes"

[①] According to Herbert Marcuse, the chief characteristic of the one-dimensional mode of thought and behavior is the repression of all values, aspirations, and ideas. The consequence of one-dimensionality is the weakening and even the disappearance of all genuinely radical critique, the integration of all opposition in the established system. See Herbert Marcuse: *One-Dimensional Man: Studies in the Ideology of Advanced Industrial Society*. Boston: Beacon Press, 2002.

(Sexton, 1985: 41). They are not enlightened with historical or national consciousness, not capable of "negative thinking" (Marcuse, 2002: 316) or critique of the society. They are people without bigger visions, taking things as they are and remaining pessimistic about things that do not directly concern their immediate wellbeing. As Herbert confesses before he cages himself, "I imagined I had no passions left except those involving shelter and the comforts of skin. I would do nothing to jeopardize either... I was going to wake each morning and gaze up at the skylight and know, straightway, what sort of day it was" (516).

Carey exposes this malady repeatedly in the text and contributes to the disillusion of the Badgerys' dream, too. It makes its initial appearance in Herbert's aviation dream when Cocky Abbots and other potential investors are reluctant to pour money into the national industry and try to talk him and Jack down to set up an agency to import British aeroplanes instead of making autonomous products. It reappears when Herbert is supposedly resounding trial flight attracts only a very moderate number of spectators. They give no care to Herbert's aviation dream. This passiveness comes into play again when former investors threaten to withdraw their capital on the bleak prospect of making profits from the national industry, which leads directly to Jack's suicide. This ill is then reflected in Emma who retreats into the cage after learning that her husband Charles has gone for enlisting without letting her know. She puts herself in the "undignified position", acts as her husband's "pet" and lives her life "so uselessly" (536). Finally, Australians' passiveness culminates in Hissao's human emporium. As they do not care about the American capital draining up the country's resources, they pay no heed to Hissao's torment or the golden-shouldered parrot and do not mind who is running the emporium, whether it be Americans or Japanese. All that they are preoccupied with is a comfy life right under their eyes, and they are not willing to take any adventure to stake it. Australians' passiveness can be best embodied in these imprisoned men and women. They are content with

> being fed and paid well... they do not act like caged people... move and talk naturally within the confines of the space. They go about their business, their sand paintings, their circumcision of ceremonies, their strikes, settlements, discussions about national anthems, arguing about "Waltzing Matilda" and "Advance Australian fair"... of course there are disagreements, fights, but no one objects. (599)

Hissao imprisons his countrymen and women out of his hatred towards their passivity, and according to Herbert's narrative, this hatred is "intelligent and necessary" (600). Passiveness is considered as "something dangerous" (595), and an ill that stops people from achieving a happy and meaningful existence and hinders a society from its multi-dimensionality. It is brought under brutal attack through the emporium fable.

To sum it up, Peter Carey reconstructs Australia's cultural memory of the twentieth century to invent its nationalist tradition through the Badgery family's utopian dreams. Carey's retrieval of the past creates a space where Australians are able to re-imagine the tradition of nationalism and mourn their compromised dream of gaining genuine independence and creating a respectable identity. It is also infused with the author's criticism of the passivity of his counpatriots as well as his hope that they overcome this social ill to seek a happier and freer existence through transformation. Apart from this nationalist aspect of Australia's collective memory, the long-denied characteristic of multi-culture is also what the author concerns himself with in this family saga.

2.1.4 Multi-cultural Genes

Jan Assmann argues that cultural memory includes those "remote, marginalized and exiled memories" (阿斯曼, 2016: 26) when compared with communicative memory. It includes those "non-instrumental, heretical, destructive and denied memory" (ibid.) when compared with collective or bonding memory. Herbert's reminiscence of his family story not only pulls out the lies and fantasies imprinted in Australia's collective identity, it also brings to the public the hastily repressed or denied memory of its multiculturality that serves as the cornerstone of Australian cultural identity. The official memory that records Australian culture as a culture of the white Europeans initiated by the landing of Captain Cook and his crew is solely part of the picture of the nation's cultural mosaic. In order to form a pretentiously consistent white identity, either the much more ancient indigenous culture or other minority cultures have long been denied by and excluded from Australian memory book. However, that does not mean they do not exist. They are just sealed in storage memory serving as the background of the White's memory performing on the stage. Now, these memories are retrieved and reconstructed in this fiction to claim their rights.

The first indisputable fact contributing to Australian multiculturality that Peter Carey aims to uncover in *Illywhacker* is Australian indigenous culture. He does this by disclosing who the genuine owner of this southern land is through Leah Goldstein's counter-narrative and Herbert's reflection. When arrogant Herbert hops up and down with his ambition to build a house on this "public land" (307) wherever he goes, Leah unmasks his false fantasy by exposing that "[T]he land is stolen. The whole country is stolen. The whole nation is based on a lie which was that the land was not already occupied before the British came here. If it's anybody's place, it is the blacks" (ibid.). She even makes this situation into quite a ludicrous analogy that Herbert sleeps with her once does not mean he owns her. Here, Leah suggests that the first culture that flourishes on this land is supposed to be that of the aborigines instead of the white Europeans and that the White appropriation of this land does not guarantee that they obtain a genuine sense of belonging. This is echoed in Herbert's confession that "I admitted I could not read and the landscape, had indeed, always seemed alien to me, that it made me, in many lights, melancholy and homesick for something else, that I preferred a small window in a house" (308). When Herbert and his family, as well as Leah, transfer from city to city and town to town to give circus performances to earn a living during the Depression, metaphorically, it is the feeling of cultural rootlessness that keeps displacing them. White people come to this land quite lately, and they change its landscape at their own will and claim to be the master of it. They "cut the arteries of an ancient culture" (553), the indigenous one that the land is born with, to establish their own culture.

It is worth noting that Carey is less progressive in representing Australian indigenous issues in *Illywhacker*. He has done nothing more than deconstruct Australian historiography as involving lies about its origin myth and suggesting that the denial of the aboriginal history problematizes the creation of Australian identity. Aborigines remain the silent Other and have not been given a voice to their sufferings or traditions to make them substantial beings. The issue is resisted and better dealt with in his later works, *Oscar and Lucinda* and *A Long Way from Home*. Australian aborigines are given a voice to gaze upon and accuse the Whites of having appropriated their land, damaged the environment, and slaughtered their folks in the former one. Their rituals and poor living conditions are further narrated in the later one.

Another significant aspect of Australian multicultural ecology represented in this fiction is the Chinese element. According to Australian historiography, the first ship of around one hundred Chinese arrived at the Sydney harbour in 1848, though some historians conjecture that the Chinese constituted one of the colonizing powers of the islands in the south seas in around the fourteenth century. (Clark, 1968: 7) Chinese Australians have made a noticeable contribution to the country's economic development and cultural ecology. However, they have been stigmatized and marginalized in Australian history and mostly silenced or misrepresented in literary works. They have been made "scapegoats", and the gazed Other by European Australians define partly who they are. (欧阳昱, 2000: 5) Chinese elements have been one of Carey's concerns in either his short stories and most prose fiction, though his representation of them is complicated. Chinese labourers are ignorable contributors to Australian modernization in *American Dreams*. However, the Chinese are associated with Communists in *Bliss*. Among his novels, *Illywhacker* has drawn the most literary attention to the Chinese element in Australian culture.

Through Herbert's reminiscence, Carey first reconstructs how Chinese Australians have been stereotyped as the Yellow Peril and lesser beings by their white folks. Herbert's father imagines himself to be a superior Englishman and shows great hostility towards other minority groups, especially Chinese. He despises them as "Chinaman" and paints pictures of their extreme "depravity" to warn his children against their "threat" (39). He never associates with any Chinese but keeps telling his children that they are barbarians who are addicted to "opium" and "ate the hands of Christian babies" (209). He indoctrinates this stereotype into his children to incite their horror and enmity towards them. Herbert's family story suggests the constructiveness, even falsehood, of memory in light of the formation of certain family traditions. Since family traditions circulate among its members to maintain cohesion, the father's understanding of life is inherited by his sons and continues to exert an impact on his grandsons. As a result, when Herbert "met my first Chinaman I expected him to kill me" (ibid.). When Herbert suggests Jack that they seek help from a Chinaman regarding the manufacture of aeroplane wheels since the Chinese are the inventors of this gadget, he does not believe that they are the intelligent type, saying, "[H]e'd be watching the snakes wheeling past and never give them a thought except eating them for his dinner. It was a wasted opportunity" (55).

Furthermore, Chinese Australians are given a voice to complain about how they have been exploited, squeezed and attacked in society. Gong Tse Ying recalls how the Chinese have plough industriously for generations on this land but suffered from horrible strikes in the anti-Chinese riots at Lambing Flat:

> They did not like the Chinese, little Englishman, because we were clever. They sold us their old mines. They thought they would cheat us, but we made money. They drew a line across the diggings and said that we must not cross it. Still we make money. We worked hard, even us children. My father was sick. He had ulcers on his feet, and still he worked. My mother worked too, alongside the men. Her feet had been bound. They were tiny pretty things, but she carried rocks in baskets and helped make the big water race. But the Englishmen thought it was all their country and all their gold and they played their band and came out to get us. They drove the Chinese down to the river bank. They had axe handles and picks. They ran over my uncle Han in a cart and broke his leg and they broke my father's head open with a water pipe. (215)

They protest the injustice white Australians have inflicted on them by writing to the legislature respectfully to claim their right to live undisturbed and to be treated fairly since they "work hard and mean no harm" (210). However, are not listened to and spared no torment from violent confrontations happening consecutively in the late nineteenth century in the gold fields in Hanging Rock (1832), Bendigo (1854), Buckland River (1857), or Lambing Flat (1861). There is no exception for Herbert, who has been brought up by Gong, that has given him much more paternal love than his biological father. He is a sympathizer of the Chinese. Still, he is ungrateful towards them. When he returns to Gong for the trick of recovering his daughter Sonia, who has disappeared owing to his abuse of "making a dragon", meaning "disappearing", and is told there is no remedy for his loss, he starts a fight, tears one of Gong's fingers off, takes it back and preserves it in a Vegemite jar.

According to Herbert's recollection, even in the mid-twentieth century, the twenty-two years old Mr. Henry Lo, a marine architect, has to seek refuge in Charles's pet shop to avoid being repatriated back to China, where the Australian government thinks he should belong. It does "not wish him to stay" owing to "the colour of Mr. Lo's skin and the shape of his eyes" (502). Though longing to walk the streets of Sydney as a free man, the predictable prospect of questioning, exportation, gaol sentence or even exile timidities him into being locked in one of Charles' cages. Even though Chinese Australians prove themselves to be even more civilized than the white ones and some of them, like Mr. Lo or Gong, have integrated themselves into the society, "had grandchildren with names like Heather and Walter... ate chips and sausages, roast beef on Sundays" (210) and even earned high social status, their skin colour might get on the white's nerves, stirring their fear and hate, at any minute. The White's xenophobia and ferocity have severely traumatized the kind and innocent Chinese, as the Englishmen's roaring bellow of "[R]oll up, kill John Chinaman" (ibid.) inhabits Gong's mind and keeps haunting him for his lifetime. The overwhelming terror he acquires in the violence teaches him the trick of "making a dragon", which is actually a PTSD (Post-Traumatic Stress Disorder), and he learns to "stand in such a manner as to be invisible" (188) to escape being mentally disturbed from that horrifying sensation.

Most of all, Carey's reconstruction destigmatizes Chinese Australians, enchanting them and recognizing the positive part that the Chinese element has played in enriching Australian culture through Herbert's counter-memory. According to Maurice Halbwachs, what family memory usually presents to us is typically "a reconstructed picture" (1992: 60). It is never static and evolves with the changing of the living environment of the family members. "We change memories along with our points of view, our principles, and our judgments when we pass from one group to the other"(Halbwachs, 1992: 81). When Herbert leaves his family at ten years old, allowing himself to be self-orphaned and suffer from starvation and finally ends up being adopted by a Chinese family, his memory of Chinese shows totally another picture.

Adopted by GongTse Ying, Herbert gets acquainted with Chinese people from various walks of life, such as herbalists whose "patients are all English gentlemen and ladies" (213), fortune-tellers, and businessmen. Family memory is "a dynamic, context-dependent construction that can change considerably over time as well as according to different settings and audiences" (Erll, 2011: 313). Since Herbert joined Gong's family, he has naturally inherited the memory of the Chinese family and its community. In his recollection, the Chinese "were nervous, polite and law-abiding" (209). Mr Lo is "nothing but a gentleman. Every evening he lowered the pink Venetian blinds so the ladies could undress in privacy, and he would inquire of them, with a small cough, before raising them each morning" (504). At Wong's house, he first sees in his piles of books the "neat rows of Chinese characters and Arabic figures" (211) and sees "children treated kindly, touched, petted and embraced so readily" (212). Though the English have treated them with hostility and caused them enormous suffering, Gong is hospitable to this little Englishman. He feeds him, lodges him and clothes him. For Herbert, Gong "had been kind to me as a father meant to kind to a son" (371), and he gets as much dotage from him as any child can get from his father, and he receives much hospitality in the Chinese community, too. In Herbert's memory, "[T]here is no kinder soul on earth than the Chinaman" (55). Gong does this out of his sympathy for orphaned Herbert because he "was once an orphan too" (211) and to show he is "not a barbarian like them (white Australians)" (212). Not only does the Chinese family provide him with everyday care and love, but it also passes on to him its traditions. Gong teaches him "how to skin a crow by blowing air into it with a bamboo ... how to fight with your feet... how to use garlic and ginger to remove pains from the head... to read and write... history and geography... everything" (211). Herbert admits that he "made use of all the things" (221) he learns from Gong in his subsequent life, which means he inherits the traditions of the Chinese family.

As Herbert's foster father, Gong is used by the author as a metaphor to show that the Chinese elements are an integral part of Australian culture and Australians have, to some extent, benefited from it. Herbert, as a production of a hybrid culture, is made another metaphor for Australian culture, which is characterized by its hybridity instead of the white's solo. Carey's representation of the Chinese elements in Australian culture is the embodiment of his intercultural conception. Australian culture and the Chinese elements, with proper communication and dialogues, can be perfectly fused to establish a symbiotic cultural ecology to nurture its people.

Peter Carey reconstructs Australia's Chinese memory in *Illywhacker* to perform multiple tasks. In the first place, the retrieved memory serves as an intertext to contradict and supplement Australian historical or cultural texts that banish or stigmatize Chinese. This intertextuality between literature and history, apart from showing the dubious relationship between historical writing and the material world it claims to signify, leads to the teetering or toppling of Australian official memory interweaved with discourse power. When Herbert reminds Jack that "by the time we arrived, we had the wheels ourselves, and gunpowder too" (55), Herbert alludes to the archaeological conjecture that Chinese people might have arrived in this land even earlier than the white Europeans. This problematizes the universal claim that Englishmen "discover" the land first and further delegitimizes their charismatic right to record its history or eradicate the existence of other races. Herbert's reminiscence of his foster father, the dignified and versatile Gong, and his genial and hardworking family and neighbours, as well as, in Leah's eyes, the "intelligent, understanding and diligent" (509) Mr. Lo, counters the prevailing stereotype blemishing Chinese. It further dismantles the foundation on which white Australians discriminate, resent, strike, dispel or kill them. By delegitimizing official memory which victimizes or excludes Chinese Australians in history, Herbert's family memory is recollected here to claim its deserved place in Australian traditions. Carey establishes, with his text, a monument to commemorate the Chinese traditions fused into Australian culture.

The author does not content himself with just exhibiting Chinese tradition as one of the elements composing an Australian multi-cultural mosaic. Under the political and social backdrop of Australia's increasing inclination to the Asian-axis as the remedy for its cultural identity, he furthers his poetic exploration of the impact that Chinese traditions have exerted on Australian culture. As Woodcock argues, Badgery's birth-father is a representation of Australia's ambivalent relationship to its British heritage in the nineteenth century, and Goon can be viewed as a representation of the equally ambivalent relationship of "white" Australia to its (much closer) Pacific neighbours in the twentieth century. (1996: 67) When Herbert admits having learned from his Chinese foster father "how to appear bigger or smaller, how to skin a crow, butcher a pig, wear expensive shoes when my suites is inferior, how to change my accent, how to modulate my walk" (221), the author indicates how Australian culture is enriched with the Chinese element and the magnificence of interculturality. This Chinese flavour is unravelled metaphorically to the most extraordinary profundity in Herbert's "bow-legs", which he contends comes from Goon's family out of "heredity" (188), and his trick of making a dragon taught by Gong, which figuratively means to bluff or tell a lie. When Herbert attributes his bow-legs combined with his compulsive, inborn liar genius to his Chinese foster father, the author points to the Chinese genes that breed Australian culture.

However, either the deconstruction of or the attack on the standardized memory, which stigmatizes or forgets the indigenous culture or the Chinese element, is unimaginable or naive for a white male author if he halts on the deconstructing or criticizing per se. As a matter of fact, it serves a more significant and more meaningful purpose to concrete Australia's multicultural identity. A bold conjecture coming from Herbert's family memory is that what problematizes Australia's cultural and national identity partially is its refusing to accept the hard truth that it is more closely connected to the peoples they despised, like the aborigines and the Chinamen, and their culture than they can imagine. European Australians have been reluctant to face the reality that the so-called "their" land actually belongs to the "little blacks" and they are the appropriators instead of original owners. They would not like to face the fact that the Chinese might have arrived earlier and that they have laboured on and contributed to this land ardently long enough to deserve a respectable place in its collective memory. Australians are told to forget the "stained" part of history, which plays a crucial role in defining where they stand. As Peter Conrad points out, "Australia is a tragic country. Its valour and virtue is its refusal to see itself that way" (Hassall, 1994: 127). Deliberate repression, even banishment of the ethnic minorities' memories, fails to stop the blood flow of the aborigines and Chinese in the veins of this land. On the contrary, the oppressed ghosts of the past frequently resurge to claim their rights. They keep bubbling up to haunt the subject, causing conflicts and even crises to its cognitive system and consequently impeding its construction of consistent identity.

The message sent here is that Australia should make peace with own past, acknowledge the "imperfections", if they are called, in its culture, and re-create a multi-cultural identify to cradle the restless souls of its people who have long been afflicted by identity anxiety and denied a proper sense of belonging. This poetic solution can lend support from Hegel, who argues that one can achieve freedom in history by "interiorizing and transcending trauma", and Freud, who contends that memory can be used to emancipate oneself by "acknowledging the scars of one's history" (Klein, 2000: 141). Not only does Carey trace his nation's multi-cultural tradition back to the nineteenth century and more previous ages to recommend Australia face up to reality to resolve identity anxiety and construct a consistent self-image, but he also travels back to the memory tunnel to explore the haunting sense of entrapment that keeps disturbing his fellow citizens.

2.1.5　Nation in Gaol

It is known to us all that Australia is initially "settled as die jail of infinite space" (Hughes, 2003: 396), which sets the tone that the mainstream white Australians have to live with a traumatizing convict memory that entraps them all their life if they do not strive to emancipate this historical legacy. As Bruce Woodcock observes, "the gaol imagery becomes expressive of the state of contemporary Australian society, trapped by history, imprisoned in its self-created present, caught by these legacies in the future" (1996: 67). It seems that for Australians, to quote Patrick White, "[A]ny manner of life is led in the cage, to pursue another is as far as I can see, merely to exchange the cage" (Hassall, 1994: 82). As a realm of cultural memory, especially those repressed and marginalized ones, literature makes itself a natural habitat of Australian captivity tradition. As Graeme Turner concludes after his delineation of Australian National Fictions, "imprisonment, convictism… provides us with a central paradigm for the depiction of the self in Australian narrative" (1986: 60).

As an author who is fed on Australian culture and assumes the mission to rediscover or invent the nation, Carey is obsessed with the prison image as one of the major motifs in his works. Peter Pierce points out that Carey concerns himself with the "investigation of kinds of captivity and escape" (2004: 72) throughout his writing career. "How do you reckon that affects you?" (342) This rhetorical question Herbert asks his son suggests how much the prison imagery stirs the author as well as his countrymen who live with this disciplinary heritage. As far as Peter Carey is concerned, the sense of entrapment has been imprinted into

Australians' flesh and bone and runs through their veins. This connection is emblemized in the bricks that Herbert uses to build his house: the die thumbprints of the convicts who manufactured them are inscribed in the bricks.

Previously, Anthony Hassall has discussed from the aesthetic perspective and points out the "prison house" (1994: 82) of narrative in which Herbert, the omniscient narrator, gaols all his characters. However, the prison image is not just poetic trickery but more of the author's thematic preoccupation. In *Illywhacker*, it serves as a thread to piece together the three sections of the fiction, each of which ends up with one form of prison or another. Book one wraps up with Phoebe's king parrot's cage built by Herbert; Book two ends up with Herbert's being imprisoned in Rankin Downs; and eventually, Book three closes with the most important emblem of imprisonment, the pet emporium. In a more detailed sense, approximately the whole list of characters of the novel is kept as prisoners, literally or figuratively, in one way or another, either by themselves or by the people they love or care. Since "[I]deas must take on a form that is imaginable before they can find their way into memory" (Assmann, 2011: 24), the gaol imagery of the novel is emblematized in the "memory figure" of the pet shop, which is given substance through its reference to Australia as a penal colony. Through the memory figure of the emporium, the author revives Australia's convict memory, which entails Australians' inveterate sense of entrapment and pins his different layers of intentions on it.

The pet emporium as a climatic symbol of the prison image includes two connotations Carey intends to convey. To begin with, it alludes to the emotional paradox of love and bondage. The pet shop initially takes its form from Charles' affection for his wife, Emma. To exhibit their token of love, the goanna, Charles builds Emma a cage to keep it. For

Emma, the caged goanna is a reminder of love and protection from her husband. When learning about Charles' unsuccessful enlisting in the army, traumatized Emma retreats into the goanna's cage, dinning and sharing a bed with the creature, and refuses to come out thereafter. This creature usurps all the care, company, and affection she is capable to offer to her husband and children. It even becomes a tool with which she inflicts sexual torture on Charles. Apparently, on the one hand, Emma's love for Charles and the intense insecurity coming from the probability of losing him has rendered her a prisoner. On the other hand, by turning herself into a caged pet animal with which her husband is fascinated, she gets command of all of Charles' attention. This can be best illustrated in Leah's complaint, "she is a great courtesan. She is not the most beautiful woman in the world. She is not endowed with intelligence. However, her ambitions are quite extraordinary — nothing less than to be adored and worshipped. She is a great artist. Her husband can think of nothing else but to love her" (536). Charles's ardent affection for his wife yields him to her clutches and turns himself into her prisoner.

The same curse occurs when Charles and Hissao try to express their love for their country. Charles attempts to stop Australia from grovelling to the imperial powers and make it matter in the world. However, his enthusiasm evolves into the pet shop that keeps what is best in the country in captivity and changes them into cheap commodities consumed mainly by the new Empire. Moreover, in order to attract investment in his business to resume his national dream, Charles has to allow himself to be led by the nose, turning himself into a slave of American capitalism. As Leah observes, it gradually ends up with "American takeovers of Australian industry" (583). Suffice it to say, Charles is ultimately not so much killed by his wife's insanity as by his guilt that the flourishment of his business has gone against his original patriotic intention and caused detrimental destruction to his beloved nation. It is not exaggerating to conclude that his love for his country and his wife costs him his life. Resolving to dedicate himself to Australian architecture and saving the golden-shouldered parrots from extinction, Hissao is even more equipped with patriotic sentiment and national awareness than his father or grandfather. However, when the parrot dies, mainly owing to the indifference of his folks, he is like a prisoner brought to display in public who becomes the target of enormous blame. His passionate love for his country is then turned into immeasurable hate and revenge for his fellow citizens, who are apathetic to his patriotic move and capable of nothing but nagging and whining. Finally, his affection "changes his natural form" (595) and converts into a prison house to keep his ambition as well as what he originally loves and strives for in captivity. Love turns out to be the shackles to yoke those who are infatuated. It is a universal paradox confusing all human beings. It is more of a dilemma that keeps disturbing contemporary Australians. They harbour such an ardent love for their home country that they are ready to share its weal and woe. However, their fates are so entangled with that of their country that its haunted ignoble past also entraps them tightly like a halo. The prison image is parodied here in allusion to the predicament shared by all Australians, at home and abroad. Moreover, the shared captivity memory is recalled to fulfil the functions of confirming Australians' collective identity, healing and criticizing the multinational capitalism.

Cliff Lobe points out the "Pet Shop itself — an analogy for Australia's international identity" (2000: 144). As a matter of fact, Peter Carey's reconfiguration of the prison memory hints at the critical dimension composing Australian identity — the sense of imprisonment. He makes it evident that being entrapped is the everyday living condition of contemporary Australians, which they are unable to escape from. As

Leah Goldstein reflects, "I want myself to be good and kind, and I made myself a slave instead" (359). It is also Peter Carey's muse: "I begin with the image of my country as a pet shop, people living in the cages, being well-fed, thinking they are happy, but denying the nature of their prison" (Willbanks, 1992: 49). Though the author has not given Australians a prescription as to how to break free from this entrapment in *Illywhacker* yet, he does create a common textual space in which the implied readers[①], regardless of their distances and social ranks, are able to concrete their singular identity, unite with each other and share the therapeutic power of the author's narrative. Since "nation-ness is assimilated to skin-colour, gender, parentage and birth-era — all those things one can not help" (Anderson, 2006: 141), people wholly unknown to each other use the convict brand to confirm that they belong to the same imagined community in the textural space. Apart from that, since the negative identification is externalized through Carey's narrative and brought from their repressed unconsciousness to the public space, the implied readers, wherever they are, share the "experience of simultaneity" (ibid: 145) provided by their reading experience. While sharing the moment of simultaneity with their imagined compatriots, they enjoy temporal, spiritual freedom, are relieved from the historical burden and, to some extent, are cured of the devastating anxiety and grief. They become the strong ones who "misprise and thereby free ourselves of our pasts in order to clear imaginative space for a present which is truly our own and our masterpiece" (53). Peter Carey returns to this motif and digs much more profound in *Jack Maggs*, in which he emancipates Australians by exonerating their convict ancestors.

---

① "The implied reader" is Wolfgang Iser's coinage. He is not the real reader but a "construct" who embodies all those predispositions necessary for a literary work to exercise its effect; this concept is a "textual structure anticipating the presence of a recipient" and "designates a network of response-inviting structures". (1980: 25)

Moreover, the pet emporium is made by the author a political allegory. It parodies the prison image to allude to the lurking political hazard of multinational capitalism in "the ear of global capitalism" (Zizek[2], 2006: 170). For this conception, I am indebted to Bruce Woodcock who has pointed out that the whole pet shop thing "is a brilliant and savage expose of contemporary corporate capitalism, how its disinformation is willingly accepted by a subject population coerced through what Noam Chomsky terms the manufacture of consent" (1996: 69-70). The pet shop is set up with Charles' nationalist intention to exhibit the singularity and beauty of Australia, however, his lack of business gifts renders it at the edge of bankruptcy. His American partners save him with their money, and, in exchange, large amounts of endangered animals and birds are shipped out of Australia, and his business partners accuse Charles himself of smuggling. Hissao sells his teetering family business to the Japanese to keep it alive, nevertheless, the capital flooding in deprives the architect of any Australian flavour and throws all his fellow folks into cages. Through the emblem of the emporium, it is not hard to infer that Peter Carey lets his anxiety over multinational capitalism walk around.

With capitalism evolving to the internationalist phase, the conventional opposition between metropolis and colonized countries disappears. What accompanies international trade emerges the new type of colonization, the "auto-colonization" (Zizek[2], 2006: 170), in which the global corporation replaces the Nation-State as the colonizing power to subordinate and exploit (economically, politically, and culturally) the colonized country directly. In the long term, as is predicted by Slavoj Zizek, "we shall all not only wear Banana Republic shirts, but also live in banana republics" (ibid.: 170). Though multinational capitalism is not the focus of *Illywhacker*, the author does prophesy that there will be "interesting times ahead" (600) at the end of the fiction. He returns to this issue with a much more profound and powerful exploration in his *Amnesia* (2014), in which he fictionalizes the sadly "interesting time" when multinational capitalism buys its way to Australian "state apparatuses and other forms of social and economic control and regulation" (Zizek[1], 2006: 375) only to jeopardize the country's political and democratic ecology, cause detriment to Australians' liberty and even claim innocent lives.

The emporium, which was first funded by the United States and then taken over by Japanese capitalism, is also the fable that Australians' passivity aids and abets new colonizing powers to take control over their culture and freedom, rendering them gaoled yet homeless. As Cliff Lobe argues, "*Illywhacker* is a novelistic record of an Australian memory disturbance — one in which convicts and capitalists play inter-connected roles" (2000: 143). The multinational capitalism encourages "[T]he colonial mentality to serve overseas interests" (Pilger, 1990: 345). Moreover, Australia will never break free from the fetters enforced on them, even in the neo-colonial era, as long as it prevails. In this sense, the gaol memory embodied in the emporium is also reconstructed for a critical evaluation, and the criticism is directed at Australians' convict mentality, which partly results from the ignoble memory. As Herbert comments in *Illywhacker*, the whole function of the pet shop

> was entrapment and its inhabitants could happily while away afternoons and years without any bigger scheme, listening to the races on the radio, reaching out for another oyster, worrying only that the beer glasses were free of detergent and kept, cold and frosted, in die fridge. They discussed the quality of harbour prawns, got drunk, and crunched the prawns' heads, imagining themselves free and happy while all the time they were servants of

die building. It made them behave in disgusting ways. (581)

This passive mentality diminishes and even eradicates people's willpower to live with sovereignty, converting them into one-dimensional men who yoke themselves in the intangible prison house to embrace the discipline of global capitalism unconsciously and venture nothing meaningful. As observed by Herbert, they imagine themselves "free and happy" while the truth is, all the time, they are "servants of the building" (581), which was built by an internationalist capital. In addition, this haunting memory compromises Australians' cultural confidence, that's why "[A] lot of Australians still see culture as something other people have. They don't consider themselves as 'cultured' types" (Burgmann & Lee, 1988: xi).

Peter Carey retrieves in *Illywhacker* Australia's cultural memories of its institutional lies, nationalism, multicultural ecology and the sense of imprisonment by way of Herbert's family memory. The author's engineering functions primarily to concrete Australian national and cultural identity through delegitimizing the official memory filled with lies. And it hampers Australia and Australians from creating a consistent identity. Then, it invents the nationalist tradition, heals Australians who are burdened by historical legacy and criticizes their passivity and xenophobia, which jeopardize Australia's maturation and independence. Carey is resolute and daring in exposing the problems lurking in the recesses of Australia's cultural memory. However, he does so more with a swelling resentment than with ready prescriptions for those problems. He also appears more pessimistic at this stage of his writing career. However, the author grows more progressive and optimistic in *A Long Way from Home*, in which he returns to Australia's problematic cultural identity with a solution. Australia's aboriginal memory is recollected not just to accuse the government's racist ethnic policy and establish a monument to the indigenous peoples but also to recommend a negotiation between Australian Whites and aboriginals.

2.2 Aborigines Remembered as Victims of European Australians' Racism: *A Long Way from Home*

The aborigines and aboriginal tradition have always been one of the two polarities that define Australia's national and cultural identity, the other being the Great Britain and the British tradition. That is why the indigenous issue has also been a recurrent motif in Peter Carey's fiction and non-fiction as well. The interaction between Australia's European tradition and its more ancient aboriginal culture has always been the core of his preoccupation. Unlike a comparatively brief and powerless reference to the downtrodden aborigines and the indigenous culture in *Oscar and Lucinda*, or later a more detailed recount in 30 *Days in Sydney: A Widely Distorted Account*, he brings the aboriginal memory to the centre of stage in *A Long Way from Home*. This section will be devoted to the examination of how Australian indigenous peoples are remembered as innocent victims of the White's unreasonable pursuit of racial purity and fear for cultural hybridity and the multiple functions that the author intends his reconfiguration to perform. Aborigines are given a voice to recount the suffering inflicted upon them by the government's White Australia policy. Their memory is restored by the author to monument the aborigines whose lands have been appropriated and whose families have been slaughtered. It is also recollected to accuse the government's racist ethnic policy and warn it against racial violence. In addition, Carey's retrieval of the aboriginal memory further serves as a starting point for his poetic exploration of the negotiation between Australians Whites and the aborigines and how the latter realize their salvation. By acknowledging the aboriginal memory as part of Australia's collective memory through negotiation, the Whites are able to atone for their sins, and the aborigines can feel a bit soothed. For the author, the only way the indigenous peoples can achieve salvation is to preserve their cultural memory. In a larger picture, through his poetic reconstruction, the author builds Australia a benign and symbiotic cultural ecology.

2.2.1 Preliminaries of the Fiction

Published in 2017, *A Long Way from Home* is another commercial success, riding into one of London's bestsellers, with a "50,000-copy first printing" (2018: 35), according to *Evening Standard*. The fiction has received very positive reviews, too. It tells the story of a short-statured Australian young couple, Irene and Titch Bobs, who take part in the gruelling 1954 Redex Trial, a contest of automobiles, in order to secure a dealership of Holden, the only Australian motor competing in the market with Ford. Along with them is their navigator, Willie Bachhuber, a history teacher, or in his own words, "a chalk-and-talker" (Carey, 2017: 9)[①] who is good at making maps and a radio quiz show whiz. As an endurance rather than a sheer speed car race, the round-Australia Redex Trial covers approximately 10,000 miles of the continent's landscape, and contestants have to drive mostly through the wilderness, field and stream to test the reliability of their cars. That makes the contest a journey through the outback of Australia, which revives the nation's collective memory of its contact with races other than the white, especially the aborigines. Most reviewers share this perspective. Connie Rockman comments that for the three protagonists, this test of endurance is more like a "journey into the heart of Australia's dark history, the treatment of

---

[①] The following quotations from *A Long Way from Home* in this section are annotated with only the page number.

its indigenous population" (2018: 114). Patrick Flanery regards this fiction a "merciless excavation of Australian history", and it "relentlessly skewers the government's racial policies towards Aborigines" (2018: 1). The *New Yorker* reviews that what lurks beneath the hero and heroine's rambunctious adventure is a "potent exploration of racial identity" (2018: 91). Hal Jensen points out Peter Carey's revisionist perspective of history embodied in this novel, arguing that he "remaps the story of Australia" (2018: 21). Erica Wagner also argues that "[T] his death-haunted history, always known yet unacknowledged, is the burden of the book" (2018: 47). Alexander Moran further contends that Peter Carey this time delves further into his "career-long fascination with the dark underbelly of Australian history powerful, pertinent exploration of race and national identity" (2017: 32).

The fiction is divided unevenly into five parts roughly based on the driving route of the Redex Trial, each consisting of twenty-three, seven, seven, three and twenty-one chapters, respectively. Most of the chapters are narrated alternatively by Irene and Bachhuber. Teeny Irene's initiative matrimony with her five-foot tree husband, Titch Bobs, wins neither her family's nor his father-in-law, Dangerous Dan Bobs' favour. But she has a prodigious will and is even more fascinated with the intoxication behind the wheel than her husband, the best car salesman in southern Australia. To help him secure a Ford car dealership and get away from his father's bullying, she moves with her husband and their children, Edith and Ronnie, to Bacchus Marsh, a small and tranquil southern Australian town neighbouring Willie Bachhuber. The first part of the fiction relates the Bobbseys' struggling yet blissful life as well as Willie's traumatic and chaotic one. Since Titch's initial dream to obtain the qualification to deal in Ford Motors is spoiled by his father, he is forced to gamble his future by participating in the Redex Trial with his wife to secure a Holden dealership instead. Hiding himself in Bacchus Marsh, Willie has been haunted by the nightmare that his wife has cheated on him since she gave birth to a black child while both of them are decedents of white Europeans. To add fuel to flames, the school suspend him for suspending a troublesome black student out of his window and then loses his championship of the Deasy's quiz show to Cloverdale out of gullibility. Amazed by his encyclopedic mastery of Australian historical and geographical knowledge, the diminutive couple decided to recruit him as their navigator. With their Holden of Redex number 92, this team of three is more than ready to embark on a trip throughout the vast wilderness of Australia, competing with Dan Bobs who drives a Ford and others.

As their car drives from Sydney to Townsville, through the Top End, and then from Darwin to Broome in the ensuing three parts, what unfolds in Irene and Willie's alternative narratives are Australia's peculiarly savage landscapes, as well as the horrible things that had happened there dozens of decades ago, for instance, the dispersion and slaughter of the aboriginal inhabitants in Horror Stretch, the violent anti-Chinese riots in Lambing Flat etc. One of the significant threads in the remaining parts is Irene's discovery of a graveyard of dead bones at a creek when she gets off to the bush to answer the nature call. She assumes the bones are the blacks'. She picks up a child's skull, puts it gently into a box and intends to turn it to the police with the hope that they will investigate the possible murder.

The last part of the novel is about two detours that culminate in the central motif of the fiction. Dropped off by Titch for the rumours that he might be a black and is involved in ignoble child-rearing issues, Willie finds himself marooned mysteriously in an aboriginal community where his biological relatives inhabit. He learns from them the secret of his birth and is revealed the truth of his abandoned black boy. He is a half-caste who happens to have lighter skin and one of the numerous victims of the White Australia Policy who is stolen from his aboriginal mother to be raised and educated in a European family. This part relates to the fierce conflict between whitened Willie and his aboriginal ancestors. He tries to flee but remains captivated and ends up spending the rest of his life in the community, teaching the children and dissertating the aboriginal culture. From the focalizations of Willie, Irene and other aboriginal folks, this part also presents the far-reaching aftermath of that policy into the 1950s, the lingering discrimination against the population with darker skin and hostile educational programs threatening to assimilate them and wipe out their culture. Irene's detour takes her to the police station, to the house of Willie's adopted parents, Mr. and Mrs. Laski, where she is informed of the truth of Willie's birth as well as his son, and then to Willie's son Neil. The last chapter of this part, as well as of the whole book, is told through Neil's voice to relate his brand new life and career, his once-in-a-blue-moon meeting with his biological father Willie under the arrangement of Irene, as well as his regular yet aloof correspondence with him.

A Long Way from Home qualifies as a neo-historical fiction in that it revisits Australia's colonial as well as nationalist history with the aim of reappraising its relationship with its old culture. Like the other texts of this genre discussed in previous chapters, this fiction also demonstrates the paradox of creating verisimilitude and revealing its status as an artefact. This contradiction can be best glimpsed from Neil's observation of his father's predicament in which he must "record the truth and keep the secret" (381). To begin with, the illusion of authenticity is produced in multiple manners. For one thing, Carey gives readers an incentive to identify the story with certain specific historical moments by his mimesis of the experiential world. The main story is set in a viral Australian public event — the 1954 Redex Trial and it precedes in an inventory of actual localities along the route, like Townsville, Darwin, Broome etc., apart from the lengthy preparation for the competition in the actual town of Bacchus Marsh where Peter Carey was born. Even the Holden, the protagonists drive for the contest, and the burned and abandoned Peugeot, which Willie has his folks repair and later tries to flee the aboriginal community with, are also the real car models used in the trial. More importantly, in the narrative detours, he makes direct references to historical events like the Lambing Flat Riots and the White Australia Policy. For another, Carey further mesmerizes readers with the sense of authenticity in the paratext of his *Acknowledgements* by revealing his reliance on aboriginal researcher Steve Kinnane, history scholars Georgine Clarsen and Hal Moloney, who write widely about the Redex Trial and Adelaide historian Tom Gara for "perfect source" (384) of relevant history involved this fiction. When it comes to the part of Captain Cook and the enigma of Willie's birth, Carey recurs to the oral history told by the survivors of the massacre and witnesses to the tragedy to enhance its credibility, giving the impression that the narrators are just dealing with the "carcass of his history" (338), "inheriting the story" (299) from his ancestors, and passing it down from generation to generation. Readers are further assured of the author's discretion of his material with the textual information that Willie Bachhubber's enormous historical knowledge is gained from his work experience as the "assistant" of Sebastian, a "Map Librarian of State Library of Victoria" (145) and then his erudition of the Redex Trial comes from his research at "the library of Melbourne" (138).

Nevertheless, Carey is contradictorily obsessed even more with uncovering the self-consciousness of the novel, on the other hand, while creating the sense of truthfulness on the one hand. Though the bulk of ficiton does not attempt to spoil readers' immersion in the verisimilitude created within the text by exposing its metafictionality potently, the latter part of it does reveal its fictive status relentlessly. To begin with, Willie, the protagonist, tells readers at the beginning of the second part that his "role" is to "write away for my own copy of the Redex rule book" (166), which is a metaphoric way to say the author is writing the fiction dealing with a household issue from a somewhat different perspective. Then, in the frame structure, Neil, the third narrator of this novel, exposes first his own status as a storyteller, addressing the readers as "professor" (381), and similarly, the fictive role of his father, Willie Bachubber, the most prominent narrator. Naive Readers are disillusioned by Neil's narration that Bachubber is, in fact, "a writer so frequently cited and so constantly belittled" who "wrote regularly for *Walkabout* magazine", and that his habitual practice is "collecting stories, making his non-maps and diagrams" (378). As a matter of fact, Bachhuber is telling stories throughout the novel. This is rather apparent in the latter half of the fiction when Bachhuber is held in captivity in Quamby Downs by his tribespeople and fed with their stories. He then becomes the storyteller who would like to "save any kartiya readers the inconvenience of learning the convention of Aboriginal English" and tell "the guts of the story" (280) in standard Australian English. He also tells readers that he has his "pencil" and "began to write down my understanding of myself, and the sentences are tangled and knotted beyond correction" (283). Carey flaunts his fictive role even by having him occasionally interact with readers, brooding aloud over what might be on their mind, "[S]urely, you will ask, I must have expected that his injury would prevent him from performing his duty?" (303) or "[Y]ou can say I was stupid to leave early" (324).

In contrast, the artefact status of the novel is more suggestive in its first half. As an erudite history teacher and a quiz show champion, Bachhuber assumes the role of educating Australians on their history and geography in class as well as in the radio. Nevertheless, he revealed to Irene that he secured the championship because he is apt at telling his own version of Australian stories, the official version. Bachhuber is the thinly disguised Carey who is offering his readers an alternative version of Australian history, only that it is an anti-official version. Some of the "knowledge" he disseminates turns out to be false in actual life, which suggests the incredibility of documented history. For example, he is judged in the show to be correct in claiming that there is an inland sea on a "certain Maslen map" while the truth is "there were only blacks and desert" (116). Absurd enough, the inland sea "exists" solely "because the madman's map was in the State Library of Victoria" (ibid.). Here, the author alludes to the power structure involved in historiography.

The self-referential tendency of the novel is not only demonstrated by its frame narrators, but also suggested by its imbedded ones. When Charles Hobbs, one of the descendants of the survivors of the aboriginal genocide, retells his version of the story of Caption Cook to the tribe and Bachhuber, it takes the place of the original one that Bachhuber has learned from the official document and taught his pupils in Bacchus Marsh. Charles "had completely inscribed the entire saga on the wall" (339). To sum it up, *A Long Way from Home* is a story about writing or telling stories. Differentiating versions of them are competing on "whose life is the least believable" (309), but it is "no longer sure which was the official route" (183). It is the embodiment that historical truth is complicated and inaccessible. Whatever any party offers is just a version of truth from their own perspective. They "showed a route but nothing was so definite in life" (186). This philosophical outlook lays the foundation for Carey's reconstruction of Australia's memory of certain key historical issues. In Joshua Finnell's words, that is his "serious ambition" (2017: 86) invested in this fiction.

Through Irene and Willie's uncovering of painful personal histories along the way of the Redex Trial, Peter employs both the imbedded structure and the multi-voice narrative to recuperate Australia's memory of its forgotten peoples and communities, reappraising its ethnic culture from the nineteenth to the mid-twentieth century. Erica Wagner applauds that this fiction "marks Carey's recognition of Australia's colonial past" and calls it "a 20th-century reprisal of the notion of *terra nullius*" (2018: 47). Apart from a critical evaluation of Australia's former racial culture, *A Long Way from Home* also has implication for the country's current preoccupations. As *Kirkus Reviews* argues, it carries "a thoroughly contemporary charge". This insight stays consistent with Carey's aesthetic obsession and can be further justified by his proposition in an interview. "It's no good not engaging with something that you've been intrinsically involved in. You wake up in the morning and you are the beneficiary of a genocide. I'm an Australian writer and I haven't written about this? Well, that just seems pathetic to me" (Wagner, 2018: 47).

2.2.2 Victims of the White's Racism

As Irene, Titch and Willie drive Holden across the savage wilderness of the underbelly of Australia, Peter Carey invites readers to travel back with the protagonists to the darkest time in the country's history to unearth Australia's memory of its violent encounter with the indigenous peoples as well as other coloured races. Although white Australians are the latecomers and usurpers of the southern land, they assume themselves to be the natural centre of the Antipodes, alienate other peoples like the black and the yellow for fear of imaginary threat, and brutalize them as lesser beings. On this adopted land, white Australians' phobia of darker races has spawned the flowers of evil, which not only poison the bodies and souls of the coloured races but also problematize, mostly unconsciously, the mental wellbeing of the whites themselves. How white Australians' uncurbed fear for the coloured races turns out to be detrimental to the poor indigenous peoples is examined in the following paragraphs.

According to the cultural memory reconstructed by Peter Carey, white Europeans land on the Antipodes with an inborn arrogance and naturally a condescending attitude. They are intoxicated with the savage beauty of exotic land, covet its bountiful resources and regard the living creatures as lesser beings that they are entitled to conquer, use and abuse. To make his retrieval of that historical chapter more compelling, Carey resorts to "communicative memory" (Assmann, 2011: 36) and allows Charles Hobbs, whose family are "descendants of survivors of a massacre" (336), to revive his living memory of the initial interaction between the white explorers and the indigenous peoples. Charles' account of Captain Cook's arrival at Downs is "a history from below" (37). It is the direct experience of his ancestors passed down orally from generation to generation until it is written into Australia's cultural memory by the author. As any memory that is revolutionary and shadowed by the subject's value preference, Charles' remembrance or Carey's reconstruction of that historical event deviates from the official memory:

> Captain Cook got a big ship. He got a jetty. He rolled down guns and he been shooting there for maybe three weeks. Shooting all the people. Women get shot [sic], kids get knocked out ... Captain Cook put the bullet in his magazine, start to shooting people ... "Really beautiful country", Captain Cook reckoned. "that's why I'm cleaning up people, take it away" ... Him been bring lotta book from Big England right here now ... And that's his Law. Book

belong to Captain Cook, that means all belong to Captain Cook … Anybody sick in the guts or in the head, Captain Cook orders: Don't give him medicine. Don't give him medicine. When they getting crook old people, you killem him first. When they on the job, that's right, you can have them on the job. But don't payem him. Let him work for free. Any children come round, you can have the stockmen killem. We'll still hold that people, and don't letem go. Any man come sick, boy, anything like that, blind man, don't give him medicine. You took him in a dry gully and knock them. (337-338)

Here in Carey's reworking, the anti-memory provided by Charles suggests that Captain Cook is not at all a discoverer of the Antipodes like what he is depicted and worshipped in the imperial as well as Australian official memory. Instead, he is an invader. He is stripped of the halo of civilization imposed by official historical narrative and brought up to readers as a complacent colonist who is eager to devour this vast new land and re-inscribe into it the imperial history, an ambitious bourgeois who is anxious to prey on free aboriginal labour force, and a bloodthirsty monster who does not hesitate a bit to wipe out all the indigenous peoples from their own land. Carey's reconstruction of Australia's memory of its initial encounter with Europeans dismantles the dichotomy between civilization and barbarianism, suggesting that white Australians are provincial and xenophobic. It is their self-righteous notion of White supremacy rather than any empirical threat from other peoples that makes them highly hostile. Nevertheless, Charles' personal memory is solely one of the many shreds of evidence that Carey wires in this fiction to prove that.

Infused with abundant historical knowledge, Willie is first presented as a prestigious historian and anthropologist in the fiction. He is the embodiment of the implied author, jumping occasionally to give commentaries on Australia's "wishful racial thinking with no basis in genetics" (30). His anti-narrative deconstructs the government's racist ethnic policy. What Charles' ancestors have witnessed is further corroborated by his extensive reading and excavation. In the reliability contest, they drive on the dangerous stretch of road along the "Crystal Highway" route, now known for the shattered windscreen glass. He tells his partners, thus readers too, that it used to be called the "Horror Stretch" (139). It is not named for the bad road conditions but for the horrible murders that happened there centuries ago. According to Willie, what is mentioned relatively lightly in the documented history as a "dispersal" (ibid.) actually involves more than three hundred people shot or drowned. In that disaster, "families had been forced off clip tops, gunned down, babies brained with clubs" (ibid.). This naturalistically stark depiction of the White's atrocity towards the aborigines instantly brings what happened in a remote time to a contemporary space, causing intense visual impact and aversion among both the listeners of the story as well as readers of the fiction. Moreover, the White's consolidated images as barbarians emerge vividly from in-between the lines. When an analogy is further made by Carey between this slaughter and the horror in the Bible, "Now therefore kill every male among the little ones, and kill every woman that hath known man by lying with him" (ibid.), the author's satirical overtone in this parody is as clear as crystal. Carey's engineering deconstructs Australian historiography, which tends to mask the ignominious chapter or paint it lightly and depict Australia's European ancestors as messengers of civilization. The documented history paints Australia as a young and promising country with a clean history that rises up to prosperity with its industrious immigrants starting from scratch in this barren penal colony of the British Empire. Nevertheless, a brief look back to Australia's growing history, as Willie concludes, will unveil the landscape as a "colonial battleground, the blood-soaked site of a violent 'contact' between the indigenous blacks and the imperial whites" (64).

The White's fear for the coloured races not just leads to their ferocious massacre of them in the early encounter. It continues to be the culprit of the White Australia policy① and subsequent assimilation policy, which leads directly to the tremendous historical tragedy of the Stolen Generations② since the first decade of the twentieth century. The cultural memory of the racial assimilation policy is constructed through multiple narrative voices. Right upon Australia's stepping into the Federation period in 1901, the Commonwealth government's vision of the country's future was "monolingual" (25) and "monocultural" (30). So, it selects "light-skinned 'Nordic types' as future citizens" (28). Above all, the racial exclusiveness of White Australia, after all, boils down to the denial of the country's original inhabitants. Unlike the racial segregation implemented in the United States, the Australian government attempts to realize the objective of racial purification through the gradual elimination of the country's Aboriginality. Aboriginal children with white genes, half-castes, quadroons, and octoroons are pinched away from their mothers and put into the welfare house where they are severed from any indigenous kingship ties and forced to abandon their native tongue, tribal customs and rituals and intermarry with non-aboriginals. They are forced

---

① White Australia policy, formally Immigration Restriction Act of 1901, in Australian history, fundamental legislation of the new Commonwealth of Australia that effectively stopped all non-European immigration into the country and that contributed to the development of a racially insulated white society. It reflected a long-standing and unifying sentiment of the various Australian colonies and remained a fundamental government policy into the mid-20th century. This racist policy was abolished in 1974.

② The term "Stolen Generations" is used for Aboriginal people forcefully taken away (stolen) from their families and raised up by welfare house or European families to eliminate their aboriginality between the 1890s and 1970s. Because the period covers many decades we speak of "generations" (plural) rather than "generation".

to acquire the English language and rituals and brought up in a European manner. All that the "Australian Natives Association" aims for is to deprive the "indigeneity" of the aborigines. (Macintyre, 1999: 145) This racial assimilation policy is genocidal in both the ethnological and the cultural sense. It also permanently traumatizes those who are forcibly taken away from their mothers and native culture and raised up in an alien and incompatible one. For those aborigines, the separation from their cultural tradition coupled with "the loss of any sensual connection with the land" is equated with the "loss of identity" (A. Assmann, 2011: 275). It contextualizes both Willie and Punka Wallah's sad life story.

  Willie's hidden story is recollected by Doctor Battery, his aboriginal uncle, who demystifies the seemingly predestined trauma stamped on his soul. Willie used to believe firmly that he is an Australian who has German ancestry, which means he understands himself and is understood to be a white man. This belief gives him a sense of white guilt about having appropriated the land from the black, as well as a sense of displacement. It also motivates him to convict his wife of adultery when she delivers a "throwblack" boy and runs away from them without hesitation, hurting both his wife and his son badly. According to Battery, Willie's biological mother is Polly, an aboriginal woman who has been promised to Battery's brother. She could have been married to the man of her own tribe and led a mundane yet steady life if she has not met Big Kev Little, the white boss of Quamby Downs, and served as his housemaid. However, peace and tranquillity have never belonged to the downtrodden blacks. Big Kev has the prevailing White arrogance, regards himself as the "King of castle" and does "not care about right ways and wrong ways" (279). He objectifies the aborigines and treats them as other natural resources he can prey on at his own will, seduces and rapes Polly While his wife goes back to England to visit her family. When he learns

Polly conceived his child, he sends for her fiancé, shoots him dead, cuts his horse and hides his body in the beast's carcass. In Battery's narrative, European Australians are brought under the gaze of the aboriginals and readers. Their pretentious cover of civilization is peeled off, and they are revealed to be barbarians who prey on the dusky race relentlessly. When Willie happens to be born "bright-skinned", his mother has to cover him with "a mud of ash and termite mound" to make him "black like coal" (281) so that he might not be stolen by the Welfare and brought up as a white man. However, the Welfare fellows, who are "worse than any eagle" (282), would not let him go even when he is badly injured from the eagle's claws. They insist on pinching him from his mother with the excuse of giving him better medical treatment. The murder of her fiancé, coupled with the robbery of her son, drives Polly into insanity. When she tries to avenge herself on the police officers by burning down their laundry hut because the law fails to do her justice, she is put into prison. Soon after, that fate repeats on her until "[S]he bin washed up, died la prison" (283).

As for Willie, he is, to some degree, a successful exemplar of Australia's racial assimilation. He was born with paler skin and has been brought up with an even whiter heart. He is obliterated of practically all memories of the indigenous customs and rituals. Although the "imagines agentes" of snakes and possums inhabiting the aboriginal landscape are passed down to his unconscious and keep recurring in his dreams, he cannot decipher them. Carey deploys surrealism here to suggest Willie's inheritance of the aboriginal unconscious as well as his rupture with the indigenous traditions. His separation from the aboriginal tradition makes either the creating of God in Aboriginal Mythology or the aboriginal dreamtime meaningless. Though extensive reading gives him an encyclopedic knowledge of Australian history, including those dark and dirty details, he has grown accustomed to the official version of it. For him, Captain Cook is the God-like man who sets the threshold of this southern continent. As a history teacher, he feels obliged to teach Australian geography according to the "map" drawn by the Whites who have cut up the land to mark their own exploration and conquer of this *terra nullius*. However, the truth is that "[B]lack fellahs got no fence. No fence and no bloody map neither" (297). When he is captivated in Quamby Downs by his own man to listen to their stories and share their sufferings and grief with them, he feels repulsed and offended by the alien culture as well as those strange men and keeps finding chances to flee from them at the very beginning. His ancestral culture has alienated him. What happens to Willie and his mother makes it undeniable that Australia's racial assimilation policy is never a mild move. On the contrary, it usually goes hand in hand with cultural genocide, trampling of human nature and often bloody murder.

However, apart from the death of his biological mother, Willie is the lucky one when it comes to the fact that he is spared from the brutal and torturous transitional life that many stolen blacks and half-castes have to spend in the welfare house. They are objectified by the Welfare fellows who deprive them of their genuine names, rename them "for things left lying in the dirt" (277), and treat them as cattle. As Punka Wallah recalls his own earlier experience, the welfare usually arrives "with a utility truck with a cage on the back, like you might use for stock" (328). The white fellows usually throw the stolen children into the cage and take them to an orphanage, where they fall victim to the white's enormous enmity towards the coloured race, suffering helplessly from the greatest of evils. They "sprayed poison on" them (328) to bleach them. Sexual abuse is also a regular occurrence. Punka Wallah recollects that he "had been used and raped night after night" (329). He gets whipped and starved and even put into jail whenever he fights them or tries to run away from school. When he finally goes back to his mother, "[H]is glistening back bore the marks of a greenhide whip, criscrossed, raised, woven into his skin" and he has "lost her language and all he had was mongrel talk". (329-330) The course of the racial purification is equated with the process of the Aborgines' body writing of trauma. The racial assimilation policy that starts with a fraudulent excuse of bettering the living conditions of the Aborigines proceeds with the annihilation of the indigenous people and their unique culture. "The Australian nation was shaped by the fear of invasion and concern for the purity of race." (Macintyre, 1999: 149)

Even in the 1950s, the Whites' prejudice against the few surviving blacks still prevailed. Black people are still considered to be less rational beings who pose a potential threat to the existing social order at any time. Strict restrictions on their behaviour are implemented wherever the black groups gather. Signs of "NO DRINKING, NO GAMBLING, NO HUMBUG" (208) are erected to warn them against misconduct. "Blacks were forbidden to visit the quarters of the whites" (327), and they still need a "certificate of exemption" (209) to appear in a white hotel or bar. Otherwise, the hotel or bar might slam the door on them, or they might end up in a lockup. As Irene observes, the Whites, including her, who is relatively liberal, are "afraid of black people" (215). To further ease their fear, white managers are appointed to run the black communities to make sure that they are under proper surveillance and control. The relationship between the white managers and the aborigines is best designated as the colonizer and the colonized. The white managers, to take Carter Cricket of the Quamby Downs for example, regard themselves as kings of the black groups, and they exercise the colonizing power over the aboriginal body. They are entitled to decide who is justified in obtaining an exemption certificate. They have the right to convict those poor blacks who rile about their white employers for payment of "communists" and shoot them or "kick the whole lot of them off the property". (258) Carter Cricket even affords the impudence to flaunt in public his sexual relationship with pupil girls like Susie Shuttle without being punished and refuses to write her a reference letter when she could have a chance to be accepted at the Perth nursing college. He has the right to have anybody who does not comply with him declared "psychotic breakdown" (372) "out of nowhere" (371) and imprisoned in a hospital.

Half castes like Willie have no better fate than their throwblack fellows at all when it comes to discrimination and persecution from the Whites. When the Bobs' friend Dunstan learns that Willie might have black blood runs in his vessels, he tries every means to talk sense into Irene that the Redex sponsors would not let a suspicious half-caste represent any crew and requires her to dismiss him immediately. When Irene refuses to do that, her husband Titch, who has just come back from his father's funeral, "flies at" (231) Willie, punches his head and eventually dumps "the best navigator in the Redex Trial" (219) halfway. All Willie, who is possessed by "deep black worry" (219), is able to do in this fight is to hold out his arms, to protest "this blatant injustice like a boy" (231). He suffers much more when encountering Carter Cricket, the white manager of the Quamby Downs. Simply because Willie is sympathetic towards Susie and insists on helping the poor girl out by writing her a reference letter, he assaults Willie ruthlessly but accuses him of "Grievous Bodily Harm" (377) and has him given the maximum sentence of ten years and locked up for in Fremantle.

Bodily persecution is only part of the enmity that the Whites have directed toward darker-skinned people. Cultural hegemony is another.

Even in the 1950s, white Australians were still obsessed with their own superior subjectivity and never tried to understand the aboriginal culture a bit. The indigenous customs and rituals remain "barbaric practices" (351) from their perspective, and white missionaries regard it righteous to take black children in to protect them from the "barbarism". With more and more young blacks pinched from the community and brainwashed into the English language and the White's customs and rituals, the increasingly withering indigenous culture is on the brink of extinction. As Willie observes, "all Aboriginal culture was based on country, on journeys, or tracks now cut up by fences ... Quamby Downs was a sort of prison where it was often impossible to honour the moral and religious obligations of singing country" (317). Even the poor and rare public education coming to the black community is concerned with the saga of Captain Cook and teaches the kids the far reaches of the Whites in English. It teaches them no practical skills to get them a proper job but things stamped with White ideology to induce them to comply with the white hegemony through this gradual infiltration. With the continuous violent oppression of the Whites and no culture to cling to, the remaining aborigines have to escape in lassitude. They become "exiles" in their own land and are "denied the meaning of their lives" (317) and experience the uttermost of nothingness.

According to the retrieved memory of Australia in the 1850s by Peter Carey, blacks are not the only people toward whom xenophobic white Australians have directed their hostility in history. Chinese who have left their home country for various reasons to earn an honest living in this strange land also fall prey to their fear of and discrimination against the coloured ethnic minorities. The signpost reminding drivers that there are sixty-three miles to the town of "Young" is an "actively effective and affective" (A. Assmann, 2011: 211) picture which stimulates Willie's "affect" (ibid.: 240) to remember the Lambing Flat Riots where thousands of Chinese miners have been cruelly beaten and expelled. "The nasty white miners had knocked the Chinese tents and stolen everything inside. There was gunfire and police sabre charges and one man was left dead" (157). While Willie provides the brutal "fact" (ibid.) of the Lambing Flat Riots, Titch's white voice fades in. He recollects his earlier life being the chauffeur of and living with a Chinese herbalist, Mr Goon, a figure Carey refers to in *Illywhacker*. In his memory, the Chinese are "clever" and gentle to other people, and they treat children incredibly "kindly" (158). The multiple narrative voices are employed to support each other and form a sharp contrast between the Chinese people's hospitality and gentleness in Titch's personal memory and the white Australians' hostility and brutality in Willie's remembrance. It creates a tension that delegitimizes Australia's xenophobia about the Chinese by exposing its complete groundlessness and fallaciousness. It also suggests that Australians and Chinese are supposed to live in harmony with and learn from each other if White Australians can afford to put aside their unreasonable fear and prejudice.

To reconstruct Australia's memory of its earlier ethnic policy of racism, Peter Carey resorts to a wide range of narrative techniques such as anti-narrative, multiple narrative voices and parody. Through the revelation of the merits of the Aborigines and Chinese, as well as the uniqueness of Aboriginal and Chinese culture, this reconstruction is aimed to delegitimize Australia's rootless fear for the coloured races. Through the unveiling of the sorrow and trauma of the blacks and the half-castes, as well as the withering of indigenous culture in the siege of the powerful white one, this reconstruction functions to criticize the evils that white Australians have committed against the indigenous people and culture due to their provincialism and racial discrimination while consoling those downtrodden black souls. As old Bachhuber reviews, they (the whites) are "white ants at the very foundations" of the blacks' lives, and they are "destroying" them (263). Most importantly, as collective memory is usually retrieved to confirm a commune's identity, this racist memory is reconstructed to remind contemporary Australians of "their place and identity", especially in relation to the "First Peoples" on his continent. (Kunc, 2018: 22) As cultural memory is frequently recalled to address present needs, Peter Carey's reconstruction of the nation's racist memory has further implications for Australia's contemporary conservative ethnic policy, which is unfriendly to the surviving aborigines and other coloured minorities like Chinese and obstructive to the prosperity of their culture. He further gives tentatively his poetic prescription within the fiction.

2.2.3 Deferred Reconciliation between the Whites and the Aborigines

Based on previous analysis, it is concluded that European Australians' self-imposed fear for the coloured race, especially the aborigines, and its thirst for racial purity have inflicted enormous detriment to the black people and their culture. To remedy the evils that white Australians have committed against the indigenous to establish their own culture and, more importantly, build a future-oriented multicultural Australia given its increasing cultural and population diversity,① Peter Carey gives the poetic prescription of reconciliation between the white and the black, or in a more general sense, between white Australians and other ethnic groups

---

① According to the 2016 Census (data collected until 30 Jun. 2016) undertaken by the Australian Bureau of Statistics (ABS), Australia had a high proportion of overseas-born population of 33.3% and languages other than English were spoken at home accounted for 27.3%. Of the 66.7% people born in Australia, there were 798,400 Aborigines and Torres Strait Islanders, accounting for 3.3% of the total Australian population. And this showed a 19% increase in the Aboriginal and Torres Strait Islander population, compared to the 2011 Census.

living in Australia. Nevertheless, it is never been a smooth way to achieve genuinely reciprocal understanding, not to say consensus, between two ethnic groups. There is, as the title of the novel suggests, still a long way for the indigenous peoples and other races alike to feel comfortable and prosper at their Australian "home".

To reconcile the whites with the black, the fundamental step suggested in the novel is to break with Australia's conservative ideology soaked with White supremacy. This vision is indicated emblematically through the dynamic relationship between Irene and her father-in-law, nicknamed Dangerous Dan, the first Australian pilot who is a little English man. He is the symbol of Australian conservative ideology. He regards England as his home and similarly, himself as "the oldest airman in the world" (17), bragging about his exploits readily as the Whites celebrate their achievements on this continent. He also has the "disease" of worshipping Henry Ford "to an extreme degree" (34) as Australians view the United States as their new master. He is a second-hand dealer selling war disposals and occassionally used cars, filling his scrap yard with bomb casings and other materials and acting out falsely this "airman nonsense as if he had really served the King of England" (14). Like Australia's European ancestors who tell lies about this *terra nuluius*, Dan is also "a 'wily prankster', a joker, a character, suspected of playing pranks with gelignite in previous car trials" (163). However, just like European Australians who will not be able to erase the fact that they are not the first owners of the Antipodes no matter how they manipulate the historical knowledge, Dan is "an artful dodger and would go to the grave without ever being an authorized dealer in anything" (34) however good at handling the newspapers he is.

More remarkably, the resemblance between Dan and the conservative white ideology also lies in his patriarchalism and chauvinism. He is somewhat tyrannical to his tiny son Titch in that he tries every means to stop him from maturing and becoming independent. He wants him to be his son, his "slave" forever, helping him sell his second-hand treasure and carrying his "propeller like a Holy Cross" (33). He is passionate about selling Ford, but tries every means to smash Titch's dream when he strives to be a Ford dealer. Even "[A]t seventy-five years of age he was still in competition with his son" (34). He "had done everything he could to keep his sonny in a cage" (188). Apart from being a manipulative father, Dan is also misogynic. He has a "low opinion of women drivers" (165) and reportedly shows "little patience for women 'cluttering up the contest'" (163). When he learns Titch and Irene are going to participate in the Redex Trial to prove the reliability of Holden, which is the embodiment of the rise of Australian nationalism, he signs up for the contest, risking his life to prevent them from making it. As far as Irene is concerned, "his father would destroy us any way he could" (163).

Irene is another typical female character of Carey who enchants readers more with her manlike vision and toughness than with her femininity. Though a teeny woman, she is determined to fight along with her husband against Dan, symbolically Australia's deep-rooted White supremacy. What Irene does symbolizes Australia's endeavour to win independence from the suffocation of the Old World. She moves with Titch to Bacchus Marsh to get away from Dan's patriarchal clutch. She casts his cherished and monstrous propeller out of her yard. She participates in the Redex Trial as her husband's co-driver to defeat him regardless of how she is judged for her inopportune transgression. As she recalls, "all my married life I had worked to protect Titch from his father's malice" (188) and prevent Titch from being "his father's dog" (171). She is aimed not just to save Titch from returning to Dan's "servitude" (33). When Dan charges at her, she never lets him win the upper hand. She is determined that "I would destroy him" (165), having him eventually "defeated, done, dusted" (185). Dan dies of a heart attack halfway through the contest, and Irene wins out so that she is able to place the bones of the little black child, and Titch becomes a Holden dealer. Irene's fight against Dan emblemizes a necessary war on and break with Australia's conservative ideology. Dan's death symbolizes the failure of this ideology, which has hindered Australia from facing reality and getting really mature.

Apart from detruding the conservative ideology, the most crucial step towards the reconciliation suggested in the fiction is to do away with the traditional subject-object model of the philosophy of consciousness and regard the blacks as equal subjects who are able to strike "internalized dialogue" (Habermas, 1987: 13) with the White. Traditionally, Australian culture stresses solely the subjectivity of the White and Christian culture while treating the aborigines and other coloured races as well as their culture as lesser beings, as unworthy objects that could be exploited to the White's hearts' content. To reconcile the Whites with the aboriginals, consciously or unconsciously, Carey recommends breaking the subject-object dichotomy and prioritizing the "intersubjectivity" of the two peoples and helping them achieve reciprocal understanding through communicative action. This vision is indicated in the fiction through the journey of rediscovering and understanding the blacks in the lifeworld of Australia.

As stated in previous paragraphs, the Redex Trial is a reliability contest around Australia, and it is also a journey diving back into the dark history of Australia. The journey of revisiting history parallels the rediscovery and understanding of the blacks, which partially lays the foundation for the reconciliation. Since the lifeworld we are in is intrinsically intersubjective, it is natural and necessary that we obtain reciprocal knowledge of our fellow men. (Parsons, 1977: 181) The cast of the black characters in the fiction are understood by Willie and Irene with considerable hospitality rather than being gazed at as the monstrous Other, and the aboriginal culture is described with a reasonable detachment, even appreciation, rather than a sentimental disgust.

Willie's first encounter with Doctor Battery gives him the impression that he has "unexpectedly delicate" feet, although he is limp (223). Irene is also convinced after a brief interaction that "[H]e can play the part of Titch" (224), meaning to drive the Holden while Titch is absent for his father's funeral. The aborigines are restored as subjects. Willie's brief contact with Quamby Downs makes him recognize that black children are "beautiful mullattos" (253). They are "lovely people" and "fabulous kids" (254). They are pure and rustic fellas who content themselves with the simple life of fishing and shooting. They are unsophisticated and grateful people. "You'll help them get bush tucker, they'll be your friends forever." (ibid.) Like her peers, the delicate girl, Susie, is also a "sneaky clever child" (361). She is able to save Willie and his car from the strong currents of the Mardowarra River single-handedly. She is intelligent and competent enough to be accepted at the Perth nursing college. As Willie acclaims, given a proper chance, she will be "an important woman" (362). With the black blood running in his vessels, Willie is even more talented. He reads widely and is erudite. Like his ancestors, he is gifted at direction and making maps. As Irene compliments him, Willie is an "expert in the required field" (125). His Redex map contributes remarkably to Irene and Titch's success in the contest. It appears to Irene that his black son, Neil, is "gorgeous-looking" (288) with "healthy brown black skin" (289). "He was a polite boy" (290) and "showed a sort of grace you would never think to see in the RACV patrol depot, or even Acland Street" (288-289). He fancies medicine and proves to be as good at it as any white boy. He gains a scholarship to pay for his education at Melbourne University. He passes his Leaving Certificate and Matriculation with first-class honours.

The fiction shows that through the interaction between the Whites and the aborigines, the intersubjectivity is generated, and the black people are rediscovered to be a different yet equally lovely race. They are not at all inferior, no matter their skin colour, disposition or intelligence. Since the intersubjectivity is "consolidated in the medium of linguistic symbols, and secured finally through cultural tradition" (Habermas, 1987: 10), Carey continues to present aboriginal culture as it is, suggesting to readers its charisma in its own unique way. The Aborigines have their origin myth that the wedge-tailed bird rides on the back of their ancestor Jila, a long-bearded snake, creating the black people and the rivers they live by from generation to generation. Singing is the language they use to approach their ancestor and they always sing "with a passion that surprised and moved" (305) people. That is why their language is "soft and indistinct", sounding more "melodic" (211) than the English Willie has been taught to speak. They have their own ceremonies and Law business to attend in the open air. They befriend nature and all living creatures inhabiting this land as if they are an organic part of them. They have considerable expertise in imitating the tracks of animals and reptiles. Pupils "ducked and dived and brushed their teeth with broken twigs and arrived clean and shinning in their desks" (351). They have their "finger talk" and "stick talk" and they can make remarkable paintings with their fingertips and sticks, recording their blissful and sad stories. (352) Scrutinized with highly-civilized and post-industrial eyes, this culture may appear raw and rough to outsiders since it evokes association of glaring primitive images with snakes and twigs and sticks and mysterious murmuring of a wizard. However, Aboriginal culture is not gazed upon in the fiction derogatorily as a barbaric practice but is depicted phenomenologically to be a singular culture with bouncing vitality. It is indicated to be a genetically constitutive part of Australian multiculture and contributes considerably, together with other minority cultures, to Australia's cultural prosperity. As Willie recollects from his earlier memory, "here were all of these lands with their diverse peoples, Germans, Magyars, Spanish Jews, Romanies and Mohammedans, which has been a wonder to my childish imagination" (97-98).

To achieve a genuine reconciliation, Peter Carey further suggests that the Whites repent of their crime and remedy what they have done to the indigenous peoples. The Whites' repentance is emblematically done by the priest, Mr. Bachhuber, Willie's foster father. Moreover, Irene's decent burial of the black skull symbolizes the compensation that the Whites are supposed to make for the slaughtered blacks. From Carey's reconstruction, Australian whites are haunted by the historical guilt of having slaughtered the first peoples of the Antipodes and appropriated their land. That White guilt turns into an incurable "grief" (146), a motif repeatedly dealt with in Carey's works, which is engraved in Australia's collective unconscious. That grief is also the collective memory of the indigenous people. It is "hereditary" (Jung, 1968: 43), like "an impersonal Karma within a family, which is passed on from parents to children" (146). It gives Willie the "instinct" (Jung, 1968: 44) that there are "things or questions which were left incomplete unanswered" (146) by his (white) ancestors. It is also the reason that Bachhuber feels conscience-stricken by the "guilty burden" (266) whenever a member of his parish asks him to hold for them something from that remote past, a letter, a little photograph that they could not bear to throw away but have to hide from their children. Those objects are actually the images that are media for Australians, especially the aboriginal memory and cultural unconscious. They arise especially in "precognitive and traumatic experiences" that "cannot be accessed by verbal processing" and their power derives from their "affective charge". (A. Assmann, 2011: 208-209) They reactivate, to quote Karl Jung, the "archetype of the collective unconscious" (1968: 48). To ease their grief, what Australian Whites should do is to confess to the brutality that they have committed, apologizing that they "did horrendous things ... There is no right thing... there are just many, many wrong things", and "pray to be forgiven". (265)

However, repentance is more of the Whites' self-redemption. They repent to redeem themselves from the historical sin and free themselves from the spiritual torture resulting from it. However, it takes their genuine actions to rectify the wrongs that their ancestors committed in previous ages. And Irene is appointed by the author to take on the mission. When Irene descends into the shrubs and grasses to answer nature's call, he finds a sickening graveyard of bones of the blacks. Sympathy and anger prompt her to excavate very cautiously a fragile and powdery skull of a little boy from the broken soil. She "nursed him" and "held him like a mother does, with my palm around the back of his head" (177), intending to take him to the police station where she is able to bring the murderer to justice. Nevertheless, it's never easy to rest the blacks in peace in their own land. She could clearly feel strangers' gawping and the sergeant's smirking and discomfort, which make her overly interfering and ridiculous woman. However, what disappoints her most is that the blatant "bullet hole" (178) on the infant skull does not suffice for the sergeant to punish whoever has committed the crime, let alone it is nothing rare in this territory. What he is capable of is to scribble a receipt and ask Irene to take the little head of the dusky race down south as a "souvenir" where "[I]t may even be worth a bob or two"

(179). Carey deploys irony to criticize the Whites' arrogance and indifference to the lives of the aborigines. Irene has to let "the victim of ignorance and murderous technology" shift in the cardboard, "sensing its historic essence, like 'wrong'" (224) throughout the Redex Trial.

The police are definitely not the only obstacle Irene encounters on her way to rest the boy in peace. She does not gain much support from her white fellows either, which is epitomized by her husband, Titch. Since the law could not do anything on the murdered little boy's behalf, Titch grows impatient and orders him to chuck the skull away or give it back to the black people. Hoveover, the blacks refuse to accept it because they "feared the evil spirits sleeping in the bones" (245). Titch becomes merciless and mean, singing a song with his rasping voice to ridicule his wife:

> *As I strolled one morning on Bondi's tropic shore*
> *I spied a huge Ardmona box like I never saw before*
> *I hauled it in and looked inside to see what I could see*
> *And there is a great big beep-beep-beep staring back at me*
> *Oh, there is a great big beep-beep-beep, it was a mystery*
> *I picked up the box and ran to town to pawn it in a shop*
> *The broker saw me coming and hollered I should stop*
> *He took his key, he turned his lock, and shouted through the door*
> *Oh, get out of here with that beep-beep-beep, before I call the law*
>
> *Oh, get out of here with that beep-beep-beep, before I call the law* (246)

Irene takes the skull to church, but Saint Peter does not let the little boy rest in either. Out of desperation, she turns to Bachhuber, the pastor in Payneham Adelaide, Willie's foster father, whom she believes she can trust completely to give the boy a proper burial. The old pastor is very friendly and sympathetic towards the black boy. However, as he tells Irene, "I cannot legally do anything for this poor fellow. We have no coroner's report, I assume, not death certificate. It's as if you found him by the road" (264). What old Bachhuber talks about is the metaphor of Australia's institutional forgetting of the dusky race. The only option left to the sympathiser is to ask Irene to leave the cardboard with him so that he can probably have him buried privately and mourn him personally. Similarly, Willie assembles all his courage and affection to tell Irene that "I would trust you with my life" (220). Irene's sweet pledge that "I wouldn't let you down" (ibid.) is solely a personal promise because she could not prevent Titch and Dunstan from fighting Willie for his black genes and turning him away ruthlessly. As neither Australian law is tolerant enough nor is Christian love as universal as it claims to be to treat the aborigines equally, the institutional forgetting of them is encouraged. There remains an enigma as to when the aboriginal souls could rest in peace in their own land. The fiction does demonstrate Carey's profound reflection on the Australian aboriginal issue. Since the indigenous people cannot count on their white folks to do them proper justice, they have to seek salvation by themselves.

2.2.4 Aborigines' Salvation by Carving Their Cultural Memory

Salvation is the keynote that the fiction as well as the ultimate poetic prescription that Peter Carey gives to Australian aborigines concerning the evils that their racist fellowmen have brought about and the genuine reconciliation between the white and the black might be put on hold indefinitely. The fiction's protagonists, either Irene and Titch or Willie, need to be saved from their messed-up living conditions. Moreover, the salvation that they strive for has both literal and metaphorical implications.

To begin with, Irene and Titch's matrimony is not thought highly of by either side of their families owing to their petite sizes. Irene's sister even derides her that she marries such a tiny Titch only to "breed a team of mice" (3). That is only part of the challenges confronting them. As is stated in the previous section, Titch, and together with his wife Irene have always been held in his father's servitude so that they are unable to have their own independent and happy life. Moreover, like his father, Titch is a super worshiper of Henry Ford and thus "a soldier in the cause of Ford" (41). His destined dream of becoming an authorized-dealer leaves him at the total disposal of the Ford Motor Company, allowing it to "go snooping through our bank account, our debts, our credit history" (34). To save them from the life overshadowed and ruined by Dan's clutch and Ford's bullying and to gain freedom and independence, they need something to "look forward to" (101). Irene steels her heart against her father-in-law and moves with her husband to Bacchus Marsh. More importantly, she persuades Titch to participate in the Redex Trial to secure the dealership of Australia's own car, the Holden.

Their salvation lies in the reliability contest. It not just "saved his (Titch's) life" (87). The whole "family's future is with Holden" (47) too. Winning the contest not just "make(s) our name" (90), which increases Titch's sales enormously and promises them the authorized dealership. It also makes him a "happy" (323) man, which is all Irene has devoted her life to making. Nevertheless, the significance of Irene and Titch's salvation does not just lie literally in the fame, money and euphoria that come along. It has a more significant symbolic implicature. As analyzed previously, Dan symbolizes the arrogant English heritage in Australian culture. Moreover, a simple delineation of Carey's works makes it effortless to infer that the wrestling between Holden and Ford emblemizes Australia's relationship with the United States. Consequently, winning the game makes Irene and Titch not just heroes of their own, but also "national champions" (322). Their determination to participate in the Redex Trial with a Holden vehicle and their ultimate triumph is not just a surmounting of a disadvantageous personal position or a pursuit and demonstration of their personal excellence. It is an emblem of Australia's overcoming of its national predicament to make a free and independent nation out of the enormous shackles imposed upon it by Great Britain and the United States. Irene and Titch's participation in the game "to 'merchandize' our famous brand" (170) and to make Holden a "household name" (92) is the author's poetic manoeuvre to make a distinguished Australia and Australian culture widely known to the rest of the world. Irene and Titch's salvation is metaphorically the salvation of Australia. It symbolizes the independence of Australia as well as Australian culture from the subordination of Great Britain and the reliance on America.

Compared to Irene and Titch, Willie has even a more wrecked life: officially claimed to be a White, he has a "deep sense of displacement" (28), with the "unshakable belief" (97) that he doesn't belong where his (white) mother has delivered him and his country lies somewhere else; he runs away from his (foster) parents in Adelaide when he should have stayed in his father's parsonage; he is haunted by relentless dreams peopled with snakes and possums that end up being born as children and dreams of rivers filled with fish broken apart like wet cardboard; he marries when he would have been a happier single; he flees his wife's adultery "like a worm" (25) thus leaves the only job that suits him to teach the worst class in Bacchus Marsh; he is suspended by the headmaster for hanging a bawling black pupil by his ankle from the second-storey window; he loses his championship in Mr. Deasy's quiz show to his rival, Miss Cloverdale, after being seduced to have sex with her. Overwhelmed by the life of "fear and chaos" (145), Willie drowns himself in grief, self-doubt, self-abasement and nihilism. In his own words, he is like a man "crouched on a lonely platform ready to spring aboard a speeding train", waiting for his "salvation ... with an impatience that made my toes squirm inside my thirsty shoes" (9-10).

Submerged by his long list of disasters, the first thought that comes to him is to "flee" (268) to avoid possible conflicts, which brings him to Bacchus Marsh, neighbouring Irene and Titch. However, escape is not conducive to his troubled mind at all. On the contrary, the idleness and the intensified loneliness allow him more time to brood over his conditions, which aggravates his anxiety, causing even physical symptoms. "I was already dizzy with sleeplessness and a sort of existential lightness in which my Self had slipped off like a shade ... like a sodden hillside after rain, I felt the danger of slide"(225). This pathological fear makes Willie lose himself. "I was unmoored, with nothing to cling to, to say 'this is who I am' with this job, this business, this belief, this wife, child, future, I was not one thing or the other" (235). But that does not exhaust the inventory of misfortunes in his young life.

As joining Irene's crew as the navigator unearths the mysteries of his birth, Willie is exposed to the most merciless reality completely. He is regarded as a white man in south Australia owing to his paler skin. However, here in the northern outback, where people hold a general discrimination against darker skin, he is convicted and treated to be a half-caste because of his slight brownness. He needs a certificate to appear in bars where white people congregate. He is sent into exile by both the white and the black. He is despised, fought, and finally expelled by Titch, who learns that he might have aboriginal genes regardless of his remarkable contribution to navigating the crew. The maltreatment and sorrow he receives owing to these confident references to his race make him extremely "irritated and unsettled" and "feared" (267). When he ends up in Quamby Downs, where he learns that he has been genuinely delivered by a black woman, he is entirely smacked by the absurdity of life all around him and "saw only death" (268). The rupture between him and the aboriginal cultural tradition has been too enormous to bridge. At the very beginning, he hates the black community and finds himself totally incompatible with the circumstances. The aboriginal culture has been severely destroyed, and what emerges in his eyes of the black community are scenes of decay and horror. People huddle together in iron shanties idly, and even the teacher's residence is scrambled on a "pioneer's ruin with a corrugated roof thrown up across its eroded walls", sending "the stink of something dead or dying". (268) He often hears something at night, like "angry shouting then some wild creature scratching at the wall" (ibid.). That is the ghost of the banished aborigines. As far as Willie is concerned, his "foreign place of birth was as depressed and mournful as a prison yard" (297). All these conditions add to his loneliness and uneasiness, making him "wake each morning frayed, disconnected and know I did not belong" (364). His loss of identity is equated with his gap with the aboriginal culture, only that he does not realize it at the very beginning.

While kept in captivity in the black community, he tries every means to seek salvation. At the very beginning, he thinks he can be cured by fleeing back into Bacchus Marsh, where he is treated as a white man. He plots to escape from Quamby Downs from time to time but ends up in failure and being accused of ungratefulness, which symbolizes his inseparable relationship with his culture. He is imprisoned in a limestone cave and condemned to be a teacher who is only able to kill time by teaching his aboriginal pupils Australian geography in English, using a usual map drawn by pioneers to show the far reaches of the Empire, but finds himself not listened to at all. Brought up in the white community, the white's ideas, images, feelings etc., have fallen upon his brain while his black ancestor has to rest in far deeper layers of the ashes. Under this circumstance, the conflict between the white tradition embodied by him and the aboriginal culture he is now faced with turns out to be an utter hindrance to his bliss, freedom or self-salvation. Finally, he has to adapt himself to the surrounding he is imprisoned in. The road to Willie's salvation is the process which he restores his sensual connection with his ancestors and their land, through which he eventually regains his aboriginal identity. Furthermore, he does this by changing himself into a proper black fellah and choosing to be the inheritor and scribe of the aboriginal cultural memory. In short, he is cured by narrative and retrieved memory.

As "a man torn apart by two conflicting desires" (378), Willie struggles between his white ego and his black id. However, he manages to cast off his white superiority and makes up his mind to inherit the "Dreaming story" of the black people. He starts from being an ignorant pupil, giving up geography, which he has been very proud to have expertise in, obliterating the state borders on his classroom map, painting out simply the coastline and leaving a perfect field of white for his pupils to draw the paths of their ancestral beings from place to place. He goes against the instruction given by the Western Australian education department that he is "not to reinforce 'backward beliefs'" (317) and pays his uttermost respect to Battery and other old men of the community to invite them to his classroom to tell the pupils the myth and Old Law of their own peoples in their tribal languages. Moreover, he drives Battery to his country, their country, so that he is able to perform his own ceremonies according to whatever aboriginal rituals are required. Not only does Willie allow ancient aboriginal culture to be passed on to its descendants and himself to be a humble student of its rituals and traditions, but he also shoulders the responsibility of being the guardian of aboriginal cultural memory and reinventing Aboriginal myth to "keep the country alive" (305). Moreover, this is generously indicated by the metaphor of Noah's Ark.

In the fiction, Carey parodies the Bible again and makes Noah's Ark a secret and scared place where black people are saved, and all Whites are drowned when a might rain of Holy Water floods the country. It is not until the last chapters that Noah's Ark is revealed to be a metaphor of Willie's narrative and symbolically Peter Carey's too. With a "hoard of notes, diary entries, tapes, accounts of a culture he has now spent a life protecting from malevolent destruction" (381), for one thing, Willie takes possession of Noah's Ark to preserve aboriginal cultural memory, thus prolonging the black people. For another, Willie, through his transcription of the courageous anti-colonial resistance that white anthropologists have hitherto denied and his reproduction of the Saga of Captain Cook and the anti-maps under his students' instruction, turns the ark into "an instrument of resistance against the white oppressors" (333). It is through his unremitting efforts to scribe, preserve and disseminate a differentiating aboriginal cultural memory to keep the downtrodden black peoples alive that Willie achieves his healing. Furthermore, his salvation has symbolic significance either to the aboriginal culture or to contemporary aborigines.

It has never been a secret that with the vast majority of indigenous people having been slaughtered and their land made unreachable, the aboriginal stories based on the country, the journeys, or the tracks have been cut up by the white's fences. Aborigines have lost sensual connections with their land, and their cultural traditions have been destroyed. What is worse, the racial purification policy, which further deprives the black peoples of most of their offspring and assimilates the rest of them through education, puts the aboriginal cultural memory on the brink of oblivion. As Punka Wallah tells Willie, as well as readers,

> The thoroughness of their [Aboriginal] forefathers has left to them not a single unoccupied scene which they could fill with creatures of their own imagination. Tradition and the tyranny of the old men in the religious and cultural sphere have effectively stifled all creative impulse; and no external stimulus ever reached Centural Australia which could have freed the natives from these insidious bonds. It is almost certain that native myths have ceased to be invented many centuries ago ... They are, in many ways, not so much a primitive as a decadent race. (329-330)

Here, an analogy is made between Willie and the status quo of the aboriginal culture, as well as contemporary aborigines. Being suppressed by another hegemonic race and culture, they have all lost their authenticity and vitality. Willie has been torn apart by the strong sense of displacement and unable to face up to his genuine identity; the aboriginal culture has lost its competence to rejuvenate or nurture the souls of the blacks; the aboriginal survivors have been living in "a sort of prison where it is impossible to honour the moral and religious obligations of singing country", becoming "exiles" on their own land and being "denied the meaning of their lives". (317) They are all in immediate need of salvation. Willie's cure emblemizes the salvation of the black people, as well as the aboriginal culture. Aborigines can only be saved when people, as indicated in this fiction, especially writers and anthropologists, are concerned with revitalizing the aboriginal culture. Moreover, it can be best revitalized through the rediscovery and the invention of its cultural memories. Though there is still a long way to go, Carey assures readers it is worth hoping for. As Willie says, "while still asleep, ... there was a time when snakes had feathers" (11).

It is not hard to detect that Peter Carey makes a pun on the title of the novel. For one thing, *A Long Way from Home* signifies the expatriate writer's unstoppable nostalgia for yet a deferred return to his home country, Australia. For another, it emblemizes the uncertainty for Australian whites and blacks to arrive at a genuine reconciliation so that the Aborigines can be equally anointed and feel at home on their own land. Like what he does in all other works, Carey perseveres passionately in his poetic exploration with both the optimism of bringing contemporary Australia any possible change and the melancholy of foreseeing the gloomy prospect of it. To express his concern as an intellectual with historical consciousness and national responsibility, he dives into Australia's cultural memory of racism that dates back to its colonial period, plagues the blacks for the first half of the twentieth century and lingers to contemporary era to bias against them and other ethnic minorities.

Carey takes the focalizations of the downtrodden blacks as well as the marginalized liberal whites so that Australia's ethnic policy is recollected to be the White demonization, massacre and assimilation of the coloured races, especially the indigenous peoples, owing to their anxiety over racial purification. This cultural memory is reconstructed in the postmodern textual space to fulfil a couple of functions. To begin with, the author aims to concrete Australian national and cultural tradition and "blame" (Antze & Lambek, 1997: Ⅶ) its racist mentality that has cost millions of innocent lives in history and still prevails among conservative politicians, historians and anthropologists. To further delegitimize this self-righteous mentality, both counter-narratives of Irene and Willie and counter memories of Doctor Battery, Charles Hobbs, Punka Wallah and Titch are pastiched to indicate the merits possessed by the coloured races and the barbarianism that the White has demonstrated either in their earlier settlement or in their ambition of ethnic purity. Simultaneously, these anti-narratives and anti-memories help to legitimize the uniqueness of the race as well as its remarkable contribution to Australian history and culture. It is one of the most telling parts of Australia and a constituent element to define what the nation is. It is safe to say that Australian culture will be eclipsed without the heavy and colourful stroke of the indigenous culture. Through the recuperation of Australia's cultural memory of its ethnic policy, which functions to delegitimize the Whites' quirk of racism and legitimize the blacks' merits and contributions, Carey aims to redefine what Australia and Australian culture is. Australia is multi-national since it has been inhabited by "diverse peoples" (97) from the very beginning, including the Whites, the aborigines as well as Chinese etc. , Australian culture is supposedly diverse, so both Christian culture, aboriginal culture and other minority culture should be allowed to prosper together. Carey's representation of Australia and its cultural status in *A Long Way from Home* is realism, and he invests his embrace of interculturality in this fiction. In a larger picture, remembering the genocidal past functions to alert contemporaries against racism.

The text serves not just as a locutionary act. It also has the illocutionary force. Peter Carey does not stop with his reconstruction of Australia's xenophobic memory, which brings out the trauma it has inflicted on aborigines and the damage it has caused to the indigenous culture. He further makes a poetic exploration of the ways to rectify this detrimental fear of the dark races to build a benign cultural ecology. As is analyzed in the above two sections, the first remedy the author gives is reconciliation. White Australians should replace their patronizing subjectivity with inter-subjectivity to achieve a reciprocal understanding with their aboriginal fellowmen. Australia's monolithic white culture should be replaced with interculturality to achieve cultural communication between the two races. The second remedy embodied by Willie is that aborigines are supposed to be healed by the author's narrative, which relates their stories and recovers their identity through restoring their connection with the land. Only when the blacks are not regarded as cannibals but subjects with equal civility and wisdom, when the indigenous culture is not viewed as a superstition but another cultural subject characterized by its primitive vitality, and when aborigines stand up to invent their own tradition which is included in the totality of Australian culture, can Australia and Australian culture acquire a fuller meaning and contemporary Australians, whatever their skin colours are, be able to break away from the restless anxiety overshadowing their identity. Peter Carey's reconstruction of the aboriginal memory is a mimesis of Australia's multicultural policy that has been implemented since 1972. It goes beyond the ethnic policy with a critical reflection and a poetic exploration of how the issues left over from history can be tackled by reconciling white Australians with the aborigines and the preservation of the singular aboriginal cultural memory.

Chapter Three Australia's Neo-colonial Memories[①] to Blame and Illumine the Present

The Commonwealth Government of Australia has switched its strategic subordination from Britain to the United States ever since the Second World War. Indignation at Britain's failure to defend Singapore, which was interpreted as an "inexcusable betrayal", coupled with fear of Japanese invasion, reduced the government to place its forces under the command of Douglas MacArthur in 1942. (Macintyre, 1999: 191) This move taken under dire emergence preludes Australia's new and constitutional subordination to the United States and constitutes a "powerful national legend" (ibid.). The shadow of the Cold War further prompted the government to cement its alliance with America to ease the fear of communist expansion. The friendship was formalised by a security treaty between Australia, New Zealand and the United States (abbreviated to ANZUS). As a consequence, Australia has to devote its obeisance to the protector and cede some of its critical territories to its

---

① By "neo-colonial memory" I mean Australia's collective memory of its political and cultural interactions with the United States which Peter Carey represents as Australia's neo-colonial experience.

control as payment for its protection. For instance, America has been allowed to build its military communication facilities at the North-West Cape since the 1960s, whereas Australia has no right to interfere. To show loyalty to its ally, Australia was consecutively involved in the Korean War and the Vietnam War. The latter event has brought about an earthquake in Australian political and cultural circles, leading to the rise of New Writing. ①

The intimate political relationship between Australia and the United States gives access to American patterns of consumption and recreation, and Australians have been intoxicated by the abundant commodities flooding in from their ally. At the same time, Australian society grows to be less critical, witnessing the "disappearance of the working-class rebel" and "reduced industrial conflicts" since the government tends to "penalise strikes". (Macintyre, 1999: 225) Intellectuals find it hard to reconcile themselves to "the dullness, the conformity and the philistinism" (ibid.: 234) of their country. Some get nostalgic for the lost national traditions and retreat into the memories of an older Australia, which is "more vigilant of its liberties" and "more independent" (ibid.: 226). Others, for instance, novelists of the New Writing, choose to play a more active role in warning their fellow men against the hazard of Americanization. Their writings show much more vigilance to and even anxiety about the relationship between Australian and American culture. Frank Moorhouse suggests in his collected short stories *The Americans, Baby* (1972) how the American consumption economy and culture has affected the Australian way of life and ideology enormously. Murray Bail implies in his prose

---

① The early 1970s witnesses the emergence of Australia's New Writing which distinguishes itself from the Realism initiated by Henry Lawson and the Modernist tradition consummated by Patrick White. Novelist of this persuasion devote themselves to literary innovations both in form and content. Representatives of this denomination are Peter Carey, Michael Wilding, Frank Moorhouse and Murray Bail. (黄源深, 2014: 221/321)

fiction *Holden's Performance* (1987) how Australians' frequent exposure to American commodities and culture gets them gradually "Americanized", alerting Australians to the United States' "cultural colonization"(黄源深, 2014:341). As the most successful author of the New Writing, Peter Carey consummates the poetic exploration of "Americanization", a motif that occurs repeatedly in his prose fiction, as well as short stories. His novellas *American Dreams* and A *Windmill in the West* depict Australians' post-war ambivalence about the American way of life and their more primitive suburban tradition and suggest how their "American dreams" are detrimental to society. In *Illywhacker*, the author explores thinly how struggling it is for Australia to get free from the clutch of American multinational capitalism. The author is dedicated to a more thorough examination of the interaction between Australian and American culture in *The Unusual Life of Tristan Smith* and *Amnesia* with reference to Australia's collective memories.

Unlike from the colonial memory, Australia's neo-colonial memory is retrieved mainly for denouncement and to lumine the present. However, Peter Carey spearheads his condemnation both to the United States for its hegemonic inclination and to Australia for its cultural cringe and forgetting traditions. He reconfigures symbolically the memory of Americanization that has prevailed in Australia since the Secoud World War in *The Unusual Life of Tristan Smith* to blame America's political and cultural hegemony and alert Australians to its colonizing hazard. In addition, that recuperation is more intended to enlighten the present. The author further offers a poetic prescription of inventing Australian culture to protect the nation from losing its identity and ending up being colonized by the new hegemonic power. Carey reworks the tradition of forgetting in *Amnesia* and relates it causally to two ignominious historical events, the Battle of Brisbane and the 1975 coup. This manoeuvre first serves to denounce the United States blatantly for taking advantage of its junior ally and interfering in its political affairs. More importantly, the author alerts his fellow citizens to the detriment of forgetting history to give access to national humiliations. Moreover, the forgetting tradition is restored to call upon Australians to resist the hegemonic power and strive for sovereignty.

Despite the functions above, Peter Carey's recuperation of Australia's neo-colonial memory is also the symbolic representation of the author's anxiety about and reflection on globalization, which might threaten to abolish the political and cultural borders between different nations. Maintaining intercuturality and resisting political and cultural hegemony are the poetic remedies that Carey offers to Australia and the world to cope with the dynamics of globalization. Detailed analysis based on the close reading of the two texts will be presented in the following two sections.

3.1 Americanization Recollected as a Crippling Force: *The Unusual Life of Tristan Smith*

The human body is a site of memory, and what is directly and indirectly written into the body is usually a "cultural script" (A. Assmann, 2011: 234). Body marks may arise out of "unconscious imprints" or "the pressure of violence" (ibid.: 231). In the fiction *The Unusual Life to Tristan Smith*, the titular hero Tristan Smith's body is inscribed into Australia's collective memory of Americanization. To quote Jacque Derrida, "[M]emory … is the very essence of the psyche: resistance" (2002: 252). Thus, in this section, I will focus my research attention firstly on the analysis of how Peter Carey reconfigures symbolically the memory of the Americanization that has prevailed in

Australia since the Second World War in *The Unusual Life of Tristan Smith* to denounce American political and cultural hegemony, blame Australians' blind and uncritical embrace of American culture and alert them to its colonizing hazard. Secondly, I will investigate how the author's recuperation is intended to enlighten the present by offering the poetic prescription of inventing culture to protect Australia from losing its identity and ending up being colonized by the new hegemonic power. After all, the past is usually retrieved to serve, to cite R. Koselleck, the "horizon of expectation" in the future.

3.1.1 Preliminaries of the Fiction

Published in 1994, *The Unusual Life of Tristan Smith* has received contentious reviews. Although the novel ends up winning only The Age Book of the Year Award in the same year presumably because of its overt political implications, it does receive lots of positive reviews. *Los Angeles Times* endorses that "[W]e have a great novelist living on this planet and his name is Peter Carey" (Carey, 1994: cover).[①] Geoffrey Dutton from *Bulletin* notes its aesthetic brilliance and its reference to the outside world and reviews that "[H]is imagination is soaring, his style beautifully disciplined, his eye for truth unblinking" (ibid.). Bruce Cook from *Chicago Tribune* identified its intertextual relationship with the pulse of the time and commented that the novel "has a wild, chance-taking quality, an eye for the grotesque, that puts him in harmony with the spirit of his age" (ibid.). Like most of Carey's early works, this unprecedented work of imagination is complete of overt fantastic and fable-like scenarios. Woodcock observes that it "might be characterized as a cross between the dystopian science fiction and the carnivalesque

---

[①] The following quotations from *The Unusual Life of Tristan Smith* in this section are annotated with only the page number.

qualities" (1996: 108).

Noticing Carey's deviation in form from his other novels, Anthony Hassall proclaims that, "Peter Carey repeats himself less, and surprises his readers more" (1994: 167). However, he fails to point out Carey's unswerving preoccupation with the Australian national psyche. Apart from delving into the complex relationship between Australia and Britain, Peter Carey has also engaged himself frequently with the exploration of Australia's national psyche entwined with American influences in his works. This can be seen from his short story *American Dreams* to novels like *Bliss*, *Illywhacker*, *The Unusual Life of Tristan Smith* and later *Amnesia*. Peng Qinglong argues that one of the sub-motifs is that "Australia, as a lonely outpost on the edge of American empire, yarns after the metropolitan culture of the centre, denies or despises its own cultural achievements" (2005: 118). However, this blind worship and dependence allows grave perils lurking around, which has aroused the interest of a couple of writers. As we have discussed in *Illywhacker*, Carey shows alert and resistance to the American capital erosion of Australia. This time, in *The Unusual Life of Tristan Smith*, he aggravates that alert and resistance by further exploring the hazard of cultural colonization and political manipulation that Americanization might inflict on Australia. As Anthony Hassall observes, this novel "takes the reader on a picaresque roller-coaster ride through contemporary neo-colonial cultural politics" (1998: 165).

This fiction consists of two "Books". Peter Carey chooses his protagonist Tristan Smith, whose name reminds us of the hero of Laurence Sterne's Tristram Shandy, as the first-person narrator to relate his life story, which is devised into the stage in Efica and that in Voorstand, in accordance with the two books. Tristan is a dwarf born with severe deformity on his face and limbs and raised in the Feu Follet, an avant-garde theatre founded by his mother Felicity Smith, the thirty-two years old Voorstand immigrant. With a triangular face without lips, strong shoulders, and withered and tangled legs, he is so grotesque that even the medical staff members suggest his mother abandon him. However, his mother insists on having him saved and cherished. Like other orphaned protagonists in Carey's writings, Tristan is not sure about who his biological father is. He is thus under the care of three men from Feu Follet: Wally Paccione, an ex-convict and now production manager; Bill Millefleur, a young and promising Efican actor; and Vincent Theroux, an Efican politician. He conceives the latter two as his mother's lovers. Their stories of Bruder Mouse, a saint mascot of Voorstand, bring him up.

The first section of the novel is set in Efica, principally in Feu Follet. Tristan takes Voorstanders as his target readers to recollect chronically what he sees and experiences in Efica. As a Voorstander, Felicity sympathises with Efica for its political and cultural affiliation to her home country and a nationalist of the Efican Blue Party. She sets up the Feu Follet to stage Efican stories and intends to get it independent of the penetration and influence of Voorstand Sirkus and change Efica's destiny by inventing its culture. However, the theatre frequently gets itself into trouble with the local authority since it also operates as a political institution and devises plays and other activities in opposition to Voorstand. It is further rendered to be on the brink of bankruptcy for capital deficiency and its inability to provide "first-rate" performances like the Saarlim Sirkus of Voorstand. It finally closes down since Felicity is funded by Vincent to act in the political theatre, that is, to participate in the upcoming Efican election on behalf of the Blue Party. However, under the manipulation of Gabe Manzini, who is a VIA agent of Voorstand, scandals of the suicide of Vincent's wife and his adultery with

Felicity get widespread in the newspaper and Felicity's political life is brought to an end even before it starts. She is schematized because she holds radical opinions against the Voorstand and struggles to get Efica free from its claw. She is eventually hung dead by VIA right at her theatre, the Feu Follet. However, with Gabe's manoeuvre, her death is reported to be an adulterer's guilty suicide. Constantly soaked in Feu Fellet and influenced by his mother's vision, Tristan has developed a passion for performance, and he is determined to be an actor to revitalize the theatre that her mother has shed her blood on despite his inborn handicaps.

The second part of the fiction is Tristan's recollection of his adult life in Voorstand. Accompanied by Wally and his nurse, Jacque, who wears the mask of Bruder Mouse to conceal his handicaps, begins his illegal journey to the enemy country to avenge his mother's death and make peace with his father Bill, Whom Felicity sends to Saarlim Sirkus to sharpen his proficiency in acting. When they arrive, they encounter a Simi, which is a robotic replica of Voorstand's saint mascot, the Bruder Mouse. It is exactly the same height as Tristan, and he takes it as a souvenir. When they are robbed of all their money, Wally guts it for Tristan to climb into the suit, and they get out on the street and put on shows to panhandle. With his small, deformed stature disguised in the full Mouse suit, Tristan can juggle, tumble and stand on one hand. He looks almost like a real living Bruder Mouse. He is loved and worshipped by Voorstanders and its fans. At the party his father holds to celebrate their reunion, his witty and humorous impromptu impresses her father's employer, Peggy Kram, a powerful Voorstand producer who owns twenty Ghostdorps and four Sirkus Domes in Saarlim city. Out of her passion and nostalgia for the Great Historical Past, Kram takes him home for company and amusement, when Bruder mouse walked among the Settlers Free. However, danger is always lurking around. VIA is suspicious of his engagement with the "January 20 group", which intends to overthrow the Voorstand government, so its operatives track him down and plot to assassinate him. Due to Kram's power and influence, he is spared from assassination, but Wally takes the bullet when trying to protect him. Intoxicated with the entertainment Tristan in Bruder Mouse is capable of, she finds him witty and sexy. He is like the incarnation of myth and legend to her. However, when Jacque removes his head mask to save him from suffocation and his true nature is revealed, Kram. is astonished and hollers: "[I]t's the Marchosias; it's Dragon; it's the hairyman; it's Red Saatanil." (411) She accuses him of being a vicious monster disguising himself as God's creature and hands in a disposition to the court for a trial while Tristan and his father have been on their way to the *Arctic Circle*.

The novel appears rather bizarre and even fable-like, with fictionalized countries like Efica and Voorstand, cities like Chemin Rouge and Saarlim, and fantastic protagonist Tristan. However, the author allows multiple of traces for readers to recognize it as a parody of the relationship between Australia and the United States. Efica is a "penal colony" whose "calendar begins with the discovery of Neufasie (later Efica) by Captain Girard" (1). It shares with Voorstand an ancestry tracing back to the "old-world". Sirkus is a parody of American Disney Land and Bruder Mouse, a parody of its archetypical character Mickey Mouse. The dependent and culturally colonized plight of Efica and the "abandoned, self-doubting" (ibid.) Eficans who find their culture inferior and obsess themselves with transformation and making their identity are obviously metaphors of Australia and Australians. As a matter of fact, when talking about his authorial intention with Robert Dessaix, Carey says, "[W]hen I began the novel, I had a site action, if you like — a field of inquiry. I wanted to write about an imperialist power like

America, or a reinvented America... so I wanted to deal with the notion of the centre and the peripheral, the large metropolitan centre and the periphery, that's obviously my cultural and life experience" (1995: 18). In a conversation with Ray Willbanks, Carey again points out the novel's reference to the experiential world, saying that "emotional engine" (1997: 16) behind the novel is the dismissal of Whitlam government. Peter Carey's neo-colonial orientation resonates with the bulk of the scholastic research of this novel. Relating interpretation to the epitext of authorial interview, James Dahlstrom argues that with *The Unusual Life of Tristan Smith* Carey "attempts to make a fictional world in order to connect with the political and social events in the real world of Australia during the 1970s" (2015: 32). Based on a close examination of the lives of the citizens of Efica, he pinpoints that this writing is an allergy "retelling the events and scandals that led to the dismissal of Prime Minister Gough Whitlam, an event which Whitlam himself describes as an 'execution'" (Dahlstrom, 2015: 32). Peng Qionglong also contends that "[T]he novel explores Australia's national psyche during the 1980s and 1990s when the country underwent dramatic changes in terms of domestic and international situations" (彭青龙, 2005: 116).

Apart from its reworking the ashes of history with the attempt to reappraise it from a contemporary perspective and at the service of the horizon of expectation in the future, this novel fits into the genre of neo-historical fiction first with its brazen and peculiar self-consciousness. The first-person narrator keeps addressing his audience as "Meneer, Madam", exposing his fictive status relentlessly. He reveals it frequently and further maintains a highly conscious interaction with readers through various manoeuvres throughout the novel. He lays bare his position of selling a story to them and invites their attention and apathy.

Meneer, Madam, forgive me — but if you had little more

> knowledge of the countries whose destiny you control, I could get on with my story. I'm eager to let you see how my mother and I abandoned the stage and retired to the tower apartment... As you yourselves were once subjects of the Dutch you will understand my passion to set this right before we move on — it is the periphery shouting at the center. (32)

The narrator even tries to control readers by guiding them to read his story in a particular way. "You know this already? Then skip ahead. There are other readers, however, to whom this may be surprising" (356). He tantalizes them and sustains their interest by deferring the part, presumably stirring their curiosity. "I am avoiding your question. You want to know why I left the place where I was safe. Why I felt it necessary to smuggle Wally Paccione into Voorstand in the first place. To tell you this I must — I am sorry — walk back into the dark closed world of the Feu Follet"(234). He raises questions for them to ask for their in-depth involvement. "If I have to choose between the Hairy Man and a fellow with TB digging three miles through solid rock, well, you tell me"(266). He warns them to be alert and keep critical of his narrative by exposing his purposeful deception. "Yes, I came to your country with my secret rage. Yes, I lied to you and said I felt no rage... But, is that not, in normal circumstances, polite?" (401)

The archetypical paradox of neo-historical fiction is also made accessible in *The Unusual Life of Tristan Smith*. On the one hand, Carey is well aware that "[N]othing could be further from the truth" (266) by exposing his novel as an artificial construct both with the provision of imaginary toponyms and characters and with the narrator's self-reflexivity. On the other hand, he appeals for an acceptance of his reconstruction as an alternative version of truth and identification with the value he is going to convey in his narrative by creating verisimilitude.

The most conspicuous strategy the author deploys to suggest its authenticity is the comprehensive use of paratexts. He frequently uses authorial annotations in the text to provide bountiful documentary supplements concerning, for instance, the history and customs of both countries. According to Gerald Genette, these notes "bear precisely on the nonfictional aspect of the narrative" and "play a corroborative role, adducing both testimony and supporting documents" (1997: 332-333). In addition, Carey puts at the very beginning of Book Ⅰ a map of the Republic of Efica, a story excerpted from a book named *Bruder Duck's Travels* with detailed edition note, and an Efican folk song with a reliable source and more detailed publication information. He also places a glossary at the very end of the fiction in which both the irregular Efican and Voorstand English vocabulary are listed and paraphrased in standard English. This prefactorial information serves as the "rhetorical apparatus of persuasion" (Genette, 1997: 198). Moreover, the narrator is arranged to negotiate with his readers to buy his story. "If I will believe that of you, then please believe the following of me: that when, a whole *twelve years* after Voorstand agents murdered my maman, I made the dangerous voyage to your fatherland, it was *not* — as Mrs. Kram would still have you believe — to do your nation harm" (231). Whether readers will take the bite is another story though.

The Unusual Life of Tristan Smith is a symbolically literary demonstration of the relationship between Australia and the United States. It brings Australia's "Americanization" under critical examination. Dahlstrom argues that "is more subtly concerned with the political influence exercised by the USA in Australia after World War Ⅱ and during the war in Vietnam, with an overarching allusion to the supposed role that America played in Gough Whitlam's loss of power" (2015: 33). Other scholars like Peng Qinglong (2005) and Antje Rauwerda (2006) who delve into the fiction from the postcolonial perspective also point to the novel's preoccupation with history and politics, which spares the novel from the denouncement of being devoid of historical consciousness and political engagement. The overflowing political overtone of the novel definitely does not accord to Fredric Jameson's criticism of postmodernism being simply "a neutral practice of such mimicry, without any of parody's ulterior motives, amputated of the satiric impulse" (1991: 17) or Terry Eagleton's accusation that postmodernism has been "depthless, styleless, dehistoricized, decathected" (2006: 128). However, pinpointing the association between the signifier manufactured within the text and the signified reality out of the text or its postcolonial stance does not exhaust the multiple facets of the novel with remarkable profundity and complexity. Through his reference to the experiential world, the author expresses his transcendental concern and his anxiety over Australia's losing of an independent cultural identity, without which it may end up with a client state of the new Empire. What he tries to revive in Tristan's individual memory is the Australian national psyche, the cultural cringe. The 1975 constitutional crisis or the historical setting is only the concrete orientation that memory relies on to create the "points of crystallization" (Assmann, 2011: 24) mentioned above.

Either for its allusion to the dismissal of the Whitlam government or its exploration of the Australian national psyche during the 1980s and the 1990s, this novel does not attempt to record historical facts as they are. Instead, the past is represented through Tristan's personal memory and written into his body. Carey deploys surrealism to tell readers that Tristan has memories before he was born. He inherits the memory of his mother's theatre and things going on there. It is an archetypical memory of his home country. It is the metaphor of Australian collective memory. Like any memory that is recalled to a second space, first and foremost, it is constrained by the social reference frame under which it is reworked. It is equally essential that it is reconstructed by the author to convey particular values and perform specific functions. That makes it unavoidably involve transfiguration, distortion or displacement. This explains why the past tends to reappear in the novel in estranged and exotic faces. In the following sections, I will take a close look at what cultural memory Peter Carey retrieves through Tristan's recollection of his personal story, how it is revived in the textual space, and the functions that it is supposed to fulfil.

3.1.2 Mania for the New Empire

As an orphan with an ignoble origin who is abandoned on the southern land by its European ancestor, Australia has been struggling hard to be accepted and petted by the world's most significant powers to save it from isolation and obscurity. Accordingly, Australia has reduced itself firstly to the Anglicization phase and then to the Americanization phase to realize its independent dream. The latter case is what Carey represents in *The Unusual Life of Tristan Smith*. The most impressive image ingrained in Tristan's memory is Efica's craze for Voorstand, which is a metaphor for Australia's mania for the United States. It was roughly initiated since the First World War, strengthened in and after the Second World War, and exploded towards the end of the 1970s. According to Stuart Macintyre, in the 1920s, "[D]espite the higher duties on non-imperial products, American goods increased to more than a quarter of all Australian imports. Despite the call for restrictions, American films, comics, jazz were avidly consumed ... Life appeared more glamorous, more real, on the other side of the Pacific" (1999: 176). Australia's growing attachment to America has been formalized and increasingly cemented through the security treaty of ANZUS, which was signed in

1952. Australia's fate was more tied to the United States when the government agreed to send troops to Vietnam as requested and allowed America to build military communication facilities at the North-West Cape and Pine Gap in the 1960s and strengthen them in the 1980s. American influence can also be found in Australia's "'New Wave' theatre movement" in the 1970s; traditional drama which features Australian nationalism is condemned to be provincial, lack of profundity and out of date; new theatres like La Mama are established, and Broadway plays are taken as their models. (黄源深, 2014: 538-540) These historical events are reconstructed in *The Unusual life of Tristan Smith*, only that they reappear in form of cultural memory, thus with an estranged face.

As Tristan remembers, Eficans hold a craze not only for Voorstand's advanced technology but also for its popular culture. They are stunned both by Voorstand's "holographs, lasers, Vids" and by its "jokes and dancers, death and beauty, with perfectly engineered and orchestrated suspense" (294). Their prevalent worship of Voorstand makes the consumption of its goods and culture their daily routine. The cultural values have infiltrated every inch of the Efican land. As Tristan remembers,

> [W]e grow up with your foreignness deep inside our souls, knowing the Bruder clowns, the Bruder tales, the stories of the Saints, the history (defeating the Dutch, tricking the British, humiliating the French, all this gets you big marks in the islands of Efica). We recite your epic poets for the same reason we study Moliere or Shakespeare, listen to your pow-pow music as we fall in love, fly your fragrant peaches halfway across the earth and sit at the table with their perfect juices running down our foreign chins. (292)

Voorstand's commodities and culture are so popular with Eficans that they find themselves hopelessly addicted to them like opium-eaters and trapped in the delusion that they are part of Voorstanders. In other words, Efica has been practically Voorstandized. To quote Tristan, "We have danced to you, cried with you, and even when we write our manifestoes against you, even when beg you please leave our lives alone, we admire you, not just because we have woven your music into our love affairs and wedding feasts" (ibid.). Eficans have gone so far in their mania that they cannot seem to demarcate which part of their role model is authentic and which is solely their own imaginary invention of it. Their inborn abjection is conducive to painting their superior counterpart with a hovering halo, and they imagine obtaining an equal sense of superiority by their affinity with it. The relationship between Efica and Voorstand is a metaphor for that between the obscure and cringing Australia and its powerful ally, the United States.

Whether for Bill, Sparrow or Roxanna, it seems every character in the novel is, in one way or another, conquered by Voorstand's charisma. Even those who are burdened with the nationalist dream of independence, like Tristan, Felicity and Vincent, have ambivalent feelings towards Voorstand, finding themselves hopelessly drawn to its mysterious sacredness. Tristan's biological father, Bill, is one of many Eficans who pin their hope for success and enormous fortune on Voorstand. He would like to do it at the cost of abandoning his mentor and lover and neglecting his paternal obligation. When Feu Follet is on the edge of bankruptcy since not many Eficans are able to afford a ticket, people flood into the theatre when the Sirkus goes on a tour in Efica. After the show, Sparrow applauds loudly for its first-class performance, elevates his compliment by associating Sirkus show with Voorstanders' impeccable moral standards, and acclaims doggedly that "[T]hey're a great people" (168). Even Tristan, the incarnation of Efica's nationalist, allows himself to be swayed in his attitude, "[T]hat is what a show like this teaches you. Theirs was a country that was founded on a principle. What you can still see in this Sirkus is their decency" (168). Eficans are impressed by and drawn to Voorstand's greatness. At the same time, their feelings of inferiority propel them to strive for superiority by socializing with Voorstanders and making themselves more like them.

 Like other Eficans possessed by the embarrassment of their ignoble birth, Roxanna, who feels "pitiful for her low level of life" (181), is fascinated with any chance for transformation and upgradation, and she picks Felicity the Voorstander as her role model. Thinking her "thick ankles" have been an obstruction to her actress dream, she imagines Felicity "could do well almost in everything" with her "very nice legs" (177). Roxanna's awkwardness towards her physical impaction emblemizes Eficans', thus Australians' feelings of inferiority, which lead to their cringing at their idols. She is suckled on the "Voorstand Dream", which is closely related to money, and she interiorizes it as an indispensable part in her life. "It is the only thing I am interested in: money. I don't like the place here. I don't like how it smells, or looks, or feels"(113). She refuses to be Wally's lover after they had sex because she does not regard him the right man for her. She also determines to find someone who thinks she is a "treasure", a "rich man". She even "promised herself she was going to marry a rich man, and there was nothing on earth — no *Pigeon Patissy*, not sex, not French champagne, not the tender feelings she had begun to engender in her breast towards Wally Paccione — nothing that would make her change her mind" (196). She is convinced that she can definitely do it "[B]ecause I decided. Because I planned. Because I have worked, and studied, and prepared" (182). She is entirely "Voorstandized". Her dream is soaked with Vooratand's flavour.

Roxanna is so desperate about her big dream that she goes with Gabe Manzini to his hotel exactly three hours after their first meeting just because he is a Voorstander, and she sees in him the sparkle of her Voorstand dream. His English, with a slight Efican accent, is "as exotic and beautiful to her ears as glass angel... She loved the way he talked. She liked the bright, clean confidence of his voice and that three-showers-a-day smell, all soap and steam and light spicy after shave" (206). She is intoxicated with the illusion that her dream is at her fingertips and persuades herself that Gabe could provide all the items she aspires in life, "a country house with a park, peacocks, a fountain... a white carpet, a brass bed with lace-covered pillows of different sizes" (ibid.). She sees him as a banker, the God, "the answer to all her prayers" (218). But, Gabe is sober. He sees in her, like all other Efican girls he has hooked, a "personal craziness matched with the craziness of the country" (202).

Voorstandization pervading Efica does not just affect its mediocre citizens like Roxanna or Sparrow. Even those with clear historical and national consciousness fall prey to its contagions. Vincent has a strong nationalist consciousness and lends his loyal support to the Blue Party. Nevertheless, he is both hostile to and affinitive with Voortand and its culture. Aware of what he and the Blue Party had been up to,

> he imagined Efica would soon be free of Voortand influence — its spies, its cables, and of the Sirkus which was then threatening to wash across us like a tidal wave. He wanted Efica to be free of Sirkus. But also — he loved the Sirkus. This was what the VIA never understood about him. He was a serious scholar of Voorstand culture, painting, music, literature. (56-57)

Moreover, Felicity, the chief director of Efican nationalist campaign, is unable to cut herself off from the charisma of her home country. On the contrary, she herself is an admirer of Voorstand's high technology and would not hesitate to apply it to the Efican milieu. More importantly, she finds it natural, consciously or unconsciously, to distort Eficans and acclimatize them to that technology. She may mean well or do all these subconsciously, but Tristan sees this through from a bystander's perspective:

> [N]o matter what her critique of Voorstand hegemony, my mama obviously held more complex feeling for Bruder Mouse than she had ever admitted to the collective... She was a creature of her culture. No matter that she denounced your country's intrusion into Efican soil, she was a Voortstander. You can see it in the Feu Follet acting style, which has its roots in the laser technology of the Sirkus. My mother pushed her actors into shapes more suitable for laser stick-and-circle figures than human beings with rigid skeletons. She would do this to herself, contort herself at the expense of ligaments, bloat or purge herself, shave her head, willingly distort her perfect future. (185)

Efica's mania for Voorstand is represented through the above characters at the level of their consumption of Voorstand commodities and its popular culture, interiorizing its mercantile value and enchanted with its dream. It is represented through Tristan more in the symbolic sense and with more profundity.

Tristan is more readily exposed to Sirkus's plays owing to the theatric milieu he was born with. In his memory, he has been brought up with the stories of Bruder Mouse, Oncle Duck, and other Sirkus characters, which are Voorstand's machines for cultural propagation and domination. As the "emblem" and "mascot" of Efican culture as well as the most ambitious Efican nationalist, Tristan himself owes half his genes to Voorstand. Though he is not sure which of the tree Efican men is his father, he is quite certain that his mother is a Voorstander and takes great pride in that. Tristan is more Voorstandized than his fellowmen in that he has Voorstand's blood flow in his vessels. Just as there is not the slighest problem with Tristan's acknowledgement of Felicity as his mother, it is out of the question for his identification with Voorstand's culture and values. This can be seen from his intoxication when he, dressed in the Simi suit, is appreciated by Peggy Kram. Instead of carrying revenge on the mind, "I was under the impression that I was a social success. I was elated, aroused, almost tipsy on her perfume" (363). This prophesies that Efican culture would be genetically transformed and replaced with the hybridity of both cultures instead of being of pure Efican flavour. This is in accordance with Edward W. Said's observation that "[P]artly because of all cultures are involved in one another; none is single and pure, all are hybrid, heterogenous, extraordinarily differentiated, and unmonolithic" (1993: xxv). This may further render any combat against the hegemony pointless and foreshadows the eventual assimilation of Efican culture into that of the Voorstand. Eficans will end up wailing helplessly about what their mania has jeopardized. That is what the author tries to warn Australia against: its excessive dependence on the United States, which invites itself to be Americanized, will lead to Australians' identification with American culture which might eventually cripple that of their own and deprive the nation of its political sovereignty.

3.1.3 Hybridized Cripple of Imperialism

Australia's apparent cringe at the United States has aroused tremendous anxiety and invited criticism and resistance of various forms, especially since the 1960s. As Carter points out, "Radicals and conservatives alike shared the fear of Americanization as a threat to the national culture, which is a foundation to construct the independent nationhood. A new left-wing critique of the US cultural imperialism developed during and after Australia's involvement in the Vietnam War" (2000: 71). The Whitlam government elected in 1972 withdrew Australian troops from Vietnam and tried to exercise control over the American military communication facilities. More importantly, flexible cultural policies and liberal political vision implemented by the Whitlam government cultivated Australia's nationalist sentiment. To quote Stuart Macintyre, "[T]he expansion of support for the arts, increased Australian content requirements for television and preservation of historical sites were among the initiatives designed to promote greater national awareness" (1999: 238). Australia's involvement in the Vietnam War has incurred national protests and stirred Australians' independent sense of nationhood. Compounded with the Whitlam government's abrupt dismissal by General Sir John Kerr, "a more general fear of rightward drift in Australian society" (Burgmann, 1988: 277) is produced. Waves to get away from American influence and achieve cultural independence rise up. Australia's ambivalence towards the United States is also reflected in the literary world. America is described as "the gleaming promise to modernity or the barbarism of economically driven consumerism" (Bell & Bell, 1993: 203). "A mythologized America is routinely deployed in media constructions of utopia and dystopia futures for Australia" (Turner, 1994: 98-99). Australia's complicated feeling towards America, as well as its anxiety about the nation's Americanization, is also reconstructed through Tristan's reminiscence of his life story.

Edward W. Said argues that imperialism lingers in the "general cultural sphere as well as in specific political, ideological, economic and social practices 'although' direct colonialism has largely ended" (1993: 9) in our time. Typically, all kinds of preparations for the enterprise of empire are made within a culture. (Said, 1993: 11) What is happening in Efican culture, the Voorstandization, prepares it for the dominance of

Voorstand, the empire. Taking advantage of Eficans' mania for its culture, Voorstand implements cultural infiltration into and domination of Efica right through Sirkus, which is the incarnation of Voorstand's ideology. It "has an ethical and religious history, something of an expert on the theology of the 'Settlers Free'" (57), and is oriented to propagate that. While Eficans are enchanted with its hilarious performance, they are unconsciously instilled in the country's values and morality. The first half of the Sirkus features hordes of clowns dressed in cast-off uniforms of conquered nations. They appear on the stage, giving an impression of "ragamuffin POWs set free in Voorstand", and at the intermission, they "became an orchestra playing wild, lonely, funny, Pow-pow music" (165). In the second half of the Sirkus show, Bruder Mouse's live and holographic dancing is shown. More than just "a logo-type, the symbol for an imperialist mercantile culture", the modern Bruder Mouse is "quick and cocky and as cruel as any animal that has to deal with survival on the farm. He had spark, guts, energy, can-do" (167). It is equipped with practically all the delicate characters of confidence, aggressiveness and toughness, which Eficans do not have and yarn for. The Sirkus show conveys the message that Voorstand is a promised land to guarantee a chance for transformation and a joyful, as well as meaningful existence of life, even for outcasts. Sirkus participates in Voorstand's imperialism by drawing Eficans to the "greatness" of the empire and creating among them a metaphysical yarning for being part of it. Tristan comments as the implied author what Sirkus is capable of through its dazzling performance is "propaganda" (166). Eficans are lured to interiorize Voorstand's values while consuming culture commodities excessively, paving the way for a bigger deception following up.

The other main course of the second half of Sirkus's performance is Irma's singing and recitation. She is a character that Sirkus managers improvise to cater for Efica's local taste. Out of their deliberate choice, she is just like an Efican, "she was not perfect. Her rose-bud lips were a little small, her neck...a little short" (167). She is made so approachable that spectators can not help but associate her with themselves or their folks. She recites Efican stories on the stage, producing the effect that "[w]e were flattered, and moved to hear our own tragedies and Pyrrhic victories celebrated in her exotic accent... Our stories seemed bigger when she recited them... each word is clear, just as she could put flesh and blood on the bones of our drowned fishermen and make us weep for our abandoned dyers" (167-168). Eficans have no idea that the careful study and respect of their mores is in essence "a 'racism with a distance'—it 'respects' the Other's identity, conceiving of the Other as a self-enclosed 'authentic' community towards which he, the multiculturalist, maintains a distance rendered possible by his privileged universal position" (Zizek, 2006: 171)

Irma is made a memory figure of Efican collective memory, which is under the command of the Sirkus. Voorstand manipulates Efica's collective memory through its control over Irma so that Efican national stories can be made "bigger" by the Sirkus actress. It points to the constructiveness of memory, as well as its alliance with power. (Assmann, 2011: 53) Irma dances with the Bruder Mouse, a quick fast Pow-pow shimmy. The differences between them and the giants they worship seem to be dismantled in the show, and Eficans are enchanted with the ecstasy that their Voorstand counterpart treats them as their equivalent, and values them and their tradition equally, if not more than they do. As Antje Rauwerda argues, with the conceiving of Irma, "[T]he 'skill' is in the manipulation of Eficans so that they feel like citizens of Sirkus, and so that they feel like they want to be Sirkus citizens" (Rauwerda, 2006: 120-121). Culture is never free from worldly affiliations, and the processes of imperialism are manifested at the level of culture. The consecutive dazzling performance of the clowns, the Bruder Mouse, and Irma, is conducive to robbing most Eficans of their reason to maintain vigilance against the imperialism and sit back obediently to resume relishing the great works of Voorstand literature as if they share the ownership of that cultural inheritance. Only very few sober ones like Tristan are aware that "it is easy enough to attribute all of this to politics and power" (168).

Through suspending their differences and creating a temporary sense of equality within a community, Voorstand mesmerizes its Efican counterparts that they are elevated through their association with them, which lays a foundation for its eventual conquer of Efica. Fed on Voorstand stories, Tristan is tutored to believe he is "different, but superior" (67). When Roxanna, the spoony Efican girl, complains tearfully to Gabe about her "fat, pork-chop, ugly" ankles and asks him not to kiss them. The hypocrite contests, "What do you know? They are beautiful feet" (201). Then he kneels on the floor and stamps his kisses on them. When Roxanna confesses that she is a pyromaniac, he regards that craziness to be part of their "sexual fizz" (202), and consoles her that it is not a problem since he can hide his watches from her. With this overwhelming sense of being treasured by a man much better than her, Roxanna completely gives herself up to him, leaving her gullibility exploited shamelessly. Gabe's respect for Roxanna's authenticity is actually his alienation from her. Eventually, her credulousness leads VIA's claw to the Blue Party's election and causes Felicity's assassination.

With the assistance of the Sirius show as cultural hypnotism, Voorstand clears the impediment to its economic exploit and political hegemony. The result is that "Efican territorial waters supplied 25 percent Voorstand's fish... the northern islands provided a safe storage place for chemical waste" (202-203). Moreover, "[T]he alliance between the parliamentary democracies of Voorstand and Efica is built on tress areas of joint cooperation — Defense, Navigation, Intelligence — DNI" (135), which proximately means Efica is giving away its military and economic power and it is surrendering the lever to negotiate anything with its ally in the future. In the narrator's words, it is like a political "fantasy" because "Efica's southern granite islands were now host to fifteen vital subterranean defence projects. Eficans would not be permitted to reject their twenty-five-year-old alliance with Voorstand" (203). However, Eficans, whose long military dependence on English and French has forged them to be pragmatic and deferent, and they, are deprived of national or historical consciousness. They are more concerned with their immediate comfort and do not possess the vision to foresee their position in the distant future, not even the intellectual minority. Voorstanders will take every means to stop any Efican resistance and attempt to threaten their vested interest. To have full command of Efica's public sentiment and "make sure the status quo is maintained" (ibid.), Voorstand taps their telephone, stops Feu Follet's performance, and burgles people's residence. When more and more people respond to the Blue Party, who are resolute in removing Voorstand's devices from Efica and Efican soil once they win the election, they plot against the promising candidate Felicity, scheme scandal, arrange assassination and plant it on her. Eventually, it kills her and fakes her death to make it appear like a suicide. The Blue Party's ambition to stand up against it is aborted in such a ferocious way.

That is not the end of the story. Since historiography always smells the stink of power, Efica's historical writing naturally falls into Voorstand's clutches, too. As Gabi flaunts to Roxanna, "I am respected... They know I am the best. I write their fucking history books" (217).

Voorstand exerts further influence on Efican public opinion by giving a false account of what actually happens. Under its manipulation, the ace, the Blues' downfall is ascribed to their incompetence and corruption; Natalie's murder is faked to be the desperate resort of a docile housewife who is tormented by her husband's unbearable adultery; Felicity's "suicide" is a notorious "adulterer's death" and "[S]he is remembered in the morass of shame that Eficans feel about this time" (223). Reality is a discursive construction. Voorstand's historical writing of Efica becomes the metanarrative that instructs people to learn what happened in this country, exerting control over its collective memory. The author makes Efican historiography a metaphor for that of Australian which is clouded by the imperial power. In a larger picture, Carey points to the discursiveness of history and memory, casting doubt on the authenticity of the grand narrative.

Ultimately, the author epitomizes Voorstand's detrimental cultural impact by the metaphor of Tristan's malformed body. The body is memory, and "bears the memory traces imprinted on it" (Clastres, 1989: 184). Body memory "may arise out of long physical habits, unconscious imprints, or the pressure of violence" (A. Assmann, 2011: 231). It could be a record of autobiographical experiences, and it could also be a "cultural script written directly and indirectly into the body" (ibid.: 234). Tristan's body is a combination of the two. Since Tristan is raised in his mother's theatre and fed on the Voorstand stories, his body is more of the receiver of Voorstand's culture and ingrained with Efica's memory of the impact of its counterpart. As body memory "never happened without blood, torments and sacrifices" (Nietzche, 2006: 38), the multiple deformities of Tristan's body stand witness to various forms of violence that Voorstand has done to Efica, reminding its people how dreadful Americanization would be.

Tristan's multiple deformities are the horrible hybrid of hegemonic Voortand culture and the dependent Efican one. When he was born, "[H]is eyes are pale, a quartz-bright white. They bulge intensely in his face. He has a baby's nose — but in the lower part of his severely triangular face, there is, it seems, not sufficient skin. His face pulls itself. He has no lips, but a gap in the skin that sometimes shows his toothless gums" (31). In his self-description, he "was, indeed, a curious-looking child-strong in the shoulders, withered and tangled in the legs. My hair was dense and blond, and the irises of my eyes — although no longer white as they had been when I was born — were now milky, marbled, striated with hair-line spokes of gold" (67). His skin is, especially, "so white" that the dazzling whiteness is genuinely horrible to look at (160). Once, running away from the theatre, he ends up being put in the burnt unit of a hospital because he is mistaken for a burnt victim. His stature is so conspicuously small that in order to escape from the hospital without being noticed, he can climb down a pipe. At the end of the pipe stand hordes of Efican and Voorstand spectators, among whom two kids, an Efican one and a white one, cry out, "a mutant", a grotesque "Phantome Drool" (157). Here, Carey parodies Frantz Fanon's record of a white child and mother seeing a 'black' man. Fanon's child says: "Look, a Negro!... Mama, see the Negro! I'm frightened." (Rauwerda, 2006: 118) The difference is what Carey's child exclaims is, "Yuk, Maman. A mutant" (157). In the author's depiction, Tristan is a Voorstand's monster in the eyes of his Efican folks and the Other in that of the Voorstanders to whom he owes half his genes to. He is the mirror image of Eficans, only that they are unconscious of that. The parody shows how Efica, as the receiver of Voorstand's hegemonic power, falls victim to the alienation both inflicted by Voorstand and by itself and eventually loses its cultural identity, just like Tristan, who is driven into exile by both worlds. Tristan's hurt is the embodiment of Efica's cultural plight, which is an analogy to Australia's predicament.

To prophesy the possible hazard of Voorstandization, thus Americanization, Carey does not stop solely with Efica's loss of cultural identity. He digs deeper. Tristan is not only grotesquely malformed in his limbs or face. With a cleft palate, he is born to be nearly aphasic, which symbolizes Efica's lost power of discourse. His speech is difficult to understand. Whenever he tries to open his "gap" to utter any word, he ends up murmuring and nobody cares what it is about. When they are in Voorstand, Jacqui gives him a Sirkus vocal patch that can resonate with the vibration on the throat and convert it to properly modulated speech. With the help of this Voorstand gadget, he makes himself intelligible for the first time in his life. However, when he is allowed to speak, he speaks in Voorstand's accent instead of his own. What comes out of his mouth are lines of Richard, the Duke of Gloucester, "[N]ow is the winter of our discontent, Made glorious summer by this sun of York" (376). King Richard Ⅲ with extreme deformity recreated by Shakespeare is a depiction of himself: grotesque, monstrous and perverse.

Even when, for the first time in his whole life, he can express himself "clearly", he is unable to utter anything against Voorstand, though he has smuggled into the country with inflaming hatred and the intention to avenge the Voorstanders who killed his mother. Having long been soaked in Voorstand culture, he has been disarmed of resistance and can not even say anything that is purely Efican. All he can do is to play Caliban, the half human half monster, who is forced into servitude on his own isle in Shakespeare's *The Tempest*. "I prithee, let me bring thee where crabs grow. And I with my long nails will dig thee pig-nuts, show thee a jay's nest, and instruct thee how to snare the nimble marmoset... I'll show thee the best springs; I'll pluck thee berries" (377-378). Here, the author makes an analogy between Caliban and Efica. Caliban's offering of the fruits, nuts, and animals of his island to his masters Prospero and Miranda metaphorizes Efica's provision of its resources to Voorstand. The instructions offered by Caliban to his masters on how to trap the marmoset of his isle is a metaphor for Efica's opening up its defence, navigation and intelligence to Voorstand only to allow the country to be cabled like a spider web, which is a recipe for future disaster. All in all, when Efica's Voorstandization encourages its culture to flourish on its own land, it begins the procedure of suffocating its own culture, which may further endanger the country's sovereignty and eventually force it into servitude without resistance. Tristan has foreseen this possible apocalyptic scene. "My life had been filled with sexual yearning, but yarning is not the same as hope ... I was someone driven by impossible desire, someone whose very soul is shaped by the sure knowledge that his dreams will not come true"(331).

When it comes to issues that might threaten Australia's creation of an independent identity, sovereignty, maturization and wellbeing, for instance, its Americanization, Carey demonstrates as much anxiety and bad-temper as he does in *Illywhacker* or *Oscar and Lucinda*. Nevertheless, he is not as pessimistic as he appears in them. On the contrary, Carey is much more progressive in exploring ways of dealing with those issues and optimistic towards his core character, Tristan's transformation.

3.1.4 Culture as Armour

It is reasonable to interpret *The Unusual Life of Tristan Smith* as a political fable of the trial of the new hegemonic power and the resistance of the peripheral to the central. However, what lies under that superficial concern is the author's persistence in the excavation of Australia's cultural memories, mostly the negative ones, discovering or inventing them, reappraising them critically, and exploring poetically possible remedies to surpass them. Following his retrieval of Australia's memory of its mania for the United States and his anatomy of the crippling hazards of Americanization to Australian cultural and political freedom, the author continues with his poetic exploration of the way by which Australia gets out of the possible entrapment. This is metaphorically embodied in Tristan and her mother Felicity's endeavour to invent Efican culture through the Feu Follet at one end and subvert that of the Voorstand at the other when he realizes "[O]ur great defence is our culture, and the brutal truth is — we have none" (231).

When most Eficans busy themselves with their intoxication with things related to Voorstand, its technology, its culture, and the government is indulged in adulation of its counterpart with an all-round alliance that buys its way to Efica's critical territories, Efica is rendered to be a lost paradise. When he wakes up every morning, what emerges on Tristan's horizon is the apocalypse scene:

> Rock-walled fields of brown grass thatched with rust like Harris tweed, ravines, dry rivers with stones like prehistoric eggs, a chalky coastal estuary... The road themselves were mostly dirt, bordered with century — old cairns commemorating famous deaths by starvation, "rot", spearing, typhoid, pigheadedness and folly. This was the country everybody felt was Efica — mostly wind, water, sky. There was an emptiness, a refusal to charm, an edge of terror in the air which cuts us to the bone. The landscape was dotted with failed attempts at European enterprise — bauxite, farmhouses, abandoned rusting windmills. The skies were a huge and empty ultramarine. (66)

This is not only a depiction of the barren landscape. It is also a metaphorical portrait of Efica's cultural infertility. Since culture is the coat of a nation, the lack of healthy cultural traditions makes it very hard for Efica to construct a mature national identity by which its people confirm who they are and nestle their souls. As Felicity says in despair and indignation,

> [N]o one can even tell me what an Efican national identity might be. We're northern hemisphere people who have been abandoned in the south. All we know is what we're not. We're not like those snobbish French or those barbaric English. We don't think rats have souls like the Voorstanders. But what are we? We're just sort of "here". We're a flea circus. (117)

However hard it is, Felicity is determined to take on the mission to invent Efican culture by building Feu Follet for its people to nestle their souls in.

Tristan is brought up seeing her mother and her colleagues being guardians and fighters of Efican culture. They are determined to change the destiny of the country with the power of theatrical arts, and devote themselves to saving their country from being assimilated and enslaved by Voorstand. Tristan describes his vision of this cause: "[I]n Efica you could have the illusion of being a warrior in a great battle, and when you toured you lived with others who shared the same illusion. When you toured, you performed as if art mattered. Doing agitprop under a petite tent you are inventing your nation's culture." (77) They turn to Efica's singular heritage for inspiration. They write crude and funny little stories based on their own life experiences. They create Efican drama. They incorporate circus skills like juggling and acrobatics into the shows. Not only do they exhibit the charisma of Efican culture, but they also disenchant Voorstand and its culture by integrating into the show their mockery of Efica's snivelling alliance with Voorstand and the subservient Red Party by parodying the canonical characters of Sirkus, like Bruder

Mouse and Oncle Duck. They deploy the tactic of, in Edward's words, "imposture" as a mechanism to fight for the survival of their own culture. By portraying Sirkus heroes as buffoons with physical awkwardness or personality defects or recasting them into different roles: "Phantome a spy, the Dog a soldier, the sharp-toothed blue-coated Mouse a paranoid — its white-gloved finger hovering above a button which might destroy the planet", they "broke the obscenity laws, the alliance laws, the secrecy laws, all in one act with two posturers" (55). While Helen Tiffin argues that the "determined dissidence" created by the colonial imposture threatens the imperial bid to secure a stable, coherent, and politically expedient subject (Tiffin, 1996: 134), the dissidence created by Feu Follet actors and actresses also problematizes the halo of the Voortand as the imperial centre and prompts critical evaluation from within Efica.

However, it is often easier said than done, and the theatre has to run with scissors. With highly inadequate raw materials in the lost paradise, it is a great challenge for actors to compose original works. Moreover, it has become even more problematic due to the lack of financial support from the government. Felicity, the founder of Feu and Follet, is more often than not out of her depth to raise enough funds to sustain the theatre and make sure her handicapped son is provided with proper medical care and education. In order to cultivate Eficans' national consciousness and mobilize them to join their team in fighting against Voorstand's cultural domination, the company may have to play agitprop at factory gates, or even street fairs. The paradox is that it is a luxury for people dwelling in those places to afford a theatre ticket. Feu Follet often fails to make two ends meet. On the contrary, the government's protective tariff policy is conducive for the Sirkus to penetrate deeply into the land. "[W]e are prohibited from placing a 2 percent tariff on their Sirkus tickets to subsidize our own theatre. They call this unfair trade, yet we know every ticket we buy to the Sirkus weaken us, swamps us further, suffocates us" (231). The theatre is almost suffocated by the conservative government and its competitive Voorstand rival. To make things worse, their programs are often under severe official censorship to avoid any blemishing of the government or degeneration of Voorstand. The theatre is under the direct surveillance of VIA, and danger, even death threats may creep up on its actors and actresses any minute before any transgression takes place. That is how Felicity's life is claimed. Her death suspends Feu Follet's endeavour to invent Efican culture. The consequence is that "[T]he Sirkus Domes spread across our little islands and the Bruders appear to spread their stories... in every corner of my nation's life" (311).

Smitten by the grief of losing his dear mother and the loss of hope to invent Efican culture, Tristan decides to flee to Voorstand to get away from the "vile octopus" (231) and resume her mother's unaccomplished mission in another way: becoming an "overman". In his enemy country, his team butcher the last Simulacrum of Bruder Mouse, a symbol of the God of Voorstand, gutting it out and fitting Tristan inside it. Tristan, the pathetic creature who had skulked inside the Feu Follet, is transformed into an "overman", "the lightning from the dark cloud", the "madness". (Nietzsche, 2006: 6/12) With his skilful cascading, juggling and tumbling tricks he learns at the Feu Follet, he wins over Voorstanders' respect. They bow to him. They send him gifts. They become "devotees, worshipers" and he is "now the object of these people's love" (398). Tristan, in the Bruder Mouse costume, becomes the one who posits the value of things. Peggy Kram, the most powerful producer of the Saarlim Sirkus, invites him to her apartment and treats him as a distinguished guest, one of her Saints. She offers him an extremely ornate room, with Voorstanders at his service. She takes him to meet her upper-class friends, and they like him too. She would like to listen to his bedtime stories. She would like to walk back and forth in front of him "with no other clothes than those her God had given her" (398). She would like to listen to Tristan's opinion on her hairstyle. She sneaks into his bed and sleeps in his arms, whispering, "This is better than a man. I'm going to keep you" (400). Tristan's disguise becomes the "Historical Past" (406), which she would like to preserve. In that costume, he is received by Voorstanders with great reverence and passion, no less than that Eficans have shown for the Sirkus.

When his true nature is revealed as Jacqui rips off his Mouse-head, for Kram, he proves to be the most horrifying creature in the world. Tristan's "performance" metaphors the different faces that Voorstand wears in the eyes of Eficans, and the authentic Tristan is in fact a mirror image of Voorstand. By revealing his own monstrous nature beneath the disguise of some Saint, Tristan demonstrates the monstrosity that his counterpart is capable of. Tristan serves as an authentic reflection of Voorstand to remind its people of what it truly is for Efica and Eficans. In other words, he subverts Voorstand's culture by his imposture of Voorstand's cultural icon, the Bruder Mouse, and demonstrates its Otherness. He avenges his mother figuratively by that subversion. Compared with his mother, who is oriented to save Efica from slavery by inventing its culture, he takes a more swerving path to resume that goal. Tristan employs imposture, an alternative for small and weak countries like Efica which do not have enough power to contend against the empire and disrupt the imperial system. Just as Peng Qinglong argues, it is "an effective counter-hegemonic strategy in neo-colonial discourse to question the consequentiality of colonial discourse and subvert within" (彭青龙, 2005: 128).

As discussed in the previous sections, Peter Carey connects his aesthetic world to Australian collective memory, through *The Unusual Life of Tristan Smith*. Through Tristan's fictional and apparently bizarre personal reminiscence of his earlier life story, he reworks analogically on Australia's Americanization partly owing to its cringe tradition. Usually, the past tends to re-emerge in literary works in an estranged way to make it possible to maintain the distance between the signified and the signifier, which facilities the author's symbolic representation of and critical re-evaluation of history. A multiplicity of textual clues suggests that the relationship between the two fictional countries of Efica and Voorstand is actually an analogy of that between Australia and America. Traces are also adequate to lead Felicity and her Blue Party to the aesthetic recreation of Gough Whitlam and his Labour Party. Tristan Smith is an emblem prophesying the possible outcome of Australia's Americanization. Here, we can see the Australian mania memory has gone through tremendous transformation and distortion, even re-invention in this novel to fulfil multiple functions.

First and foremost, Australia's collective memory of Americanization is restored and amplified for a critical re-evaluation. Australia's excessive and uncritical attachment to America is represented by Carey as extremely hazardous. Excessive worship and consumption of American advanced technology and popular culture might result in a growing dependence on them. The concomitant legacy would be the worshipers' and consumers' identification with American culture and values. Just as what is portrayed in the novel, proximately the whole list of characters, Roxanna, Bill, and even the ambitious nationalistic protagonist Tristan, are deeply affected by American mercantile culture and interiorize it as their own. However, that is only part of the whole threatening picture. The plight might be unimaginably aggravated when more competitive American culture is given free rein by the government. As depicted in the novel, the Efican government places no tariff on imports from Voorstand. While American culture is thriving in Australia, the nation's own culture is diminishing and even facing the danger of withering away, which is bound to pose a threat to Australia's cultural independence. This observance is in accordance with Carey's authorial intention in an interview. "I am concerned with the difficulties the little theater being able to invent a culture for its country in the face of the big slick machine of Sirkus. It's not so much that I'm personally worried about the input of ideas from Sirkus or its values, but it suppresses the emergence of other culture"(Willbanks, 1997:15).

Self-inflicted cultural colonization is only half the jeopardy of Americanization. Its far-reaching, devastating influence also lies in its complicity with American cultural and political hegemony. Australian government's fawning policy to allow American corporations to stick to the country's vital departments such as defence, navigation, and intelligence may mean that it will eventually relinquish the country's political sovereignty and end up as a subservient client state. The overthrow of Efica's Blue Party and the assassination of its candidate, Felicity, serves as the embodiment to illustrate the detrimental consequence of American clutches at Australian intelligence. This plot is a symbolic representation of the Australian constitutional crisis in 1975. It is reconstructed along the line of "conspiratorial interpretation of political activity" (Macintyre, 1999: 242). The motivation for Carey's engineering lies in the thrust to deconstruct the official memory, which stigmatizes the Whitlam government by attributing its dismissal to its dangerous incompetence in tackling the national issues of inflation and unemployment. Simultaneously, it legitimizes the alternative version of American interference provided in the novel. While claiming its rights to be included in the nation's collective memory, this alternative version serves to stand witness to American political hegemony over Australia, remind Australians of America's wilful trample upon their country's sovereignty, and foment possible actions to fight against it to avoid future plight.

Secondly, the Americanization memory is revisited to denounce the United States as the new imperial power that deploys jointly the measures of cultural transmission and political alliance to plunder, annex and colonize weak and small countries. Americanization is a reflection of Australians' unsettling sense of belonging. As Tristan whines in grief, they are northlanders who are cast off on the south land. The insecurity coming from the sense of rootlessness and the fear of isolation by its neighbours drives them to seek refuge from some powerful country, Britain in the past and America for now. However, Peter Carey disillusions this wishful thinking and warns Australia against it by laying bare its doomed detriment. No matter how much Australians hold dear the imperial culture, and value and practice it as their own, they remain the inferior Other from the periphery. As Bill, who is thought by his folks to be a very successful Efican admits, however hard he has laboured for the Sirkus, he is still regarded in Voorstand as "an Ootlander, a horse rider, a barbarian" (404).

"Appeals to the past are among the commonest of strategies in interpretations of the present"(Said, 1993: 3). Apart from preaching his moral lessons, the ultimate purpose of Carey's retrieval of the Americanization memory is to explore possible ways for Australia to get rid of American imperialism. Tristan's unusual adult life can be taken as a further exploration of the possible actions that Australia is encouraged to take. With severe deformation and voice deprivation, Tristan has been made entirely powerless to retaliate, and the only option he can count on is to flee from imperialism. As Tristan notes before he sets foot in Voortand, "if we wish to escape the vile octopus, our escape must be total" (231). However, fleeing is an escape. The best remedy is the invention of culture as an enclosure. As Efica has gone through tremendous hardship, even sacrifice, to have its own tradition established despite Voorstand's suppression, it is supposed to be a similarly rocky road for a country like Australia, which has such a short history to create its own culture to resist American imperialism. Luckily, Carey's narrative enlightens his protagonists like Felicity, Tristan and Wally by the nationalist consciousness so that they are pretty aware of the critical importance of developing their own culture to maintain an intact national and cultural identity. Tristan has an even more acute political awareness of safeguarding the nation's sovereignty by fighting against the empire's interference. Even Bill, who initially pins his dream of enormous success and good fortune on the Empire, eventually experiences a catharsis leading to his understanding that his career and identity are not in Voorstand but in Efica. That understanding spurs him on his ultimate decision to reconcile with his ugly son and return to his tatty home country Efica. There they "have a whole damn country to invent" (53) and a lot to accomplish.

The idea of having Australian culture as armour to protect the country from being enslaved by the new imperial power is solely part of Peter Carey's poetic conception of the relationship between Australian and American culture. He conducts a more profound exploration of this issue and offers more progressive solutions to the predicaments facing Australia.

3.2 Ally Recalled as the Imperialist: *Amnesia*

Australia has switched its dependence on Britain to its subordination to the United States, especially since the Second World War. The friendship from the powerful ally has eased Australia's insecurity resulting from the Cold War. However, Australia also has a cost to pay for the protection. Peter Carey dives into the recesses of history to re-examine the relationship between the two countries, and the "ally" is represented as an imperialist for a poetic trial. The Australia-US relationship is only part of the signified of the author's symbolic representation. The Australian tradition of forgetting, which partly results from cultural cringe, is reconstructed to be partly the cause of Australian historical humiliations, thus complicit in American imperialism.

It is widely known that man's basic and natural disposition favours forgetting rather than remembering. Owing to the stained chapters in its history, either institutionally or personally, Australians tend to selectively forget their ignoble past to construct positive national and individual images. This forgetting tradition partly defines what Australia is since, according to Benedict Anderson, the essence of a nation is that its individuals choose to have many things in common and at the same time, choose to forget many things. (2016: 194) "Amnesia" as a collectively shared secrecy among Australians has been inscribed into their tables of memory. For Friedrich Nietzsche, forgetting is a capacity and the way through which happiness becomes happiness. (1998: 4) However, for Peter Carey, it is an emblem of cowardice and cultural cringe that will trap Australia in more political humiliation. He imaginarily deploys the 1942 Battle of Brisbane and the sacking of the Whitlam government in 1975, events which he calls "the traumatic injury done to my country by our American allies" to illustrate his above anxiety. What is worse, this negative national psyche will jeopardize Australia's identity construction. Textual clues suggest that Carey would like Australia to develop, to quote Nietzsche, "a memory of the will" (2006: xxii) to resist the empire and avenge the humiliations it has inflicted on it instead of burying the ignominious past in oblivion.

I will analyze in this section how Peter Carey revisits Australian forgetting tradition by relating it with Australia's memory of two historical events and WikiLeaks to primarily denounce the imperialism of the United States and and Australian cultural cringe. Moreover, I will also examine how the author uses his recuperation as a threshold to explore further how Australian "overmen" can draw power from its antiauthoritarian tradition to fight against the new colonizing power to fight for the country's political sovereignty. Last but not least, this section and this chapter as well will wrap up with the argument that the author's reconstruction of Australia's neo-colonial memory is also the symbolic representation of the author's anxiety about and reflection of multinational capitalism, which might threaten to abolish the political and cultural borders between different nations to become a new colonizing power. Maintaining interculturality and resisting political and cultural hegemony are the poetic remedies that Carey offers to Australia and the world to cope with the dynamics of the global trend.

3.2.1 Preliminaries of the Fiction

Amnesia, published in 2014, proves to be Peter Carey's another effective endeavour to delve into the recesses of Australian collective memory and associate it with present preoccupations. Though having not garnered any major literary awards, it is applauded by positive reviews. Writer and former Poet Laureate, Andrew Motion, reviews that by introducing new inventions and new possibilities in his narrative lines, Carey makes himself "Dickensian", and "[N]o other contemporary novelist is better able to mix farce with ferocity, or to better effect"

(Carey, 2014: trailer page). [1]Luke Harding, a British journalist of *The Guardian*, acclaims that the novel is "written with forensic precision. The story of WikiLeaks as if [it is] transmogrified by Dickens and turned into a thrilling fable for our post-Edward Snowden era" (ibid.).

Australian cultural memories have always been Peter Carey's preoccupation. Having delved into the nineteenth century to revisit the nation's convict past in *Jack Maggs* and Irish settlers in *True History of the Kelly Gang*, he switches his interest to more recent Australia history in *Amnesia*, such as the Battle of Brisbane, the 1975 coup and Julian Assange's cyber-activism, directing them to the relationship between Australia and the United States. To trace Australian memory from the 1940s onwards, Nicholas Birns comments that Carey "gives a panoply of Australia over the past several decades" (2015: 206). Having reconfigured Ned Kelly to be an Australian soldier, a fighter who stands up against imperial suppression in the nineteenth century, Carey reconstructs the fictionalized Julian Assange to be a soldier of modern Australia who always bears in mind what the new imperial power has done to his country and takes his revenge fearlessly.

Amnesia encompasses bountiful motifs. It deals with cybercrime, geopolitics, marital relationships, as well as the relationship between Australia and the United States, which Carey has probed into symbolically in *The Unusual Life of Tristan Smith*, in its surface narrative. However, underneath that surface layer, as is suggested by its title, it also resolves around forgetting and remembering. It is an exploration into human freedom, unabashedly questioning "the freedom of choice: the choice to forget, to resort to the comforts of collective amnesia, and the choice to sacrifice a nation's freedom and in doing so substitute the influence of one

---

[1] The following quotations from *Amnesia* in this section are annotated with only the page number.

imperial power for another" (Kampmark, 2015: 102). The core character of the novel is the heroine, Gaby Baillieux, whose story draws on some of the experiences of Julian Assange, the founder of WikiLeaks. Delivered into the world at 4:40 p.m., November 11, 1975, which is right at the moment of the dismissal of the Whitlam government, she is suspected of releasing an Internet virus code-named "angel" to breaking into the Australian incarceration system, which resulted in the unlocking of countless prisons and the infection of "117 US federal correctional facilities, 1700 prisons, and over 3000 county jails" (1). She is thus called a "traitor" by the federal government of the United States, which orders the Australian government to extradite her to America to serve the death penalty. This incident introduces the other central character of the novel, Felix Moore, a journalist and writer. The novel consists of two parts, each of which adopts the Chinese box structure. Although the embedded structure in each part is devoted to different stories, the two parts are connected by the frame narrative, which relates how Felix is hired by his mate Woody Townes and his old friend Celine, Gaby's mother, to "Australianise" the young lady through writing so that she will be exonerated from the death sentence.

The first part of the novel is composed of twenty-six chapters. In the frame narrative, Felix, the first-person intradiegetic narrator, relates his currently awful conditions as a journalist, focusing on how he accepts Woody's commission to exonerate Gaby. Then, the embedded narrative is first devoted to Felix's reminiscence of the Australian constitutional crisis in 1975, in which the implied author is convinced that "American hands pulled the strings, [and] that the CIA had an active role in the 'complex storm system' that brought down an elected Australian government" (Romei, 2014). Then, it also details Celine's recollection of what her family encountered during the Battle of Brisbane. The second part of the novel is made up of thirty-nine chapters. The frame narrative employs the third-person omniscient narrator to relate how Felix lives up to the confinement and maltreatment to invent Gaby's story. Then, in the embedded narrative, both Celine and Gaby are given voice to tell their own life and family stories, focusing on how Gaby grows to be a rebellious juvenile cyber hacker, as well as Celine's unhappy marriage with her husband Sando Quinn, a Labour member of the parliament. Towards the end of the novel, the main plot reverses with Felix's betrayal of Woody and Celine to victimize Gaby according to her own wishes and out of the journalist's nationalist fever. He conspires with Gaby and her mates by packaging the "Amnesia Worm" (306) inside the PDF file of his book named "life and crimes of Gabrielle Baillieux" (305). This name of the virus is actually an embodiment of the hazards of forgetting. Owing to Felix's role in "destroying all records, memory and production processes of certain global corporations and their lawyers" (307), he is arrested immediately after the digital version of the book is released and put into the Barwon Prison. Though Gaby and Frederic are sentenced to life imprisonment based on the one hundred and fifteen charges, the novel closes with their being brought forth three years later by the updated version of the Angel worm released by their supporters. Their present whereabouts remain unknown and "an American grand jury is still empanelled" (307).

Reviewing *Amnesia*, Nataša Kampmark points to its political and moral edge and sees it not only as a "literary thriller", "a murder mystery" with regard to its dealing with the "murder of Australian democracy", but also as "a morality tale with the theme of psychomachia at its core" and a "textbook example of ... the actions of Julian Assange". (2015: 102-103) Julieanne Lamond (2015) makes comparison between the novel with the genre of "contemporary Australian fiction of the 'War on Terror' era" and with that of "hardboiled detective fiction". Martin Staniforth approaches it as a "historical fiction" and argues that it uses "the conventions of the convict novel to examine more recent periods of Australian history" (2017: 478) and "it looks forward to his nostalgic and rose-tinted reconstruction of 1970s Australia as a lost world" (ibid.: 485). While Nataša Kampmark and Julieanne Lamond allude to the novel's reinterpretation of certain historical events in their comments, Staniforth Staniforth argues *Amnesia* is Carey's "rose-tinted reconstruction" (2017: 585) of the 1970s Australia in a "historical fiction" (ibid.: 578). That makes it self-evident that *Amnesia* is a neo-historical fiction in which it evokes Australia's memory of the Battle of Brisbane and the constitutional crisis and the more recent event of Julian Assange's hacktivism to launch a reinterpretation of those events in the light of Australian forgetting tradition. It inherits the paradox of claiming truth in a self-referential manner.

To begin with, the author deploys various techniques to create a sense of authenticity within the text. At the end of the novel is an italic introduction of the protagonist Felix Moore: "*a writer living in Denison Street, Rozelle. His early novel* Barbi and the Deadheads *is soon to be a motion picture.*" (307) This annotation gives readers an illusion of reading a biography and meeting people and things that really exist in the experiential world. The author fortifies his mesmerism by giving a physical description of how he obtains the sources for his writing: he "plays", "pauses", "ejects", and "forwards" the "tape recorder" to note down the information from the "tape" and "cassette" Celine gives him. Readers are lured to the impression that what they are fed is a documentary account of Gabe's life and experiences. Moreover, Carey also employs the old trick of letting his narrator declare that he is "a servant of the truth" (6) and nick-named Felix "Moore-or-less correct"

(174).

In addition, Carey sells his authenticity by making his protagonist a journalist, an occupation supposedly to report the truth. This "socialist" (6) is made to be his mouthpiece for truth. He exposes "lies" and digs out what is masked and forgotten. He gives evidence that Australia has been toyed with and exploited by the United States during the Second World War; he convinces readers that the government of Gough Whitlam does not topple owing to its incompetence in dealing with domestic crisis as is disseminated by the documented memory; rather, the nation's democratically elected government is dismissed by the Governor General, the representative of the Queen of England; it is overthrown by the alleged workings of the CIA because the Whitlam government withdraws from Vietnam Australian soldiers which threatens to hinder American interest (this reconstruction is in line with that of *The Unusual Life of Tristan Smith*); he tells Gaby's true story at the risk of being revenged by Woody and Celine. All the above tricks convince the reader of his honesty in telling Australian history. As Nataša Kampmark contends, Carey makes public the truth in his novel by pointing out "the voids, absences and silences in Australian historical records as he diagnoses the nation with collective amnesia" (2015: 103). It is in the sense of telling the truth that "*Amnesia* is hacking back into the system of the supreme power using the avenues of computer technology in the way *Jack Maggs* is writing back to the imperial power employing 'the master's tools', that is, language and literature" (Kampmark, 2015: 103).

While suggesting there is historical knowledge to strive for through creating verisimilitude, Carey also paradoxically calls the objectivity of knowledge into question by deploying the textual strategy of metafiction. Felix, the novel's protagonist and narrator as well, makes clear at the threshold of the novel that he is a "journalist", a word Carey uses as the synonym of writer. He clarifies to Patrick Allington in an interview what he means by this trade, "there is a sort of a tradition of writers of Felix's age who would be deemed gonzo journalists, who would make up all sorts of shit. In other words, reimagine scenes, and so on" (2015: 144). Apart from exposing the narrator's status as an author, Carey provides readers with more detailed information to highlight the fictionality of his story. Felix is made an unreliable narrator in the first part of the book by informing readers that he is bribed by Woody to assume his commission to write Gaby's story, to "Australianise her" to "[M]ake it up, and most of all make the bitch lovable" (43). He further tells readers that the reason he has accepted that job is that he needs the money his mate offers. What Carey calls into question here is the authenticity of his story as well as that of all historical narratives. He further suggests the possible elements that might bias memory, individual or collective alike. Eventually, the artificiality of his work is consummated when he warns readers to be cautious about following him since, despite the unavailability of her background resource, all he is going to do is to "pitch that story. He can do it standing on his head" (31). Carey's alternative version of truth is not spared from being contested and undermined by the narrator's highly self-referential inclination coexisting within the text. The metafictional strategy that the author deploys problematizes the documented memory of the Battle of Brisbane and the 1975 coup as well as the historical narrative. Taking it together with his creation of verisimilitude, we may find the inaccessibility of authenticity, as well as the value of keeping seeking it.

Though the timeline in *Amnesia* may vary a bit from that in his previous novels of the same genre, Carey clings to his fascination for what is engraved in the nation's cultural memory. Nataša Kampmark argues that it is the toppling of the Whitlam government in Australian history, "which Carey wants to bring back to cultural memory deploying a 'pocomo blend' of literary genres and strategies" (2015: 102). However, the 1975 constitutional crisis is only one of the memories that Carey revives and an even smaller part of the big picture of the reconstructed Australian tradition of amnesia. All of them are brought under examination in the sections following up.

3.2.2 Forgetting as a National Ill

When discussing the significance of forgetting in the ethics of memory and memory politics, Avishai Margalit argues that "An ethics of memory is as much an ethics of forgetting as it is an ethics of memory" (2002: 17). Amnesia forms itself owing to both psychological and social motivations. It has long been a consensus in psychology or sociology that memory is closely connected to identity, individual memory or collective memory alike. Experimental evidence from psychology suggests that memory selectivity bears a close relation to self-concept and self-esteem. Constantine Sedikides and Jeffrey D. Green find that individuals tend to activate what they call the "inconsistency-negativity neglect model" when favourable views about them are "questioned, contradicted, impugned, mocked, challenged, or otherwise put in jeopardy" (2000: 909). To elaborate, an individual is motivated "to neglect the processing of information that challenges their positive self-conceptions... to maintain the stability of the self-concept" (Sedikides & Green, 2000: 909). Other studies conducted by Romin W. Tafarodi, Tara C. Marshall and Alan B. Milne suggest that "[A]ccording to the mood-congruence model, activation of either dimension of self-esteem (self-competence or self-liking) produces an affective state that facilitates retrieval of traces that are consistent with that state while hindering retrieval of traces that are inconsistent" (2003: 29). In brief, forgetting takes place when memory threats an individual's construction of a favourable self or the maintenance of high self-esteem.

However, forgetting is also "a social phenomenon" and it takes place when a society's "referential frames of the communicated reality disappear or change" (Assmann, 2011: 23). As is claimed by Maurice Halbwachs, what shall be remembered in a society depends on the social frame of reference. This holds true to what shall be forgotten. Subjects of memory are always individuals who organize this memory based on that "frame". Individuals, and societies alike, are only able to "remember what can be reconstructed as a past within the referential framework of their own present, then they will forget things that no longer have such a referential framework" (A. Assmann, 2011: 22-23). In other words, an individual's memory takes its shape through his or her involvement in the communication with the social groups he or she belongs to. This could be a very small community like his or her family. It could also be a bigger one like a religious group or a nation. Memory that is regarded helpful to legitimate a political power, to consolidate a stable and unified group and to establish favourable image in cross cultural communication will be stored in functional memory as a meaningful lesson, concept or symbol of a society. On the contrary, memory that is considered detrimental to the regime power, to the stability or unification of a group, or to the construction of positive self will be excluded and left to gather dust in memory box.

Lack of great men or heroic deeds or worthy sacrifices, there seems to be nothing much in Australian early history that its people can take pride in. On the contrary, Robert Hughes confirms in his *The Fatal Shore*, that Australia does have a great deal to forget in its past. He argues that "the desire to forget about our felon origins began with the origins themselves" (Hughes, 2003: 12). This consciousness is shaped so thoroughly that it lurks under the national psyche like a "national pact of silence" (ibid.: 13). "Amnesia seemed to be a condition of patriotism, and this pervaded attitudes toward the writing and teaching of Australian history" (ibid.: 14). However, convict stain is not the only thing that Australians want to blot out from their collective memory. The genocide that White exploration has caused to the indigenous people is another taboo prevailing among Australians. Forgetting is like a "disguised form of religion" (Margalit, 2002: 10). As is mentioned in the previous discussion of *Illywhacker*, every Australian is taught to forget about that part of the history, "[A] liar might be a patriot" (Carey, 1985: 456). If the convict experience is a traumatic memory that Australia's forefathers used to be felons who are chained and worked like cattle, the aboriginal genocide is no less than another fatal moral stain of their great grandfathers who are supposedly messengers of civilization. Those memories are disadvantageous to Australia's construction of a positive national identity and international image and consequently lose their relevant referential frameworks of the present day. They wind up being cast in oblivion. Similar cases happen to other cultural memories. There are even things in modern times that Australians "forget in order to survive... They're trauma victims and that's how they behave" (Allington, 2015: 142). Carey makes an analogy to illustrate this point: "we're like a woman whose husband is a notorious womanizer and we just can't afford to see that. So we pretend it's not happening and we continue to have the, let's say, privileged life we've been having." (ibid.) In *Amnesia*, Carey unearths the inclination of forgetfulness of ignoble and traumatic past lurking in Australia's national psyche to, in his own words, "remind us that we have forgotten" (ibid.). Indeed there are more significant tasks he intends his recuperation to perform. I will have a close examination into how and why Carey reconfigures the Australian tradition of amnesia in the following paragraphs.

Carey revisits the forgetting tradition symbolically through the way in which the four woman characters, Doris and her mother, Celine and Gaby, deal with their family history. Doris' personal story is part of the history of the battle of Brisbane. When Doris, Celine's mother, is brutally maltreated by his partner Hank, the African American soldier who is sent to Australia during the World War Ⅱ to protect the country and its people from the Japanese invasion, and gets infected with a STD (Sexually Transmitted Disease), she chooses to hide the ever raw abrasion and her disease from her mother. For her, there is no need to make a fuss as long as she leaves it covered by her silk dress since "[N]o-one saw" (79). More absurdly, she does so because both she and her mother are worried that Hank will not get the blame but kill them if his brutality is exposed. This is a double satire on both Australian government which cares his ally more than its own citizens and the imperial United States. Moreover, when her mother learns that young Doris' "patriotic duty... to entertain some officers" (63) gets her pregnant by accident, what occupies her mind is not her daughter's health or safety or reputation but to conceal the scandal even from her family. She asks her daughter to flee home in case her father finds the truth: "We've got no choice, my titchy mouse. You'll have to be gone before he arrives home."(81) The attitude of Doris and her mother towards her scar inflicted by Hank symbolizes the Australian acquiescence to the injustice that the new empire has done to them. Here comes the ghost of cultural cringe. Since Australia is looking up to the United States to shelter it from its Asian enemies, it has no choice but to swallow the insult and humiliation silently, consigning all of them to oblivion.

When Felix Moore acts as a time traveller on Celine's behalf to uncover the mystery of her birth, he discovers that her biological father is

Hank, the American rapist and brownout strangler. Celine almost collapses on hearing the truth. She loses her sleep and turns up the other day with an "acid breath... blackened eye, the hard contusion in her cheekbone, the awful puce in the soft cave of the orbit" (83). However, her torment does not come from the truth itself but from Felix uncovery of it. She does not bear resentment towards the rapist who has victimized her mother or the United States which has invaded Australia in the name of ally or Australian government which is complicit in the crime. Instead, she spearheads her enmity against the truth-teller, reproaching Felix for having written things that is "reprehensible" and "hurts everyone", slandering him to be a "liar" (ibid.), jerking her rifle at him and throwing his scripts into the flames. The analogy is made here between Celine's family memory and Australia's collective memory. And her reaction to Felix's digging of her shameful family skeleton is the embodiment of Australia's conservatism towards its stained past. They tend to cover the ignoble history up and suppress it into oblivion. As the narrator reflects in self-pity, "the truth is ugly and often frightening. We have placed truth in our stained-glass windows but when it arrives in person, unwashed and smelly, loud and violent; our first act is to pull a gun on it" (ibid.).

When Gaby learns that Celine has cheated on her husband and commited an affair with another actor, she feels it a disgrace to continue sharing a roof with her mother and feels her obligation to get everything related to her out of their house. She displays a sort of moral vanity. "She fetched the black rubbish bags from the kitchen and stuffed them full of Celine, five full bags of them and tied them up with yellow ties" (178), and later throws them out of that house. Gaby has "vanished" (184) her mother, pretending she has never existed. Since "[W]e only remember what we communicate" (Assmann, 2011: 23), Gabe's estrangement from her mother makes the memory of the scandal impossible, which metaphorizes how Australian blotted past is forgotten: people are not allowed to talk about it. The documented memory tends to gloss over those ignoble chapters, eradiating their possible traces and pretending self-deceivingly that nothing has ever happened. However, as Carey quotes William Faulkner as the epigraph of *True History of the Kelly Gang*, "[T]he past is not dead. It is not even past". This is better elaborated through Celine's reflection, "[T]he whitewash only served to emphasize the jagged shadow where the floorboards failed to meet the walls. As everyone said, the house has good bones: large square rooms and massive sash window and once the filth was scrubbed off or covered up, it should felt wonderful" (185).

Nietzsche, in his *Untimely Meditations: On the Use and Abuse of History for Life*, eulogizes the power of forgetting as a capacity for human beings to protect themselves from being distracted or damaged by their memory of the past. He considers forgetting equally essential with remembering for the health of an individual, a people, and a culture and argues that it is right through forgetting that happiness becomes happiness.

> As the active person is always without conscience ... He forgets most things in order to do one thing; he is unjust towards what lies behind him and knows only one right, the right of what is to come into being now ... this condition — unhistorical, thoroughly anti-historical — is the birthing womb not only of an unjust deed but much more of every just deed. (Nietzsche, 1998: 5)

However, what Nietzsche sees as a positive force, Carey reconfigures as a humane flaw to criticize. Whatever motivations lying behind Australian memory selectivity, Carey doesn't seem to take the bite.

For one thing, that undesirable memory can be covered up or

repressed for the time being does not mean it disappears forever. Instead, as Felix recalls, "[A]ll my buried past turned sticky, cloying like spoiled velvet, dead roses" (50). Censored by the ward of consciousness and not allowed to prank, the undesirable memory remains suppressed there in the unconsciousness and waited to be evoked. As Celine reflects, "[Y]et even when the morning sun washed across the hallway floor, it was clear that something awful had happened there" (185). Different from Nietzsche's claim that forgetting is beneficial to human beings and a culture's health, psychological evidence shows that repressed memory may cause physical dysfunctions which Carey discusses in *Jack Maggs*. Deliberate memory selectivity may cause identity crisis for individuals and groups as well. The genuine healing power, as Freud argues, lies in bringing those repressed memories to the light of consciousness, which echoes Gnosticism' purport to "offer knowledge of the hidden truth about reality as the key to man's salvation" (Margalit, 2002:1).

As is evidenced in his other novels, Carey follows the progressive camp to advocate that historical writing should not "mince matters when it comes to the imperfections and defects of their nation's story" (Gaile, 2010: 4). Forgetting, as is implied in this fiction, is far from being a wise move to bring forth salvation. Instead, it embodies, for a nation, cowardice and escape from the problem itself, which will suffocate the chance for introspection and maturization and result in cultural cringe leading to more humiliations. This is what concerns Carey most in his recuperation of Australian "amnesia" tradition. If favourable memory nurtures a nation with its warm and inspiring force, unfavourable memory could be a mirror image which provides a referable Other upon which it depends to reflect on what it should or should not do under a particular circumstance and recreate identity through technologies of self. Carey's revisiting of the "amnesia" tradition brings this national psycho under re-examination. Forgetting in his reconstruction is not the least a redemptive power. Instead, it is the threshold leading to endless humiliations coming after. Carey's insight echoes Hegel's argument that one "achieved freedom" in history by "acknowledging the scars of one's history" and "by interiorizing and transcending trauma". (Klein, 2000: 141) The author continues his poetic investigation of the detriment of the forgetting tradition and the ensuing section will be devoted to a discussion of his exploration.

3.2.3　Cost of Oblivion — Carnival of Humiliations

Carey is apt at representing the marginalized and downtrodden figures and weaves into their stories his perception of human conditions and insight of the predicaments facing contemporary Australians. In *Amnesia*, he makes a pastiche of Celine's birth, Felix's cowardice, and Gaby's cybercrime. And through that pastiche he revives Australian buried memories of the Battle of Brisbane, the 1975 constitutional crisis as well as Julian Assange's hacktivism. These seemingly isolated stories from different periods of time are collaged together in the space of the text to put on show a carnival of shame both at the personal and the national level. Deploying the "dual narrative dynamics" (申丹, 2013: 47), the three characters' personal shame is made the metaphor of Australian national humiliation. The plot development relates the shame the individuals are afflicted with. Yet, paralleling that plot development is the "covert progression" (ibid.) of Australian national humiliation. Moreover, these seemingly irrelevant stories are not just scratched from Australia's cultural memory and piled up randomly in the text in the diachronic manner. Indeed, the author engineers them into a causal continuum and what threads these humiliating events that initially take place in different times and space is Australian forgetting tradition.

Since Australia feels itself betrayed by Britain in the defence of Singapore in its initial experience of the Second World War and Japanese has launched raids on Pearl Harbour, the government is so much seized by the reinforced fear of the Asian invasion that John Curtin places Australian forces under the command of Douglas MacArthur. (Macintyre, 1999: 191-199) Here the author lays the background of Celine's traumatic birth and offers readers a counter memory that is silenced in official narrative. When Australia cedes its military power to the command of America and looks up to its protection, it is bound to assume the responsibility of feeding and provisioning the American servicemen, most of whom passing through the cities to their front. Consequently, Australian women are "instructed to welcome 'Yanks' into their homes", and they learn that it is their daughter's "patriotic duties to be the 'Victory Belles'" (63). Australians are mesmerized by the government's patriotic propaganda. Countless women, like Celine's grandmother Doris, rush to express their wishes to "entertain some officers" (ibid.). Like other folks, Celine's grandmother does this out of her gratitude of the Americans and she is quite convinced her passion is "well based" (ibid.) considering the dire situation facing Australia. Though she doesn't want her daughter to entertain those "black" US soldiers, Doris is "wilful to a genetic degree" (66) to perform the task. Here emerges symbolically from Carey's narrative Australian genetic cringe at big powers. Through Doris' focalization, the narrator juxtaposes the Aussie servicemen with their American counterparts. Those Aussie boys, their cheeks "sunken", their teeth "pulled out", they wear the "awful uniforms that the mingy government provided, not tailored, not slick, not even the right size" and they are dying for their country. (65-66) In contrast, those black men from America, they have "tailored uniform" and lovely teeth. (66) They stay in Australia "with one thing on their minds" and they are allowed to "look for entertainment". (ibid.) While those Aussie soldiers are starving from basic provision, their American counterparts have "higher pay, superior conditions and access to luxury goods" (Macintyre, 1999: 197). They turn out to be more attractive to local girls who are "examined like livestock in an auction" (68). Carey satirizes that Australian cringe is both a national and individual complex which seems to have been inscribed into the collective unconscious.

Doris is picked by Hank, one of the African American servicemen and she takes pride in that, describing it as an elevation of her status. She loves the stockings and the parachute silk that he brings her in exchange for her fresh and budding body. People spit on her cheek, when she walks along the streets with her hands in his pockets, laughing hilariously. She understands she is judged for a "tart", a "traitor with a Yank" (72), but she takes is lightly. On the bus back home, "[S]he folded her hands in her lap, covering her ring finger, pretending to herself they were engaged, going to live in Detroit, no longer Doris Crook, something better, safer, clearer, richer" (ibid.). However, when she takes him home, he reveals his true nature, regarding her as nothing but an object to vent his libido and abusing her with heinous brutality:

> [H]e had shoved her head onto the chopping block... He was pushing and breaking and her tummy was filled with hurt but she dared not scream. His hands around her neck. He said, 'You better sing.'... She could no longer breathe but she did 'Danny Boy'. The air came through the words and the air was ripped-up rags. His hands were large and very strong and she finally understood, without a doubt, he would kill her when he'd finished. (74)

Shortly after their dating, Doris finds that Hank also gives her blisters "down there" and his baby in her womb. Unaware of the hurt and disease Hank has brought her, she is still immerged in the illusion of envisioning a future with him. Nevertheless, she happens to see him on the front page of the Courier-Mail: sentenced to death for raping six girls, strangling and mutilating them. Doris' innocence is juxtaposed with Hank's brutality to create tension to satirize Australian wilful sacrifice and accuse America of exploiting its young ally. That baby girl is delivered secretly, and her name is Celine. Individual memory only takes place when it is helpful to build a favourable image. Having a father of notoriety is undoubtedly the last thing to celebrate. To cover up her relationship with the brownout strangler, Doris gives her daughter a French family name, Baillieux. Consequently, it is not until Felix unearths the whole mystery that Celine finds out from her mother about her father that he is an American, the "most decent man you could never know" (76). The constructiveness of memory plays a part when Doris invents a false memory in order to build a positive image for herself and her daughter.

Again, through Doris' focalization, Carey juxtaposes the Australian vision of the Japanese atrocity with the actual brutality Hank inflicts on Doris and other Australian women to create an enormous tension. Compared to what they are instilled to believe that the Japanese "bayoneted men tied to trees, they raped and chopped heads" (63), the American soldiers exercise their inhumanity more perversely. Doris's relationship with Hank severs as a metaphor for Australia's alliance with the United States. Doris' initial passion for doing her part to be a patriot, her subsequent sick flattering to seek protection, and her resultantly trampled body and soul serve as an emblem of Australia's disadvantageous, even humiliating position, in the so-called ally. Australia has put an end to its subordination to Britain yet created a new dependence on the United States since the Second World War. However, it is still relegated to an auxiliary role in the new alliance. It has surrendered much of its significant territories to America's deployment yet has been scarcely consulted on crucial issues as agreed in the treaty. What the alliance functions for Australia is to justify American "friendly invasion" (Macintyre, 1999: 197). The so-called ally is, in fact, an imperialist. Doris' shame, which reveals itself progressively with the plot development, is Australian national humiliation unfolding in the covert progression, as well as in the course of history.

To strengthen the tension between what Australia sacrifices and what it gets from its American ally, Peter Carey first juxtaposes what American soldiers are provided with and that of Australian soldiers to suggest the government's disgusting cringe. In addition to that, the author provides another counter-narrative through his journalist narrator Felix. The United States has not dispatched a large army to secure Australia from Japanese invasion as the government claims, "[T] here is only one American soldier who'd been photographed in Brisbane. The rest were Melborne" (77). Worst of all, there was a clash between Australian soldiers and civilians and American service members in the streets of Brisbane, which is known as the Battle of Brisbane. Those American soldiers who are supposed to go off to New Guinea to fight the Japanese turn their guns to Australians, and the battle lasts for two days. Australia's cringe is brought in sharp contrast to the infidelity and invasion of its new ally, culminating in Australia's national humiliation. As is concluded by the narrator, "[T]he Americans were a knife twisted in their guts" (66). However, it is the government that controls the official memory, and this event is understated as a "brawl" started by "[T]he stupid Australians" who are "jealous of the Yanks" for their sexual attractiveness to Australian girls. (26-27)

It is through collective memory that the individuals of a group consolidate their identity, so Felix, in his own words, has a "shambolic self" (4) and unavoidably lives a life of "disgrace" (23). All his shame and helpless fury result from his lame conduct in 1975, which he defines as cowardice. When the Australian elected government is deposed in the coup, he intends to go to the premise of ABC (Australian Broadcasting Corporation) to call for a strike. However, he allows himself to be talked out of the idea since he is fearful of the possible consequences. He sees this as the greatest shame in his life and despises himself for being such a coward. He confides to readers, "the events of 1975 have been the obsession of my erratic and mostly unsuccessful life" (117). Felix's shame is an emblem of Australian national humiliation brought about by the constitutional crisis. Through counter-memory, the 1975 coup is reconfigured by Carey to be a conspiracy schemed by the CIA in collaboration with General Kerr and Australia's conservative opposition. Their joint efforts have murdered Australian democracy. The Whitlam government brought Australian soldiers from the US war in Vietnam, denounced its friend Nixon for bombing North Vietnam, and threatened to permanently terminate the lease on the Pine Gap since Australia is kept from what the United States is doing on its territory. However, the people's government gets "punished" for its "mad idea" (113) of speaking up for its own wellbeing and defying its ally. It gets dismissed for the idea of changing its status as a client state of America. What is more humiliating is that Bob Hawke abuses his moral authority to prevent the unions from having a general strike for fear of conflict. It turns out that Australia allows its government to be stolen in plain sight by its American ally from its people without even a protest against this unconstitutional brutality. Felix concludes, "we have displayed this awful level of cowardice, brown-nosing, criminality, mediocrity and nest-feathering"

(6). Obviously, Australia fails to take any lesson from the long-forgotten memory of the Battle of Brisbane. As for this humiliating dismissal of its own government, again, Australia "forgot it right away" (113).

The implied author relates the constitutional crisis to the Battle of Brisbane and considers it "part of 'The Great Amnesia'" (5). However, they do not exhaust the list of humiliations that forgetting history has brought to Australia. As a wanted law perpetrator, Gaby is surely a stain of her family. But, her supposed extradition adds one more case to the inventory of Australian national shame. When Gaby hacks into the Australian incarceration system, which implicates thousands of American federal and state prisons, the United States declares her a "traitor" and orders the Australian government to turn the fallen angel to it for the death penalty. To aggravate her crime, American politicians even frame a case against her. "They say she infected their base at Pine Gap" (88). The United States exposes its imperialist status blatantly in this event. It shows no respect for Australian sovereignty but regards it as a client state that should behave as the metropolitan commands. Felix contradicts the absurdity by saying that "the American politicians who did not seem to understand she was not their citizen and therefore could not be their traitor any more than she could be their patriot" (42). More absurdly, the Australian government responds cooperatively like a client state to America's unreasonable demand to extradite its own citizen and Gaby, the authentic Australian, needs a writer to "Australianise her" (43) to spare her from this disaster. Carey weaves into Gaby's personal experience of Australian status as a colony without the "colonizing Nation-State metropole" (Zizek, 2006: 170).

Through Carey's reconfiguration, the Battle of Brisbane, the 1975 coup and Julian Assange's cyber activism takes on a new look that is differentiated from the official narrative. During the Second World War,

America's supposed assistance with Australia is transfigured into a friendly invasion; the constitutional crisis is transformed into a political conspiracy; Julian Assange's network perpetration is reconstructed to be a political wrestling between Australia and the United States. All the events are recuperated as witnesses to Australian's national humiliations. Moreover, the author of all these humiliating memories is the detrimental national psyche — amnesia. As "writing is a far more effective weapon against the second or social death, which is oblivion" (A. Assmann, 2013: 171), the first function that Carey intends his reworking of those memories to fulfil is to revive them to the foreground of the nation's memory book to remind Australia what its ally has inflicted upon it and blame the United States for its political hegemony. Furthermore, these memories are also retrieved to give a critical re-evaluation of Australian forgetting traditions that partly result from cultural cringe. History is like a mirror. It records where we are from and what we could be. Forgetting history means denying the future. In addition, Carey's reconstruction of the memories by unearthing the hidden secrets, tearing them apart and making them public serves as a therapeutic force for Australians haunted by their repressed memory since "[M]aking the traumatic, repressed communal memories open, explicit, and conscious is said to have healing power" (Margalit, 2002: 5). Ultimately, presumably the most critical function that Carey's reconfiguration is supposed to perform is directed to Australia's future. As Heiner Muller argues, "[O]ne function of drama is to conjure up the dead — the dialogue with the dead must not break off until they have yielded the future that had been buried with them" (A. Assmann, 2011: 165). Carey's reminiscence of the humiliating Australian past in light of the forgetting tradition is revolutionary. Through his poetic reconstruction of the past, he attempts to find his nation poetically a way out of its contemporary impasse. Furthermore, the prescription he writes out for Australia is to remember what they have been inflicted upon and pluck up the courage to fight against the new empire as well as any power that threatens to murder Australian political sovereignty. The ideal image of the heroic model Carey sets is embodied in Gaby, the juvenile girl.

3.2.4　Birth of the Overman

Carey invents the Australian nationalist tradition in *Illywhacker* and later the antiauthoritarian tradition in *True History of the Kelly Gang*. He revives them in *Amnesia*. The implied author embodied in Felix argues in retrospect, "[W]e have a history of courage and endurance, of inventiveness in the face of isolation and moral threat" (6). Carey is not the only one who observes that Australia has a tradition of standing up to tyranny. Nataša Kampmark also contends that "[B]ravery, endurance, and antiauthoritarianism are actually displayed in the actions of Australians, not solely found in the nation's foundational myth" (2015: 104). *Amnesia* is consistent with *Illywhacker* and *True History of the Kelly Gang*, especially the latter, in that the author has those traditions come into play in this fiction in which Australia is represented to be under the threat of the new colonizing power in the era of global capitalism. Peter Carey has created Ned Kelly to be such a "soldier" (Allinton, 2015: 152), who rises up single-handedly in revolt against the tyrannical colonial government. Although Carey does not admit that he has such a hero on his mind when composing *Amnesia*, he does affirm that it is "very reasonable" (ibid.) for Gaby to define herself as a "soldier" (275). It is not a coincidence that Gaby was born right at the minute when the Australian elected government was removed from power. The author invests in this character his political vision. Felix sees her as a hope to rewrite the history of 1975 in another way, the rebellious way. Thus, he views Gaby as an Australian with the will to power and her hacking as a deliberate "attack on the United States" and a "retaliation" (5) for the 1975 events. Consequently, Gaby, the outlaw and fallen angel in the eyes of the government and the United States, is reconfigured to be a fearless fighter that the dire circumstance of Australia calls desperately for.

Gaby's obsession with cyber games originates from the solitude and melancholy she is rendered by her parents, who are busy with politics or social activities. There is a parallel between the juvenile girl and the obscure Australia, a foster child of Great Britain before and the United States now who finds itself totally unloved and ignored. The "immensely pleasurable" time Gaby spends with her mate Frederic in the virtual world drives away their loneliness and illuminates their boring life. They use code as a language to talk to people and machines. Different from their conditions in the actual world, they have absolute sovereignty in the virtual world. As long as they like it, they can invade any network and rule it, write new tunnels and caves, introduce new characters and rename the old cast, just like God. Through writing software, they invent meanings and define the world. Different from their fathers, who are possessed by passivity and insensibility, they transform themselves into "builders" (266) and intoxicate themselves with the unprecedented "total ownership" (191). They rename the identity of "Thief" into "Dad" (193), which is just an appetizer of their new life unfolding in front of them. What Gaby is capable of symbolizes the author's political imagination of Australia, in which it is reborn as an "overman" who has transcended historical shackles and gained complete sovereignty over itself.

Born into "the Anthropocene age" (299), Gaby is well aware that the presence of human beings who pursue maximum profit from nature has caused environmental detriment. She thus has enormous enthusiasm for environmental protection and chooses to play an active part in ecological activism. Seeing the dying gardens on McBryde Street, she grows skeptical that the murky liquid that Agrikem factory drains into the sewer is poisonous, though its chemical analysis released on MetWat (portal of the Department of the Environment and Energy) shows no trace of dioxin in its effluent at all. When she learns from her friends that Agrikem is issued a secret license by MetWat to "release 'limited quantities'" (260) of dioxin into the creek, she decides to dig out the dirty details to "obliterate the corporatists" (261). She goes to nag her father to interfere in this incident since MetWat is under his immediate purview. However, Sando is not aware that he is fed with the wrong information, which is presumably arranged by the minister. He swears to her daughter that there are no poisonous chemicals in the effluent, criticizes her friends as "real radicals" and "vandals" (242), and transfers her to a remote high school to avoid their ill influence. However, Gaby is unstoppable. She and her friends take the effluent sample to the environmental science lab of Batman Institute Technology for a test, and the result indicates that Agrikem has discharged into the creek dioxins and furans that are "one hundred times Agrikem's allowed limit of their Trade Waste Agreement" (268). As a matter of fact, dioxins and furans are so dangerous that even a very small amount of them is poisonous enough to pollute the environment. However, the analysis report is rejected by the parliament because it is not officially signed by BIT. Feeling she and her partners are toyed by MetChat, Gaby goes to its office, where she finds that the officials who are entrusted to guard their water turn out to be "corporate advisors specializing in debt, performance improvement" (271). She learns that multinational capitalism has bought its way into the Australian government, and they are joining hands to exploit the country, pollute its environment, and interfere in its politics. Gaby makes up her decision to take extreme measures to fight against them.

To prove that Agrikem's affluent is poisonous and MetChat is deceiving the public by releasing forged analysis, she risks her like fearlessly. Gaby turns herself into a guinea pig, striping her undies and rolling on the poisoned soil. She is taken to the hospital by ambulance, and a month later, her skin is blemished with "chlordane bubbles and pustules" (274). Her whole action is recorded in a Cannon film by Frederic, which she hopes to expose on television. Gaby is young but has strong historical and political consciousness. When her parents denounce her for being such a "masochist", she refutes, "I would have been a hero for putting my body at risk for the greater good. But I was just a girl and so I must be a masochist" (275). However, the film is confiscated by their teacher, Crystal and handed to her father, who will be promoted to minister next year. For the benefit of his future in the government and out of his love for his dear daughter, he does not allow the dirty secrets to see the light of day. In despair, Gaby and Federic hack into WetMat and obtain its memoranda to evidence that WetMat is indeed colluding with corporations and issues them secret waste-disposal licenses. Despite Celine's warning that she is going to pay the price for the crime, Gaby tells her mother clearly that "she would manage an event which would force the government to act" (289). They sabotage the WetMat dragline, which instructs the plant to expose itself on the portal until it is closed by the government out of public pressure. Unlike her parents, who have long been accustomed to coming to terms quickly with their fate "to love that abused landscape, in spite of the evidence before our wind-wet eyes" (289), Gaby is convinced that she and her mates are "making history" (288). Although their fathers fail, they assume their responsibility to make some changes. Moreover, she regards it as their "public power" (297) to turn off Agrikem's toxic affluent or close any corporation that pollutes the environment or jeopardizes the wellbeing of Australian people. She does not weigh the consequences. She tells Felix with resolution, "I wanted to be responsible" (296).

Environmentalism is far from being the only issue that concerns Gaby. Compared to her parents, she is more equipped with historical consciousness, political sensibility and the bravery to act responsibly. She interprets it as a "shame" that the Labour Party failed to call a general strike in the constitutional crisis and call those politicians, including his father, "cowards" (241). She recognises the liaison between Australian manipulative politics and the "capitalists" (240) who play a part. She understands "that the enemy was not one nation state but a cloud of companies, corporations, contractors, statutory bodies whose survival meant the degradation of water, soil, life itself" (299). She assumes that it is her responsibility to fight against domestic corruption and American hegemony as well as to defend her homeland. Even though her parents hire Felix to exonerate her so that she is spared from extradition, Gaby herself "had no wish to be innocent, it was her job to be the guilty one" (265). She is resolute and gallant. As she tells Felix, "[F]ear is not helpful to anyone" (109), and she is ready to take the price for venturing some change for her nation. She believes she is ploughing in the "*Field of Dreams*, if you build it they will come" (292).

Gaby is not the only hero that Carey configures in this fiction. Felix is represented as an Australian intellectual who is as gallant as Gaby when it comes to resisting imperialism and maintaining Australian sovereignty. As he says, he is allowed the privileged role of being "both a witness and participant in a warfare where the weapons of individuals could equal those of nation states" (111). As a journalist and an author, he considers representing as his "trade" (4), embodying an ideal intellectual that Australia might need. Like what Edward Said prescribes for intellectuals who are supposed to "represent all those people and issues that are routinely forgotten or swept under the rug" (1994: 11), Felix insists on unearthing Australian long-buried memory of the Battle of Brisbane and the 1975 coup which the authority would instead cast into oblivion. He is pretty aware of the frequent alliance between memory and power and its detriment and he is determined to fight against it and be a truth-digger. As he depicts, the three corporations who control "the flow of information" also have the capacity to "manipulate the 'truth'", he "did his best" to contest the authoritative version of truth. (6) He chooses to be a "shit-stirrer, a truffle hound for cheats and liars and crooks amongst the ruling class" (111). He gives voice to the quietened figures like Doris, which allows her to relate her personal memory of the Battle of Brisbane, interpreting the so-called American assistance in official memory as a friendly invasion. Since he is seized by the outrage at Australian fawning and its ally's imperialism during the 1975 coup, he preoccupies himself with "the metaphysical passion" of publishing books and features and columns to denounce them and enlighten the public out of "disinterested principles of justice and truth" (Said, 1994: 6). Felix's action also suggests that the competition between memories is in essence the wrestling between powers.

Owing to his assiduous exposure of corruption and lies, as well as his ruthless denouncement of those in power, Felix frequently earns himself charges, cells in prison and even death threats. His "alternative and more principled stand that enables them in effect to speak the truth to power" (Said, 1994: 97) also renders him homeless, down and out. His undomestication drives him into a genuine fugitive writer, in Edward Said's words, an "outsider" and "exile". (ibid.: 52-53) After learning Gaby's real intention and seeing in her the bravery and endurance to rejuvenate their nation, he decides to betray his mates by victimizing his subject, whom he is paid to exonerate from conviction. Although his wife begs him to edit his scripts as his patron requires so that he and his family can be spared from danger, "he can't be changed" (265). He insists that "an honourable writer needs to be a scorpion as well. A writer serves the story. He dare not weigh the private consequences" (23). Felix is in line with Edward Said's definition of a real intellectual who "does not respond to the logic of the conventional but to the audacity of daring, and to representing change, to moving on, not standing still" (1994: 63-64). He is well aware that it takes sacrifices to change, and he is ready to face the consequences. Like his young female protagonist, he does not wish himself to be innocent. He wants to be "fearless, guilty of courage, of principle" (254). He does not care that his writing would get his name on the so-called "Disposition Matrix". The change he is presumably to bring forth is worthy of all the pains he takes.

  Carey recuperates the Australian forgetting tradition in modern space primarily for a critical re-evaluation. Forgetting means moving away from traumatic memories to avoid re-confronting the hard truth. It is represented not the least as a therapeutic force for traumatized minds but as an escape from reality. It results partly from cultural cringe and abets it in return. It deprives Australia of any chance for introspection and superiority and thus becomes the root of its consecutive political humiliations. Secondly, Carey's retrieval of the forgetting tradition revives Australia's collective memory of the Battle of Brisbane and the constitutional crisis as well as Julian Assange's cyber activism, which the author reconfigures to condemn American imperialism. Carey's engineering delegitimizes Australian official memory, which prioritizes American contribution to ensuring Australian security from the bloodthirsty Japanese during the Second World War or ascribes the collapse of the Whitlam government mainly to its incompetence to cope with the domestic economic. Based on the deconstruction, it denounces the United States as an imperialist who is colonizing Australia economically and, politically in the name of alliance and with its multinational capitalism.

Memory often comes into play whenever "actions are motivated" (Assmann, 2011: 55). When amnesia is reinterpreted as an opposing force to induce consecutive political humiliations, Carey broods on a change for Australia's future, which is the third as well the most important function of his engineering. Gaby, the transfigured Julian Assange, comes into the picture to symbolize the author's poetic prescription for the predicaments facing Australia. As "[M]emory breathes revenge as often as it breathes reconciliation" (Margalit, 2002: 5), Gaby carries the humiliating memories on her mind and is determined to revenge herself on the victimizer. Unlike her cowardly forefathers who take whatever they are fed by fate, she is resolute and fearless in defending her nation and people from degeneration. Unlike her improvident forefathers, who concern themselves mainly with the profits coming from capitalists, she envisions how multinational capitalism might jeopardize Australian political sovereignty. What the author intends his reconstruction of memory to be, to quote Jan Assmann, is a "mythomotor". Memory is used here as a subversive force, a "directional impetus" (Assmann, 2011: 63).

Amnesia envelops bountiful themes. Carey pours into this fiction his reflection on the relationship between Australia and the United States and Australian forgetting tradition, which is interrelated with its cultural cringe. America emerges from its representation as a new colonizing power instead of an ally of Australia. Australia, to some extent, conspires with American colonization of itself with its forgetting of history. With multinational capitalism flooding into the country, Australia is facing the danger of being auto-colonized by the new empire. That makes it necessary to revive the antiauthoritarian tradition to resist the imperial power and maintain its sovereignty. Different from the melancholy tone pervading his works in the previous phase, for instance, *Illywhacker*, Carey culminates his optimism towards the Australian future in *Amnesia*. As Nataša Kampmark observes, "[W]hile Felix sells his signed copies of Manning Clark's History of Australia to get the means to check into a hotel, Gaby and her friends do not shy away from leaving homes for the streets, renouncing comfort for beliefs, which is one of the most optimistic views Carey expresses about the future of Australia" (2015: 103-104). *Amnesia* is a symbolic representation of Carey's historical as well as political conception in the era of global capitalism. The prescriptions of remembering history and resisting imperialism he writes for Australia, to some degree, have their universality in the increasingly globalizing world.

Conclusion

As grand narrative is dismantled worldwide and more and more witnesses to two World Wars pass away, historiography has turned to narrative and memory ever since the 1980s. Those social and intellectual milieus give rise to the cultural memory theory. In Australia, contended views concerning how to interpret the country's past and what should be inscribed into the official memory have arisen among historians and politicians of the conservative and the progressive camps and have finally evolved into "history wars" since the mid of 1990s. Australian writers like Peter Carey, David Malouf, and Rodney Hall also engage in the historical conversation with their neo-historical fictions. Among them, Peter Carey is the most successful.

Peter Carey is apt at revisiting Australian history for a critical reappraisal and enjoys the reputation of the "spokesman of Australian culture" and "Australia's national Myth-maker" in academia. Nine of his fourteen fictions to date fall under the neo-historical fiction genre. And seven of them are involved with the author's interpretation of Australian experience, namely *Illywhacker*, *Oscar and Lucinda*, *The Unusual Life of Tristan Smith*, *Jack Maggs*, *True History of the Kelly Gang*, *Amnesia* and *A Long Way Home*. This research deploys the cultural memory theory to investigate Peter Carey's reconstruction of Australia's cultural memories in the seven texts with reference to related paratexts and historical intertexts. Specifically, it is oriented to examine what cultural memories Carey has retrieved, how they are reconstructed in the textual space and what functions such recuperations are supposed to fulfil.

The first chapter is a study of how Carey reconstructs Australia's memories of the imperial expedition, the convict stain and the bushranging legend in *Oscar and Lucinda*, *Jack Maggs* and *True History of the Kelly Gang*, respectively to demonstrate the consistency between Australian culture and the British and Irish culture, re-evaluate critically the advancement of the European civilization in Australia, the Transportation System and the Empire's ruling of Australia, and invent the antiauthoritarian tradition. The second Chapter is oriented to examine the recuperation of Australia's memories of the national lies, the nationalism, the multiculturalism, the sense of imprisonment and the Aborigines in *Illywhacker* and *A Long Way from Home*. The analysis goes to how the above memories are retrieved to concrete Australia's multicultural identity, invent the nationalist tradition, soothe those souls that burden the historical weight, and explore how Australia is able to transcend its historical conservatism and provincial ethnic policies to build a harmonious and symbiotic multicultural ecology via dialogue and negotiation between White Australians and the Aborigines. The third chapter investigates mainly how Australia's "Americanization" and "ally" memories are reconfigured in *The Unusual Life of Tristan Smith* and *Amnesia* by the author to condemn the United States for its "auto-colonization" of Australia through cultural input and multinational capitalism, blame Australians for forgetting history and cultural cringe, and explore how Australia is able to get rid of the American hegemony by constructing cultural subjectivity and active resistance.

Studies of the above issues lead to the following findings.

First and foremost, Peter Carey's neo-historical texts are not only narrative but also distinctively performative. Australia's colonial memories, original memories and neo-colonial memories are reconfigured for the construction of Australian cultural subjectivity. Moreover, Australian cultural subjectivity consists of both the internal and the external dimension. In terms of its internality, it concretes the European origin of Australian culture by root-seeking, upon which Australian antiauthoritarian and nationalist traditions are created; it establishes a harmonious and symbiotic multicultural ecology through dialogue and negotiation between Australian Whites and Aborigines; Australians who are freed from historical burdens through a critical re-evaluation of its cultural heritage and narrative therapy overcome the cultural inferiority complex and their limitations, restore their cultural confidence, and strive for superiority. From the external perspective, the subjectivity of Australian culture is closely linked to the criticism of and resistance to American hegemony and has a distinctive anti-neo-colonial characteristic. Considering the enormous impact that British and American cultures have exerted on the Australian culture owing to historical reasons, Carey's poetic construction of Australian cultural subjectivity usually parallels the deconstruction or subversion of the imperial, as well as official narrative.

Secondly, Carey's neo-historical fictions have distinct postmodern and existentialist flavours. The writerly strategies he deploys in the texts, such as metafiction, parody, pastiche and magical realism manifest both their consistency with the postmodern intellectual milieu and the author's historical and philosophical conception. He juxtaposes the self-consciousness of metafiction and the verisimilitude of historical fiction to create a tension highlighting the complexity, ambiguity and inaccessibility of historical truth. At the same time, he is in pursuit of that truth unremittingly, like the indefatigable Sisyphus, prioritizing the meaning of pursuing itself.

Thirdly, the diachronic delineation of the seven texts also indicates that Carey has played an overtly more progressive role in reconstructing Australia's cultural memories ever since the early 1990s. He has shifted his preoccupations from a pure disenchantment of the imperial and official memory to taking this engineering as a threshold to launch further a poetic exploration of Australia's way out of its current predicament. Carey's neo-historical fiction are a symbolic literary demonstration of Australian cultural memory ecology in the multicultural and global capitalism context. The poetic construction of Australian cultural subjectivity in his works is also the wisdom of interculturalism that the author contributes to the world.

The findings above lend themselves to further implications. To begin with, neo-historical fiction distinguishes itself as a new realm to realize poetic democracy and poetic justice by redistributing the sensible to the previously excluded and marginalized subjects to make the invisible visible, the unspeakable speakable, and the wronged rectified. Moreover, the alliance between the fictionality of literature and the constructiveness of cultural memory does not mean that cultural memories reconstructed in neo-historical texts should be despised as falsehoods. Indeed, societies' recollected past through narrative reconstruction has an illocutionary force. It offers an alternative epistemology of groups' experience and could also be a mythomotor serving as either a directional impetus or a subversive power.

With the findings ventured above, this research is significant and suggestive in the following ways. First of all, employing cultural memory to study the author's reconstruction of Australia's cultural memories in his neo-historical texts is conducive to broadening the research horizons of Carey critics at home and abroad. In addition, the holistic and diachronic delineation of Carey's neo-historical fiction helps to deepen Carey criticism in that it facilitates a fuller comprehension of his thematic preoccupations and a more dynamic grasp of his writing career. Furthermore, this research contributes to the discussion of how cultural memory theory interacts with literature more effectively and how societies recollect their past in literary space. With more and more history, for instance, the two World Wars, the holocaust, the assassination of J. F. Kennedy, the 1975 constitutional crisis and the "9·11" etc., finding their habitats in literature, this burgeoning interdisciplinary theory might have a more significant part to play in the interpretation of literary works. Last but not least, the excavation of Carey's efficient textual techniques in light of expressing thematic visions may offer a feasible reference for novelists to tell their national stories in their writings.

However, owing to the inadequacy of the research horizon and scholarly attainments, this study unavoidably has limitations, even slips, that need further polishing and exploration. For a start, this research has not made an adequate investigation of the narrative techniques of the selected texts since the large bulk of research attention has been drawn to their political and ethical edge. Textual strategies like parody, pastiche, surrealism and magic realism that have been touched on lightly in this book can be explored further to excavate the politics of literary forms. Other formal features prevailing in the selected texts, such as the multiple narrative voices and the embedded narrative, are also worthy of future exploration to investigate their possible connection with the manifestation of the author's thematic preoccupations. In addition, this research has brought only seven of Carey's nine neo-historical fictions under investigation. The other two are excluded either because they are majorly concerned with artistic authenticity or American democracy. However, it might be meaningful to examine the two texts to explore their consistency with or discrepancy from the selected texts with regard to the author's artistic conception or the relationship between Australia and the United States, which is his crucial preoccupation in *The Unusual Life of Tristan Smith* and *Amnesia*.

Reference List

[1] Abbott, H. Porter. *The Cambridge Introduction to Narrative*. Cambridge: Cambridge University Press, 2002.

[2] Adler, Alfred. *What Life Could Mean to you*. Los Angeles: Business and Leadership Publishing, 2014.

[3] Ahearn, Kate. "Peter Carey and Short Fiction in Australia." *Going down Swinging* (Melbourne) 1 (1980): 16-17.

[4] Allington, Patrick. "Patrick Allington in Conversation with Peter Carey." *Kill Your Darlings* 20 (2015): 139-160.

[5] Anderson, Benedict. *Imagined Communities: Reflections on the Origin of Nationalism*. London and New York: Verso, 2006.

[6] Antor, Heinz. "Voice, Authority and the Law in Peter Carey's *True History of the Kelly Gang*." *Pólemos* 9. 1 (2015): 131-155.

[7] Antze, Paul, and Michael Lambek, eds. *Tense Past: Cultural Essays in Trauma and Memory*. New York and London: Routledge, 1997.

[8] Ashcroft, Bill, Gareth Griffiths, and Helen Tiffin. *The Empire Write Back: Theory and Practice in Neo-colonial Literatures*. London and New York: Routledge, 2002.

[9] Ashcroft, Bill. "Against the Tide of Time: Peter Carey's Interpolation into History." *Writing the Nation: Self and Country in Neo-

colonial Imagination. Ed. John C. Hawley. Amsterdam: Rodipi, 1996. 194-213.

[10] Ashcroft, Bill. "Reading Carey Reading Malley." *Australian Literary Studies* 21. 4 (2004): 28-39.

[11] Ashcroft, Bill. "Simulation, Resistance and Transformation: The Unusual Life of Tristan Smith." *Fabulating Beauty: Perspectives on the Fiction of Peter Carey*. Ed. Andreas Gaile. New York: Rodopi, 2004. 199-214.

[12] Assmann, Aleida. *Cultural Memory and Western Civilization: Arts of Memory*. New York: Cambridge University Press, 2011.

[13] Assmann, Jan, and John Czaplicka. "Collective Memory and Cultural Identity." *New German Critique: Cultural History/Cultural Studies* 65 (1995): 125-133.

[14] Assmann, Jan. *Cultural Memory and Early Civilization: Writing Remembrance and Political Imagination*. New York: Cambridge University Press, 2011.

[15] Barthes, Roland. "The Discourse of History." *The Rustle of Language*. Trans. Richard Howard. Berkeley and Los Angeles: University of California Press, 1989.

[16] Bennett, Bruce, and Jennifer Strauss. *The Oxford Literary History of Australia*. Melbourne: Oxford University Press, 1998.

[17] Birns, Nicholas. *Contemporary Australian Literature: A World Not Yet Dead*. Sydney: Sydney University Press, 2015.

[18] Bishop, Catherine, and Angela Woollacott. "Business and Politics as Women's Work: The Australian Colonies and the Mid-Nineteenth-Century Women's Movement." *Journal of Women's History* 28.1 (2016): 84-106.

[19] Bliss, Carolyn. "'Lies and Silences': Cultural Masterplots and Existential Authenticity in Peter Carey's *True History of the Kelly Gang*." *Fabulating Beauty: Perspectives on the Fiction of Peter Carey*. Ed. Andreas

Gaile. New York: Rodopi, 2004. 275-300.

[20] Bohmer, Elleke. *Colonial and Postcolonial Literature*. Oxford and New York: Oxford University Press, 1995.

[21] Bone, Martyn. "American-Australian Relations and the Battle (s) of Brisbane in Peter Carey's *Amnesia* and John Oliver Killens's *And Then We Heard the Thunder*." *Journal of American Studies* 52. 3: 626-634.

[22] Botton, Alain de. *Status Anxiety*. New York: Vintage Books, 2005.

[23] Boym, Svetlana. *The Future of Nostalgia*. New York: Basic Books, 2001.

[24] Brady, Veronica. *Can These Bones Live?* New South Wales: The Federation Press, 1996.

[25] Brown, Ruth. "English Heritage and Australian Culture: The Church and Literature in England in *Oscar and Lucinda*." *Australian Literature Studies* 2 (1995): 135-140.

[26] Brydon, Diana, and Hellen Tiffin. Decolonizing Fictions. Sydney: Dangaroo Press, 1993.

[27] Burgmann, Verity, and Jenny Lee, eds. *Constructing a Culture: A People's History of Australia since 1788*. Fitzroy: McPhee Gribble Publishers Pty Ltd, 1988.

[28] Byrne, Trevor. *The Problem of the Past: The Treatment of History in the Novels of Peter Carey and David Malouf*. Adelaide: Adelaide University, 2001.

[29] Byrne, Trevor. "The Road to Babi Yar: Anti-historicism in Recent Australian Fiction." *Association for the Study of Australian Literature* 2 (2013): 209-215.

[30] Callahan, David. "Peter Carey's *Oscar and Lucinda* and the Subversion of Subversion." *Australian Studies* 4 (1990): 20-26.

[31] Camus, Albert. *The Myth of Sisyphus*. Trans. Justin O'Brien. New York: Penguin Classics, 2000.

[32] Carey, Peter. *Bliss*. New York: Vintage Books, 1981.

[33] Carey, Peter. *Illywhacker*. London: Faber & Faber, 1985.

[34] Carey, Peter. *Oscar and Lucinda*. London: Faber & Faber, 1988.

[35] Carey, Peter. *The Tax Inspector*. New York: Alfred A. Knope, 1991.

[36] Carey, Peter. *The Unusual Life of Tristan Smith*. Queensland: University of Queensland Press, 1994.

[37] Carey, Peter. *Collected Stories*. London: Faber & Faber, 1995.

[38] Carey, Peter. *Jack Maggs*. London: Faber & Faber, 1997.

[39] Carey, Peter. *True History of the Kelly Gang*. London: Faber & Faber, 2000.

[40] Carey, Peter. *30 Days in Sydney: A Wildly Distorted Account*. New York: Bloomsbury, 2001.

[41] Carey, Peter. *My Life as a Fake*. Sydney: Alfred A. Knope, 2003.

[42] Carey, Peter. *Wrong about Japan*. New York: Vintage Books, 2004.

[43] Carey, Peter. *Theft: A Love Story*. London: Faber & Faber, 2006.

[44] Carey, Peter. *His Illegal Self*. London: Faber & Faber, 2008.

[45] Carey, Peter. *Parrot and Oliver in America*. New York: Alfred A. Knope, 2010.

[46] Carey, Peter. *The Chemistry of Tears*. London: Faber & Faber, 2012.

[47] Carey, Peter. *Amnesia*. Toronto: Random House Canada, 2015.

[48] Carey, Peter. *A Long Way from Home*. London: Faber & Faber, 2017.

[49] Carter, David. "Australian Popular Culture: Models of Cultural Influence and Originality." *New Directions in Australian Studies*. Eds. Cynthia Vanden Driesen and Adrian Mitchell. New Deli: Prestige Books, 2000. 68-81.

[50] Clancy, Laurie. "Selective History of the Kelly Gang: Peter Carey's Ned Kelly." *Overland* 175 (2004): 53-58.

[51] Clark, Manning. *A History of Australia*. I vols. Sydney: Melbourne University Press, 1968.

[52] Clark, Manning. *A History of Australia*. III vols. Sydney: Melbourne University Press, 1973.

[53] Clark, Manning. *A History of Australia*. IV vols. Sydney: Melbourne University Press, 1978.

[54] Clark, Manning. *A History of Australia*. V vols. Sydney: Melbourne University Press, 1981.

[55] Clastres, Pierre. *Society against the State: Essays in Political Anthropology*. Trans. Robert Hurley Abe Stein. New York: Zone Books, 1989.

[56] Coad, David. "Book Review of *True History of the Kelly Gang*." *World Literature Today*. Spring 2001: 314.

[57] Craven, Peter. "My Life as a Fake." *Sydney Morning Herald* 12 Jun. 2003: 14-15.

[58] Dahlstrom, James. "The Unusual Life of Gough Whitlam: Peter Carey's Tristan Smith." *Journal of Language, Literature and Culture* 62. 1 (2015): 32 - 47.

[59] Daniel, Helen. *Liars: Australian New Novelists*. Haimondsworth and Middlesex: Penguin, 1988.

[60] Darian-Smith, Kate, and Paula Hamilton, eds. *Memory & History in Twentieth-Century Australia*. Melbourne: Oxford University Press, 1994.

[61] Delfabbro, Paul, and Daniel King. "Gambling in Australia: Experiences, Problems, Research and Policy." *Society for the Study of Addiction* 107 (2012): 1556-1561.

[62] Derrida, Jacque. *Of Grammatology*. Baltimore: Johns Hopkins University Press, 1976.

[63] Derrida, Jacque. *Archive Fever: A Freudian Impression*. Trans.

Eric Prenowitz. Chicago and London: The University of Chicago Press, 1998.

[64] Derrida, Jacque. *Writing and Difference*. Trans. Alan Bass. London: Routledge, 2002.

[65] Dessaix, Robert. "An Interview with Peter Carey." *Australian Book Review* 18 Jan. 1995: 18-20.

[66] Dingley, Robert. "Playing the Game: The Continental Casinos and The Victorian Imagination." *Cahiers Victoriens and Edouardiens* 44 (1996): 17-31.

[67] Don. "Peter Carey Does a Wonderful Thing." *Sydney Morning Herald* 20 Feb. 1988: 71.

[68] Dowling, Andrew. "Truth and History." *Heat*, New series 1 (2001): 249-254.

[69] Eagleton, Terry. "Capitalism, Modernism, and Postmodernism." *Jean-Francois Lyotard: Critical Evaluations in Cultural Theory*. 2 vols. Eds. Victor E. Taylor and Gregg Lambert. London and New York: Routledge, 2006. 127-141.

[70] Eagleton, Terry. *After Theory*. New York: Basic Books, 2003.

[71] Edwards, Brian. "Deceptive Constructions: The Art of Building in Peter Carey's *Illywhacker*." *Fabulating Beauty: Perspectives on the Fiction of Peter Carey*. Ed. Andreas Gaile. New York: Rodopi, 2004. 149-170.

[72] Eggert, Paul. "The Bushranger's Voice: Peter Carey's *True History of the Kelly Gang* (2000) and Ned Kelly's *Jerilderie Letter* (1879)." *College Literature* 34. 3 (2007): 120-139.

[73] Eliot, George. *Middlemarch*. New York and Boston: H. M. Caldwell Company Publishers, 2008.

[74] Erll, Astrid, and Ansgar Nu nning, eds. *Cultural Memory Studies: An International and Interdisciplinary Handbook*. Berlin and New York: Walter de Gruyter, 2008.

[75] Erll, Astrid, and Ann Rigney. "Literature and the Production of Cultural Memory: Introduction." *European Journal of English Studies* 10. 2 (2006): 111-115.

[76] Erll, Astrid. "Locating Family in Cultural Memory Studies." *Journal of Comparative Family Studies* 42 (2011): 303-318.

[77] Evans, Morton. "Carey Reaches a Blissful Peak in his Literary Career." *The Australian* 26 Jul. 1984: 8.

[78] Fazilleau, Sue R. "Bob's Dreaming: Playing with Reader Expectations in Peter Carey's '*Oscar and Lucinda*'". *Rocky Mountain Review of Language and Literature* 59. 1 (2005): 11-30.

[79] Fidyk, Barbara. *Rewriting Scapegoat Texts: Mimetic Desire and the Dynamics of Rivalry in Michael Ondaatje's In the Skin of a Lion and The English Patient, and Peter Carey's Jack Maggs and True History of the Kelly Gang*. Newcastle: Newcastle University, 2009.

[80] Finnell, Joshua. *Library Journal*. 1 Dec. 2017: 86.

[81] Flanery, Patrick. *Spectator*. 13 Jan. 2018: 1.

[82] Fletcher, Don. "Utopia in Peter Carey's *Bliss*." *Social Alternatives* 26. 1 (2007): 39-42.

[83] Fletcher, Lisa, and Elizabeth Mead. "Inheriting the Past: Peter Corris's *The Journal of Fletcher Christian* and Peter Carey's *True History of the Kelly Gang*." *Journal of Commonwealth Literature* 45 (2010): 189-206.

[84] Foucault, Michel. *Language, Counter-Memory, Practice: Selected Essays and Interviews*. Trans. Donald F. Bouchard and Sherry Simon. New York: Cornell University Press, 1980.

[85] Freud, Sigmund. *The Complete Psychological Works of Sigmund Freud*. Trans. James Strachey. London: Hogarth Press, 1974.

[86] Freud, Sigmund. *The Interpretation of Dreams*. Tans. James Strachey. New York: Basic Books, 2011.

[87] Gaile, Andreas. "Re-Mythologizing an Australian Legend: Peter Carey's True History of the Kelly Gang." *Antipodes* 15. 1 (2001): 37-39.

[88] Gaile, Andreas, ed. *Fabulating Beauty: Perspectives on the Fiction of Peter Carey*. New York: Rodopi, 2004.

[89] Gaile, Andreas. *Rewriting History: Peter Carey's Fictional Biography of Australia*. New York: Rodopi B. V., 2010.

[90] Genette, Gerard. *Paratexts: Thresholds of Interpretation*. Trans. Jane E. Lewin. Cambridge: Cambridge University Press, 1997.

[91] Gilmour Robin. "Using the Victorians: the Victorian Age in Contemporary Fiction." *Rereading Victorian Fiction*. Eds. Jenkins A. and John J. Palgrave Macmillan: London, 2000. 189-200.

[92] Gong, Jing. "Gender and Genre in Peter Carey's *True History of the Kelly Gang*." *Comparative Literature: East & West* 2 (2011): 26-31.

[93] Habermas, Jürgen. *The Theory of Communicative Action: Lifeworld and System: A Critique of Functionalist Reason*. Trans. Thomas McCarthy. Boston: Beacon Press, 1987.

[94] Habermas, Jürgen. "Modernity — an Unfinished Project." *Croatian Political Science Review* 46. 2 (2009): 96-111.

[95] Halbwachs, Maurice. *The Collective Memory*. Trans. Francis J. Ditter, Jr. and Vida Yazdi Ditter. New York: Harper & Row. 1980.

[96] Habermas, Jürgen. *On Collective Memory*. Ed. and Trans. Lewis A. Coser. Chicago: University of Chicago Press, 1992.

[97] Hall, Stuart, and Paul de Gey, eds. *Questions of Cultural Identity*. London: Sage, 1996.

[98] Hassall, Anthony. "A Tale of Two Countries: *Jack Maggs* and Peter Carey's Fiction." *Australian Literary Studies* 18. 2 (1997): 128-135.

[99] Heilmann, A. and M Llewellyn. *Neo-Victorianism: The Victorians in the Twenty-First Century*, 1999-2009. Basingstoke: Palgrave Macmillan, 2010.

[100] Hergenhan, Laurie, ed. *The Penguin New Literary History of Australia*. Ringwood and Victoria: Penguin Books, 1988.

[101] Hickey, D. J., and J. E. Doherty. *A New History of Irish History from 1800*. Dublin: Gill and Macmillan, 2003.

[102] Highfield, Jonathan. "Suckling from the Crocodile's Tit: Wildlife and Nation Formation in Australian Narratives." *Antipodes* 20. 2 (2006): 127-140.

[103] Ho, Elizabeth. *Neo-Victorianism and the Memory of Empire*. London: Continuum, 2012.

[104] Hobsbawm, Eric, and Terence Ranger, eds. *The Invention of Tradition*. Cambridge: Cambridge University Press, 1983.

[105] Hoefferle, Caroline. *The Essential Historiography Reader*. Boston and MA: Pearson, 2011.

[106] Huggan, Graham. *Australian Writer: Peter Carey*. Melbourne: Oxford University Press, 1996.

[107] Huggan, Graham. *The Postcolonial Exotic: Marketing the Margins*. London: Routledge. 2001.

[108] Huggan, Graham. "Cultural Memory in Postcolonial Fiction: The Uses and Abuses of Ned Kelly." *Australian Literary Studies* 20. 3 (2002): 141-154.

[109] Hughes, Robert. *The Fatal Shore: The Epic of Australia's Founding*. New York: Vintage Books. 2003.

[110] Hutcheon, Linda. *A Poetics of Postmodernism: History, Theory, Fiction*. London: Routledge. 1988.

[111] Iggers, Georg G. *Historiography in the Twentieth Century: From Scientific Objectivity to the Postmodern Challenge*. Hanover and London: Wesleyan University Press, 1997.

[112] Iser, Wolfgang. *The Act of Reading: A Theory of Aesthetic Response*. Baitimore: Johns Hopkins University Press, 1980.

[113] Iser, Wolfgang. *The Fictive and the Imaginary*. Baltimore and London: Johns Hopkins University Press, 1993.

[114] Jacobson, Howard. "Dirty Very Old Man." *New York Times* 17 Nov. 1985.

[115] Jacques, Le Goff. *History and Memory*. Trans. Steven Rendall and Elizabeth Claman. New York: Columbia University Press, 1992.

[116] Jameson, Fredric. *Postmodernism, or, the Cultural Logic of Late Capitalism*. Durham: Duke University Press, 1991.

[117] Jenks, Chris. *Transgression*. London and New York: Routledge, 2003.

[118] Jensen, Hal. "Race, Chase and Walkabout: Peter Carey Remaps the Story of Australia." TLS. 19 Jan. 2018: 21.

[119] Jones, Russell. "Democracy's Discontents." *Times* 23 Jan. 2010: 5.

[120] Jung, C. G. *The Archetypes and the Collective Unconscious*. Trans. R. F. C. Hull. Routledge: London, 1968.

[121] Kammen, Michael. *Mystic Chords of Memory*. New York: Vintage, 1991.

[122] Kampmark, Nataša. "Where Angels Do Not Fear to Hack Back: Review of *Amnesia*, by Peter Carey." *Journal of the European Association for Studies of Australia* 6. 1 (2015): 101-105.

[123] Kane, Paul. "Postcolonial/Postmodern Australian Literature and Peter Carey." *World Literature Today* 67. 3 (1993): 519-522.

[124] Kaplan, Fred. *Dickens and Mesmerism: The Hidden Springs of Fiction*. Princeton and NJ: Princeton University Press, 1975.

[125] Kenneth, Pellow C. "Peter Carey's *Jack Maggs*: Re-Doing Dickens's Re-Doings of Dickens." *Papers on Language & Literature* 49. 1 (2013): 86-108.

[126] King, Francis. *Spectator*. 12 Dec. 1981: 21.

[127] Kirkus Reviews. 15 Dec. 2017.

[128] Klein, Kerwin Lee. "On the Emergence of Memory in Historical Discourse." *Representations* 69 (2000): 127-150.

[129] Krassnitzer, Hermine. *Aspects of Narration in Peter Carey's Novels: Deconstructing Colonialism*. Lewiston and Queenston: The Edwin Mellen Press, 1995.

[130] Kunc, François. "Finding myself through First Peoples' Stories." *Eureka Street*. 2 Sep. 2018: 22-24.

[131] Lacan, Jacques. *The Four Fundamental Concepts of Psychoanalysis*. Trans. Alan Sheridan. New York: W. W. Norton & Company, 1998.

[132] LaCapra, Dominick. *History, Politics, and the Novel*. Ithaca: Cornell University Press, 1987.

[133] Lamb, Karen. *Peter Carey: The Genesis of Fame*. London: Angus Robertson, 1992.

[134] Lamond, Julieanne. "Nothing Too Serious: Review of *Amnesia*, by Peter Carey." *Sydney Review of Books* 20 Feb. 2015.

[135] Larsson, Christer. *The Relative Merits of Goodness and Originality: The Ethics of Storytelling in Peter Carey's Novels*. Uppsala: Uppsala University Press, 2001.

[136] Lobe, Cliff. *Un-settling Memory: Cultural Memory and Neo-colonialism*. D. Edmonton: The University of Alberta, 2000.

[137] Lobe, Cliff. "Reading the 'Remembered World': Carceral Architecture and Cultural Mnemonic in Peter Carey's *Illywhacker*." *Mosaic: A Journal for the Interdisciplinary Study of Literature* 35. 4 (2002): 17-34.

[138] Lyotard, Jean-François. *The Postmodern Condition: A Report on Knowledge*. Trans. Geoff Bennington and Brian Massumi. Minneapolis: University of Minnesota Press, 1984.

[139] Macfarlane, Robert. "Dangerous Inventions." *Times Literary Supplement*. 12 Sep. 2003: 23.

[140] Macintyre, Stuart, and Anna Clark. *The History Wars*. Carlton and Victoria: Melbourne University Press, 2003.

[141] Macintyre, Stuart. *A Concise History of Australia*. Cambridge: Cambridge University Press, 1999.

[142] Marcuse, Herbert. *One-Dimensional Man: Studies in the Ideology of Advanced Industrial Society*. Boston: Beacon Press, 2002.

[143] Margalit, Avishai. *The Ethics of Memory*. Cambridge: Harvard University Press, 2002.

[144] Marshall, Brenda K. *Teaching the Postmodern: Fiction and Theory*. New York and London: Routledge, 1992.

[145] Martin, Luther H., Huck Gutman, and Patrick H. Hutton, eds. *Technologies of the Self: A Seminar with Michel Foucault*. Amherst: University of Massachusetts Press, 1988.

[146] Marx, Bill. "Dystopia Down Under." *Nation* 254. 10 (1992): 346-348.

[147] Mathews, Peter. "On the Genealogy of Democracy: Reading Peter Carey's *Parrot and Olivier in America*." *Australian Literary Studies* 27. 2 (2012): 68-80.

[148] May, Rollo. *The Meaning of Anxiety*. New York: W. W. Norton & company, 1996.

[149] McCormack, Leah. "Reclaiming Silenced & Erased Histories: The Paratextual Devices of Historiographic Metafiction." *Making Connections* 14. 2 (2013): 37-54.

[150] McCrum, Robert. "Robert McCeumTalks to Peter Carey about Wrestling with a National Myth: 'Reawakening Ned'." *The Observer* 7 Jan. 2001.

[151] McCrum, Robert. "The 100 Best Novels: No. 100 — *True History of the Kelly Gang* by Peter Carey (2000)." *The Guardian* 16 Aug. 2015.

[152] McHutchion, Benjamin. "Derision and Demography: New South Wales and the Irish Orphan Girls of the Earl Grey Immigration Scheme, 1848 to 1850." *Constellations* 6. 2 (2015): 18-34.

[153] Mitchell, Kate. *History and Cultural Memory in Neo-Victorian Fiction: Victorian Afterimages*. Basingstoke: Palgrave Macmillan, 2010.

[154] Moran, Alexander. *Booklist*. 15 Nov. 2017: 32.

[155] Motion, Andrew. "*Amnesia* by Peter Carey Review — Turbocharged, Hyperenergetic." *The Guardian* 30 Oct. 2014.

[156] Moya, Paula M. L., and Michael R. Hames-Garcia, eds. *Reclaiming Identity: Realist Theory and the Predicament of Postmodernism*.

Berkeley: University of California Press, 2000.

[157] Mundow, Anna. http://randomhouse.com/knopf/authors/carey. Accessed on 28 Oct. 2018.

[158] Munro, Craig. "Building the Fabulist Extensions: An Interview with Peter Carey." *Makar* 12. (1976): 3-12.

[159] Munro, Craig. *The First UQP Story Book*. Saint Lusia: University of Queensland Press, 1981.

[160] Myers, Janet C. "'As these fresh lines fade': Narratives of Containment and Escape in Peter Carey's *Jack Maggs*." *The Journal of Commonwealth Literature* 46. 3 (2011): 455-473.

[161] Natale, A. Riem. "Harry Joy's Children: The Art of Storytelling in Peter Carey's *Bliss*." *Australian Literary Studies* 16. 3 (1994): 341-347.

[162] Neumann, Birgit. "The Literary Representation of Memory." *Cultural Memory Studies: An International and Interdisciplinary Handbook*. Eds. Astrid Erll and Ansgar Nunning. Berlin and New York: Walter de Gruyter, 2008. 333-344.

[163] *New Yorker*. 19 Mar. 2018: 91.

[164] Nietzsche, Friedrich. *Untimely Meditations: On the Use and Abuse of History for Life*. Trans. Ian C. Johnston. Columbia: Malaspina University College, 1998.

[165] Nietzsche, Friedrich. *On the Genealogy of Morality*. Trans. Carol Diethe. New York: Cambridge University Press, 2006.

[166] Nietzsche, Friedrich. *Thus Spoke Zarathustra*. Trans. Adrian D. Caro. New York: Cambridge University Press, 2006.

[167] Nora, Pierre, ed. *Realms of Memory: Rethinking the French Past*. Volume I: Conflicts and Divisions. Trans. Arthur Goldhammer. New York: Columbia University Press, 1996.

[168] O'Farrell, Patrick. *The Irish in Australia: 1788 to the Present*. Sydney: University of New South Wales Press Ltd., 2000.

[169] O'Hara, John. *A Mugs Game: A History of Gaming and Betting*

in Australia. Kensington: New South Wales University Press, 1988.

[170] O'Reilly, Nathanael. "The Influence of Peter Carey's *True History of the Kelly Gang*: Repositioning the Ned Kelly Narrative in Australian Popular Culture." *The Journal of Popular Culture* 40. 3 (2007): 488-500.

[171] O'Reilly, Nathanael. "Mythology, History, and Truth: Teaching Peter Carey's *True History of the Kelly Gang*." *Antipodes* 29. 1 (2015): 71-81.

[172] Osteen, Mark. "Hideous Progeny: Forgery, *Frankenstein*, and Peter Carey's *My Life as a Fake*." *Papers on Language & Literature* 53. 4 (2017): 347-382.

[173] Parsons, Talcott. *Social Systems and the Evolution of Action Theory*. New York: Free Press, 1977.

[174] Pellow, C. Kenneth. "Peter Carey's *Jack Maggs*: Re-doing Dickens's Re-doings of Dickens." *Papers on Language & Literature* 49. 1 (2013): 86-108.

[175] Pierce, Peter. "Preying on the Past: Contexts of Some Recent Neo-Historical Fiction." *Australian Literary Studies* 15. 4 (1992): 304-312.

[176] Pierce, Peter. "Kinds of Captivity in Peter Carey's Fiction." *Fabulating Beauty: Perspectives on the Fiction of Peter Carey*. Ed. Andreas Gaile. New York: Rodopi, 2004. 71-82.

[177] Pilger, John. *A Secret Country*. London: Vintage, 1990.

[178] Pons, Xavier. "The Novelist as Ventriloquist: Autobiography and Fiction in Peter Carey's *True History of the Kelly Gang*." *Commonwealth: Essays and Studies* 24. 1 (2001): 61-72.

[179] Porter, Peter. "New Worlds for Old." *The Australian's Reviews for Books* 7 Aug. 1997: 5.

[180] Qinglong Peng. *Writing Back to the Empire — Textuality and Historicity in Peter Carey's Fiction*. Shanghai: East China Normal University, 2005.

[181] Qinglong Peng. "Memories and their Literary Representations: A Comparative Reading of Red Sorghum and True History of the Kelly Gang." *Comparative Literature Studies* 54. 1 (2017): 177-194.

[182] Rabinow, Paul, ed. *The Foucault Reader*. New York: Pantheon Books, 1984.

[183] Rancière, Jacques. *Dissensus: On Politics and Aesthetics*. Ed. & Trans. Steven Corcoran. London and New York: Continuum, 2010.

[184] Rancière, Jacques. *The Politics of Aesthetics: The Distribution of the Sensible*. Ed. & Trans. Gabriel Rockhill. London: Bloomsbury Academic, 2013.

[185] Ranke, Leopold Von. "Preface: Histories of the Latin and Germanic Nations from 1494-1514." *The Varieties of History*. New York: Meridian Books, 1957.

[186] Rauwerda, Antje. "Multi-Nationality and Layers of Mouse in Peter Carey's *The Unusual Life of Tristan Smith*." *Antipodes* 20. 2 (2006): 117-123.

[187] Renk, Kathleen J. "Rewriting the Empire of the Imagination: The Post-Imperial Gothic Fiction of Peter Carey and A. S. Byatt." *SAGE Publications* 39. 2 (2004): 61-71.

[188] Rockman, Connie. *Booklist*. 1 Jun. 2018: 114.

[189] Romei, Stephen. "Peter Carey Maintains the Rage." *The Australian* 4 Oct. 2014.

[190] Rousselot, Elodie, ed. *Introduction: Eroticizing the Past in Contemporary Neo-Historical Fiction*. New York: Palgrave Macmillan, 2014.

[191] Rubik, Margarete. "Provocative and unforgettable: Peter Carey's short fiction — A Cognitive Approach." *European Journal of English Studies* 9. 2 (2005): 169-184.

[192] Said, Edward W. *Culture and Imperialism*. New York: Vintage Books, 1993.

[193] Said, Edward W. *Representations of the Intellectual*: *The Reith Lectures*. New York: Vintage Books, 1994.

[194] Sawer, Marian. "Misogyny and Misrepresentation: Women in Australian Parliaments." *Political Science* 65. 1 (2013): 105-117.

[195] Schmidt H., Barbara. "The Writing-Back Paradigm Revisited: Peter Carey, *Jack Maggs*, and Charles Dickens, *Great Expectations*." *Fabulating Beauty*: *Perspectives on the Fiction of Peter Carey*. Ed. Andreas Gaile. New York: Rodopi, 2004. 245-262.

[196] Seal, Graham. *Ned Kelly in Popular Tradition*. Melbourne: Hyland House Publishing Pty Limited, 1980.

[197] Sedikides, Constantine, and Jeffrey D. Green. "On the Self-Protective Nature of Inconsistency-Negativity Management: Using the Person Memory Paradigm to Examine Self-Referent Memory." *Journal of Personality and Social Psychology* 79. 6 (2000): 906-922.

[198] Sexton, D. "Interview with Peter Carey." *Literary Review* 15 Apr. 1985: 41-42.

[199] Shilling, Jane. "Racing round Australia and Uncovering the Truth about its Past." *Evening Standard* 25 January 2018.

[200] Smyth, Heather. "Mollies down under: Cross-dressing and Australian Masculinity in Peter Carey's *True History of the Kelly Gang*." *Journal of the History of Sexuality* 18. 2 (2009): 185-214.

[201] Staniforth, Martin. "'Shades of the prison house': Reading Richard Flanagan's *The Narrow Road to the Deep North* and Peter Carey's *Amnesia*." *Journal of Postcolonial Writing* 53. 5 (2017): 578-589.

[202] Svevo, Italo. *Death — Short Sentimental Journey and Other Stories*. Trans. Beryl de Zoete, L., Collinson Morely, and Ben Johnson. Berkeley: 1967.

[203] Tafarodi, Romin W., Tara C. Marshall, and Alan B. Milne. "Self-Esteem and Memory." *Journal of Personality and Social Psychology* 84. 1 (2003): 29-45.

[204] Taylor, Beverly. "Discovering New Pasts: Victorian Legacies

in the Postcolonial Worlds of *Jack Maggs* and *Mister Pip.*" *Victorian Studies* 52. 1 (2009): 95-105.

[205] Tautsky, Thomas. "Getting the Comer Right: An Interview with Peter Carey." *Australian and New Zealand Studies in Canada* 4 (1990): 27-38.

[206] "Jack's 'Great Expectations'". *The New York Book Review* 8 Feb. 1998: 10.

[207] Thieme, John. Postcolonial Con-Texts: Writing Back to the Canon. London: Continuum, 2001.

[208] Thompson, Della, ed. *Concise Oxford English-Chinese Dictionary*. Beijing: Foreign Language Teaching and Research Press, 2004.

[209] Tilney, Martin. *The Politics of Postmodernism*. London and New York: Routledge, 2002.

[210] Tilney, Martin. "Cohesive Harmony and Theme in Peter Carey's *The Last Days of a Famous Mime*." *Language & Literature* 27. 1 (2018): 3-20.

[211] Tocqueville, Alexis de. *Democracy in America*. Ed. Eduardo Nolla. Trans. James T. Schleifer. Indianapolis: Liberty Fund, Inc., 2010.

[212] Turner, Graeme. *National Fictions: Literature, Film, and the Construction of Australian Narrative*. Sydney: Allen & Unwin, 1986.

[213] Turner, Graeme. "Nationalizing the Author: The Celebrity of Peter Carey." *Australian Literary Studies* 16. 2 (1993): 131-39.

[214] Wachtel, Eleanor. "'We Can Really Make Ourselves Up': An Interview with Peter Carey." *Australian and New Zealand Studies in Canada* 9 (1993): 103-105.

[215] Wagner, Erica. "Land Built on Bones." *New Statesman*. 26 Jan. 2018: 47.

[216] Wagner, Jodi L. *Gambling and Risk in Victorian Literature and Culture*. West Lafayette, IN: Purdue University, 2008.

[217] Wellek, Rene, and Austin Warren. *Theory of Literature*. Portsmouth: Peregrine Books, 1985.

[218] White, Hayden. "Interpretation in History." *New Literary History* 4 (1973): 281-314.

[219] White, Hayden. *Metahistory: The Historical Imagination in Nineteenth-Century Europe*. Baltimore: Johns Hopkins University Press, 1975.

[220] White, Hayden. *Tropics of Discourse: Essays in Cultural Criticism*. Baltimore and London: The Johns Hopkins Univeristy Press, 1978.

[221] White, Hayden. "The Value of Narrativity in the Representation of Reality." *Critical Inquiry* 1 (1980): 5-27.

[222] White, Hayden. "The Politics of Historical Interpretation: Discipline and De-Sublimation." *The Content of the Form: Narrative Discourse and Historical Representation*. Ed. Hayden White. Baltimore: The Johns Hopkins University Press, 1987.

[223] White, Michael, and David Epston. *Narrative Means to Therapeutic Ends*. New York: Norton, 1990.

[224] Wigston, Nancy. "A Respected Outlaw: An Interview with Peter Carey." *Books in Canada* 31.1 (2002): 13-15.

[225] Willbanks, Ray. "Peter Carey." *Speaking Volumes: Australian Writers and Their Work*. Ringwood: Penguin, 1992. 43-57.

[226] Willbanks, Ray. "Peter Carey on *The Tax Inspector* and *The Unusual Life of Tristan Smith*: A Conversation with Ray Willbanks." Antipodes 11 (1997): 11-16.

[227] Williams, James. "Jean-Francois Lyotard." *Key Contemporary Social Theorists*. Eds. Anthony Elliott and Larry Ray. Oxford: Blackwell Publishers, 2002. 210-214.

[228] Woodcock, Bruce. *Peter Carey*. Manchester and New York: Manchester University Press, 1996.

[229] Wroe, Nicholas. "Fiction's Great Outlaw." *The Guardian*. 6

Jan. 2001: 6.

[230] Wood, James. "Tocqueville in America." *New Yorker*. 17 May 2010: 104-109.

[231] Zizek, Slavoj. *The Parallax View*. Cambridge: MIT Press, 2006.

[232] Zizek, Slavoj. *The Universal Exception*. Eds. Rex Butler and Scott Stephens. London: Continuum, 2006.

[233] 阿莱达·阿斯曼.回忆空间:文化记忆的形式和变迁[M].潘璐,译.北京:北京大学出版社,2016.

[234] 埃德蒙·怀特.将自己的心灵印在文学的版图上:彼得·凯里访谈录[J].晓风,晓燕,译.外国文学,1990(4):70-71.

[235] 白曼曼.重述他者与自我:论《杰克·迈格斯》对《远大前程》的颠覆[D].合肥:安徽大学,2016.

[236] 贝奈戴托·克罗齐.维柯的哲学[M].柯林伍德,译.陶秀璈,王立志,译.郑州:大象出版社,2009.

[237] 本尼迪克特·安德森.想象的共同体:民族主义的起源与散布[M].吴叡人,译.增订本.上海:上海人民出版社,2016.

[238] 陈栩.《杰克·迈格斯》中的家庭叙事及其政治隐喻[J].当代外国文学,2019(1):73-79.

[239] 范丹丹.从空间叙事角度分析《奥斯卡与露辛达》中的爱情悲剧[D].绵阳:西南科技大学,2016.

[240] 冯亚琳.德语文学中的文化记忆与民族价值观[C].北京:中国社会科学出版社,2013.

[241] 冯亚琳.文学与文化记忆的交会[J].外国语文,2017(2):48-54.

[242] 耿占春.回顾或展望:作为一种话语的文学[J].南方文坛,2019(2):5-9.

[243] 龚静,向晓红.论《杰克·迈格斯》的男性气质[J].当代外国文学,2012(1):127-134.

[244] 龚静.销售边缘男性气质:彼得·凯里小说性别与民族身份研究[M].成都:四川大学出版社,2015.

[245] 郭梅.永远在路上:《杰克·迈格斯》中文化身份的解读[J].外语研究,2012(6):98-101.

[246] 郭梅,陈丽辉."我们将书写自己的历史":《凯利帮真史》的双声语解读[J].华夏文化论坛,2014(1):255-261.

[247] 胡鸿.颠覆与重构民族身份:从后殖民角度解析彼得·凯利的《凯利帮真史》[D].合肥:安徽大学,2007.

[248] 花娟.不同的创伤,共同的身份追寻:后殖民主义视域下的《奥斯卡和露辛达》和《我的位置》[J].宜春学院学报,2018(4):95-97.

[249] 黄洁.内德·凯利传说的当代阐释:《凯特妹妹》与《凯利帮真史》的比较分析[J].外国文学,2017(4):36-45.

[250] 黄艳红."记忆之场"与皮埃尔·诺拉的法国史书写[J].历史研究,2017(6):140-157.

[251] 黄源深.澳大利亚文学史[M].修订版.上海:上海外语教育出版社,2014.

[252] 加里·古廷.20世纪法国哲学[M].辛岩,译.南京:江苏人民出版社,2005.

[253] 江丹丹.流变的身份:彼得·凯里《凯利帮真史》之文化研究[D].杭州:浙江工商大学,2014.

[254] 金寿福.扬·阿斯曼的文化记忆理论[J].外国语文,2017(2):36-40.

[255] 利奥塔尔.后现代状态:关于知识的报告[M].车槿山,译.南京:南京大学出版社,2011.

[256] 李明星.《奥斯卡与露辛达》后殖民写作研究[D].桂林:广西师范大学,2014.

[257] 李晓娟.重塑澳大利亚国家身份:析彼得·凯里之著《杰克·马格斯》[D].呼和浩特:内蒙古大学,2008.

[258] 李友梅.文化主体性及其困境:费孝通文化观的社会学分析[J].社会学研究,2010(4):2-19.

[259] 刘海婷.记忆、身份认同与文学演示[J].外国语文,2017(2):55-60.

[260] 刘阳.无法穿越的"玻璃教堂":论《奥斯卡与露辛达》中的沟通

交流屏障[D].洛阳:河南科技大学,2014.

[261] 米歇尔·福柯.性经验史[M].佘碧平,译.上海:上海人民出版社,2000.

[262] 欧阳昱.表现他者:澳大利亚小说中的中国人 1888－1988[M].北京:新华出版社,2000.

[263] 彭刚.历史记忆与历史书写:史学理论视野下的"记忆的转向"[J].史学史研究,2014(2):1-12.

[264] 彭青龙.是"丛林强盗"还是"民族英雄"?:解读彼得·凯里的《"凯利帮"真史》[J].外国文学评论,2003(2):30-36.

[265] 彭青龙."魔术师"的谎言与牢笼[J].上海师范大学学报(哲学社会科学版),2006(3):79-84.

[266] 彭青龙.《我的生活如同虚构》:一部后现代理论小说[J].外国语文,2011(3):7-13.

[267] 彭青龙.《幸福》:游离于地狱与天堂之间的澳大利亚人[J].外国文学研究,2008(5):168-173.

[268] 彭青龙.《奥斯卡与露辛达》:承受历史之重的爱情故事[J].当代外国文学,2009(2):125-132.

[269] 彭青龙.历史小说的嬗变与文学性特征[J].英美文学研究论丛,2010(2):12-20.

[270] 彭青龙.彼得·凯里:从新派小说家的代表到民族神话的制造者[J].当代外语研究,2011(2):26-31.

[271] 彭青龙.彼得·凯里小说研究[M].上海:上海外语教育出版社,2011.

[272] 彭青龙.超越二元、以人为本:解读彼得·凯里小说文本中的伦理思想[J].外语教学,2015(4):77-85.

[273] 彭青龙.后殖民主义语境下的当代澳大利亚文学[J].外国语,2006(3):59-67.

[274] 彭青龙.《杰克·迈格斯》:重写帝国文学经典[J].外国文学评论,2009(1):191-201.

[275] 彭青龙.解读《"凯利帮"真史》的"故事"与"话语"[J].华东师范大学学报(哲学社会科学版),2005(1):75-79.

[276] 彭青龙.论《"凯利帮"真史》的界面张力[J].外语与外语教学,2013(1):83-86.

[277] 彭青龙.论《税务检查官》中的人性沉沦与救赎[J].解放军外国语学院学报,2010(3):93-98.

[278] 彭青龙.写回帝国中心,建构文化身份的彼得·凯里[J].当代外国文学,2005(2):109-115.

[279] 彭青龙.新世纪中国澳大利亚文学研究的趋向[J].当代外国文学,2014(3):165-176.

[280] 皮埃尔·诺拉.记忆之场:法国国民意识的文化社会史[C].黄艳红,等译.2版.南京:南京大学出版社,2017.

[281] 申丹.何为叙事的"隐性进程"? 如何发现这股叙事暗流?[J].外国文学研究,2013(5):47-53.

[282] 沈坚.记忆与历史的博弈:法国记忆史的建构[J].中国社会科学,2010(3):205-224.

[283] 沈忠良.后殖民视角下《凯利帮真史》中的文化身份探究[D].杭州:浙江大学,2018.

[284] 斯维特兰娜·博伊姆.怀旧的未来[M].杨德友,译.南京:译林出版社,2010.

[285] 托克维尔.论美国的民主[M].董果良,译.北京:商务印书馆,2019.

[286] 王丽亚."重写小说"中的"重读"结构:以《杰克·麦格斯》和《匹普先生》为例[J].外国文学,2017(2):3-13.

[287] 王蜜.文化记忆:兴起逻辑、基本维度和媒介制约[J].国外理论动态,2016(6):8-17.

[288] 王珊珊.凯利的追寻:《凯利帮真史》中的身份认同问题研究[D].杭州:杭州师范大学,2017.

[289] 维柯.新科学[M].朱光潜,译.北京:人民文学出版社,1986.

[290] 扬·阿斯曼."文化记忆"理论的形成和建构[N].金寿福,译.光明日报,2016-03-26(11).

[291] 扬·阿斯曼.什么是"文化记忆"?[J].陈国战,译.国外理论动态,2016(6):18-26.

[292] 叶胜年.风格和主题:彼得·凯里小说刍议[J].外国文学,1992(4):89-92.

[293] 叶胜年.当代澳大利亚小说中的殖民主义意义[J].当代外国文学,2008(1):91-100.

[294] 约恩·吕森.历史思考的新途径[M].綦甲福,来炯,译.上海:上海人民出版社,2005.

[295] 张计连.谁是米里亚姆·查德威克?:从接受理论看《奥斯卡与露辛达》[J].理论界,2011(4):155-157.

[296] 张计连.彼得·凯里小说中的民族认同问题研究[J].西北民族大学学报(哲学社会科学版),2014(5):106-111.

[297] 张计连.彼得·凯里笔下的"美国梦"[J].沈阳大学学报(社会科学版),2015(1):117-120.

[298] 张计连.彼得·凯里小说对认同问题的解构与重构[J].阴山学刊,2015(1):46-50.

[299] 张计连.彼得·凯里小说认同问题研究缘起[J].怀化学院学报,2014(7):80-84.

[300] 张计连.彼得·凯里小说中的母亲形象研究[J].滁州学院学报,2015(1):12-15,19.

[301] 张计连.镜观物色:彼得·凯里小说中的认同问题研究[M].北京:中国社会科学出版社,2015.

[302] 张加生.互文、戏仿与解构:论《杰克·迈格斯》对《远大前程》的文化反戈[J].外语研究,2016(2):97-101.

[303] 张明."新派"先锋彼得·凯里:评澳大利亚作家彼得·凯里的小说创作[J].外国文学,2001(4):16-20.

[304] 赵晶.后殖民主义视域下《杰克·迈格斯》和《凯利帮真史》的对比研究[D].合肥:安徽大学,2018.

[305] 郑海婷.文学介入理论研究:以萨特、阿多诺、朗西埃为样本[D].福州:福建师范大学,2016.

[306] 周宪.文学与认同[J].文学评论,2006(6):5-13.

[307] 祖华萍.孤独的心灵,不屈的抗争:小说《奥斯卡与露辛达》的女性主义解读[J].长春理工大学学报(社会科学版),2014(4):156-158.

[308] 祖华萍. 彼得·凯里小说《凯利帮真史》的狂欢化精神探究[D]. 合肥:安徽大学,2015.